Praise for *On the Line*

"You will feel all the things on the emotional rollercoaster that is *On the Line*! Amanda is absolutely masterful in the art of angsty romance. You can't help but root for Lexie and Mitch."
—Meredith Wallis, alpha reader/early reviewer

"It's difficult to articulate just how totally, entirely, wholly, and completely I loved this book."
—E.K. Larson-Burnett, author of *The Bear & The Rose*

"The perfect steamy must-read with characters you'll fall in love with more and more after each page."
—Kelsey Whitney, author of *In the End*

"*On the Line* is heart-wrenching, achingly beautiful, and addicting."
—Madison Wright, author of *Just Between Us*

"*On the Line* gives readers so much more than a hockey romance. Mitch and Lexie's story is one of passion: for life, for their careers, for their friends, and most importantly, for each other."
—Jennifer Rockey, alpha reader/early reviewer

"*On the Line* will have you smiling, blushing, crying, and smiling all over again."
—Juliana Smith, author of *Baggage Claim*

"This book wasn't long enough and I don't know if it ever could be. I want to live with these people forever."
—T.M. Ghent, author of *Lume*

"Amanda absolutely knocked it out of the park with this one. This one really put my emotions through the wringer, but in the absolute best way possible."
—Kenna Holman, early reviewer

"This book was incredible and I know it will always have a special place in my heart. From page one, these characters had my heart and their hold on me only grew. I loved For the Boys so much, but I somehow loved this sequel even more."
—Abigail McMillon, early reviewer

"If you are looking for a fun, heart wrenching, steamy romance with sports wrapped in, this book will not disappoint."
—Nicole Wood, early reviewer

"Everyone, this book was IT! I've been anticipating Lexie and Mitch's story ever since meeting them in *For the Boys*. Chaperon took everything I loved about FTB and delivered a more emotional, funny, steamy and heartbreaking follow up that's, dare I say, even better than book 1."
—Aaron Farrelly, early reviewer

Also by Amanda Chaperon

ON THE Line

AMANDA CHAPERON

To the people who don't believe in love.
I promise you it exists.
I hope you find it.

PROLOGUE
Mitch

OCTOBER 29, 2020

The lights in the club were low, and the entire place smelled of stale beer, body odor, and cheap perfume. Brief flashes from the strobes overhead illuminated the bodies on the dance floor, where a hundred girls screamed the words to every song the DJ played. The scene instantly transported him back to those early days after high school.

Mitch hadn't gone to college, choosing instead to jump right into junior hockey and work his way up through the various leagues until landing in the pros. He was no stranger to hard work, just as he was no stranger to letting loose. Any free time they had, even before he'd been legally old enough to drink, Mitch and his teammates found themselves at a bar in whatever city they were playing in, tying one on and fucking around with the locals.

Now, at thirty-two, he realized he was far too old for places like this. The girls here were far too young, and he wasn't entirely sure how he'd let Parker talk him into coming to Contour in the first place.

Usually, Mitch Frambough found his size to be a detriment in crowded public spaces like these. On the ice? His six-foot, five-inch frame was perfectly intimidating and great for knocking around opponents, making him extremely good at his job. But in a club packed wall-to-wall with bodies, the bulk of them female who were much, much smaller than him? It proved to be more of a hindrance than anything. About all he was good for in these situations was pushing his way past the throng to reach the bar.

Once he had secured a few beers, he made his way back to a table at the edge of the dance floor where his teammate, Parker Graff, and his friend Jay were seated.

"Don't you own anything other than flannel?" Parker asked with a groan, as if finally realizing what Mitch was wearing despite the hour they'd already spent together tonight.

"What's wrong with my flannel?" Mitch replied, glancing down at his faded red and white shirt with a frown.

"Nothing, except we're at a club, not a rodeo."

Mitch smacked Parker on the back of the head before sliding his beer in front of him. "Graff, the day I start taking fashion advice from you is the day someone should put a bullet in my head."

Jay snorted, and Parker shot him a dirty look, rolling his eyes as he said, "I'm just saying, you look ridiculous."

Mitch sat down and looked around, capturing the heated glances of several women. "I hate to break it to you bro, but this right here?" he said, gesturing to his body. "This is perfection, and the females here tonight agree."

Parker followed Mitch's gaze around the room and groaned. "I don't know how you pick up so many women looking like a farmer."

"It's less about the clothes and more about what I look like under them," Mitch said with a smirk. "I could wear a garbage bag and I'd still get more ass than you, Graff."

Parker threw a balled-up drink napkin at him. "Shut up."

Mitch's smirk bloomed into a smile, and he turned his gaze to the dance floor. Secretly, he loved to dance, and as he sat there watching the bodies writhing on the platform in front of him, he desperately wanted to get up, find a girl, and drag her out there. Instead, he settled for finishing his beer and wading through the crowd to get another.

With a second drink in hand, Mitch turned from the bar, nearly plowing over a tiny blonde girl. Easily over a foot shorter than him, Mitch hadn't seen her until he bumped into her.

A tall brunette entered his vision, presumably the girl's friend, and Mitch froze. The two stood there staring at each other, his green eyed-gaze locked on her hazel one for far longer than was appropriate given the fact that they were strangers.

Thanks to all of the social media sleuthing his teammate Brent had him doing lately, Mitch knew exactly who she was. Her name was Lexie Monroe, and he had to clamp his lips shut tight to prevent himself from letting out a low whistle at his first full look at her in the flesh.

Pictures truly did not do the woman justice. Her miles-long legs were clad in black denim and stuffed into a pair of white sneakers. A black sweater hung loose on her thin frame and draped off her shoulder, giving Mitch a tantalizing glimpse of smooth, tan skin. Her hair fell in a long, straight curtain down her back. As he gave Lexie a head-to-toe inspection, she returned the favor, a small smile playing on her lips.

This meant the little blonde standing in front of him was Berkley Daniels, the object of Brent's attention. Without breaking eye contact with Lexie, he tapped Berkley on the shoulder, and she whipped around. "What can I get you guys?" he asked.

If she was as big of a Warriors fan as Brent claimed she was, he had no doubt she recognized him. His suspicions were confirmed when she stood staring up at him, mouth open in shock. He couldn't help but grin down at her, waiting for her to have her fangirl moment.

But it never happened. Instead, Lexie came to her rescue, saying, "Would you mind terribly getting us a couple beers, please?" She batted her eyes at him, and he practically snorted. Clearly, she had no idea who he was, and she was laying it on thick, but who could blame her?

Mitch's physique was solid muscle, built more like a football linebacker than a hockey defenseman. His green eyes, the straight, white smile he paid a lot of money for after signing his first big contract, and even that scar slicing through his left eyebrow had earned him a romp in the sheets with a lot of women.

He couldn't help hoping Lexie would be next.

He held Lexie's gaze as he said, "Comin' right up."

Mitch turned back to the bar, towering over the men and women standing there, gawking at him. "Two more beers, please!" He yelled at the bartender over the music. The guy gave him a thumbs up and returned a moment later with the drinks.

He handed them to the girls, then stepped around them and inclined his head, urging them to follow.

When they arrived at the table, Mitch cleared his throat and said, "Ladies, I'd like you to meet my teammate, Parker, and my buddy, Jay. Parker and Jay, I'd like you to meet..."

"I'm Berkley, and this is Lexie," Berkley said.

Lexie's gaze locked onto Mitch's, a hint of mischief glinting in their depths.

Oh yes, he thought. *Tonight is going to be fun.*

"You're coming home with me, right?" Lexie whispered to him several hours later. Three empty pizza trays littered the table in front of them, along with half-drank bottles of beer and grease-covered napkins. Jay had disappeared hours ago, Berkley had gone to the bathroom, and Parker was so drunk he was half passed out across from them.

"Hell yes," Mitch said without hesitation.

Her answering grin was devilish enough to make his dick instantly hard.

It took every single ounce of restraint Mitch had not to paw her in that cracked leather booth, but he managed.

Barely.

When the Ubers arrived, they climbed into theirs after seeing Berkley and Parker off in the opposite direction.

Mere seconds after the doors closed, Lexie climbed half into his lap and pressed her mouth to his.

Not exactly how Mitch pictured his night going, but he couldn't deny that it was a *very* welcome turn of events.

Lexie was sexy as hell, with ridiculously long legs and bright golden eyes, and finally getting to tangle his fingers in her long, dark hair had him groaning against her mouth.

And that *mouth*. Her full lips were as soft as he'd imagined while staring at her all night, and he couldn't wait to feel them on other parts of his body. Her hands were everywhere, gripping his shoulders, trailing across his biceps and forearms, and knocking his hat off his head so she could rake her fingers through the shoulder-length, thick blond strands of his hair.

Mitch had to admit, he'd never been into girls touching his hair. But when Lexie did it, he was seconds away from coming undone.

He pulled away from her, gasping for air as she continued to press kisses along the column of his throat.

"Lexie," he rasped. "We have to slow down."

"Why?" She asked, and he was pleased to find her voice as wrecked as his. Was she as turned on as he was? He desperately wanted to shove his hands in her pants and find out if she was as wet as he was hard.

"Because if you don't stop doing that," he whispered as she gently bit down on his earlobe, "I'm going to make a mess in this backseat."

Lexie backed off, eyes wide, if a little unfocused, and the passing street lamps cast an eerie glow on her tan skin.

"My building is right there," she said, pointing to a high-rise two blocks away. "I think you can make it."

As if she was purposely trying to make him lose control in this cab with a perfect stranger three feet away, she leaned forward and pressed her mouth to his again, dropping one of her hands to palm his dick through his jeans.

"Goddamnit, woman," he hissed, pulling back from the kiss and locking his fingers around her wrist, stopping her, even if her touch had his eyes rolling back in his head. "Are you trying to kill me?"

"Maybe a little," she said, smiling against his mouth. "I've been waiting all night to do this."

When she licked the seam of his mouth, he opened for her, that first touch of her tongue on his causing him to groan low in his throat. And he lost himself in that kiss, unable to remember why he'd wanted to slow down moments before.

The car finally pulled to a stop, the driver braking hard enough to jar them from their embrace.

They couldn't keep their hands off each other in the elevator, and by the time they reached Lexie's door, Mitch was so beyond turned on—his restraint moments from snapping—that he lifted her off her feet and backed

5

her into the wall just outside her apartment. Her legs went around his waist instantly, and he pressed into her.

It amazed him how well, how easily, they fit together.

"Are you going to let me open the door, or are you going to fuck me right here?" Lexie asked, breathless, as he trailed his tongue along her exposed collarbone where her sweater had slipped off her shoulder. "I don't mind, but I'm not sure my neighbors would appreciate it."

She nodded at a camera over his left shoulder, and added, "The security guard might enjoy the show, though."

Mitch growled but set her down, every inch of her slowly sliding against him as he did, his chest rapidly rising and falling with the effort of holding himself back.

He was a hockey player, damnit. Making out should *not* be making him this breathless.

But, as he studied her from behind while she punched her code into the door and stalked inside, he realized her ass had spelled trouble from the beginning.

When she faced him again, he was leaning against the doorframe, a wicked grin splitting his face.

"What are you doing?" she asked, cocking a hip and setting her hand on it.

"Admiring the view," he said.

She smirked. "Well, I can assure you it's a lot better when it's not covered in all this denim," she said, gesturing to the jeans that molded perfectly to her, like a second skin.

Closing the distance between them in one long stride, he hooked her by the belt loops and pulled her flush against him. Mitch dwarfed normal women, but Lexie was tall enough that he hardly had to duck to kiss her. Tipping his head toward hers, she greeted him hungrily, shoving her hands under his shirt and scratching her nails down his back.

Mitch groaned as his skin pebbled. "Bedroom. Now."

"Awfully bossy for someone who doesn't live here," Lexie said, her words a whisper.

"Lexie," he growled.

She pulled back with a smirk but grabbed his hand and turned, pulling him through her apartment.

Before they stepped inside, Mitch pushed her up against the wall outside her bedroom door and slid his knee between her legs, reaching around to cup her ass. She arched into him and whimpered as she ground her center onto his thigh.

The sound nearly undid him, his cock hard as a rock, his balls aching, begging for release.

But for some reason, Mitch felt compelled to savor this. To wring every last ounce of pleasure from Lexie before giving in to his own. Once he was buried inside her, he wouldn't last long anyway.

And that would be embarrassing.

He needed to take care of her first.

Several times.

"I know, baby," he said, sliding his hands under her sweater and pulling it over her head. "Let's get you out of these clothes first."

He unbuttoned her jeans, pulled down the zipper, and dug his hands inside to slide them past her hips—

And her phone rang.

He pulled one hand out of her jeans and slid it from her back pocket, seeing Berkley's name on the readout. Lexie snatched it from his hand.

"Berk," she said when she answered, putting the phone on speaker. "I'm in the middle of something here."

Mitch laughed, and Lexie smacked him as Berkley's voice echoed between them. "I...something happened."

"What? Are you okay?" Lexie asked, her face leached of all color.

Little alarm bells went off in his brain, the adrenaline coursing through his veins shifting in a heartbeat from wanting to rip Lexie's clothes off to wanting to protect Berkley. All thoughts of taking Lexie to bed flew out of Mitch's head, the lust he was feeling moments ago replaced instantly by concern.

As a man who had spent his entire career protecting his teammates and as one who understood how it felt to need protecting, the need to be there for Berkley after whatever had happened tonight came as naturally as breathing.

Plus, sticking around should earn him some major brownie points with her best friend.

Mitch's mind was spinning. Something had happened in the twenty minutes since he and Lexie had left her, bad enough that Berkley was shaken.

When they had left her, Berkley had been with Parker, so if something happened...

Berkley's voice, low and shaky, filtered from the phone. "I don't know. Lex, I know you're with Mitch, but I can't be alone right now."

Lexie's gaze shot up to his as she said. "He'll be gone when you get here. Whatever it is, Berk, it's gonna be okay."

"I know," Berkley said quickly. "I'll see you soon."

Lexie hung up and said, "You need to leave. Now."

"Like hell I do," he said, crossing his arms over his chest. "If something happened between us leaving her at the bar and now, there's only one person to blame."

His rat bastard teammate. Mitch shouldn't be surprised, given Parker spent the entire night talking about how he would take her home, even though Mitch had been very clear that she was not to be touched.

She was Jean's. They all knew that even if she didn't.

"Mitch, I'm serious. I'm sorry that whatever this is," she said, gesturing between them, "got interrupted, but Berkley needs me right now. You can't be here."

"Look," Mitch said, stepping forward to twine a lock of Lexie's silky hair around his finger. "I know I just met y'all tonight, but I've heard a lot about Berkley from Jean. And after this sexy little makeout session, we're friends now, aren't we?" He gave her a sly grin, which she returned.

"Yes, I suppose so. Although I was really hoping for some benefits," she said.

"Me too," Mitch told her honestly. His dick was still straining against his jeans, and he looked down to where her own was hanging open, a glimpse of red lace barely visible. She followed his gaze and hastily zipped herself back up. "But if Parker had something to do with this," Mitch continued, "I want to be there for Berkley. Since Jean can't."

Lexie studied him, her eyes flitting across his face as if looking for some insincerity in his words. When she didn't find it, she said, "Okay. Let's go down to wait for her. She can't be far away."

She turned from him, and he reached out to clasp her wrist in his hands, pulling her in for a searing kiss. They both breathed heavily when he broke away, leaning his forehead against hers. "I promise there will be plenty of time for benefits later."

She threaded her fingers through his and made their way down to the street.

A few minutes later, Berkley arrived, and apparently, the ashen quality of her skin gave Lexie second thoughts about his presence because she said, "You can go."

He ignored her, walking up to the cab to help Berkley out. She was shaking so badly that he half-carried her onto the sidewalk where Lexie was standing. "Are you okay?" He asked.

Berkley shook her head, eyes wild, blonde hair flying in the light breeze. "I don't want to talk about this here. Can we just go upstairs?"

"Of course," Lexie said, reaching out for Berkley's hand. "Mitch, you can leave."

"No!" Berkley said, the word loud and laced with fear but firm. "I want him here. I..." She broke off, and tears spilled down her cheeks. Mitch pulled her to his chest as the first sob tore free from her throat.

"Oh, honey," he said, gently rubbing circles on her back.

Lexie stepped up next to him, and they wordlessly helped Berkley up to the apartment.

Once inside, Berkley shrugged them off and made a beeline for the kitchen, pulling a bottle of tequila from the freezer, then removing a shot glass from the cupboard.

Mitch guessed this wasn't the first time Berkley participated in this particular ritual.

After Berkley had downed a shot, Mitch said, "Okay, what the fuck is going on?"

"Parker tried to assault me." The words were flat, cold, and detached. It had happened less than twenty minutes ago, and Berkley was already stoic.

Mitch, on the other hand, was neither cold nor detached. The instant the statement fell from Berkley's lips, Mitch's cheeks heated as his anger spiked.

"He WHAT?" He and Lexie yelled in unison.

Berkley briefly recounted the events of the cab ride.

"I'll kill him," he said when Berkley finished, already moving toward the door, teeth ground together, fists clenched.

Berkley raced toward him and grabbed his arm as if that alone could hold him back. He was over a foot taller and at least a hundred pounds heavier and had rage on his side. And almost nothing could stop a pissed-off hockey player.

"No, Mitch, please don't," she begged him. Tears welled in her eyes again, the lines of her face etched in distress. "I can't have anyone finding out."

"And why the hell not?" Lexie asked. "I see no reason why you shouldn't let Mitch go to his place right now and rip his balls from his body."

Mitch nodded, Lexie voicing his thoughts exactly. Parker was going to pay for this, one way or another.

A small giggle bubbled from Berkley's throat, presumably at the vision that conjured, but there was no mirth in it. "Lexie," she said, turning to her friend. "No one is going to believe me, for starters. Second, it's just not worth it. Nothing happened. I'm okay, if shaken up. I'm safe. All I want to do is curl up on the couch and watch Clueless."

Mitch could get on board with some Alicia Silverstone action. "I love that movie," he said quietly.

Berkley gave him a small, sad smile. "Me too. So let's just forget about this and move on."

Lexie appeared unconvinced, and Mitch waited to see what she would do. "Are you sure you don't need anything from us? Like Mitch taking Parker's head off?"

Berkley shook her head, and Mitch had to admit, he was disappointed. After what he'd just learned about his teammate, he was spoiling for a fight.

If it were up to him, Parker would already be in handcuffs, and from the murderous gleam in Lexie's eye, he guessed she felt the same.

But it wasn't up to them. This was Berkley's call, and even though it went against everything Mitch stood for as a man and hockey player, he had to respect that.

But he would be keeping an extra close eye on Parker Graff from now on.

A shiver raced down his spine, and Mitch had an inkling that he was living one of those nights he would look back at and say, "That's when it all changed."

Berkley spoke again, pulling Mitch from his thoughts. "What I need from you both is to just sit with me and keep me company. I can't be alone right now. That's why I didn't go home."

"We can do that," Mitch said quickly, willing to do whatever it took to make Berkley feel safe. Lexie raised an eyebrow at him, dubious.

Berkley's grateful smile was the first real one he'd seen on her face since before he and Lexie had left her in Parker's incapable, slimy hands.

Once Berkley was comfortable in and over-sized t-shirt and pair of sweatpants she rolled several times at the waist, they curled up together on the couch, marathoning early-2000s chick flicks into the wee hours of the morning. Berkley fell asleep with her head on his lap, feet on Lexie's, and when she was out cold and snoring, Lexie turned to him, her eyes shining with gratitude.

"You didn't have to stay," she whispered.

He shrugged. "I wanted to."

"I'm sorry we got interrupted, but I'm very much looking forward to getting you naked in the near future."

Mitch laughed, a low rumble deep in his chest. "That makes two of us."

It was nearly four in the morning when Lexie's eyes fluttered shut and breathing evened out. Only then, when she and Berkley were safe in their dreams, did he dare leave.

But not before he rifled through the drawers in Lexie's gigantic kitchen, which was all sleek white granite countertops, chrome appliances, and matte black hardware, wrapping around a massive island—honestly, what did this girl do for a living?—and found some scrap paper and a pen.

He scrawled his message and sat the note on top of her phone, so she'd find it as soon as she woke up, then crept out of the apartment and into the night.

CHAPTER ONE
Lexie

TWENTY-TWO MONTHS LATER...

L exie cracked open an eye, instantly blinded by the sunshine streaming through the blinds on the window across the room. She slammed her eyes shut against the sudden brightness and deeply inhaled, taking a survey of her body.

Head? Surprisingly not achy.

Back and chest? Slightly sore from too much laughing and screaming the words to early-2000s hip-hop at the top of her lungs last night.

Legs? A little stiff from dancing on the patio.

Feet? Grimy, but nothing a quick shower won't fix.

Stomach? Grumbling, begging for food.

Then there was the matter of the strong, heavy arm thrown across her middle. That was enough to keep her in this bed a little longer.

In fact, after their romp in the sheets the night before, when he got her off not once but twice, wildly jerking himself while he licked her through the second orgasm, Lexie was ready and willing to return the favor.

So she tossed the covers back enough to roll her naked body toward him and pressed her chest and stomach along his warm side, slinging her leg over his thigh. His arm, still draped over her, tightened, and a deep sigh emanated from his chest.

She leaned forward to press open-mouthed kisses across his chest, flicking her tongue over a nipple, and his hand floated down her back to cup her ass.

"Good morning," he mumbled, not bothering to open his eyes as Lexie sat up to straddle him and slid down his body until she was eye-to-eye with her favorite appendage.

Instead of responding with her own greeting, she traced the head of his cock with her tongue and giggled when his whole body twitched.

"Lexie," he hissed. "Don't play with me."

"You love it when I play with you.".

He looked down at her, brown eyes glowing in the morning sun, and said, "You're always so sassy. I should spank you."

"Later," Lexie said and wrapped her mouth around him.

Afterward, they made their way downstairs, where her best friend Berkley and Berkley's fiancé Brent were already in the kitchen, the latter at the stove, frying up a mountain of scrambled eggs, and the former at the counter, cutting up strawberries.

"Morning Lexie, morning Chris."

Lexie's companion mumbled a response as he sank onto a bar stool.

Chris Murphy. What could Lexie say about Chris Murphy?

For starters, he was no Mitch Frambough, which was a point in his favor most days. Truthfully, Chris was Mitch's opposite in many ways. Where Mitch was tall, fair-haired, and green-eyed, Chris was average height—which was actually the same height as her—with curly chocolate brown hair and eyes that turned molten in the sun, like hot cocoa with a splash of cream. He didn't have a professional athlete's physique but took excellent care of himself. In casual conversation, he was quiet and thoughtful, but behind closed doors...well, Lexie was pleasantly surprised the first time she got him into bed, and what she expected to be a quickie turned into a two-day sexual bender.

The boy did incredible things with his tongue.

They had been at the Jean family cabin in upstate New York for a week, enjoying some downtime with Brent and Berkley before training camp started, and Berkley went back to school. Seven days together, and Chris still could barely look Brent in the eyes. Lexie had failed to clue Chris in on exactly who Brent was on purpose, wanting to see what kind of reaction he would have when he discovered she was friends with a professional athlete.

It didn't go well, as was evidenced by the fact that even now, a week later, Chris was still starstruck.

Lexie didn't feel anything in particular for Chris one way or the other outside of the fact that he was easy to spend time with, and the sex was incredible.

But there was a new tension between them, and Lexie knew the moment was coming when he'd ask her for something more serious.

Something she couldn't give him.

Not after Mitch.

It was wild to compare her life from twelve months ago to her life now. A year ago, she had spent this very week, the week of Brent's then-thirtieth birthday, in this exact same cabin. She had shared the same guest room with Mitch, woken up next to him, and done all the things with him that she'd done with Chris this morning.

Berkley held a mug of coffee out, and Lexie took it gratefully, allowing the too-hot sip to chase away those memories of last summer and all the ones before and after that involved Mitch Frambough.

Lexie padded back across the kitchen, with its white-washed everything and giant windows that overlooked the lake, to set up camp on the bar stool next to Chris while Brent and Berkley finished making breakfast.

The foursome chatted about nothing, the conversation stilted, lopsided, mainly Lexie, Berk, and Brent carrying it while Chris sat awkwardly, sipping his coffee.

Chris wasn't Mitch, and Lexie hated herself for constantly comparing the two. Sometimes, she couldn't help it. Mitch had, up until four months ago, been a huge part of her life. She couldn't just erase that from her memory, as badly as she wanted to.

Once breakfast was finished, Lexie and Chris followed Brent and Berkley out to the patio to eat, where Brent, bless him, tried desperately to get Chris to open up about his life in Detroit, how he and Lexie met, and what his hobbies were outside of work. Unfortunately, Chris wasn't interested in making small talk with the star hockey player, and would rather stare at him in awestruck silence.

Lexie struggled not to roll her eyes.

By the time they finished their meal, Lexie's shoulders were burning from tension, and she loosed a large sigh of relief when Chris, surprisingly, trailed inside after Brent to clean up.

"You're going to end things with him, aren't you?" Berkley asked the moment they were alone.

The situation was hardly comical, yet Lexie couldn't help but laugh. She had always been a master of schooling her features, keeping her true feelings locked away and maintaining a calm, cool, and collected exterior.

Rarely, if ever, did Alexandra Monroe let anyone close enough to know what she was truly thinking.

But Berkley could read her like a book. It was a testament to the strength of their friendship that Berkley inherently understood things about Lexie that others never did and never would.

"Alexandra," Berkley scolded. "This isn't funny!"

"I know it's not, Berk," Lexie said with a sigh. "It's just funny how easily you can read me."

Berkley giggled. "Sometimes I wish I couldn't. And let's not forget you're not *always* easy for me to read."

Lexie tried not to wince, but her eyebrows drew together anyway. "I don't want to talk about him."

Berkley reclined back in her chair and took a sip of her coffee, giving Lexie a knowing look. "You never do. But one day you're going to have to."

"Well today is not that day."

The screen door from the kitchen slid open, and Chris asked, "Not the day for what?"

"Jet skiing," Lexie lied easily. "Berkley and I are going to go into town and do some shopping so you boys can bond."

Berkley raised an eyebrow at Lexie, dubious. "We are?"

Lexie silently pleaded with Berkley to go along with this ruse. She needed time away from Chris, from this cabin, for a few hours. If only so, she could regain some piece of her sanity.

Chris opened and closed his mouth a few times, and Lexie held her breath, waiting.

If he fights me on this or shows any inkling that he has a backbone, I'll reconsider ending things. Just...please, Chris. Give me something to work with here.

In the end, all Chris did was nod and turn to go back inside.

"Okay," Berkley said. "I can see why you're ending it."

"Right? Thank you," Lexie said with a laugh.

"I mean...when we were younger, a dude that let us get away with shit always seemed like the dream, right? But now..."

"But now, I don't want some docile man who never wants to stand up to me."

"Exactly. Trust me, that one fights with me constantly," Berkley said, tilting her head toward the kitchen window at Brent, looking out at them and sticking his tongue out. "But it's good for me. Keeps me honest. If I had a man who just let me have free reign over our entire lives, I'd be a horrible person. Especially considering the type of money mine makes. If Brent and I were different people, that could be dangerous."

Lexie snorted. Berkley had never wanted or needed Brent's money. She worked her ass off in undergrad to put herself through law school, with a little help from her parents and a trust fund, and in the year since graduation, she had been doing very well for herself, working for the same firm that represented Brent.

Except now Berkley was going back to school. Berkley's dream has always been to be an agent and represent athletes like rookies and women who tend to be taken advantage of in contract negotiations. She would still be practicing law part-time while she took business and other necessary courses at Wayne State so she could open her own agency, and Brent was bankrolling the entire thing.

When she told Lexie about it, Lexie genuinely thought it was some big joke. The Berkley from two years ago would never. But she and Brent were getting married eventually, and what was his would soon be hers anyway.

It was a big moment for Berkley and said so much more about how safe she felt with Brent and how much she loved him than words ever could.

"You know what else we can do today?" Berkley asked, dragging Lexie's attention back to the present.

"I'm assuming this is a rhetorical question," Lexie said.

Berkley rolled her eyes but said, "We can start wedding planning!"

That got Lexie's attention. "You two finally settled on a date?"

"Sure did," Berkley said proudly. "July 22, 2023."

God, a year from now. Where would Lexie be then? Would she still have the same job? Would she even still be in Detroit? She wasn't worried about her friendship with Berkley; it was the strongest she'd ever had in her life, and she knew they could withstand anything, no matter how far apart they were.

"That's a long engagement," Lexie said, thinking about how it had already been a year since Brent proposed. "What if I'm not around next year?"

"You better be!" Berkley said. "I can't get married without my maid of honor."

Lexie's eyes widened. "Maid of honor? Are you sure? What about your sister?"

"I love Jessica," Berkley said, "but she's not my best friend."

The proclamation was completely unexpected and rendered Lexie momentarily speechless. Tears pricked her eyes, and she heaved a deep breath, composing herself.

"Is that a yes?" Berkley asked, smiling widely.

"That's a *hell yes!*" Lexie exclaimed, jumping up from the table to hug her best friend.

"So now you're obligated to help me plan this thing. And unfortunately, because of Brent's job, it's going to be fancy."

"Unfortunately?" Lexie asked with an eyebrow raised.

It was a well-known fact that Berkley Daniels hated surprises, but she loved throwing parties and getting the chance to plan a wedding with a star-studded guest list was right up her alley. Her apparent distress surprised Lexie.

"Yes, unfortunately," Berkley echoed. "I've planned parties before, but never a wedding. And never for people who are stupid rich."

Ahh, the money. It always came back to the money for Berkley. Brent was obscenely wealthy, and it had always been a sticking point for Berkley. When she agreed to marry him, Lexie assumed she'd loosen up a bit. And she had, if her going back to school and letting Brent foot the bill was any indication. So why was this tripping her up now?

"What's really going on?" Lexie asked, knowing her friend well enough to know there was more to this story.

"I just…" Berkley trailed off, eyes darting to the serene surface of the lake and remaining fixed there as she continued. "I just wish we didn't have to make such a spectacle of it. This place is only so big. I wanted something low key and romantic. I never envisioned having to plan the wedding of the century."

"Well first off, it will hardly be the wedding of the century," Lexie told Berkley, satisfied when Berkley huffed out a laugh. "I'm pretty sure that honor belongs to William and Kate. But Berk, have you mentioned it to Brent?"

"Well, no…"

"Not this again," Lexie muttered.

In the early stages of their relationship, Brent and Berkley had textbook miscommunication issues. Or, in Berkley's case, complete lack of communication a lot of the time.

"Truthfully, Lex, I just came to this conclusion like five minutes ago. The more time I spend up here, the more I can picture the wedding. And the wedding I want isn't some grand affair. It's our families, our friends, a small group of Brent's teammates—past and present. It's turning this patio into a giant dance floor with a buffet that people can pick at all night instead of a sit down dinner. It's intimate and romantic, with crisp white flower arrangements accented by blue and red, and twinkle lights covering every inch of this place. It's a DJ playing all of our favorite songs and us dancing into the wee hours of the morning. It's falling into bed with Brent at the end of the night and not having to worry if I made a fool of myself in front of some important league official. It's just…simple. Elegant. Perfect."

"Is that really what you want, babe?"

Lexie and Berkley whirled toward the screen door, where Brent was standing, arms folded across his chest, a small smile playing on his lips.

Lexie watched as Berkley swallowed hard and nodded.

Brent walked toward them and bent down to give Berkley a quick peck on the lips. "Then that's what you'll get."

Lexie's heart swelled. Brent had always been wonderful to Berkley, their relationship the stuff of fairytales despite their hardships. Lexie was incredibly happy for her friend, but she couldn't ignore the pang of longing that echoed through her chest.

She'd had that with Mitch, hadn't she? She had tried so hard to keep him at arm's length when they first met, distracting him with her body before he could weasel his way into her heart. But when he finally had, Lexie couldn't figure out why she'd fought it for so long.

For nearly two years, Mitch had been the sun around which Lexie's universe revolved. And when he'd gone, everything turned dark and cold.

She was happy for Berkley, but she could admit that she was still crawling out of that hole she'd dug to protect herself when Mitch had left. She knew it was going to take some time before she could have conversations about weddings and love stories and not mourn what she had lost.

"So where are you jetting off to next?" Berkley asked her, steering the conversation toward safer waters.

"Phoenix," Lexie said quickly.

"Who are you recruiting this time?"

"Some financial whiz a company in Indiana wants to bring on as their new CFO," Lexie told her. "I'm not sure how long I'll be gone. All depends on how amenable this kid is to the offer."

Berkley smirked. "Well, you *are* Lexie Monroe. And no one walks away from what Lexie Monroe is offering."

Lexie gave Berkley a smile that didn't quite reach her eyes.

No one walked away from Lexie Monroe, she thought. *No one except Mitch Frambough.*

CHAPTER TWO
Mitch

M itch dropped the barbell back onto the rack and sat up, reaching for a towel to wipe the sweat from his face and naked chest.

"So what're you and Kiera up to tonight?" His teammate and defensive partner, Gabe Huntley, asked.

"I think she put together some listings for me to go see," Mitch told him.

"Finally gonna put down some roots out here?" Gabe asked with an eyebrow wiggle.

Mitch fought a smile as he snapped the towel in his direction. "Maybe."

Truthfully, Mitch had fought finding a new apartment for as long as possible. But it had already been six months since the trade, and he figured it was probably time to stop renting month-to-month.

Although that was far preferable to his first two months in the City of Angels, during which he lived out of a hotel room.

It had been easier than acting like this place was home now, but he couldn't avoid it any longer.

But nothing permanent; he would not be *buying* anything. To him, living in LA still felt like a bad dream, although he'd never admit that to Gabe.

Some mornings, he still woke up and experienced a split second where he expected to open his eyes and find himself back in his condo in Detroit, Lexie naked and passed out next to him, that vanilla and cinnamon lotion she favored clinging to his sheets around her, sticking in his nose.

But a blink of his eyes always placed him in a barely recognizable room, in an apartment he lived in like a ghost, no trace of that girl or her warm and spicy scent anywhere to be found.

And his heart broke a little more each time.

Shaking his head, he returned his attention to Gabe as he laid down on the bench and pumped the bar loaded with heavy plates up and down.

Their first game of the season was the next day, and the Knights were out for blood after being knocked out of the playoffs in the Western Conference Finals the year before.

God, it's insane how much has changed, he thought.

Once Gabe finished his sets, wrapping up his and Mitch's strength training regimen for the day, they opted to head outside for some early-morning cardio.

Most hockey players hated it, but running had always relaxed Mitch. While being on the ice was akin to breathing for Mitch, something about running was soothing. He loved emptying his mind of everything but focusing on his breath and putting one foot in front of the other.

As hockey players were creatures of habit, Mitch and Gabe always ran the same route: northwest up Figueroa Street and farther away from the ocean until they met Temple, where they took a right and followed that until they hit Spring Street. Mitch loved jogging along Spring Street. To his left was the massive thirty-two-floor, Art Deco-inspired Los Angeles City Hall building. And to his right was the Grand Park pet park and playground, where the sounds of dogs barking and children squealing filled the morning air. Past that, they hooked a right onto West Second Street and continued along until it connected up with Figueroa again, where they would turn left and head back to the arena.

A little over five miles later, they stumbled into the locker room and collapsed at their stalls. The few teammates still milling around from that morning's weight lifting session chuckled at their expense.

"I don't know why you guys torture yourself like that," Cally said. "You know running and skating are not the same kind of cardio. You're wasting your time."

"Speaking as your captain, Cally," Gabe said, followed by a desperate gasp for air, "kindly fuck off."

Connor "Cally" Callahan snorted. Cally was a rookie phenom and had spent most of the previous season with the Knights' AHL team in Ontario. He'd been called up to Los Angeles the same day Mitch was traded.

The kid had all the makings of a superstar career, but he had a bad habit of not being able to keep his mouth shut.

Cally stepped close to Gabe and leaned down so they were nearly eye to eye. "Say it to my face, old man."

Case in point.

He also hated being called "Cally," so the guys did it every chance they got.

Mitch snapped his towel in the kid's direction. "Get lost, Cally."

He turned on Mitch and opened his mouth.

Mitch stood. At six-five, he towered over the five-eleven forward.

Cally backed away and turned to exit the locker room, looking like a dog with its tail between its legs.

Gabe looked at Mitch. "We really gotta teach that kid a lesson about that mouth of his one of these days."

"I'm in," Mitch said.

Gabe barked out a laugh. "That easy, huh?"

"That kid is a nuisance, and it's going to be our asses on the line when he says something stupid on the ice and can't defend himself."

Gabe nodded in agreement. "I'll let you know what I come up with."

Mitch held out his hand and bumped his fist against Gabe's.

An hour later, Mitch was freshly showered and dressed in an outfit he probably would not have been caught dead in back in Detroit.

Especially not in October.

But his change of scenery had also necessitated a change of wardrobe, and he had always loved shopping for clothes, even if he favored flannels and jeans. He was now the proud owner of approximately ninety percent of the men's clothing Bonobos offered, having quickly discovered that their clothing fit his oversized frame well, and he looked good in it.

Today he was sporting a pair of their heather azure blue performance link shorts and a Riviera cabana shirt that was a light linen material with a little palm tree where a breast pocket would be.

He bumped fists again with Gabe after they exited the arena and reached the player parking lot, agreeing to meet early tomorrow to go over a game plan before their season opener in Anaheim.

When he walked into his apartment, Lizzo was filtering through the television speakers, there were bags of God only knew what on his kitchen counters, clothes strewn along the floor in the hallway, and the bathroom light was on.

Which could only mean one thing: Kiera was here.

He dropped his bag by the door and stalked forward, taking a deep breath before peeking his head around the bathroom door. There Kiera stood, in a pair of soft gray shorts and a white sports bra, a chunk of hair wrapped around her curling wand, the counter in front of her littered with cosmetics.

"Hey babe!" she said, stepping up to him and raising on her tippy-toes to give him a quick peck on the lips. "How was practice?"

"It was good," he said slowly. "How did you get in? Not that I'm not happy to see you..."

Kiera giggled a stupid, vapid sound that grated on Mitch's ears. "You gave me a key like a month ago, silly."

Mitch raised an eyebrow, but she had already turned away. He knew he hadn't given her a key, but because she was his real estate agent, she had probably sweet-talked his super into making a copy.

Kiera Lawrence was also Mitch's sort-of girlfriend.

Sort-of because things weren't that serious, and he had been thinking about breaking it off with her for a while.

Kiera and Mitch had met during his third month in LA. The Knights had been knocked out of the playoffs the week before, and hotel living was growing old. The Knights' management set him up with a real estate company, and Kiera became his agent. They went out for drinks to discuss what he was looking for in a place, and because Mitch was still nursing his broken heart over Lexie and needed the distraction, he didn't turn down her advances.

She went home with him that night and never left.

Kiera was the opposite of Lexie in every way: short, blonde, even-tempered, gave her affection freely from the beginning, but also incredibly high-maintenance.

He was dreading this evening of apartment hunting with her. He only hoped that she had actually taken his list of must-haves to heart and not selected listings based on what she thought he wanted.

Kiera finished getting ready minutes or hours later—Mitch stopped paying attention—and emerged from the bathroom looking like a totally different person.

Incredible what caking on powder and foundation and some eyeshadow and mascara could do for a woman.

Not that Mitch had anything against women who wore makeup. But Kiera didn't wear makeup; makeup wore her.

"You can't keep living in this apartment," Kiera said, turning a tight circle in his sparse living room, surveying Mitch's utter lack of interior decorating.

The room contained a couch and a TV, which was all he really needed.

And again...he had no desire to put down roots. But he couldn't very well tell her that, so he said, "I didn't know if the Knights were going to keep me around after the season was over. Renting this place month-to-month seemed like a smart decision."

Kiera rolled her eyes. "You're going to love the houses I found for you. They're spectacular."

Mitch sighed, zeroing in on the words *houses* and *spectacular*. "I don't need some big fancy house," he said. "I'm hardly ever home. What I need is something low maintenance."

She waved her hand dismissively, which quite frankly pissed Mitch off, but he held his tongue.

"You only think you want low maintenance because you've been living like a monk for the last six months. But you're with me, aren't you? I think that decision speaks for itself," she said with a wink.

The girl had a point. Her clothes were designer, her car had cost enough to make even Mitch balk when she'd told him, and she lived in a sprawling high-rise apartment complete with a doorman and all other bougie ameni-ties a woman like her could want.

Now that he thought about it, it was possible her motivation to find him a home wasn't entirely altruistic.

Add that to the list of reasons to end this relationship.

"Are you ready?" he asked, steering her from the apartment with a light hand on her lower back before she launched into another one of her monologues about the future.

A future that she seemed to think included him.

Mitch had never intended to lead her on. At first, she was someone to have fun with, and the sex was enthusiastic. From where he was standing, this wasn't anything serious, and it was never meant to be.

He didn't think he'd ever be able to do *serious* again.

But as the days rolled by, Mitch got the impression that Kiera expected more from him than he could give.

Which meant he really had to end it.

He would do it tonight after she showed him whatever listings she had pulled. Before they came back to his spartan apartment and he buried himself in her. He didn't need sex bad enough to warrant fucking her then dumping her. Truth be told, there were plenty of women that would gladly take her place at the drop of a hat, ones who wanted far less of him.

They headed outside and approached Kiera's car, Mitch folding himself into the low-slung vehicle, practically kneeing himself in the chest.

I fucking hate this car, he thought.

He missed his Suburban back in Detroit. After the move, he sold it and bought a sporty little Range Rover. It felt more...LA Mitch.

Kiera sped away from the curb and down the road, turning up into the hills instead of toward town, where all the high rises were.

"Kiera," he said. "Where are we going?"

She glanced sideways at him, an attempt at a sexy smile playing on her lips. If Mitch wasn't Mitch, if his chest wasn't full of the broken pieces of his heart, it probably *would* have been sexy. But all it did was irritate him.

"You'll see," she said innocently, a wicked gleam in her eyes.

She navigated them away from the city's bright lights and onto quieter residential streets, babbling the whole time about how one of the agents at the brokerage had poached a wealthy client from another and the drama it caused at the office.

Finally, she turned onto a tree-lined street broken by driveways veering off into the distance.

"We're almost there," she promised. "There's this gorgeous house up here that I think you'll love. Great for entertaining. I've been informed you like to throw a lot of parties for your teammates."

Mitch groaned. "I already told you I'm not in the market for a house. I was hoping for an apartment near the arena. Somewhere that requires minimal upkeep since I'm gone so much."

Kiera side-eyed him. "You have an entire off-season to spend here. And trust me, summers in LA are the best. You're going to want a house. Trust me."

Mitch checked another groan before it escaped, settling for rolling his eyes and hoping she didn't see. She had an incredibly annoying habit of saying phrases like *trust me* and *believe me* twice in a row as if it would make him do either.

But he didn't bother to fight her, knowing she was used to getting her way. There was nothing he could say or do to get her to turn this car around and head back down the hill. He was stuck. So he would just have to tell her he hated the house and politely, sternly, ask her to find him an apartment downtown like he wanted in the first place.

At this point, he'd be better off finding a new real estate agent altogether. Preferably a man.

Kiera turned up a cobblestone drive shaded by towering palm trees and lined with big, full rose bushes. The house came into view a moment later, and Mitch couldn't help himself: he gasped.

Kiera looked smug. "Told you."

The exterior was wide plank siding painted a bright white, the windows and doors trimmed in black. It consisted of two wings connected by an open-air breezeway. A detached garage sat off to the side, large enough to fit at least four vehicles.

Mitch knew instantly it was way too much, but while they were here, he might as well see the interior.

And it was just as spectacular inside as out: light and airy, with vaulted ceilings in the common areas and doorways large enough for him to enter rooms without ducking. The floors were a sandy oak that ran through both levels. Kiera informed him that it had four bedrooms, five and a half bathrooms, a giant kitchen and dining room, a great room, and a home theater.

It was way more space than he would ever need.

"Kiera," he said as she turned to take him upstairs to the master suite and two of the guest rooms, babbling about square footage and comparable properties in the neighborhood, "I really appreciate you showing me this place. But it's way too much space for me."

"No it isn't," she insisted, frowning at him. "You're a big guy. You've got lots of teammates, and they've got families and friends. So do I. We'll be able to keep this place filled all the time with no problem."

Her use of *we* had Mitch internally cringing, knowing that was the final nail in the coffin of this relationship. She was a sweet girl and wildly energetic in bed. He never wanted to hurt her feelings but couldn't lead her on any longer. Not when she was clearly much more serious about this relationship than he was.

"That's the thing, Kiera," he said, hoping his constant use of her name would force her actually to hear what he was saying. "I don't want to entertain."

"You...what?" She asked, looking for all the world like he had just sprouted a second head from his neck.

"I don't want to entertain," he repeated.

"But why not? I was under the impression that entertaining was like...your thing."

"Not anymore."

Kiera stepped close and slid her arms around his waist, bending her head back to look up at him. Mitch met her gaze. "You never talk about it, you know."

"About what?" He asked.

"Michigan. Your life before you came here. You act like you were born the second you set foot in LA, that there's nothing to talk about from your past. But there is, and I wish you would share it with me."

Mitch melted a little under her gaze, surprised she had been paying that close attention to him. He tucked his hand under her chin and bent to kiss her. "I'm sorry," he said. "I'm just not ready."

Kiera nodded and stepped out of his arms. "Come on, let me show you the home theater."

He reached out his hand, and she took it, towing him along behind her as she passed through the massive rooms of the home. Even though he had every intention of ending their relationship tonight, looking at her now, seeing her face lit up as she discussed the specs of the house, he knew he couldn't. Having a companion, someone to wake up next to in the morning and come home to after a road trip or a long day at the rink, wasn't something he was ready to part with.

Kiera wasn't his usual type, and she was no Alexandra Monroe, but she was exactly what he needed right now.

CHAPTER THREE
Lexie

A few rows behind her, a baby let out a piercing wail. The couple next to her winced, and Lexie clicked up the volume on her audiobook.

While the narrator of *The Stranger in the Mirror* by Liv Constantine prattled on about the main character not recognizing herself or her life, Lexie rested her chin on her hand and turned her attention out the window.

She often felt like a stranger these days, too.

Lexie had always loved flying. As a child, it was the only opportunity she had to spend uninterrupted time with her parents, though even then, they ignored her in favor of in-flight cocktails and reviewing the materials for the next big deal they were heading off to close.

The thought of her parents made her heart sink, as it always did, and gazing at the clouds as they floated by wasn't helping matters, so she returned her attention to her iPad. Before she could settle back into reviewing the contract she had pulled up on the screen, the faint ding of the plane's intercom system sounded over the noise from her AirPods.

"If you all could return to your seats and fasten your seatbelts, we're beginning our descent into LAX. We'll have you on the ground and on your way in no time."

LAX.

Los Angeles.

Lexie's heart sank further.

LA was the absolute last place Lexie wanted to be right now, but the mechanical engineer she was recruiting for a medical equipment production company in Chicago lived here. After weeks of endless email correspondence, texts, and phone calls, she was certain he was about to jump on her hook at any moment. Traveling to LA was her way of sealing the deal, that final interaction, the face-to-face connection with Lexie that would finally get him to sign the contract and move to Illinois.

The second she deplaned and set foot on LA soil, she couldn't stop herself from picturing Mitch. He was here, somewhere in this vast metropolis. The chances of running into him were pretty damn slim, but nothing about their relationship had ever made much sense. She wouldn't put it past karma, the gods, or fate to intervene.

When she reached baggage claim, she found Kimber waiting for her looking tan and trim despite her natural curves, blonde hair flowing brightly in waves around her bare shoulders.

After a year and a half apart—since Kimber had moved back to California from Detroit—Lexie could barely contain her excitement. It was the only thing getting Lexie through the three days she had planned to spend in LA. Had Kimber not been here, Lexie wasn't sure she would have made the trip, wasn't sure she *could* have. No matter how small, the possibility of seeing Mitch again had nearly given her a panic attack on more than one occasion the last few weeks.

"Lexie!" She yelled, rushing up to crush her in a hug. Lexie squeezed back, then pulled away to study her.

"Girl, you look amazing."

Kimber spun in a circle, grinning wide. She had always been beautiful, but returning to her hometown had turned her into a smoke show. "Thank you. Being back in California has done wonders for me. Not that I don't miss you guys, but have you seen my ass? You could bounce a quarter off of it. When I'm not at work, I'm always outside. Hiking, surfing, yoga on the beach. You name it. I haven't been this happy, or this toned, in a long time."

Lexie smiled; Kimber's mood was contagious despite the storm cloud that had followed Lexie since Mitch left.

But she wasn't going to think about that. She was here in LA and was going to enjoy this time with her dear friend, pretending that Mitch Frambough didn't exist.

Once Lexie had checked into her hotel—much to Kimber's annoyance; she had offered several times to let Lexie stay with her—they went to Kimber's favorite Mexican restaurant for lunch, chowing down on fish tacos and catching up on their lives since Kimber had moved away from Detroit.

Which, truth be told, was a lot. It *had* been over a year.

"So are you seeing anyone?" Kimber asked.

"Nope," Lexie told her. "I've been super busy with work. Traveling a lot. The usual."

Kimber shook her head. "You never did know how to slow down."

Lexie laughed. "I still don't. And speaking of work, how is your dream job treating you?"

"It's been amazing. Those kids," Kimber paused, swallowing hard and clutching her chest, "inspire me every day. It's been a big motivating factor behind this transformation. I want to live a long, healthy, happy life. So getting my shit together was the first step."

"That's amazing, Kimber, truly." Lexie sipped her margarita. She couldn't imagine what it must be like, going to work every day to take care of sick children, some of whom would never leave the hospital alive. "What's the next step?"

"Vacation," Kimber told her. "I've been working at least six days a week for a year and a half. I want to experience the world. So for my two year work anniversary, I'm taking a trip."

"To where?"

"South America. I'm going to backpack around and do nothing but sight-see for a month."

"An entire month?" Lexie asked, incredulous. "By yourself?"

Kimber nodded. "All alone. It's going to be incredible."

"Sounds terrifying to me," Lexie said, which was ironic as hell coming from the girl who had basically raised herself. She had spent the bulk of her life alone, but never in a foreign country, with nothing but her wits to protect her.

Kimber was far more brave than Lexie would ever be.

"I'll admit, I am a little afraid, but not so much that I don't want to. do it. I owe it to myself, and those children in the hospital, to go on this adventure."

Lexie lifted her glass, and Kimber mirrored the gesture, clinking them together. "I'm proud of you," Lexie told her. "It seems like getting out of Michigan was exactly what you needed."

"It has been life-changing, to say the least. Who knew coming home, to the place where I grew up, could change me so much."

"Something to consider," Lexie said with a small smile, although she didn't have a home in the way that Kimber did.

Lexie and her parents had moved around so much during Lexie's formative years that she truly didn't understand the meaning of the word, or what it would feel like to have that one place where she could go to and always feel safe and loved.

For Lexie, home wasn't a place. It was people.

And Detroit was where those people lived.

So Detroit was her home now.

Lexie spent the next day with Steve, another engineer she was recruiting, endlessly studying the contracts she needed him to sign. Lexie had even called Berkley several times, grateful to have a best friend that was an attorney who specialized in contract law. Between the three of them, they reworked the deal until Steve was satisfied with the terms. Thankfully, Lexie had been given carte blanche to make changes as necessary. Her boss's exact words had been, "Show him your tits if you have to. Just get him to sign the damn deal."

Had a man said those words to her, she would've quit on the spot. But her boss was a woman–and a badass one at that—who took no prisoners and could slice you in half with a single sharp look.

Lexie wanted to be her when she grew up.

Though Lexie's company had in-house counsel, Lexie allowed Berkley to pass the revised contract off to her boss to redraft it. The following morning, Steve promised he would sign it.

Lexie had one final night in LA, and all she wanted to do was have an early dinner, go out for some drinks, and return to her hotel early.

Kimber, of course, had other plans.

As they wove in and out of the traffic clogging up downtown, Lexie asked, "Where are we going?"

"You'll see," Kimber said in a sing-song voice.

A few blocks later, a large event venue came into view, dominating the sky across an entire square city block.

"You didn't," Lexie said.

"Surprise!" Kimber said as she turned into a parking lot across the street. "We're going to a Knights' game!"

The LA Knights. Also known as the team Mitch had been traded to back in April.

Lexie struggled to keep the panic from her face as Kimber parked the car and got out, chatting excitedly about how much Lexie would love the arena and wasn't it so fun that they were going to a hockey game together, just like old times?

Lexie could think of a thousand things that would be more enjoyable than willingly putting herself in a position where she would have to see Mitch Frambough.

Getting a root canal.

Having her vagina waxed.

Scooping her eyes out of her head with rusty spoons.

Lexie hadn't laid eyes on the man in six months, and she wasn't entirely sure she was ready.

At least she wouldn't actually have to speak to him. Surely simply seeing him while he worked couldn't be *that* bad.

After all, it *had* been six months. Sure, the mention of his name still caused her heart to constrict, and she'd moved into a new condo, the old one holding too many memories for her sanity. But she was fine.

Really. She was *fine*.

Except, naturally, he was the first player out of the tunnel. And naturally, when he skated onto the ice, he headed directly for where she was seated right on the glass, Lexie had to admit, she was the opposite of fine.

Stunned, she couldn't tear her gaze away from him fast enough, and they locked eyes when he was about a foot away, separated only by the boards and a thick sheet of Plexiglass. When he skated away without recognition dawning, her shoulders relaxed. And then he spun back so fast, he nearly fell over. One of his teammates—the back of his jersey read Huntley—bumped into him and urged him along.

Mitch's mouth hung comically open as he skated backward. Having missed the entire exchange, Kimber turned toward the ice right as Mitch turned his back on them, completely oblivious that Lexie's heart was a brick beating against her ribs.

"Oh hey," Kimber said. "I forgot Mitch Frambough played for the Knights now. Remember when we used to party at his loft? I wonder if he recognized us."

"I don't think so," Lexie said, entire body wrapped in a cold embrace that had absolutely nothing to do with their proximity to the ice.

Kimber didn't know about the...*thing* with Mitch. Truth be told, when she moved away, they had all sort of lost touch with her. Berkley had taken the bar, passed, started her career, and gotten engaged. Amelia had landed a gig with a travel magazine, going from a small-time blogger to a big-time feature columnist.

Lexie had...well, she had her job, which she loved mostly because she was good at it and she made a lot of money doing it. And she had her friends, like Berkley and Amelia. In the wake of Mitch leaving the way he did, she had gotten closer with Brent and his teammates like Cole, Rat, and Grey out of necessity. They had bonded over their shared sadness of Mitch being gone.

Before, she'd had Mitch. That was an accomplishment to be proud of, simply because somehow, some way, a man like him had loved her.

Had loved her. That was, of course, before she fucked it all up.

And then he left, and that was the end of that.

So Lexie sat in the front row of the arena, watching Mitch in pure agony as he skated around the ice, laughing with his teammates, sweating, checking opponents, and looking sexier than ever.

Honestly, in quiet moments after he'd left, when the utter shock had worn off and she'd taken a break from drowning her sorrows in sex and tequila, she realized she would've given long distance with him a shot. She had acted hastily in pushing him away after their last fight; she knew that now. That last fight had been a desperate attempt to save herself. She hadn't yet been willing to put her heart on the line for him, not completely. Or rather, she *had*. She *had* been willing, and it scared her so much she'd lashed out.

When she stopped to consider what she'd done, only then could she admit to herself that she would have been willing to put everything on the line for him.

Everything.

But the way he left had made his feelings on the matter perfectly clear: he wasn't interested. He hadn't been willing to fight for her, so why would she fight for him?

So she picked herself up, dusted herself off, and put herself back together. After those awful early days, once she'd gotten her shit together—with the help of her friends—she had worked so hard to mend her broken heart, doing everything she could think of to distract herself from the pain. She'd gone out on dates, a few even lasting longer than a night, drank less, and threw herself into her work. She had even started going to the gym with Amelia, Berkley, and Brent, using her frustration, anger, hurt, and sadness as motivation.

All she wanted was to become a better version of herself. Maybe that version had been shaped by her relationship with Mitch, by being loved romantically by someone for exactly who she was for the first time in her life, but she was also becoming a version of herself that Mitch wouldn't recognize anymore.

And she was so proud of herself.

But sitting here tonight, with him mere feet away for the first time in months, she was instantly transported back to all those sleepless nights after he left. All those mornings she woke up next to someone whose name she didn't remember, with only flashes of memory from the night before to guide her through the awkward dance of getting them to leave.

And then even further, to being that little girl whose parents were never around, who only cared about her when they needed something from her.

She was reminded how easy she was to leave, and that thought was a knife to the heart.

Breaking down in front of Kimber and an arena full of people at a professional hockey game was not an option, though, so Lexie buried her feelings deep inside her heart, shoving them back in that box she kept them in, locking them up, and throwing away the key. This was simply a bump in the road. From here on out, it would surely be smooth sailing.

The first cut is the deepest, right? And this *was* the first cut. The first time she saw him. It had to be like ripping a bandage off; once she did it and got it out of the way, she'd feel so much better afterward.

Lexie was antsy as hell for the entire game, which Kimber chalked up to Lexie not being a hockey fan. Naturally, regulation ended in a 2-2 tie, and Lexie's anxiety continued to climb. Being near him, even in this massive, crowded arena, made it hard to breathe.

Thankfully, the Knights scored shortly into overtime on a goal assisted by none other than Mitch.

The second the goal horn sounded, Lexie was out of her seat, hustling Kimber down the row and up the stairs to the concourse level.

"What the rush?" Kimber asked. "I wanted to celebrate!"

"We can go out for drinks to celebrate," she said. "I want to beat the rush out of here. You know how I hate crowds."

Kimber smiled indulgently and hurried after Lexie.

That night, Lexie got drunk. Drunker than she had been since the early days after the trade when numbing herself was preferable to the pain.

Apparently, old habits really *did* die hard.

It certainly didn't help that Kimber was all for it, ready to cut loose to celebrate the Knights' win and Lexie's last night in the city.

So she danced her feet off, grinding her ass into the lap of a perfect stranger. And when he slipped his hands around her waist and spun her to face him, she kissed him, knowing it wouldn't make her heart race or her toes curl. Not like with Mitch. No one made her feel the way he did. But it had been so long since she had connected physically with someone, since she broke up with Chris two months before, and despite the fact that there was no spark whatsoever, his lips felt good on hers.

After Mitch, the string of endless guys had never inspired the kind of physical reaction that he had. They had simply been a means to an end—a way to lose herself in the feel of someone's hands on her body, overwriting all of the times Mitch had done the same thing, until hopefully, one day, she would forget how it felt for him to hold her. But she constantly worried that there would never be another Mitch again, that no man would ever put his hands on her and elicit the same reactions Mitch had been able to.

She wouldn't be going home with this stranger, but she could let herself have this one makeout session, this one night of very public intoxication, in this dim LA club with EDM pounding from the speakers, drowning out the constant noise in her head.

Tonight, she could let herself slip. Just this once.

Tomorrow, she'd get her head back on straight.

Back in Detroit later that week, Lexie found herself at the gym with Amelia. Brent, Berkeley, and Cole usually joined them, but the boys were on a road trip to Canada, and Berkley flew up for a few days to watch their game in Toronto, so it was just them.

Amelia had an exercise science degree and had become the de facto personal trainer for Lexie and Berkley. After forcing Lexie through an exhaustive lower body strength training session, they were now on the floor in front of the wall of mirrors at their gym, moving through a yoga flow to cool down.

"So, how was LA?" Amelia asked conversationally as she pushed back into downward dog. Lexie's quads were screaming at her, but she followed Amelia's lead, grateful for the stretch she felt along the backs of her legs.

"It was good," she said on an exhale as Amelia lowered them into a plank position. "It was really great to see Kimber."

"Aww, I bet. I'm glad she's doing so well. I miss her, but it's good to see her thriving."

"Yeah, she definitely is. Obviously her pictures on Instagram are veritable thirst traps, but seeing the transformation in person was pretty shocking."

Amelia smiled as she effortlessly lifted into cobra. "I'm proud of her. She actually reached out and asked me for some tips when she decided she wanted to get back into shape."

It irritated Lexie how easy Amelia made this fitness stuff look, but she supposed she'd been doing it long enough that it was almost second nature now.

"Yeah, she told me when she's not working, she's always outside, biking, surfing, those sorts of things."

"Okay that's good. Diet and exercise are important, but they have to be done right," Amelia said. "I saw you guys went to a hockey game, too," she added.

"Ames..." Lexie warned. "Leave it alone."

"What?" Her friend asked innocently. She smoothly pushed back into downward dog again, then dropped down onto her hands and knees; Lexie followed her lead, thankful to give her arms a bit of a break.

Amelia slowly rounded her back and curved it inward in cat-cow but gave Lexie a sidelong glance, waiting for Lexie to tell her about the game Kimber had dragged her to.

"The hockey game was fine," Lexie said, watching in the mirror that dominated one entire wall of the gym as her biceps flexed and extended.

"Did you..." Amelia broke off as she pressed back into child's pose. This position was Lexie's favorite when she was allowed to let her upper body drape over her lap, stretch her arms above her head, and relax into her breathing for a few moments.

Then Amelia pushed back up, dusting her hands off. She turned to Lexie on her mat, biting her lip, clearly debating whether or not to ask the question Lexie knew she was dying to ask. But Lexie refused to give her the satisfaction of helping her out, so she waited, taking several long pulls from her water bottle to pass the time.

Finally, Amelia said, "Did you see Mitch?"

A pang shot through Lexie's heart at the sound of his name. "I saw him on the ice while he played, yes."

"That was it?"

"That was it."

"How did he look?"

Lexie sighed. Amelia wasn't going to let this go. "He looked fine. In case you forgot, he was the one who left. He decided his life would be better without all of us in it. I don't understand why you care."

Amelia cast her gaze down, chastised, but said quietly, "I don't understand why you don't. You love him, Lex. Or at least, you did."

"No I didn't."

Amelia made a face, clearly unimpressed with the lie. "Don't bullshit me, Lexie."

She met Amelia's eyes then and saw the sadness and pity and worry there. Tears welled in her own in response, and she turned away, lifting the hem of her shirt to wipe them away, playing it off as though she was mopping sweat off her face. "I don't want to talk about this."

"You never have." Amelia's tone indicated an eye roll had accompanied the statement.

Lexie turned on her and pinned her with a glare. "What's that supposed to mean?"

"It means it's been six months, Lexie! And not once have you ever wanted to sit down and talk to me about what happened. How everything went so horribly wrong! And you never let me talk about Mitch. In case you forgot, in your own sad, selfish bubble where that part of your life just ceased to exist, Mitch was my friend too. We all lost someone when he left, but you want to pretend like it never happened. I know it was different for you, but...we're all working through something here."

Amelia stood up quickly and stalked away from Lexie as though she couldn't bear to be near her right now.

"I'm sorry," she said quietly.

Lexie walked over to her, and Amelia wrapped a sticky arm around Lexie's shoulders. "I know things haven't been easy for you. And I've been trying to be a good friend, but I feel that in not pushing you on this, I've been a bad one instead."

"You've never been a bad friend a second in your life," Lexie said, sliding an arm around Amelia's shoulders and squeezing her to her side. "I'm just...hurting."

"I know you are. But I need you to lean on me. On all of us," she said. "We'll get through this together."

Lexie nodded, pulling away. "What do you say we grab a couple bottles of wine, some Chinese takeout, and have a movie night?"

"Your place or mine?"

"Definitely mine," she said, thinking of the little six hundred-square foot apartment Amelia moved into after Kimber left.

Later, when they were set up in her living room on her roomie cloud-like couch, takeout containers and bottles of wine littering the glass-topped coffee table in front of them, the weight that had settled on her chest in Los Angeles lifted. Being here with Amelia reminded Lexie of the old days, back before she and Berkley met Mitch, before Berkley started dating Brent, and everything changed, back when it had just been them against the world.

Too bad it couldn't have stayed that way.

CHAPTER FOUR

Lexie

TWO YEARS AGO...

All night, Lexie had tried, and failed, not to track Mitch's movements from across the crowded room. The loft was huge and full of people; there was absolutely no way she should have been able to find him every time she lifted her eyes to scan the space.

And yet, that's exactly what happened.

And more often than not, she found him already looking at her. Butterflies had set up camp in her stomach because she knew what came next, what all this dancing around each other would lead to, especially after their first attempt had been interrupted.

Not that she was blaming Berkley for that. Never. Her friend had needed her, and Mitch had endeared himself to both of them that night by being so sweet and gentle. He didn't have to stay and help Lexie take care of Berkley, though she couldn't deny that she was glad he did.

But now, Lexie wanted him to take care of *her*.

And not in the friendly, big brother kind of way he'd used on Berkley.

She was standing near the bar, making small talk with a few of Mitch and Brent's teammates, still nursing the same beer she'd asked the bartender for an hour before.

When she turned away from Rat—or Grey; she got them confused more often than not—her eyes immediately latched onto Mitch's.

Lexie had moved around a lot as a kid, and seen and been with many attractive men. Through all of that, she could honestly say she had never found herself sexually attracted to a man who rocked flannel.

Mitch Frambough was proving to be the exception.

Every single thing about the man drew her in, from his long, thick legs that strained against the seams of dark jeans, to the way his red checked button up shirt was thrown so casually over a white tee with a vee deep enough to offer a tantalizing glimpse of the strong column of his neck and lines of his collarbones and the dip of his sternum between his pecs, to the sleeves rolled to his elbows, showing off strong forearms dusted with hair.

And his hair. Lord, that man's hair. Before tonight, she'd only ever seen him with a Warriors ball cap settled backwards on his head, the thick dirty blond strands falling straight to brush the collar of his shirt. But tonight, he'd forgone the hat and tied it into a low bun at the base of his skull. Lexie's fingertips itched to pull the elastic free, grip a handful, and beg him to make her come.

As her gaze connected with his again, a small smirk tipped up one corner of his mouth, as though he could read her thoughts clear across the room.

Not that she minded, especially not when his eyes slowly cast down then back up, and she could practically feel his perusal like a brand on her skin.

She so badly wanted his hands to follow the trail his eyes raked across her body.

By the time Mitch detached himself from his conversation and made his way toward her, Brent, Berkley, Kimber, and Amelia had left. Only a small handful of people remained, not a single one paying them any attention. When he was close enough, Lexie reached out and grabbed Mitch's hand, tugging him into her. Not that it mattered if anyone saw them together. Berkley already knew about this *thing* between them, but Lexie was a private person. And they were just getting started. She didn't want or need to be broadcasting to the world that she was sleeping with a Warrior.

Well, *hopefully* sleeping with a Warrior.

Even if all she wanted from him was his dick—and tongue and teeth and lips and fingers—she preferred her sex life to stay between her and whoever was sharing her bed.

"Hey you," he said, settling a hand high on her thigh, right where her leg curved up to her ass. His palm warmed her skin through her jeans, a sensation that worked its way up to her core and spread, adrenaline spiking her blood.

Good god. Even a simple touch from this man had her squirming.

"We should get out of here," she told him, tired of dancing around how badly she wanted him.

"It's my party," Mitch said, a twinkle in those green eyes. "I can't just leave."

"Yes you can. We were interrupted last time, and that was weeks ago."

"Someone is awfully needy," he said, turning to survey the room, a small smile on those full lips.

"Are you trying to tell me you haven't thought about that night at all?"

He leaned close, his lips brushing the shell of her ear, hot breath on her neck. "I have taken my hand to myself so many times replaying that night, Lexie."

She smirked as goosebumps broke out across her skin. "Me too. So let's get out of here!"

Mitch looked around as if weighing whether or not it would be safe to leave. The majority of people had cleared out, leaving only a few of his teammates and random women. "Okay."

The second the word left his mouth, Lexie laced her fingers through his and practically sprinted for the door.

"For what it's worth," she said as she pulled him along, the feel of his palm against hers spreading warmth through her body, "I've only had two beers since we got here." He shot her a questioning look, and she added, "I wanted to savor this, and I didn't want to forget a single second."

Mitch grinned at her. "Me too."

When they reached the street, Mitch dug his key fob out of his pocket and pressed the unlock button, the lights on a big black Chevy Suburban flashing in front of them.

"This is a surprise," Lexie said as she climbed into the plush leather passenger seat. "I always pegged you for a sports car kind of guy."

Mitch started the vehicle and pulled away from the curb. "We live in Michigan, Lex. Not ideal for sports cars."

"True, true," she said, heart thumping harder at the use of a nickname. *Lexie* was already a nickname, but the way he shortened it further had her wanting him to call her all kinds of things, if only to hear what they would sound like with his slight Southern accent. Hell, he could read her a grocery list and she'd be begging him for more. This was Mitch, the one guy in a long time that had captured her attention beyond a passing interest in getting him naked.

Not that she didn't desperately want to get him naked, because she did.

"I moved around a lot as a kid, so I never even had my own car until I left for college," she blurted. Lexie was never the type to babble, but the anticipation of what was to come made her itchy and had her volunteering up information she normally wouldn't.

Mitch briefly glanced sideways at her. "Army brat?"

Lexie rolled her eyes. "I wish. My parents are venture capitalists, so we were constantly moving around to help launch whatever their latest startup was."

"I assume that means they're successful?" Mitch asked.

"Extremely. I never wanted for anything as a kid."

Except love and affection.

"So you're like loaded," Mitch said.

"No, *you're* loaded. My parents are loaded. I'm...well off. All of my money is my own, and I've worked my ass off for every penny."

"What exactly do you do for a living, anyway?"

"I'm a headhunter for the largest employment recruiting company in the Midwest."

"So what, you travel around the country trying to convince people to take jobs?"

"Pretty much," she said. "You've seen *Friends with Benefits*, right? With Mila Kunis and Justin Timberlake?"

"Yes."

"I do what Mila's character does. Only it's not nearly as glamorous as the movie makes it seem. And I have yet to fall in love with one of my recruits."

Why had she added that last part?

Mitch, missing nothing, raised an eyebrow. "Yet?"

Lexie sighed. "I don't believe in love."

His fingers, drumming on the steering wheel along with the Def Leppard song on the radio, stilled. "You don't believe in love."

It wasn't a question.

"No," she said firmly, leaving no room for arguments or further conversation on the matter. "So don't get any ideas. This is just sex."

Mitch held a hand up, pinky extended. "Just sex, I promise."

Surprised, she looped her finger around his, her skin tingling at the contact.

Fuck, she couldn't wait to get this man naked.

While he navigated the streets in the direction of his apartment, she openly and greedily traced his profile with her eyes.

He had a long, straight nose, perfectly pouty lips with a strong chin, and sharp jaw covered in dark blond scruff. His cheekbones were high, but not in a feminine way. More in a way that made him resemble a Greek god. Lexie could easily picture his likeness rendered in marble and displayed in a museum somewhere.

Chiseled. That's what he was. And Lexie couldn't wait to take him for a test drive. Her fingers itched to tunnel into his hair, and her sex ached to be filled by his.

When they arrived at his building and made their way upstairs, Lexie purposely stood as far away from him as she could get in the elevator. There would be no interruptions this time, and she loved the way his eyes darkened as they scanned her from head to toe. Her heart beat faster in anticipation, and by the time they were safely ensconced in his condo, she thought she might explode if he didn't touch her.

After kicking off her shoes, she stalked up to him and ran her hands up the planes of his stomach and chest. He sucked in a breath, and she smiled, grasping the back of his neck and burying her fingers in his hair like she had been dying to do all night.

"You know," he said as he bent down to trail his lips down the side of her neck, "I've never liked girls touching my hair."

"Except me," she said, nipping at his jaw.

"Except you," he agreed.

"Your hair is fucking amazing," she said, pulling back to look at him. Mitch was huge, but she fit against him perfectly, grateful, for once, for her height.

"So is yours," he said, grabbing a handful and gently pulling her head back to return his attention to her throat. He nibbled on the soft spot where her neck met her shoulder, sucking her skin into his mouth and releasing it with a small *pop*.

She shucked her sweater off, needing to feel the heat of him against her skin. With a groan, he kissed her then, backing her into the wall so their bodies were flush, every ridiculously hard, warm inch of him pressed against all of her soft ones.

Now it was Lexie's turn to groan. In the weeks since they met, she had forgotten how good his soft lips felt when they slanted over hers. How hot it was when he trapped her bottom lip between his teeth and pulled. Their tongues tangled, and before long, she found herself with her legs wrapped around his waist, his strong arms cupping her ass.

"Are you going to fuck me right here?" she asked, an echo of that first night outside her apartment, as he bent his head to suck on her neck again. Surely she would have a hickey tomorrow, and she found herself looking forward to it, excited about the prospect of wearing the evidence of what this man did to her like a brand.

And where the *fuck* had that thought come from?

"Thinking about it," he said, his voice husky.

He stepped forward, pressing her even further into the wall, his thick erection coming into contact with her center. She gasped at the pressure, her control snapping. Lexie reached between them, and Mitch got the idea quickly, backing off a bit to give her access. She worked his zipper down and dove her hand inside, finally grasping the hard length of him.

She worked her hand up and down a few times, the movement awkward and stunted by their position and his clothes, but his answering moan told her she was doing just fine.

So she continued to move her hand over him, squeezing a bit tighter when she reached his head and swiping her thumb over the moisture collected there, earning her a bite on her shoulder for her efforts.

"If you don't stop that," he ground out against her skin, "I'm going to make a mess all over our clothes.

Lexie chuckled. "I don't mind."

To showcase her point, Lexie unwrapped her legs from around his waist and he set her on the floor. Making quick work of her zipper, she shoved her jeans and panties to the floor, stepping out of them before reaching for his.

His unbuttoned jeans and bunched boxers gave her a tantalizing glimpse of the head of his cock, thick and smooth and beaded with pre-cum. Greedily, needing to see more, she pushed his bottoms over his thighs and to the floor.

From the waist down, the man was a work of art. Thick thighs bigger than her head, with a dick she desperately wanted inside her.

She stepped closer to him and palmed him, eliciting a hiss from his clenched teeth.

"There's a condom in my wallet that you should probably grab," he said, voice strained as he braced his hands on the wall.

She knelt and dug through his jeans pockets, pulling the foil packet from his wallet, wasting no time ripping it open with her teeth.

Before sliding it on him, she ran her tongue along his length once, twice, three times, his groans filling the space between them.

It should be weird that she was still wearing her bra, and he was fully clothed from the waist up, but the need to have him buried inside her trumped all awkwardness.

The second he was wrapped, he pulled her off her feet again, and wrapping her legs tightly around his waist felt like the most natural thing in the world. One again he backed her into the wall, snaking one arm behind her and gripping tightly to her hip, anchoring her in place as he pushed inside her without warning, slapping the palm of his other hand onto the wall beside her head as he filled her.

Lexie's eyes rolled back and she bit down hard on her bottom lip, a moan escaping her. In this position, he was so fucking deep he managed to hit that spot that other men rarely ever found, and Lexie knew neither of them was going to last long.

As if to prove her point, Mitch pulled out slowly and slammed home again, dropping his head onto her shoulder with a groan.

"You are so fucking tight," he said. "God, you're going to ruin me, aren't you?"

She chuckled, the clenching of her muscles around him only adding to the euphoric sensation of finally having this man buried inside of her. She reached down and dug her fingers into his ass, urging him on.

He enthusiastically obliged, his restraint snapping as he relentlessly claimed her, pounding in and out in quick, fluid movements. Lexie clung to his shoulders, marveling at the way the muscles of his shoulders bunched under his shirt in time with his thrusts. She dropped her head back against the wall, panting as he picked up speed.

"Lexie, I..."

"I know," she breathed. "Me either. Just come with me, Mitch."

The arm around her waist tightened and the one by her head dove between them, finding her clit easily despite how closely they were pressed together.

It wasn't the most skilled approach, but Lexie felt her release build low in that spot where his thumb applied pressure against her, and she cried out as it barreled through her moments later, thighs tingling and toes curling.

"That's it," Mitch said, voice low and rough. "One more."

He widened his stance and lifted Lexie off him an inch, giving him better access to her clit, which he used to put even more pressure on, pressing his thumb hard into the bundle of nerves and rapidly moving it in tight circles while he still moved in and out of her.

How did this man know exactly how to touch her, exactly what she needed from him to push her over that edge? Because there was no way any man, let alone one who hardly knew her, should be capable of making her feel this way. Mitch shouldn't just inherently know that Lexie wasn't the kind of woman who got off from penetration alone, that she needed that extra stimulation to get her there. And when she felt her second orgasm start to build from that spot where his thumb was still circling her, she knew.

She was going to let this man ruin her.

Lexie clawed at his back, surely leaving scratch marks that she'd kill to hear him explain to his teammates in the locker room later. Mitch's athletic lifestyle paid off in spades in those moments, when the pace he kept working in and out of her while also standing and supporting her weight would've tired a normal man long ago.

Mere minutes after the first one, Lexie came again, biting down on Mitch's shoulder, pulsing around him as his own release found him shortly after. He came with a yell, throwing his head back to shout "holy fuck" at the ceiling.

His movements slowed, then stopped completely before he pulled out of her. They remained wrapped around each other for several long moments, breathing heavily.

When Lexie's heart rate had calmed significantly, she unwound her legs from Mitch's waist and slid down to the floor.

She bent down and quickly stuffed her legs back into her pants, tucking her thong into her pocket before padding away from him to retrieve her sweater from across the room.

"Well, this was fun," she said, standing on her tiptoes to peck him on the cheek before strutting toward his door.

"Wait..." Mitch said, catching up with her and snagging her wrist in his hand. "That's it?"

Lexie nodded. "That's it. What did you expect? I told you this was just sex."

"Well, yeah, but I didn't think that meant we'd fuck like animals against a wall and then you'd walk out."

Lexie shrugged. "Then what did you think? That we'd crawl into bed and cuddle and talk?"

"I mean not exactly but I figured we'd go more than one round."

"Look I'm sorry if you thought this was going to be something different, but I warned you."

He was dumbfounded, a deer caught in headlights. "I suppose you did," he said quietly.

She nodded. "See you later."

In the hallway, she made her way to the elevator, smirking to herself as she waited for it to reach Mitch's floor. She got exactly what she had come here for: multiple orgasms with a ridiculously sexy man and no emotional connection. It had been quick and dirty, exactly how she liked it.

Or...how she *usually* liked it. Quite frankly, she was proud of the display she had put on when walking out of his apartment. The outwardly cavalier attitude she had given him was completely at odds with the tangle of emotions that had set up camp in her chest and stomach. Sex against a wall should not have been good enough to get her off even once, let alone twice, especially not so quickly. It was a feat no man before Mitch had ever accomplished; Lexie had long gotten good at faking it.

Something about Mitch was different. They hardly knew each other, but some piece of him spoke to some long-buried piece of her—a piece she hadn't even known existed.

Leaving the way she did wasn't something she was proud of, but...it was the only way to protect her heart.

But despite, or perhaps *in spite* of, the foreign clench in her chest, Lexie knew she'd be back for more.

CHAPTER FIVE
Mitch

It had been a few weeks since the first—and last—time Mitch had fucked Lexie, and he couldn't stop thinking about her or that night. Every time he walked into his apartment, he was greeted by the blank stretch of wall where it all went down, and his dick instantly hardened with the memories that flooded in.

He had to have her again.

Soon.

Immediately.

It was New Year's Eve, and the Warriors had a game at home that night against the New York Lakers, so Mitch decided it was the perfect opportunity to get Lexie in his bed afterward.

She hadn't spoken to him much since the night they hooked up. Though he had texted her a few times trying to make plans, she was never available, citing being out of town for work or simply too busy.

Given that she traveled about as much as he did, he was willing to take her word for it, but he couldn't help feeling she was blowing him off. Especially after the way she had left his apartment that night.

He was completely on board with a purely physical relationship between them. That wasn't the thing that was tripping him up about this girl. No, what was tripping him up was the way she had so brazenly taken what she wanted from him—two incredible orgasms if he did say so himself—and then bounced without a backward glance.

Given the number of times he had done that exact same thing to women, it was unsettling to be on the receiving end of such behavior.

But that was beside the point. Tonight, he would have Lexie wet and willingly spread out underneath him. And then he was going to take his time with her, teasing her until she was begging him to make her come.

Payback and all that.

He called the box office at the arena and had the attendant set aside two tickets for her and a friend. Berkley was out of town, but Mitch figured Lexie wouldn't want to show up alone to a hockey game anyway.

Then he texted her.

> Hey, left two tickets at will call for you for tonight. I promise I'll make you come later if you come to my game ;)

By the time Mitch needed to leave for the arena or risk being late for pregame warm-ups and meetings, she still hadn't responded, but he refused to read too much into it. It was last minute, and maybe she had other plans.

The promise of sex should be a sure-fire way to guarantee she showed up, so Mitch put the worries out of his mind. Without a doubt, he knew the sex between them was different. It had never been like that with anyone else before, and he wanted more.

But even if she didn't show up, it was New Year's Eve, and Mitch was young, undeniably good-looking, and in the prime of his life. If Lexie didn't want what he was offering, he knew several women who would.

With Brent out for an undetermined amount of time, thanks to the concussion he'd sustained a few weeks before, quite a bit of the Warriors' offensive production had gone with him. That night, the team had to find new ways to score, and when the final buzzer sounded in a 5-1 victory for the home team, Mitch, as an alternate captain, couldn't help grinning at his teammates.

Not only because they had won, though that was a huge mood booster, but because they had been firing on all cylinders, garnering goals from all four lines. They played a well-rounded, clean game, and now Mitch wanted to celebrate.

When he reached his stall, he didn't even sit before reaching for his phone, checking to see if Lexie had texted him.

She hadn't, but one of the will-call workers had let him know that his tickets hadn't been used.

Lexie hadn't shown up.

Mitch gripped his phone in frustration, barely withstanding the urge to chuck it at the wall.

Then he took a deep, centering breath, realizing there was no reason to get worked up. From the beginning, she had made it clear that it was just sex between them, that she didn't want and couldn't give him any more than that. So why was he suddenly pissed off that she wasn't accepting his advances?

"Cole!" Mitch yelled, whirling around and pinning his friend with a look across the room.

"Yes?" Cole asked.

"What're you doing tonight?"

Normally, Brent would be Mitch's wingman, but Brent was gone, up in Traverse City surprising Berkley so they could spend New Year's Eve together.

Cole was the perfect substitute.

"I had plans to go to the bar," Cole said. "See what kind of trouble I could get into."

Mitch widely grinned. "I'm in."

By the time Mitch and Cole walked into the club, it was nearing eleven o'clock, and the dance floor was a wall of bodies. The lights pulsed in time to the bass-heavy music, and men and women in all shapes and sizes were on the prowl, searching for someone to share in a midnight kiss.

"This place is a madhouse!" Cole yelled over the sound of Doja Cat blaring from the speakers.

Mitch glanced appreciatively at a curvy brunette girl in front of him who smirked and winked before following her friends into the crowd of people. "Just the way I like it!" Mitch yelled back.

They worked their way through the crowd and stepped up to the counter, the bartender instantly recognizing them and abandoning the girls he was flirting with to take their orders. Cole ordered a beer, and Mitch settled on two fingers of Johnnie Walker Blue Label on the rocks.

If he was going to forget that Lexie had blown him off tonight, he would need something stronger than his usual Miller Lite.

When the bartender slid his drink in front of him, he downed it in one gulp and signaled for a refill.

"Alright," Cole said, stilling Mitch's hand as he reached for his second drink. "What's your problem?"

"I don't have a problem," Mitch said, shrugging off Cole's touch and throwing his scotch.

"You only drink like this when something is going on with you," Cole said. "Tell me what's up."

"Female problems," Mitch told him.

"Ahh, that girl you're spun out over but won't talk to any of us about. Makes sense. What happened?"

"I left her tickets for our game tonight and she blew me off."

"Well, fuck her," Cole said. Mitch had half a mind to punch him for insulting Lexie that way, but seeing as how Cole didn't know who he was talking about, he let it slide. "It's New Year's Eve, we're young, good looking, and rich professional athletes. You can't be moping about some chick all night. So here's what's going to happen. I'm going to pick a girl and you're going to blow off some steam."

Mitch only wanted Lexie, but he didn't see any way out of this without spilling the beans, so he said, "Deal."

The men stood in companionable silence for a few minutes while Cole glanced around the bar, surveying the women in attendance. Then he chuckled and said, "What about her?"

On the edge of the dance floor, clad in a scandalously short red dress, was a tall brunette girl. She had her arms loosely draped around the neck of a guy who was skating his hands up and down her sides, tugging her closer so they could grind together. The guy was dressed in dark skinny jeans, a white button-down, and a black tie.

Skinny jeans.

And a fucking tie.

At a club.

Mitch instantly saw red.

"Isn't that Lexie?" Cole asked, knowing full well it was.

Mitch sucked in a deep breath through his nose and exhaled slowly, begging his heart rate to settle before he did something stupid, like walk up to them, toss Lexie over his shoulder, and carry her out of here.

He didn't know Lexie all that well yet, but he knew without a doubt that that sort of behavior would not be well-received.

"It sure is," Mitch said.

"You should go talk to her. That guy looks like a dweeb."

Cole was unaware that Mitch was already intimately acquainted with Lexie. None of his teammates knew, mostly because it wasn't worth mentioning at the moment and because he was too embarrassed to admit to anyone how she'd acted toward him.

Brazenly, she had used him to get herself off and walked out the door without thinking twice. Her behavior was equal parts aggravating and intriguing.

And looking at her now, across this crowded bar with some other guy's hands running all over her body, all over places where his own should be, had Mitch setting down his drink on the bar beside Cole and striding toward her before he could give it a second thought.

Over the shoulder of the guy she was dancing with, Lexie caught his gaze, and her eyes widened. He didn't miss the way her lips formed his name, and a jolt of satisfaction shot through him.

"What?" The guy she was dancing with yelled at her.

"She was talking to me, dude," Mitch said when he reached them. He looked down his nose at the guy. "Get lost."

"Holy shit, you're Mitch Frambough."

Mitch's eyes never left Lexie's as he said, "I know. Now beat it."

"Possessive asshole isn't a good look on you," Lexie said once the guy had disappeared into the crowd.

"And you ignoring me isn't a good look on you, so I guess we're even."

Lexie snorted. "Not even close."

She spun away from him and snaked through the crowd, Mitch's large body making it easy to follow.

When they reached a quieter corner, Mitch reached out and snagged Lexie's wrist. "Why are you always running away from me?"

Lexie rolled her eyes. "I'm not running from you. I don't know how many times I have to tell you that anything that happens between us is just sex. It's purely physical. So you don't get to dictate what or who I do with my time."

"Didn't you have a good time with me that night?" Mitch asked, wincing at how whiny his voice sounded. Who the hell was he turning into? He had never chased a woman in his life, nor had he ever been so used and tossed aside by one. Now he was the one pining, all in his feelings about the fact that she wanted nothing to do with him outside of using his body.

If it was his body she wanted, he would gladly oblige.

It was time to give Lexie a little taste of her own medicine. If she wanted to play games, she was messing with the wrong dude.

Without a word, he gripped her wrist tighter and pulled her down the long hallway at the back of the club, searching for a secluded spot. They came upon an empty supply closet, and Mitch shoved Lexie inside.

"What the fuck do you think you're doing?"

Mitch unbuckled his belt and lowered the fly of his jeans. His dick was already rock hard, had been since the moment he first laid eyes on her tonight. "What do I look like I'm doing? If all you want from me is sex, then here you go."

Lexie stood there arms crossed over her chest, studying him with a narrowed gaze, for several long, excruciating moments.

If she said no and turned him down right now, he would die of embarrassment on the spot.

Instead, she leapt at him, and Mitch barely caught her before she was crashing her mouth to his. He spun them so her back was against the door.

Their kisses were hungry, desperate. If Lexie wanted to act like this thing between them was only about sex, then that's exactly what he would give her. He would treat her like another warm body, even if his stupid heart rebelled at the thought of using her like that.

Mitch pulled away from her mouth and trailed kisses across her cheek and jaw, bending to suck on her neck while he reached between them.

A moment later, her skimpy panties were nothing but shredded lace in his hands and her tight little dress was bunched around her waist.

"I really liked those," Lexie said as she knocked his hat off and tunneled her fingers in his hair, pulling his head back so she could press her mouth to his again.

"Too damn bad," he said, reaching between them once more and gripping his cock, sliding it through her warmth. "God, you are so wet. Don't tell me all of this is for that dweeb on the dance floor."

Lexie shook her head. "It's not."

"Tell me it's for me."

"It's for you."

"Have I told you before that you're going to ruin me? Because damn, baby...you are."

He pushed into her then, and they both groaned, Lexie dropping her head back on the door with a *thunk*.

He drove in and out of her relentlessly, knowing he wasn't going to last long. Lexie was too tight, too warm, too wet, and the sounds she made as he picked up the pace, those little whimpers in his ear, her begging him *please please more more* drove him insane.

The moment she slipped her hands under his shirt and scratched her nails down his back, he was a goner.

Though the noise from the crowded club was enough to mask what they were doing back here, Mitch still buried his face in Lexie's neck when he came, groaning loudly into her skin. She followed him down, back arching her breasts up into his face as she chanted, "oh god oh god oh god."

When their breathing slowed, Mitch pulled himself free and set Lexie on her feet. She turned away from him and put herself together, pulling the skirt of her dress down and finger-combing her hair. Then she withdrew her phone from a small clutch he hadn't even noticed she'd been carrying, turning the camera on to check her appearance in the dim light.

He took the moment to shove his dick back in his pants and readjust himself.

Once she had reapplied her lipstick and sufficiently straightened her clothing, she turned toward him, glaring daggers.

It was impressive to him that he had just gotten this woman off and she still managed to be pissed at him.

"I'm on birth control, by the way. Thanks for asking."

All the blood drained from Mitch's face. "Oh my God, Lexie. I'm so sorry. I didn't even think. I just wanted—"

Raising a hand, she cut him off. "I don't want to hear it. Get out of my way."

"Why?"

"I'm leaving."

"There you go running again," he said under his breath.

It must have come out louder than he intended because she said, "Mitch, we both got what we wanted. Don't make it a big deal."

And then, exactly like she had a few weeks before, Lexie spun on her heel away from him, opened the door, and stalked out into the club without a backward glance.

Mitch bent to pick his hat up from the floor and settled it back on his head, his movements slow and dazed.

What the fuck just happened? He had dragged her back here intending to give her a taste of her own medicine, showing her that blowing him off had been a bad move, proving to her that she needed him, that the sex was too good to walk away from.

In the end, it seemed as though Lexie had won yet another round, and Mitch was left standing with his dick in his hand like a dumbass.

Lexie

Lexie moved as fast as her unsteady legs would carry her away from what she would forever refer to as "the scene of the crime." She would never be able to enter this bar again without thinking about what happened in that darkened supply closet. The dim lighting snaking under the door had all but stripped her of her eyesight, forcing her to rely on her other four senses, which only heightened the experience.

That was, bar none, the hottest sex of her life. Putting herself back together afterward, acting like she didn't want to take him home and strip them down completely so she could ride him all night, took a level of self-control Lexie hadn't been aware she possessed.

She was proud of herself, but she was also ashamed. Mitch got to her so easily, could somehow break down the walls she had so carefully constructed around her heart.

It was good that he hadn't been able to see her when they had just come together because she was afraid that he would've been able to look into her eyes and know that her man-eater mentality was all an act. There had never been anyone like Mitch before. Never had she reacted so strongly to the sheer presence of a man, as though she was drawn to him like a magnet.

For that reason, Lexie had been shooting him down every time he tried to make plans, and why she had refused to use the tickets he had offered her to his game that night.

Over the last month, keeping him at arm's length had become increasingly more difficult.

Getting close to people wasn't something she did, save Berkley, Kimber, and Amelia. Call her crazy, but she had an inkling that if she carried on like this, if she let Mitch have even one small piece of her outside of her body, she would come to regret it.

He kept telling her that she was going to ruin him, but the simple fact was that he had no idea he held all the power. He had no idea he could very easily ruin her, too.

She intended to keep it that way.

CHAPTER SIX
Mitch

Now...

T wo weeks after the Knights' home opener, Mitch still could not believe he'd skated out on the ice and found Lexie sitting in glass seats, staring wide-eyed at him. As if she was surprised to see *him*.

Who did that?

He hadn't even paused to see who was seated next to her, to see if it was anyone he knew. Brent had his own season to worry about, which meant Berkley wasn't going to any games her fiancé wasn't playing in any time soon. Chances were high Lexie was on the road for work, but with the way they had ended things, what made her decide to show up at his game, where she knew she'd see him, if only from afar?

Thankfully, as a professional athlete, he had long since mastered the ability to compartmentalize, and had played a near perfect game despite her reappearance in his life.

And then he, Gabe, Cally, and some of the other guys had gone out that night and got absolutely shitfaced. Mitch half expected the crowd in the club they were in to part and find her standing there, exactly like New Year's

Eve two years before. Thankfully, she'd never appeared. Mitch had no idea what he would've done if she had.

When he was traded, he had left her without a word, and there wasn't a lot he could say to her to come back from that.

But she had pushed him away before that.

Truthfully, they had both messed up, and now he was living with the consequences.

Gabe hadn't asked any questions, though Mitch was sure he had known something was up when Mitch skated away from the boards where Lexie was seated, pale as a ghost.

And Mitch hadn't wanted to talk about it anyway.

"Game time, boys!" Gabe yelled, pulling Mitch from his inner turmoil. Mitch stood and walked past his teammates, tapping each of their sticks with his own as he did before joining Gabe at the head of the line.

Gabe grinned widely at Mitch, and asked, "You good, bro?"

Mitch only nodded and turned toward the tunnel, all business as he led the Knights from the locker room and onto the ice. That night, they were playing the San Jose Wolves.

As an athlete, he fed off the energy of the crowd, and that night, the air was buzzing with hostility. He couldn't figure out why, but he experienced a prickling sensation along the back of his neck the moment he skated onto the ice.

"Something feels wrong," he told Cally and Gabe when they lined up for the National Anthem.

His teammates exchanged a look. "I'm sure it's fine, bro," Cally said.

The last time they played the Wolves, Mitch had got in a fist fight when one of the Wolves' players had laid a bad hit on Knights' forward Cooper Barrineau, forcing him to miss fifteen games with a concussion and partially separated shoulder. The Wolves' player had only received a five-game suspension. It was hardly fair, and tonight, the air in the arena was hostile, fans and players buzzing with animosity.

Something bad was going to happen. Mitch could feel it like a weight on his bones.

When the puck dropped to start the game, Mitch and Gabe did what they did best: they patrolled their defensive zone, blocking shots, protecting Evan Powell, their goalie, and running interference for any other teammates who managed to get themselves into defenseless situations. It was back-breaking work, trying to be everywhere at once while skating for only forty- or fifty-second shifts at a time, but Mitch had been born and bred, grown and matured as a hockey player for nights like this.

Late in the third period, San Jose was down by two and pulled their goalie for an extra skater. Three possessions in a row, one of the Knights' forwards iced the puck, which meant Mitch had been on the ice for nearly two minutes and counting. He was in the best shape of his life, no small task for being thirty-four years old, but he could only endure so much. At that moment, his lungs were burning, quads shaking with each glide of his skates. He was on the far side, away from the circle where the next face-off took place and closer to the San Jose bench. Cally won the draw, but a Wolves' player quickly stole it. Shortly after, Gabe intercepted a tic-tac-toe pass between three of the Wolves' players, and Mitch saw an opening for an easy empty net goal.

Despite the fact that he was completely gassed, he turned on the jets, using every last bit of strength he could possibly muster, skating hard and fast through the neutral zone as Gabe and Cally skated up ice with him, defended by two Wolves' players. The three made crisp passes back and forth, trying to keep the Wolves guessing. Once they passed through the neutral zone, Huntley chipped the puck at the San Jose net, where it sailed just wide. Mitch followed it into the corner, angling himself sideways to slow his momentum so he could make a quick turn toward the net.

He had nearly reached the puck when a stick slammed into his ankles, sending him sprawling at an awkward angle into the boards.

Hard.

His final thought before everything went black was, *I guess this is why I had a bad feeling about tonight.*

Mitch regained consciousness as he was being loaded onto a stretcher. A cervical collar immobilized his neck, arms and legs strapped tightly to a backboard to restrict his movement.

"How bad is it?" He asked the paramedic nearest his head, his voice rough and cracking.

"We won't know exactly until you've had some x-rays and more tests run at the hospital," the kid said and reached down to hold Mitch's left eyelid open while tracking the responsiveness of his pupils with a penlight. He repeated the process on the right. "The fact that you're awake and coherent is a good sign. For your brain anyway."

For your brain anyway.

That statement led Mitch to believe they weren't particularly concerned with his brain health at the moment.

"Mitch, can you feel this?" Another voice—this one female—asked. Without being able to move his head, he couldn't be sure, but he guessed the woman was standing at his feet.

"Feel what?" He asked.

Mitch knew that was the wrong answer when he watched the paramedic in his line of sight share a deeply concerning look with whoever was out of it.

"Look," Mitch said, voice surprisingly steady despite the panic building in his chest. "I know we won't have the whole picture until I get x-rays and all that other shit done. But tell me, what do you think happened?"

"From the angle of the hit and the fact that you can't feel Vanessa pinching your big toe right now…"

"Just tell me."

"I'm no doctor," the paramedic said. "But I'd guess a lower spinal fracture. Most likely lumbar region."

A spinal fracture?

Fuck.

He couldn't feel his feet; that much was clear. This prompted him to take inventory of the rest of his body. He knew he had legs, with kneecaps and bones, and a dick that hung between them, but they may as well have been gone. He shifted his upper body as much as he could on the stretcher and heaved a massive sigh of relief when his abs constricted, the straps biting into his arms through his jersey. He also knew every uncomfortable place where the cervical collar dug into his shoulders, collarbones, the back of his head, and his chin.

It seemed the paramedic was correct: Mitch currently had no feeling below his waist. Some sort of trauma had occurred to his spine.

Would he ever…

No.

He wasn't going there. Not yet. He was going to let these kind paramedics take him to the hospital, get all of the necessary tests run, then consult the best orthopedic surgeon this state, hell, this country, had to offer until he got the feeling back in his legs.

In his years as a professional athlete, Mitch had spent time with all manner of people suffering from all diseases and injuries imaginable. He knew from those interactions that the mind was powerful, and attitude was everything. He'd had minor setbacks before in his career, and the absolute belief that he would rehabilitate and find his way back onto the ice, come hell or high water, was always a given.

He was a hockey player, damnit. They didn't make athletes any tougher than that. Physical and mental toughness were part of the job description and an intrinsic piece of his genetic makeup.

He *would* walk, and he *would* skate again.

Anything less was unacceptable.

The next several hours passed in a blur of beeping, buzzing, clanking machines, needles poking him, and nurses and doctors prodding at him, asking him thousands of questions about his lifestyle, injury history, and drug and alcohol habits.

Exasperated, Mitch finally yelled, "I am a professional athlete, not a fucking junkie! Will someone please tell me what the fuck is wrong with my legs?"

A team had gathered around him in the private room he'd been given, and several nurses stepped back at his outburst.

"I'm sorry," he said quietly. "I would just like some answers."

"We'll go get the doctor for you."

One by one, the crowd exited the room, giving Mitch his first moment of peace and quiet since he left his apartment earlier that day to head to the arena.

In the way that always happened when he had a few silent moments to himself, Mitch's thoughts turned to Lexie.

Had she heard about his accident? Would she be worried? Would she even care?

That last thought wasn't fair. For all her faults, most of them completely internalized, Lexie was one of the most loyal people Mitch had ever met.

He would bet she did care, if only because she never liked to see anyone in pain.

And what about his former teammates?

And, *fuck*, what about his current ones? Mitch experienced a pang of guilt that they weren't his first thought. He wasn't an egotistical man; he knew hockey was a team sport, and as long as they all did their jobs right, they would win more often than not. But he also didn't have any delusions about how big of a part he played in changing the tide of a game when he was on the ice.

Had they won tonight? Were Gabe or any of the other guys outside waiting for news on his condition?

And his mom? Another stab of guilt that *she* wasn't his first thought. God, she was probably beside herself with worry. She wasn't a huge fan of flying, and being the sole owner of a successful accounting firm kept her insanely busy, even months before tax season really ramped up, so she typically only attended games near Ann Arbor—Detroit, Chicago, Columbus, sometimes Minnesota.

His heart rate kicked up at the thought of her and the panic she must be experiencing, and a nurse rushed through the door at the monitor's increased beeping.

"Sir, are you alright?"

"I'm fine," Mitch said. "I need a phone."

The nurse walked up to him and reached for his hand, turning it palm up and pressing her cold pointer and middle fingers to his wrist, a ministration Mitch found odd considering he was connected to a machine that gave a digital readout of his pulse.

"You need to relax," she said as she turned to leave.

"No, I need a phone. Please."

She spun to face him, crossing her arms over her chest. "Give me one reason why?"

Mitch found her behavior incredibly odd and briefly wondered what he'd done to piss her off. "Look, my mom lives in Michigan. I'm her only child, and she likely watched my game tonight and saw her son be carted off the ice on a stretcher. And you know how the media can be. They're probably spinning all sorts of crazy tales about my condition. I just want to let her know I'm okay."

The nurse stared at him for several long moments, then said, "I suppose that's a good enough reason to give you special treatment."

"Special treatment?" He blurted, incredulous. "It's not like I'm in prison, miss. I just want to call my mom."

She rolled her eyes but stalked from the room, returning a short while later with a cell phone. "You can use this," she said. "Assuming you know her number by heart."

The open hostility grated on Mitch, whose mood given his current circumstances wasn't exactly glowing to begin with, but he accepted the phone gratefully. "Thank you," he said.

She nodded and remained in the room, staring at him expectantly.

"Uhm...can I have some privacy, please?"

She gave him a withering look before turning and leaving the room, shutting the door hard enough to rattle the window inside.

Mitch tapped in his mother's number and took deep breaths, bracing himself for the crying and yelling and endless questions about his health he was about to endure.

Being the parent of a professional athlete meant his mother rarely answered the phone for numbers she didn't recognize. Reporters regularly managed to dig up her contact information and attempted to weasel information from her. Still, he had long ago spoken with her about it, and thankfully, the number of reporters that got through to her these days—as far as he knew—was next to zero.

He hoped she recognized the area code and picked up just this once.

When the phone rang several times, and Mitch was certain he was going to reach her voicemail, a click came through the phone, followed by a tentative, "Hello?"

"Mama," Mitch breathed.

"Mitchell!" She yelled in his ear, loud enough that he had to pull the phone away for a moment. "Oh my gosh, I've been so worried about you. What's going on? What happened? That hit was horrible. The refs immediately kicked that little shit off the ice. Gabe looked ready to take his head off. I hope he gets suspended for a good long while."

Mitch smiled, instantly relaxing. While their move from Georgia to Ann Arbor when Mitch was fifteen hadn't allowed his own accent to root too deeply in his speech—he still had a slight twang and was partial to the word y'all—his mother was all Georgia peach, her twang even more evident when she was upset.

No joke, his grandparents had literally named her Georgia.

"I'm okay, Mama," he said when she finished prattling on about player safety.

"What's the prognosis?" She asked.

"I'm not sure yet..." he trailed off, unsure of whether or not he should tell her just how bad he suspected his injury was.

He should've known she'd hear something wrong in his voice because she said, "Mitchell Devan Frambough, you tell me what's going on right this instant."

"Before they brought me to the hospital, they ran a few field tests on me," he said. "I...I can't feel anything below my waist."

"Paralyzed?" She wailed. "Oh my lord, my baby is paralyzed. Keith, c'mere. It's Mitch on the phone and he says he's paralyzed!"

Mitch could hear his stepfather's soothing murmurs in the background, talking his mother off the ledge from which she was about to throw herself.

"Mama!" Mitch said loudly, attempting to be heard over her frantic prayers.

"Yes?" She said quietly. The silence on the other end of the line following that word was near deafening after the chaos of the first few minutes of this phone call.

"I'm okay," he said. "I'm alive. I will walk again. Try not to worry too much."

"Boy," she said, exasperated. "Telling a mother not to worry is like telling a pig not to enjoy rolling around in shit."

Mitch boomed out a laugh, his spirits lifting.

"I love you, Mama," he said.

"I love you, too, baby," she replied.

A sharp knock came at the door to his room, and he said, "Sorry, I think the doctor is here. I'll call you later, once I have my own phone back, and let you know what he says."

He ended the call with his mother just as the doctor strolled in.

He was a younger guy, probably not much older than Mitch, with wavy brown hair starting to go grey at the temples. "Mitch," he said, stepping forward and extending his hand. "James Rogers."

Mitch shook his hand, impressed by the strong grip. Then again, if this man was a surgeon, maybe it shouldn't be all that surprising.

"So I'm just going to cut to the chase here, Mitch," Dr. Rogers said. "There's some good news and some potentially bad news."

"Start with the bad news," Mitch said.

"Bad news is you suffered a vertebral fracture in your L2, which in turn put pressure on your spinal cord, explaining the loss of feeling in your lower extremities."

Mitch nodded, having already figured this was the case. "So what's the good news then?"

Dr. Rogers walked over to a screen and computer setup along the far wall and tapped the keyboard a few times. A moment later, several images popped up, showing Mitch's spine exactly as it was at the moment.

He had to admit, that break looked nasty.

"The good news is that the area is currently suffering from a lot of swelling. Think of it as your body's way of protecting your vertebrae and spinal cord. I can't give you a definite prognosis at the moment, but based on the clean break of your L2 and the fact that you're in peak physical shape, I would say your chances of regaining feeling in your legs are very high once the swelling goes down."

"And skating? Will I be able to do that again?"

A pained look flashed across the doctor's face before he schooled his features into that eternal calm all medical professionals exuded. "Let's take this one day at a time," he said. "I'm not saying no, but I'm not saying yes either."

Mitch tried to suffocate the bubble of hope that welled in his chest like a balloon. According to the doctor, he had every right to assume things weren't as bad as they seemed. He couldn't allow himself to believe he was in the clear. Not yet. Not until the swelling in his back went down and he could roll his ankles, flex his calves, and tense his quads of his own free will.

Not until he was up, walking.

He reached across his body with his right hand and pinched his left forearm, certain he was dreaming. Even the potential that he could walk again was enough to lift his spirits considerably.

Nope, definitely awake.

Dr. Rogers smiled at him, turning to leave the room. "I can assure you this isn't a dream. Of course, I can't say for certain until the swelling goes down and we can get a better idea of the whole picture, but I'm optimistic." Almost immediately after Dr. Rogers walked out the door, Kiera came rushing in.

"Oh my God, babe," she said, crawling onto the bed next to him without regard for his injured state. "What happened? I got the update that you were carted off in the middle of showing a house and came straight here."

Looking at Kiera, Mitch wondered where that fondness he'd experienced for her that day in the hills had gone because right now, she was pissing him off.

"Kiera," he said firmly. "I have a back injury and I really need you to get off this bed."

His patience for this girl had gone down with the feeling in his legs.

"Oh my God, I'm so sorry." She quickly scrambled off and pulled a chair up next to him, reaching out to tightly grip his left hand in hers. "What's going on?"

"I'm paralyzed," he said flatly.

Since he'd woken up in the hospital, he'd had some time to think, and those thoughts brought him to the realization that everything in his life was about to change, things he had absolutely no control over.

But one thing he did have control over? His relationship with Kiera. The road from this moment on was going to be difficult, and the companionship he'd needed from Kiera a few weeks before simply didn't play a role in the new scope of his life.

Was there a softer way he could've told her what was happening with him? Yes.

Could he have told her about the doctor's news, that he would most likely walk again? Also yes.

But he didn't.

"You're paralyzed?" She repeated, face leached of all color. "As in...you can't walk?"

"Correct," he said.

"Like...ever?"

"I don't know," he said. "My back is broken. I currently can't feel anything below my waist."

"Not even your dick?" She blurted.

Mitch rolled his eyes, not bothering to bury the impulse like he normally would. "Not even my dick."

"Well what the fuck am I supposed to do now?"

"I'm sorry?"

"I mean...my boyfriend can't walk, can't even use his dick. We don't know if you'll ever get that feeling back." She hopped up from her chair and started pacing. "What am I going to do?" She wailed.

Mitch almost laughed. Truth be told, he had expected this reaction. It didn't surprise him that while he was the one laid up in a hospital bed with a fractured spine and no feeling in his lower extremities, Kiera was making it all about her.

"Look," he said calmly. "Things are going to be really hard for me while I get used to my new normal. I think it's best if we break up."

Kiera stopped her pacing and faced him, narrowing her eyes. "You did this on purpose."

Well, he certainly hadn't expected *that*. "I broke my back on purpose?" He asked, incredulous.

"Yes," she said. "You've never been all the way in this thing with me, and this is the perfect excuse for you to cut ties and run. Well fuck you, Mitch. I'm breaking up with you!"

Mitch laid there, blinking slowly at her, stunned. "Get out."

"What?"

"Get out of this room right now. I can't believe you just accused me of breaking my back to get out of this relationship. Get out, and don't ever come back."

Kiera at least had the sense to look embarrassed, the blush creeping into her cheeks until they were sunburn red. After one last long look at him, as though she were gearing up to say something, she spun on her heel and left, the door slamming shut behind her.

Mitch closed his eyes, suddenly exhausted, but the door opened again moments later.

"What the fuck did you do to her?" Someone asked.

Mitch opened his eyes to find Cally and Gabe standing at the foot of his bed, Cally staring expectantly at him.

"I could ask you the same thing," he said. "That nurse out there had been a nightmare since I got admitted."

"Ahh, yeah..." Cally said, trailing off. "Black pixie cut? Blue eyes? Looks like she eats men for breakfast?"

"That's the one," Mitch said.

"So...I might have slept with her a while back and then never called her again," he said, a sheepish grin overtaking his features.

"Turns out she's taking her anger at Cally out on all hockey players," Gabe said. "She gave us a major attitude when we came in looking for you."

"Sorry about that, man," Cally said.

Mitch waved a hand dismissively. "It's fine. Just apologize to her or something. I don't know how long I'm going to be here and I can't have her trying to kill me in my sleep. What are you guys doing here anyway?"

"We came to check on you!" Cally said brightly.

"Plus I brought you some stuff."

Gabe held up a duffel bag and set it next to Mitch.

"Is my phone in there?" He asked.

"Sure is."

"Thank God," Mitch said. "I had to ask that nurse to borrow hers so I could call my mom, and she was really mean about it."

His teammates laughed, and Mitch chuckled with them. "What's the prognosis anyway?" Gabe asked.

"L2 fracture. At the moment I..." Mitch's throat closed up, choking off the words he'd been about to say.

"You what?" Cally prompted.

Mitch swallowed hard and croaked out, "I can't walk."

Tears pricked his eyes, and he threw his forearm over his face lest he start crying in front of his teammates.

"Holy shit," Cally breathed. "Like...not at all? Ever again?"

"I don't know about ever again," Mitch said, voice muffled by his arm. "The doctor seemed optimistic that in a few days, when the swelling around the break goes down, I'll regain feeling."

"So you'll be back on the ice in no time," Cally said, reaching out to punch Mitch on the arm. Gabe reached over and smacked him upside the head.

"One day at a time, bro," Gabe said. "Whatever happens, we're here for you."

"Thanks man, I appreciate that."

The door to Mitch's room swung open and in walked the nurse Cally had slept with. "Visiting hours are over," she said flatly. "Leave."

Cally turned back to Mitch, who mouthed, "Fix this!" at him.

Cally rolled his eyes, and Gabe chuckled.

"We'll be back tomorrow," Gabe told him.

"Sounds good. Thanks for coming by."

His teammates shuffled from the room, and Mitch closed his eyes again, thinking about all of the things he'd be doing right now if he could walk. Soon, he was asleep again, dreaming of happier times.

CHAPTER SEVEN
Mitch

TWENTY MONTHS AGO...

As he stepped out of the arena in Dallas, shielding his eyes from the watery late-February sun, Mitch's phone buzzed in his pocket. He pulled it out, surprised to find a text from Lexie.

Good game tonight

Since when do you text me if it's not for sex?

Since now

Mitch huffed out a laugh, and Brent looked at him questioningly. Mitch waved him off and turned away from him to shield his phone. He wanted to keep this thing between him and Lexie, whatever it was, *between him and Lexie* for as long as possible.

> I wish you were here. You know...so you could show me just how great you think I played tonight ;)

Mitchell Frambough, are you trying to sext me right now?

> Definitely. Is it working?

> Also I love that you just called me Mitchell

Careful with that L word, big guy. I might get the wrong idea, and it'd be a shame to end this thing between us so soon

So now it was a thing, Mitch thought. *I'll take it.*

> What're you wearing?

Nothing ;)

> Prove it

Come meet me and I will

Mitch's eyes widened, his fingers clumsily flying across the screen as he typed out his response.

Ur in Dallas?!

Sure am :)

Tell me where and I'm there

Lexie sent him a pin of her location, and the second the bus pulled up to the team's hotel, he was off like a shot, sprinting up to his room. He quickly changed into jeans and a flannel—his uniform of choice outside of the rink—ordered an Uber, and set off for downtown.

Lexie was staying at the Kimpton Pittman Hotel and told him to meet her at the pool. He had several ideas of how she would appear to him when he showed up, but having never been to this particular hotel, he was surprised by what he found.

The Deep End was a swanky outdoor bar with casual seating surrounding a pool filled with scantily clad women and men who, from Mitch's professional athlete standpoint, spent a little too much time on the abdominal exercises and not enough on arms or legs. Lexie was seated on a tall stool, belly up to the bar, a margarita sweating on the counter in front of her. Compared to the rest of the patrons, she was wildly overdressed, her long, sexy legs clad in black skinny jeans topped with a silky black tank top, feet wrapped in black closed-toe stilettos with red bottoms.

Mitch prayed that getting a drink right now was simply foreplay, that Lexie was trying to play it cool before taking him upstairs so he could strip her naked and spread her out underneath him. All he wanted was to press his mouth to hers and capture those sounds she made when she came, giving her orgasm after orgasm until the team caught their flight back to Detroit tomorrow morning.

He desperately wanted to fuck her in a bed, something she had so far managed to avoid.

By the time he sat next to her and surreptitiously adjusted his fly, he was already sporting a halfie. He signaled the bartender for a beer.

Lexie turned to him, her knee pressing against his thigh, and Mitch swore. With that simple touch, his dick got harder, once again prompting an adjustment.

"Hey stranger," she said, a mischievous grin tipping up one corner of her mouth.

"Mitch," he said, sticking his hand out for her to shake. A little role-playing sounded fun, as long as the night ended with her screaming his name.

"Lexie," she said, her grin growing as she grasped his hand and pumped his arm up and down a few times. The press of her skin had him remembering what her hands felt like on his dick, and scratching down his back, and there he went again, getting all hot and bothered.

It was the purest, sweetest form of torture.

"What brings you to Dallas, Lexie?"

"Work."

"What do you do for a living?"

"I'm a model," she said, so nonchalant, not a flicker of the lie showing in any line of her entire body.

And it very easily could have been the truth, Mitch realized. She was tall, lean, her face nearly perfectly symmetrical, the exception being her left eyebrow, which sat a touch higher than her right, as if she were in a perpetual state of dubiousness.

"I believe it," he said, taking a swig of his beer.

She smirked. "And why are you here? Are you a local?"

"Sure am," Mitch said. "I work in the financial district."

"Let me guess," Lexie said, leaning closer and dropping her voice. "You're some big wig at a bank. You've got a sexy assistant that you sometimes fuck in the board room after hours, you sleep three hours a night, and survive on black coffee and Clif bars."

Mitch laughed, a loud bark that was instantly swallowed up by the chatter around them. She had clearly put a lot of thought into this, and the longer they sat here playing this game, the more his skin tightened, the situation in his pants growing more and more dire by the second.

This little role play game was so fucking hot, and Mitch was going to make tonight *so fucking good* for her.

"Close," he said. "I'm a hedge fund manager."

She smirked. "That was going to be my next guess. So you wear a suit every day?" He nodded, and she leaned close enough that he could peer down her shirt and see her boobs. Those perfect, perky, ridiculously soft mounds he wanted to put his mouth all over.

"I'd love to see you in a suit," she whispered and reached out to run a finger along his dick through his jeans. His back stiffened and he hissed out a breath.

"Lexie..."

She pulled away with a laugh that was borderline maniacal.

This woman was going to kill him.

"Let's go get dinner," she said, abruptly downing the rest of her margarita in three quick swallows and looking expectantly at him.

"You want to go get dinner," Mitch said dumbly. "Right now? With all...this...going on?" He gestured at his lap, the zipper of his jeans straining against the *very* hard flesh underneath.

"I want to go get dinner," Lexie confirmed. "I'm assuming you got off the bus, changed, and came right here, which means you haven't eaten yet. And I'm starving," she said, with a pointed look at his lap followed by that sexy little smirk again.

Mitch slowly blinked at her, and when she apparently got tired of waiting, she picked up his beer, drained the remainder of it for him, and stood, holding out her hand.

In a daze, he grabbed it and let her lead him out of the bar and hotel and onto Elm Street. She turned left out of the door and, at the end of the block, took a right. A few moments later, they turned onto Main Street.

Main Street was teeming with nightlife, couples, families, and groups of men and women coming in and out of all the bars and restaurants. Lexie started up the street, still holding Mitch's hand. Bending down so he could whisper in her ear, he said, "This feels an awful lot like a date, Lexie. I thought you didn't do love?"

She spared him a glance and an eye roll, gaze returning forward so she could navigate the crowded street, and said, "I don't. But we're not in Detroit, and I wanted to hold your hand. If you have a problem with that..."

When she went to pull her hand free, he held tight, quickly pulling her into his side and tossing his arm around her shoulders, grinning at how she molded perfectly into him.

I'll take whatever you'll give me, he thought.

"What kind of food do we want?" She asked.

"I would kill for a burger right now," he said.

They walked a few more blocks until they came to a classic American-style restaurant and stepped inside. It was dim, the walls decorated with sports memorabilia, the tables packed. A hostess took Mitch's name, handed them a pager, and told them it should only be about ten minutes.

So they stepped back outside and sat on an unoccupied bench along the exterior wall of the building to wait. Needing to touch her, he slung his arm around her shoulders again, toying with the ends of her hair.

"Why didn't you tell me you were going to be in town tonight?" Mitch asked her. "I would've got you tickets to the game."

Lexie shrugged. "I had tickets anyway."

Mitch looked at her, eyebrows drawing together in confusion. "And I repeat: why didn't you tell me you were going to be in town tonight?"

"I went to the game because I was trying to sign someone, and he's a big hockey fan."

"*He,* huh?" Mitch asked, jealousy spiking through him.

Lexie glared up at him. "Don't get all jealous on me, *Mitchell,*" she said, and his dick, which had sufficiently calmed down on the walk here, twitched.

"I'm not jealous," he said, though he could admit to himself that he definitely was a little bit. "I just wish you would've told me you were going to be around."

"I'm here now," she said, looking up at him. Her eyes caught the waning sunlight and glowed. "Isn't that enough?"

He nodded, face splitting in a grin. "Absolutely."

She beamed back. "Good."

"So, did you sign the guy?"

She nodded, satisfaction at a job well done lighting her face. "I have to bring him the contract in the morning."

He squeezed her shoulder. "Proud of you."

"Thank you," she said, smile turning shy.

A moment later, the pager buzzed in her hands.

Once they were seated, drinks in front of them and food ordered, Mitch asked, "How did you even end up as a headhunter anyway?"

Lexie laughed, a little incredulously. "I'm still not entirely sure, to be honest. I have a business degree from Michigan State. At the start of my last semester of school, there was this big job fair they held at the Breslin Center that Amelia and I both attended. I wasn't really sure what I wanted to do with my life at that point. I just knew, since I had grown up with parents who were venture capitalists, that a business degree made a lot of sense. I just never really planned for what I would do once I got it."

"You've mentioned before that you moved around a lot," Mitch said. "That had to be hard."

Lexie waved him off. "It was, but that's not the point of this story. The point is, there was an employment recruitment company recruiting employees—trust me, the irony of that statement is not lost on me—and I thought, headhunting? Why the fuck not? So I interviewed a few days later and they hired me on the spot. I actually started working for them before I even graduated. Turns out I'm really good at it."

"That doesn't surprise me one bit," Mitch told her. "How did that all work while you were still in school?"

"There was a woman that took me under her wing. Taught me everything she knows. During the week, I would go to classes, study, and work at their office in Lansing. Pushing paper and answering phones. That type of bullshit. Paying my dues. Then on the weekends, we'd jet across the country."

"Didn't that get stressful? Trying to balance all of that?"

She shook her head vehemently and took a long swallow of her beer. "I was made for this kind of lifestyle," she told him.

"In what way?"

"I grew up traveling constantly, for starters," she said. "And I don't like being stuck in one place for too long. It makes my skin itch."

Mitch had often experienced that same sensation, and he told her so.

"What was your childhood like?" She asked.

Not great, he wanted to tell her. Instead, he said, "It was okay. I grew up in Georgia, near the Florida state line. My parents had me young, so my dad worked while my mom stayed home with me. When I was old enough to start school, she started taking classes at the local community college. She got her accounting degree, and now owns her own accounting firm in Ann Arbor."

He couldn't, wouldn't, tell Lexie about those dark years when his father chose to drink away their money instead of taking care of his wife and son. When their neighbors would take pity on him and his mom and invite them over for a warm, home-cooked meal. How embarrassing that had been for him.

How his father would beat up on him, and when Mitch got big enough to start hitting back, he threatened his mother to keep Mitch in line.

"How did you end up in Michigan, then?" Lexie asked.

This wasn't a conversation he was prepared to have with her tonight. It brought up far too many bad memories.

If he hadn't been picked up by the US National Team Development Program in Ann Arbor when he turned fifteen, if he and his mother hadn't moved to Michigan, leaving his piece of shit father behind, Mitch would not be where he was today.

And his mother would probably be dead.

So he told Lexie the truncated version, without all the sad sack bullshit about how hockey had saved his life.

But hockey *had* saved them.

The pain and anger of those years before they left must have shown on his face because Lexie said, "Where's your dad?"

"He's dead," Mitch said, no emotion in the words. "My mother remarried an amazing man who cherishes her, and I couldn't have asked for a better stepfather."

"I'm sorry," Lexie said, reaching across the table to squeeze his hand.

"Thanks," Mitch said tightly.

Their food arrived then, saving Mitch from having to dredge up more bad memories from the first fifteen years of his life.

Instead, they chatted about nonsense things: what time their flights back to the city were tomorrow, how Berkley was handling law school, if Mitch thought the Warriors had a shot at the Cup this year.

When they finished eating and their drinks were gone, Lexie's gaze caught Mitch's, eyes flaming.

Finally.

He paid quickly, dropping far more money on the table than was strictly necessary, rushing from the restaurant behind Lexie. Once they reached the sidewalk, he snagged her wrist and pulled her back into him, sealing his mouth over hers.

She nibbled at his bottom lip, and he opened up for her, their tongues moving together in an already well-choreographed dance.

When he pulled away, they were both breathing hard. "What is it about you that turns me back into a horny teenager?" He asked against her lips.

She pressed her pelvis into him, sighing into his mouth when his hard length pressed against her stomach, a sentiment he echoed. "I don't know, but I sincerely hope we never grow out of it."

"That's a bold statement for someone who doesn't believe in love," he said, stepping away and sliding his hand into hers, withstanding the urge to pick her up and run them back to her hotel.

Lexie stopped in the middle of the sidewalk, staring at him, an unrecognizable look clouding her features. "Just because I don't believe in love doesn't mean this thing between us isn't the best...whatever...I've ever had."

He dug his fingers in her hair and slanted his mouth over hers in a searing kiss, loving how her groan reverberated against his chest. "Same," he said when he broke away, unable to come up with anything more articulate, her intoxicating vanilla and cinnamon scent invading his senses, wiping his mind clean of anything but the feel of her, the taste of her.

This time, she captured his hand in hers and power walked them back to her hotel, his mind spinning the entire three blocks.

He couldn't be the only one feeling this, right? This pull between them? For all her talk of not believing in love, of wanting to keep things casual, of it being *just sex*, tonight had been wildly different than he was expecting. They had finally started to open up to each other, acting more like a couple than a couple of fuck buddies.

He never wanted it to end.

But he knew he had to handle her with kid gloves. There were things she wasn't telling him, a story behind her disbelief in love, and he was willing to bet good money on the fact that it had something to do with her parents. If she wasn't ready to tell him, that was fine. He wasn't exactly jonesing to tell her about his abusive, alcoholic father and the scars that had left on him, the damage it had done to his psyche.

"So what do you want to do now?" Mitch asked when they strode into the lobby, still hand in hand.

Lexie glanced up at him and licked her lips. "I think you know."

Mitch needed no further encouragement, practically running as he tugged her toward the elevator.

Once inside, Lexie backed him against the wall and leaned into him, running her hands up and down his chest.

He bent forward to press his mouth to her neck, his voice already wrecked when he asked, "What floor are you on?"

"The ninth," she said, voice just as husky as his own.

Spinning them so Lexie was the one backed against the wall, he punched the button for her floor, then ran his hands up and down her body, relishing the feel of her soft warmth. And as badly as he wanted her right now, this would not be a repeat of the first two times when he couldn't control himself and took her against a wall.

As if sensing the direction his thoughts had gone, she reached forward, tugging on his belt and going for his fly. He snagged her wrists in his grasp and stretched her arms above her head, marveling at how massive his hand looked against her thin, delicate wrists.

"Lexie," he said in warning. She looked up at him, blinking, eyes wide, pupils blown with desire. "I'm fucking you in a bed this time."

She nodded once and pulled her hands free of his grasp, tunneling them under his shirt and lightly scraping her nails down his back.

He shivered in response, his restraint nearly snapping. Thankfully, they reached Lexie's floor, and the doors opened. This time, she threaded her fingers through his and tugged him down the hall, pausing in front of a door and fishing a key card from her pocket.

The second they were safely inside, Mitch wasted no time, scooping her up off her feet and carrying her across the room. Unceremoniously, he dumped her on the king-sized bed and stared down at her, studying her: the dark hair fanned out on the bed around her, in stark contrast to the crisp white comforter, those hazel eyes of hers, like rich, liquid gold, that long, lean body.

He couldn't wait to have those legs wrapped around him again.

"You are exquisite," he said softly, meeting her gaze. "Perfection."

A blush crept to her cheeks, and she tore her eyes away, mumbling, "Thank you."

"And now I'm going to unwrap you like the fucking gift you are."

Mitch skated his hands down her sides, then back up, lifting her silky top over her head.

"Please," she said. She got up on her knees, and Mitch reached behind her to unclasp her bra, trailing his fingers up her back and over her shoulders to push the straps off. When they were bared, he reached up to cup her breasts, his giant hands dwarfing them, and she arched into the touch.

This was the first time he had seen her completely topless, and he greedily looked his fill.

"So beautiful," he whispered as he flicked a nipple with his thumb, then bent and sucked it into his mouth. "And so soft."

Lexie moaned, and when he pulled away to give her other breast the same attention, the scraping of his teeth over her nipple had her bucking against him.

"God," she groaned. "Never stop doing that."

He lifted his head to meet her gaze, a small smile tipping the corners of his lips up. "Never?"

"Never," she repeated, raking her hands through his hair, brushing it out of the way so she could press her lips to his neck, biting and sucking.

"Not even for this?" He asked, trailing a hand down her stomach and palming her through her jeans. She was impossibly warm, and he groaned when she ground into his hand.

"Okay, definitely for that." She threw herself back on the bed and wriggled out of her jeans, underwear now the only thing keeping her from fully exposing herself to him.

Mitch's eyes widened and, methodically, he stripped out of his clothes.

He slowly unbuttoned his flannel, peeling it off his shoulders to reveal a white t-shirt that molded to his chest, pulling tight across his shoulders and biceps. And when that shirt came off, Lexie's breath hitched.

Mitch was a big man; he knew this about himself. On skates, he was close to seven feet tall, and he had checked himself out naked enough to know that his bronzed, heavily muscled body could be quite intimidating.

He'd also had women tell him so, afraid he would crush them in the throes of passion. Mitch had worked incredibly hard since he was a teenager to keep himself in peak physical shape, growing steadily from the too-tall, gangly teenager to the chiseled man Lexie was currently staring at, slack-jawed.

"Jesus Christ, you're like a fucking statue."

Mitch chuckled, unzipping his jeans and pushing them over his thighs, leaving him in only blue plaid boxers.

"And you could actually be a model," he said, eyes trailing from her toes to her face.

Lexie rolled her eyes with a laugh. "Get over here."

He crawled onto the bed and lowered his body onto hers, his biceps flexing as he held himself back from crushing her completely under his weight. "You're so damn bossy."

"You don't even know the half of it," she said, running her hands up his back and tunneling her fingers in his hair again. "I want your head between my thighs," she said, grasping a fistful of the sandy locks. "I want all of this hair brushing my thighs. *Now.*"

Mitch growled in response and kissed her, a rough press of his lips against hers, trying to brand the feeling on his skin. Then he pulled away, trailing kisses down her neck and across her collarbones, pausing only briefly to lavish her chest before continuing south. He reached her sex and groaned.

"God, you're so wet," he murmured as he ran a knuckle over her soaked panties.

"You should do something about that," she told him, propping herself up on her elbows to watch.

He gave her a wicked grin. That was one order he would gladly obey without argument.

"You're going to ruin me, aren't you?" He asked, pushing her panties to the side with one finger and blowing air over her slit. She gasped, and her arms gave out, dropping her head back onto the bed.

"You keep saying that," she ground out. "Stop talking and put your mouth on me."

"Say please."

"Please," she breathed. "God, *please.*"

And he obliged, flicking his tongue out and tracing a path around her clit.

With the first taste of her, Mitch moaned nearly as loud as Lexie did, his eyes rolling back in his head.

He toyed with her at first, trailing lazy circles around and teasing her by slipping the tip of his pointer finger into her opening. Soon, she was gasping, wriggling around so much he had to place a hand on her stomach to hold her down.

Then he went to work, inserting two fingers into her warmth. His mouth and hand worked in tandem, sucking and nipping, pumping in and out of her, faster and faster until she was coming apart, arching her back off the bed, fingers clutching the sheets. She clamped her thighs around his head, holding him there, yelling his name at the ceiling. And he let her, allowing her to ride the orgasm out on his fingers and tongue.

When she had calmed, he slipped his fingers out and sat back on his heels, licking them clean.

"Jesus Christ," Lexie whispered, eyes wide as she watched him.

Mitch chuckled and crawled up her body, giving her a sweet kiss.

"Definitely going to ruin me," he said against her mouth.

"That makes two of us."

The admission from her surprised him, given how hard she had worked to that point to keep things between them as casual as possible. Could it be that their pseudo-date and finally fucking in a bed were melting this ice queen?

All thoughts abandoned Mitch the next moment when Lexie reached between them and dove her hand into his boxers, cupping his dick in her palm. He backed away from her and worked his boxers down, kicking out of them and standing before her completely naked for the first time.

She responded by shimmying out of her panties and tossing them across the room to join the rest of their discarded clothing.

Mitch's mouth went dry. Lexie was stunning, and knowing he got to enjoy her all night long had him rock hard. He brought his hand to his cock and pumped it a few times. "Lexie..."

"Yes?" She asked, getting up on her knees and coming toward him so she could replace his hand with her own.

"Since we're not at my hotel, I don't have any condoms."

Lexie stilled, and when she stroked her thumb absently across his head, Mitch's hips jerked.

"In case you forgot," Lexie said, moving her hands around his neck, "we've already fucked without a condom."

Mitch winced. Truthfully, he had been trying to forget about it for the last two months. His behavior on New Year's Eve had been inexcusable, so the fact that Lexie was here with him now, that she had been the one to initiate this entire evening, was a blessing.

And further proof that she was softening toward him.

"I am so sorry about that night," he said quietly. "I don't know why you even forgave me."

Lexie snorted. "You think some jealousy, your possessive attitude, and taking me without protection one time was going to stop me from coming back for more?" She grasped his chin and looked deep into his eyes when she said, "That was the hottest sex of my life. I've been thinking about it every day."

Given her reaction at the time, he was pleasantly surprised to hear that, so he whispered, "Me too."

"Plus...have you seen yourself?"

"I *am* pretty impressive," Mitch said, feigning nonchalance. Lexie laughed, smacking him. "And you haven't even seen me in bed yet." He leaned forward and trailed his tongue along the column of her throat. "Where I can spread you out and take my time." He nipped at her jaw, smiling when she shuddered. "Where we've got all night to play." He brought his mouth to hers, stopping a hair's breadth away from pressing them together. "Those other times were just the preview, honey," he said quietly. "It's time for the main attraction."

Lexie's breathing picked up, desire blowing her pupils wide as she gnawed on her lower lip.

"You're either going to be the best or the worst thing to ever happen to me," she whispered.

Unsure how to respond, Mitch closed the remaining distance and caught her mouth in a kiss, running his tongue over the spot she'd been chewing on. She opened for him, and as their tongues tangled, his hands came up to fist in her hair. Walking her backward and climbing onto the bed beside her, he laid her down, their mouths still fused.

Then she pulled away and said, "What are you waiting for?"

It took Mitch's brain a moment to catch up, to cycle back through their conversation.

When he did, he crawled between her legs and, grasping his dick at the base, lined it up with her entrance. One swift pulse of his hips was all it would take.

But that was up to her.

"I need you to say it, Lex," he said. "Tell me it's okay to fuck you without a condom. Say it and I'm yours."

She settled her hands on his shoulders and wrapped her legs around his waist, digging her heels into his ass. "Please, Mitch."

A second later, he was buried to the hilt inside her.

CHAPTER EIGHT
Lexie

Now...

About three years ago, before Brent, before Mitch, back when it was just Lexie, Berkley, Amelia, and Kimber, fresh out of college and ready to take on the world, Amelia got it into her head that she wanted to become a blogger. The girls indulged her, never really pressing her for more info on what exactly she would blog about. Or why she even wanted to in the first place. It was right around the start of the Instagram craze when normal women from across the globe started monetizing their social media presence. They all assumed that was what Amelia was trying to accomplish.

That was, until one day, about a year later, Amelia announced that she had received a job offer with a travel magazine based in Los Angeles. They loved her fresh take on traveling as a single woman and how she had shown her readers the best ways to get the most bang for their buck in cities across the country. Plus, they were allowing her to remain in Detroit, using the hub city as a home base.

Berkley and Kimber were understandably excited for her, asking what the pay and benefits package was like, what sorts of places she was going to travel and write about next, and if her company had any plans to send her on overseas vacations—and if they could join. But something about the entire thing had needled Lexie. At that time, Berkley, Kimber, and Amelia were living together, and it struck Lexie as odd that neither Berkley nor Kimber ever mentioned Amelia traveling frequently. Especially not when Lexie herself was only in Detroit about half the time; the other half she spent...traveling for work.

Exactly like Amelia claimed she was doing.

When Lexie brought this up to Berkley, her friend waved her off, claiming Amelia had been gone quite a lot. They figured it was a new boyfriend—they knew how Amelia could get when a new guy entered her life.

"She probably didn't tell us because she was afraid she might fail," Berkley said to Lexie matter-of-factly. "Or maybe she just didn't want us trying to tag along."

Lexie scoffed, unconvinced, but didn't press Berkley any further.

For some reason, she still couldn't let it go; something about the entire thing felt very off. So she decided to dig into Amelia's blog and quickly discovered one thing: all of the places Amelia claimed to have traveled happened to be places Lexie had been for work. And not only that, but it seemed as though Amelia had been blatantly stealing Lexie's experiences and passing them off as her own.

Lexie had no choice but to confront her.

"Okay," Amelia said a few days later when Lexie finally managed to corner her, hands raised in surrender. "Before you fly off the handle, just hear me out. This isn't how I wanted you to find out."

"I don't understand, Ames. Why are you stealing my travel stories and pretending they're your own?"

Resigned to her fate, knowing she wasn't going to get out of this without an explanation, Amelia told her the entire story.

She wanted to open a gym. And not just any gym, but a fitness center exclusively for women. Amelia had an exercise science degree from Michigan State, and recognized that there was a massive need in the market for fitness programs that focused on women's health. The only problem was, she didn't have the capital to make her dream a reality, which is why she decided to start blogging.

"I've been seeing influencers on Instagram make crazy money over the years, and I didn't think it would be that hard. Only...it was."

"I still don't understand. If you want to open a gym, why not blog about fitness? Why travel?"

"Things were taking too long to take off, okay! And you know me. I'm impatient. I didn't want to wait months or even years to start monetizing my online presence. So I cheated."

"And what made you think stealing my travel stories and using them as fodder for your own brand would be the thing to take off more quickly than the fitness stuff?"

Amelia huffed out a large sigh, clearly exasperated with Lexie, although Lexie had no idea why. "Because you already were getting a ton of attention for your travel posts! And you weren't even capitalizing on it."

Lexie crossed her arms over her chest and looked her friend in the eye. "I have no idea what you're talking about."

"Alexandra," Amelia said, scolding. "Don't play dumb. It's not a good look on you. We all know about the brand partnerships you've been offered over the years. And yet, you refuse to accept a single one. Why is that?"

Lexie sighed, unwilling to get into the entire sordid tale. She had never accepted a single one of those offers because she wasn't about to go back to the days of people using her for her image. She would not allow these companies to whore her out like her parents had done her entire adolescence.

So instead, she told Amelia, "I already make plenty of money from my actual job. And I'm busy enough from that as it is. Why would I want to add more to my plate?"

Amelia appeared unconvinced but plowed ahead with her story anyway. "Well, regardless...you weren't taking advantage of the golden, six-figure opportunity that had literally fallen in your lap, so I did."

Lexie shook her head, a million questions swirling through her mind. "How did you get away with posting travel photos without actually leaving the state?"

"Google," Amelia said. "And I sometimes would go to the airport and pay random travelers to take pictures of me outside, posing with an empty suitcase."

Lexie let loose a humorless laugh and scrubbed a hand down her face. "Ames," she said, exasperated. "Berk and Kimber said you've been gone a lot..."

"I've been going up to TC," Amelia said, and when Lexie gave her a withering look, she added, "I know, I know. I really went out of my way to make things as difficult as possible for myself."

"You sure as shit did," Lexie said. "Especially when I would've been more than happy to help."

"I was afraid and embarrassed," Amelia said. "And I know you're mad and probably want me to stop. I'm making better money now, but still not great. I guess I could move some stuff around, starting taking a few trips..."

Lexie watched as Amelia dug her phone out of her pocket and started rapidly typing on it, talking quietly to herself, lost in whatever scheme her brain was concocting to get her out of this mess now that the ruse was up.

And Lexie knew what it was like to have dreams and want so desperately to make them come true that she'd been willing to do anything she could to make them happen. In Lexie's case, she had been doing whatever she could to destroy her good girl image, forcing her parents to let her live her life apart from them instead of parading her around like some prized show pony.

And Amelia? Well, Amelia had lied to kickstart a career that would ultimately allow her the financial freedom to start her gym.

Lexie may be an ice queen, but she wasn't heartless, and she couldn't fault Amelia for doing what she needed to succeed.

"You can keep using my trips for your columns," Lexie said at last.

Amelia looked up at her, that deep blue gaze narrowing. "What do you get out of it?"

"Can't I just help a friend in need without having an ulterior motive?"

"Normally, I would say no," Amelia said, and Lexie smacked her. "But in this case, I really can't see how any of this benefits you."

"I'm sure I'll think of something eventually," Lexie said with a smirk. "But for now, I'll send you anything you need when I'm on the road for work. We look enough alike from a distance that carefully angled photos and filters should make it relatively easy to pass me off as you."

"Don't you think Kimber and Berkley will notice?"

"If they do, we come clean," Lexie said with a shrug. "But until then, it's our little secret."

Amelia stepped forward and wrapped Lexie in a hug. "Thanks, Lex. I appreciate this so much."

Lexie pulled away and looked her friend in the eye. "I've got your back, always."

Amelia nodded. "I know."

And that was that. Over the course of the last two years, in addition to her travel for work, Lexie had begun taking trips for Amelia. Thanks to her trust fund—which her parents finally released to her after one too many drunken exploits in her late teens, when they realized Lexie was harming their precious image more than helping it—and ridiculously large salary from her job, she had a lot of disposable income. It didn't make sense to either of them for Amelia to blow her nest egg on traveling when Lexie could handle it.

And she was glad to. She had spent the bulk of her life alone, thanks to her parents' careers and their general refusal to acknowledge they had a daughter unless they needed her for their perfect family facade.

She truly loved traveling and felt most like herself when she was exploring some new city and experiencing new things.

Lexie was yet again on the road this week, back in Dallas of all places. The last time she was here, she hadn't exactly been paying attention to the nightlife and family-friendly events, so Amelia suggested she come back and actually experience the city and not having sex with Mitch while *in* the city.

Every time she came to Dallas for her day job, the company put her up in the Kimpton Pittman Hotel, and despite being in here on her own dime this time, she booked a room there again. The location was unbeatable, since it was right off Main where a lot of the Dallas nightlife was located, but not *right* on the main drag so she could still escape the noise. Her first steps into the hotel lobby nearly suffocated her under the memories, though—most of them bittersweet now. When she'd arrived the night before, she wandered out onto Main Street, remembering being here with Mitch. The way his hand dwarfed her own when she slid her palm against his and intertwined their fingers. How they had spent all night long in bed in this very hotel, limbs tangled, making each other come with mouths and hands and...other things.

How something between them had shifted that night.

Lexie was jarred from her daydream by her mother's voice as she and her father approached the table in the restaurant Lexie had selected for lunch.

Lexie hadn't seen her parents since the ill-fated day they met Mitch, and she would've preferred to go even longer between visits. But when they figured out she would be in Dallas for work at the same time as them–thanks to the fact that her father's assistant routinely stalks her on social media–they insisted on a meal together.

"Like one big happy family," her mother had said on the phone two days before.

Right. As if her parents knew the meaning of the word "family".

"Hello, darling," Christina Monroe said when she stopped in front of her daughter at the table, giving her an air kiss on each cheek.

"Hello, mother," Lexie said, attempting to rein in her temper. She would sit through this farce of family dining, pretending as though she liked her parents if only to get them off her back for the next...forever.

Actually, forever might be too soon.

Robert Monroe reached out and gave Lexie's shoulder a squeeze. "How you doin', kiddo? You look good."

"You do look good, Alexandra," her mom said. "You've lost some weight. I'm proud of you."

Lexie gave her a tight-lipped smile and sat down. She had always been thin, so if she'd lost any weight, it certainly hadn't been on purpose.

The moment they were settled and comfortable, a waiter appeared, and her mother ordered a bottle of Chardonnay for the table.

Lexie hated Chardonnay.

"I can't drink, mom," Lexie said. "I have work to do."

"Who are you recruiting this time?" Her father asked.

"It's not..." Lexie trailed off, unsure how to explain the blog to them. "It's not for the head hunting job. I started a travel blog with a friend, so I'm here working on our next post."

"A travel blog?" Her mother asked, turning up her nose as if she smelled something rancid. "Why ever would you want to be a blogger?"

"First of all, bloggers make really good money. And second, maybe I don't want to headhunt forever."

"And why the hell not?" Her father boomed, dark eyebrows drawing together. "You're making excellent money. You practically run the place. Hell, in five years you'll probably own it. Why throw all of that away for some pipe dream?"

And this was the problem with her parents: the only thing they cared about was money.

"I'm not planning on quitting my job anytime soon," she said, choosing not to mention that she wasn't making any money from the blog anyway.

Or the fact that the longer she did this, and the more she traveled without the weight of some deal hanging over her head, the more she could genuinely see herself doing this full time.

That was a conversation for another day.

Or if she was really lucky, never.

She was an adult now, had been for a long time, and thus capable of making her own decisions. But she couldn't help that small piece of her that perked up in her parent's presence, desperately begging for some shred of praise from them.

"Okay good," her mother said, taking a big slug of her wine. "You know we just want the best for you."

Lexie nearly snorted but passed it off as a cough at the last second.

"So are you seeing anyone new?" Her mother asked. "You haven't been with anyone seriously since that Matt guy."

"His name is Mitch," Lexie ground out, jaw aching under her clenched teeth. "And no, I'm not seeing anyone."

"Well, darling, you're not getting any younger. You're looking a lot more fit these days, but you should try doing something different with your hair. And start wearing some makeup."

Lexie had been blessed with a clear complexion, thick and perfectly sculpted dark eyebrows that matched her father's, and a fringe of lashes normal women paid good money to achieve. Her physical appearance was about the only thing her parents had given her that didn't make Lexie want to punch a wall in frustration.

"I like my hair the way it is," she said, tugging on a long, straight lock. "And I don't need to wear makeup."

Truthfully, she used to wear makeup, more as armor for her emotional baggage than because she wanted to boost her physical appearance. Being with Mitch had made her confident enough to stop, especially when he had reminded her daily how beautiful she was without it.

"Still," her mother said, jarring her from her memories yet again. "You should change up your look. Try something new. That's probably why that Matt guy left you, you know. He got bored with the same old, same old."

Lexie opened her mouth to respond, but her father cut her off. "Although, I suppose you dodged a bullet with that one anyway. He's got a long, difficult road ahead of him."

Lexie blinked, unsure she heard him correctly. "What are you talking about?"

"You haven't seen the news?" Her father asked. "Mitch—his name is Mitch, honey, not Matt," he added to her mother, "took a nasty hit in a game last week and has been in the hospital ever since. Sources say he's paralyzed, and the doctors are unsure if he'll ever walk again."

All the blood drained from Lexie's face, and she was glad to be seated, knowing full well her legs would've given out from under her otherwise. A roaring filled her ears, drowning out her parents as they continued to chat about nonsense bullshit, completely unaware that their daughter's world was falling apart.

"Lexie?" Her father's voice cut through her thoughts. "Are you alright?"

"I'm fine," she said, standing quickly, grabbing her purse and jacket from the back of her chair. "I have to go."

She power-walked from the restaurant, on the verge of running, ignoring her parents as they called after her.

Her phone was in her hand, dialing Berkley's number before she even reached the sidewalk.

"Hey, Lex," Berkley said. "How's Dallas?"

"What happened to Mitch?"

Berkley was silent for so long that Lexie pulled the phone away from her ear to make sure the call hadn't dropped.

"Berkley," Lexie said, voice barely above a whisper. "What happened?"

"We didn't know how to tell you..." her friend trailed off, still not answering the question.

"We'll circle back to *that* later," Lexie said, voice rising with impatience and anger and worry. "What the fuck happened?"

"He took a bad hit last week when they played the Wolves. Some asshole hooked him and he went into the boards at a really weird angle. It's been almost impossible to get information on his condition, but Brent threw his weight around and someone finally talked. He fractured his L2. Initially, he had some really bad swelling and I guess the break was doing some weird shit to his spinal cord because he lost feeling in his legs." Berkley paused for a moment, and Lexie could hear murmured voices in the background. She came back with a sigh. "I should've just had Nate explain this to you. But basically, he broke his back and might have been paralyzed. Now that the swelling has gone down, he's regaining feeling thankfully. Next steps are preventing further nerve damage while he rehabs."

Lexie took a deep breath, the weight on her chest easing some. She breezed through the doors of her hotel and made a beeline for the elevator. "So that's good news, right? He can walk. He'll be back on the ice in no time."

More silence followed that statement, and when Berkley spoke again, it wasn't Berkley at all, but a man. "Hey, Lexie."

Lexie, unfortunately, recognized that voice instantly, though the memory of that night is a tequila-soaked mess of bad decisions and regret. Thankfully, she had just reached her hotel room and keyed the door open, dropping her purse and coat on the floor before sitting down at the foot of the bed. "Hi, Nate."

"Okay, so look...as Brent's brother and a future doctor, I've sort of been the Warriors sounding board for all things medical over the last few years before seeking an opinion from one of the team doctors. And Mitch...when he was a teenager, he was in a bad car accident."

Lexie knew the one.

"He's going to be able to walk, right?" She asked Nate, afraid of where this conversation was going.

"Yes," Nate said. "Certainly. The only problem is, despite the fact that in all other aspects of his physical health, he's in his prime, his back has suffered enough trauma over the years that, at this point, he's one bad hit away from legitimately never walking again. His playing days are over."

His playing days are over.

Those words bounced around in Lexie's brain.

God, he must be devastated.

In a daze, mind and heart swirling with a million thoughts and emotions, Lexie disconnected from Nate and flung herself backward so she was sprawled across the plush white comforter.

The urge to call Mitch over the last several months had always been there, like a low level hum in the back of her mind. She had come close a few times, going so far as to type his number in before remembering he had changed it.

Right now, more than ever, she wished she could call him. She wanted to tell him she was thinking about him, that everything was going to be okay, and that he'd find meaning in his life without hockey. That he'd be successful in whatever he chose to do next.

But she couldn't do that. Not just because he had changed his number, but because he had left her. He didn't want her anymore.

And she had no one to blame but herself.

CHAPTER NINE
Mitch

M itch nearly cried with relief the week after his injury when the swelling on his back had gone down enough for him to regain feeling in his lower limbs.

"I need you to exercise caution, though," Dr. Rogers said after a thorough examination of his latest X-rays and test results. "You can walk again, yes. But you need to take it easy. Your spine suffered some serious trauma, and coupled with your old injuries, it's going to take time before you're back to normal."

"Don't worry, Dr. Rogers," his mother said, squeezing Mitch's hand, "I'll make sure he goes slow."

Mitch smiled up at her, thankful she had come out to LA to be with him.

"So what exactly are my next steps?" Mitch asked.

"Rehab, of course. We've got a couple options where that is concerned. We can transfer you to an in-patient facility here in the city where you'll have round the clock care, or you can return to your own home here and we'll have in-home care, plus transportation for appointments and such.

It's entirely up to you. I will say, in-patient care is what I would recommend simply because it'll be a lot less stressful on you, both physically and mentally, to have everything you need be the press of a button away."

His mother looked down at him, a gleam in her pale green eyes. As his mother, she would undoubtedly have strong opinions moving forward regarding his care. "What do you want to do?" she asked.

"Honestly, I'm not sure." He looked at Dr. Rogers. "Can I think about it?"

"Of course," the doctor said. "Take your time. We'll be keeping you here for a few more days for observation anyway, so you've got some time before you absolutely have to make a decision."

"Thank you, Dr. Rogers," he said, and the man nodded and left.

Mitch scrubbed a hand over his face. Being able to walk again was good news—the best news—but...his career was over.

"Are you okay, sweetheart?" His mom asked softly.

He shifted his body on the hospital bed so he could look at her and found tears welling in her eyes.

"I don't know," he told her. "I'm only thirty-four years old. What the hell am I supposed to do with the rest of my life?"

Tears welled in his own eyes and slipped silently down his cheeks as his mother crawled up next to him and wrapped her arms around his shoulders. "You have your whole life ahead of you, Mitchell. I raised you to be strong and smart and resourceful and successful. This is a bump in the road. There is more to life than hockey."

"That's easy for you to say," he *told her, his voice muffled against her neck. "My entire life for the last twenty some odd years has been* hockey." He lifted his head to look at her. "And now it's just all gone? What the fuck am I supposed to do with that?"

"Language," his mother said absently, as she'd done a million times before. "But you're honestly telling me you've never, not once, considered what you'd do if you were no longer playing hockey?"

"No," he said stubbornly, and she gave him a look that said she knew he was lying, but she would let it slide anyway. "I don't know, Mom. I just got this news. I need time to adjust. I need to get back on my feet. Rehab, all of that stuff, just like the doctor said."

After giving him a long look, she crawled off the bed, gripping his hand tight in hers once she was on her feet. "I'm going to get some coffee," she said. "I'll be right back."

His mother had always known him better than anyone, and he knew for a fact the cafeteria coffee in this hospital was disgusting; she told him so herself. Her leaving now was her way of giving him a few moments to himself.

When she was gone, he reclined back onto the pillows, his lower back tight and throbbing. This bed was so damn uncomfortable, and no amount of adjusting his position alleviated his pain. It was incredible to him that a medical system touted as having state-of-the-art *everything* couldn't install some more comfortable beds for their spinal trauma patients.

He had half a mind to call a nurse and beg for a mountain of pillows, but distracting himself with such a menial task would only last for so long.

At some point, he would have to face the fact that he would never play competitive hockey again.

Thanks to this recent fracture, and trauma he had suffered earlier in his life, there was too much nerve damage and scar tissue in his lumbar region. It was concerning enough that Dr. Rogers didn't feel comfortable clearing him to play, stating that the chances of suffering permanent loss of feeling in his lower limbs were much higher the longer his career continued. Professional athletes put their bodies through hell, and hockey was far more physically taxing than most sports. It wasn't how he wanted to go out, but he had to trust his doctor on this one.

So what the fuck was he supposed to do now?

He supposed the only saving grace was that he didn't have to figure it out right this second. What he really wanted was a nap.

And a drink.

And unfortunately, alcohol was currently out of the question.

Mitch's mind spun, his chest grew tight, and the sight of his mother slipping back through the door was the only thing that saved him from a full-blown panic attack.

Something about her was different, as though she'd had an epiphany while on her walk to the cafeteria and back, and it reminded him of that gleam in her eyes while the doctor was speaking to them earlier.

"You know..." she said, and Mitch grinned.

"I knew you were cooking something up in that mind of yours," he said. She laughed and pulled up a chair next to his bed. "It's just...I live in Ann Arbor."

"I'm aware," Mitch said drily.

"Don't sass your mama," she scolded him. "But Ann Arbor is home to one of the best medical systems in the country."

She had a point. The University of Michigan medical system *was* world-renowned.

"I'm assuming they have some sort of in-patient rehab facility?"

"Of course they do," his mother said, bending down to withdraw a sheaf of papers from her bag. "I printed out all sorts of literature on it before I flew out here. I figured something like this would be necessary and...I was hoping I could convince you to come home."

Home.

Mitch had assumed it would be a good long while before he called Michigan home again, but he couldn't deny the prospect of returning to the Mitten excited him. He'd be close to his mom again—only a phone call away if need be—and...well, he could work on repairing his friendships. He missed his former Warriors teammates.

And he missed Lexie.

Despite the painful way it happened, he couldn't pass this opportunity up when it had fallen right in his lap.

Maybe this was exactly what he needed. Maybe being back in Michigan would provide insight into what the fuck he was supposed to do next.

"I would love to come home," he told his mom, and she gave him a wide smile as a tear trailed down her cheek.

"It's going to be so good to have you back."

"I think I'd still like to do in-patient, though," he said. "It makes the most sense."

"I agree," his mom said. "As much as I'd love to have you living under my roof again, our house is only so big, and adding your giant self plus in-home care to the mix wouldn't work out well for any of us."

"Then it's settled," Mitch said. "I'm moving back to Michigan."

"Should I get the doctor back in here to clear it with him?"

"Yeah, I suppose that's a good idea," Mitch said, and his mother exited the room, returning a few minutes later with Dr. Rogers in tow.

"I understand you've made a decision," the doctor said. "That was fast."

"Well yes, and no. I guess we need to clear this with you first. My mom lives in Ann Arbor, and we were wondering...would it be possible for me to move back to Michigan? The University of Michigan medical system is one of the best in the country, and I think it makes the most sense to be close to my mom and stepdad while I rehab."

The doctor considered him for a second, then said, "I think that should work fine. Had I known you had ties to the area, I would've suggested it myself. We'll have to figure out logistics for getting you there, of course. Although I would prefer it if you didn't fly, that many hours in a car would be a major setback so I believe it's our only option."

"I'll fly first class," Mitch assured him. "Make it as comfortable as possible for myself."

The doctor nodded. "Then yes, I see absolutely no reason why you shouldn't be able to return to Michigan with your mother. As I mentioned before, we want you to remain here for a few more days. But I think Friday we can get you discharged and on your way, as long as we don't have any setbacks between now and then."

Two more days until Mitch was heading home to Michigan.

Two days in which he needed to get his apartment packed up, wrap up any loose ends in LA, and sit down with the Knights.

That last one wasn't going to be easy, but he owed them a face to face conversation before he left the city.

After all, it's not like he would ever be returning to their roster.

His mother, who had always known him better than anyone and could always read his mind, squeezed his hand again and said, "What do you need me to do?"

"I need a pad of paper and a pen," he said. "It's time to make a list."

Three days later, Mitch found himself seated in one of the meeting rooms inside the Knights' arena, gathered around a table with his coach, the President and Vice President of the organization, the General Manager, a public relations representative, his agent, and Gabe Huntley, acting in his official capacity as the Knights' captain.

"So you're just moving back to Michigan?" Gabe asked once Mitch said his piece.

"Are you sure you can't play?" His coach asked.

"What about your contract? We just signed you to an extension."

Leave it to the President to only be worried about money at a time like this.

"Look," Mitch said, scrubbing a hand down his face and reclining in the plush leather chair, trying to ease some of the tension in his back. "This isn't how I wanted to go out. But my career is over. I have to rehab this injury, and I have to figure out what the fuck I'm going to do with my life once I'm on my feet again. My mom lives in Michigan. Ann Arbor is home to one of the best in-patient rehab facilities in the country. It makes the most sense for me to move back. I know this isn't what you had planned when we signed my extension. I can assure you I expected to be playing well past the age of thirty-four. But it's the hand I was dealt, and I can't do anything about it now. All I can do is move forward. I'm here as a courtesy. Void my contract, do whatever you have to do to make yourselves feel better or whatever makes the most sense for the club. But I'm leaving tomorrow, so we need to get this shit sorted now."

Those gathered at the table stared at him, blinking in stunned silence. Since his move to LA, Mitch had been a quiet but reassuring presence in the locker room. He had never been known to raise his voice or lose his temper off the ice, and the guys had often referred to him as a gentle giant.

It was a far cry from the man he'd been in Detroit, and only Gabe knew how he truly was, having gotten drunk with him enough times for the old Mitch, the real Mitch, to resurface.

"We're not going to void your contract just because you got injured," the President said. "We'll continue to pay you out on it subject to the terms agreed upon."

A diplomatic answer, but one that made Mitch's shoulders relax a bit. Not that he was hard up for money, but his medical care wouldn't be cheap, and it was nice to know he'd be taken care of while he figured his shit out.

"Great," Mitch said, making to rise from his chair, heavily relying on the cane now permanently attached to his hand. He was walking, which he was eternally grateful for, but it was slow and laborious. "Now if that's all, I have a lot of shit to do before I fly out tomorrow, so I need to go. But I just want to say thank you for giving me a shot these last few months. I loved playing here, and I'm sorry my time with y'all had to come to an end like this."

Those gathered simply nodded before turning toward each other, murmuring in low voices as Gabe helped Mitch from the room.

"I can't believe you're leaving," Gabe said. "Now who am I going to get Friday night margs with when we're not on the road?"

Mitch laughed. Friday night margs had become a tradition with them, born from Mitch's first week in the city when he and his teammates were just getting to know each other, and Gabe took Mitch to dinner to size him up.

"You can always take Cally," Mitch said with a smirk, and Gabe lifted his arms to shove Mitch, stopping at the last second as if realizing what a mistake that would be.

"Over my dead body will Cally *ever* be invited to Friday night margs."

Ann Arbor.

Mitch genuinely couldn't believe he was back in the Mitten. When he left the previous spring, he had burned so many bridges—truthfully, all of them except the one that led to his mother and stepdad.

It had been three weeks since his accident, and he was back on his feet. Tentatively.

But he was walking. And that was enough.

Even if his career as a professional athlete was over.

At thirty-four, he was already washed up. It would be a knife to the gut a million times more painful if he couldn't walk on top of it.

He wasn't exactly an invalid, but living at the facility while he regained strength in his back and legs made the most sense. Everything was available via phone call or a short walk down the hallway.

His room was nice, if sparse and a bit suffocating sometimes. There was a comfortable bed topped with memory foam that cushioned his body like a cloud, relieving some of the strain on his lower back while he slept, and a large comfortable chair in the corner that looked out over the parking lot.

The television had access to all manner of channels, and he found himself watching a lot of comedy movies late into the night when he couldn't sleep.

Rehab was going well, but for someone used to moving about the world when and how they pleased, it was also moving so slowly it bordered on frustrating.

His strength flagged easily, and too much time spent on his feet or in an upright position caused persistent tightness and stinging pain in his back. There was always a cane or wheelchair nearby for particularly bad days.

"Good morning, Mr. Frambough!" The woman at the desk said when he exited his room and shuffled past, on his way down the hall for strength exercises with his physical therapist.

"I don't know how many times I have to tell you, Denise," Mitch said as he hobbled by, "you can call me Mitch."

"Never," she said with a wink. "You've got some visitors today."

"Visitors? What, more doctors that want to poke and prod me and study my back?" He groused as he made his way into the rehab room halfway down the hall.

Mitch's cane clattered to the floor when he stepped inside and found himself face to face with Brent Jean and Cole Reid.

"Hey, Mitch," Brent said with a sheepish smile on his face.

"What the fuck are you guys doing here?" He asked, turning away from them and slowly making his way to a chair at the edge of the room. His back wasn't in good enough shape to bend over and retrieve his cane, so it lay there on the floor, abandoned like an out-grown child's toy.

Cole stepped forward and picked it up for him, walking it over to where Mitch sat.

Mitch angrily swiped it away from him. "I asked you a question," he said, not meeting either of their gazes.

"We wanted to come see how you're doing," Cole said.

"How did you even know I was here?"

"Jean might have called your mom to check on you, and she gave us the scoop," Cole said. "We would've called you directly but your bitch ass changed your number when you left."

When you left.

The words hung heavy in the air between them, and Mitch had no doubt they were chosen carefully.

"I was traded," he said lamely.

Brent snorted. "You could've stayed in touch after the trade, bro."

Mitch heaved a sigh. "It was just...easier."

Mitch looked up then and met Brent's gaze. Those blue eyes, cold in appearance but the exact opposite if one knew the man underneath, bored into his own. "I know you don't want to talk about...her," Brent said. "That's not why we're here anyway. We came to check up on you."

"I don't need you checking up on me."

"You can knock the attitude off right now because you're not getting rid of us until this PT session is over," Cole said.

"And even then...we know where you live."

"So what, you're here because you wanted to come make fun of me? The thirty-four year old washed-up hockey player?"

"No," Brent said. "We genuinely wanted to check on you. Seven months is too long to go without talking, man."

"Oh god," Mitch said, eyes growing misty. "Don't get all cheesy on me. The last few weeks have been absolutely brutal on my emotions."

"Fine," Cole said as Mitch's physical therapist came into the room. "Then let's get to work."

For the next two hours, while Mitch worked through his physical therapy routine, Brent and Cole worked right alongside him. It was almost familiar, as though they had done this before.

And that was because they *had* done this before. For years, side by side in the weight room, on the streets around downtown Detroit, on different sheets of ice across the country. They had sweat and bled and cried tears of joy and disappointment together.

The fact that Mitch had thrown that all away because his heart was broken...he'd never forgive himself for the lost time.

But it seemed as though not all was lost, not if Brent and Cole were here now, making an effort to bridge this gap between them.

When his PT session wrapped up, Mitch sat on a chair and chugged half a bottle of water.

"We're going out," Brent said without preamble.

"So you're kidnapping me now?"

"Not kidnapping. First of all, you're a giant. You'd be impossible to hide. And second, we're going to lunch. Together. And we're going to talk."

"Goodie," Mitch said under his breath, heaving himself off the chair and ambling behind them toward the elevator.

The elevator ride down the car was quiet and tense, as was the ride from the rehab center into downtown Ann Arbor, where Brent steered them in the direction of a hole-in-the-wall diner, navigating them around on Mitch's clipped directions.

When they parked and made their way into the restaurant, Brent settled them at a table that would offer plenty of legroom for the three men, who combined for nearly nineteen feet of height.

A waitress came over, took their orders, and then left them to their own devices.

"So, spill." Brent said. "What's the prognosis? And what the fuck happened in April?"

"Prognosis is I'm never going to play again. I got in a car accident when I was fourteen that fucked up my back the first time. Twenty straight years of playing hockey after that, combined with this L2 fracture, caused nerve damage severe enough that I risk permanent paralysis if I ever try to play competitively again at an elite level."

"Damn," Cole said quietly. "That's brutal, man. I'm sorry."

Mitch waved him off. "It is what it is," he said. "Who knows how much longer I would've been playing without the injury anyway. It's not how I wanted to go out, but my career was going to end eventually."

Brent and Cole shared a look, as though they couldn't quite reconcile the version of Mitch sitting in front of them with the one that had left all those months ago.

But surprisingly, mentally, Mitch felt fine. He had always been realistic about the longevity of being a professional athlete. He knew it wasn't going to last forever, and that he was going to have to find some way to fill his time for the rest of his days when it was all said and done.

The rest of his days were just starting sooner than he expected.

And that was fine. Like he had just said, it is what it is.

"So what's next?" Cole asked.

"Next, I learn how to walk again without taking this stupid fucking cane with me everywhere," Mitch said, glaring daggers at the curved aluminum tube as though it had gravely offended him.

"And after that?" Brent asked.

Mitch and Lexie had this conversation once, and it was honestly the only reason he could answer Brent now.

"I think I'd like to get my real estate license."

"Damn," Brent said. "That's a big change."

"Not really," Cole said. "He's owned and rented the loft out for years. Going from property management to real estate sales seems like a natural step. He's personable and highly recognizable, so he should be making good money in no time."

Brent and Mitch stared at Cole in stunned silence.

"That's..." Mitch said, sputtering, trying to find the words. "I think that's the nicest thing you've ever said about me, Cole."

Cole shrugged. "It's true."

"Speaking of the loft," Mitch said to Brent, "did y'all ever use it while I was gone? The team real estate agent told you I added you to the title, right?"

Brent and Cole exchanged another look, and Brent said, "She did. But no, we didn't. It never felt right without you."

Mitch blinked slowly. "You mean to tell me...that building...has been sitting empty and unused for *seven months*?"

Most people thought Mitch only rented or leased the floor the loft was on, but in fact, Mitch had owned the whole building. He'd always dreamed of renovating the lower floors into...something. But he'd always been so busy with hockey that he never found out exactly what.

Maybe now was his chance.

But back to the matter at hand.

The guys shrugged at his outburst, and Mitch's temper rose. "What the fuck is wrong with you? You should've been partying there every weekend. Every night. Y'all love the loft."

Cole sighed, and Brent said, "What you're failing to realize is that the loft isn't the same without you. You made that place somewhere for us to go unwind after a win, or blow off some steam after a bad loss. Without you around it was just...sad."

Mitch shook his head, biting back a smile. "I ghosted the entire team, the entire damn city of Detroit, and you couldn't even step foot in the loft because it wasn't the same without me? I'd be flattered if I didn't think that was the most ridiculous thing I'd ever heard."

Brent shrugged again. "We missed you. And speaking of ghosting us...it's time to spill the beans."

Mitch's eyebrows raised, knowing where this line of questioning was headed. "Lexie didn't tell you what happened?"

Brent shook his head. "I don't even think Berkley knows the full story."

Mitch considered that. If Lexie hadn't even bothered to discuss what went down with them that night, there had to be a good reason. And just because they weren't speaking didn't mean he didn't still care about her, so he wasn't about to air their dirty laundry to Brent and Cole.

He would *always* care about her.

Hell, he would always *love* her.

So instead, he said, "I don't want to get into the whole story right now. Maybe one day. But there's too much other shit going on. It boils down to we had a fight, we both handled it badly, and I left."

Brent opened his mouth as though he wanted to press Mitch for more details, but snapped it shut and nodded. "Fair enough."

"Now that that's over with," Cole said, sitting up straighter and rolling his shoulders back, "there's another reason we came to see you today."

Mitch leaned back in his chair and said, "Lay it on me."

"We're here on official Warriors business," Cole said, tone turning serious. "We know you're technically still on the Knights' roster."

"More of an honorary title than anything at this point," Mitch said, gesturing to his near-useless body. "They've agreed to pay out my contract according to the agreed terms, but they understand that I have to move on with my life."

"Management in Detroit is interested in bringing you back into the fold," Brent said.

Mitch's eyebrows scrunched together in confusion. "In what capacity, exactly? Because we all know damn well I'm not a player anymore."

"First of all, you'll always be a hockey player. That shit doesn't just stop being simply because you're injured and can't play professionally anymore," Cole said in a rare display of impatience from the most laid-back guy Mitch had ever met.

"Okay, okay," Mitch said, holding his hands up in surrender.

"They want you to come back as a consultant," Brent said.

"A consultant?" Mitch asked, lip curling.

"Consider it more like a coaching position," Cole added quickly at the disgusted look on Mitch's face.

Coaching?

Interesting.

It wasn't an avenue Mitch had ever considered before. Unlike Jean, who had his whole life after hockey planned out, Mitch was more of a go-with-the-flow kind of guy. And outside of maybe getting his real estate license, he'd never given much thought to what else he would do with his time once his career ended. He had always expected to play until he was at least forty, maybe longer.

Obviously, his back and that prick from San Jose had other ideas.

But *coaching*...it would be a way to stay connected to the game he loved so much, the game that had given him everything.

"I can't skate," Mitch blurted. "I can barely walk."

"We know," Cole said. "Management wants you working with the defenseman. Sharing training tips and dissecting video with them. Hanging out on the bench during practice and yelling shit at them when they fuck up."

"What's the catch?" He asked.

"There is no catch, bro," Brent said. "Management sees this as an opportunity to right their wrong in trading you."

Desperately, more than anything, Mitch wanted to agree. But he held his tongue, not wanting to look too eager, and said, "I need some time to think about it."

"Fair enough," Cole said. "Take all the time you need."

CHAPTER TEN
Lexie

Three weeks had passed since Lexie found out about Mitch's injury, and she was ashamed to admit that her phone had been permanently attached to her hand during that time, as she was constantly scouring the internet for updates on his condition.

She still regularly had to fight off the urge to reach out to him or call his mother since she couldn't speak to him directly. Georgie Scott had, surprisingly, adored Lexie from the moment she met her, and Lexie had no doubt she would be glad to hear from her, even if things between her and Mitch hadn't worked out.

But she couldn't bring herself to make that call. She was still healing; allowing Mitch, or anyone close to him, back into her orbit now would feel like a giant running leap backward. For the sake of her sanity, she had to be strong.

Now, it was a Friday night, and Lexie was at dinner with Berkley, Brent, Cole, and Amelia, a tradition they had adapted in the wake of Mitch's trade to check in with each other once a week, as long as they were all in town.

It was mid-November, and the few trees dotting the sidewalk outside the restaurant were covered in leaves in shades varying from bright yellow to deep orange, red so vibrant it bordered on pink, and brown, indicating the leaves were seconds away from falling to the pavement below.

Seated around a large circular table in the bustling dining room of an Italian restaurant downtown, the five of them caught up on Lexie's work, Amelia's magazine column, Brent and Cole's season, and Berkley's struggles to balance both a full-time course load and part-time legal work.

"I keep telling her she should just quit her job completely, but she refuses," Brent said to the group.

"I don't understand why you keep asking," Berkley said with an eye roll. "You know it's never going to happen."

"I can't believe, two years later, you idiots are still having the same argument about money."

Berkley giggled uncomfortably, and Brent directed a sheepish grin at his lap, chastised. "It's not about the money so much as it is about the fact that I want to be working. I'm learning a ton from Lippett, and the more experience I have drafting contracts will only benefit me in the long run when it comes time to open my own agency."

"Will you take me on as a client when you do?" Cole asked her.

"Sure," Berkley said after swallowing down a large mouthful of wine. "But what's wrong with your current agent?"

"He's a nice guy and all," Cole said, "but he's kind of a kiss-ass. I need someone who is going to tell it like it is and go to bat for me when I need them to."

Berkley quirked an eyebrow. "And you think that's me?"

"Hell yeah I do."

Berkley smiled, her cheeks turning red. "I'm flattered, Cole."

Brent cleared his throat. "Hey, Reid?" He said.

"Yeah, bro?"

"Stop hitting on my fiancé."

The table erupted into laughter, and Cole's cheeks blushed to match Berkley's.

"I wasn't hitting on her," Cole said quietly. "I'm only trying to help her get her agency off the ground. Why aren't *you* asking her to be your agent?"

Brent and Berkley shared a look, alerting Lexie to the fact that they'd had this conversation before. If Lexie knew anything about Berkley, she knew chances were high that Brent had asked, and Berkley shot him down.

"We don't want to mix our business and personal lives," Berkley finally said.

Bingo.

"Besides, I'm happy with my current agent. I'll let Berkley handle those less fortunate than me," Brent said with a pointed look at Cole.

Cole opened his mouth to say something but snapped it shut. Finally, he muttered, "I hate that you make more money than me."

The whole table laughed again, but the mood quickly soured when Amelia asked, "Has anyone heard any news on Mitch?"

Lexie felt as though all of the air was sucked from the room. Brent and Cole looked at each other, and Cole's eyes widened, as though pleading Brent not to do whatever he was about to do.

"Actually..."

"He's back in Michigan," Berkley blurted.

Lexie reared back as though she'd been slapped.

He was back?

"And you didn't tell me," she said flatly.

"We didn't really know how," Berkley said.

"And to be honest, we weren't sure you'd care..." Brent said.

Lexie turned in her seat and glared at him, pointing her finger in his direction. "I have never, not for a single second, not cared about that man. I've been out of my mind, worried sick about him. And you didn't know how to tell me he's back in the fucking state? First you didn't tell me he got hurt and now this? What the fuck is wrong with you guys?"

In her hysteria, Lexie's voice rose. People gathered around the other tables in the dining room were glancing their way, sharing hushed words behind their hands at her expense.

She couldn't find it in herself to care, not when her best friend just dropped this massive bomb on her.

"Lexie, please calm down," Amelia said, reaching out to grab Lexie's hand under the table. Lexie had half a mind to pull away but chose not to, allowing the physical contact to ground her.

Sucking a deep breath in through her mouth, she slowly let it out through her nose and tried again. "Of course I care about Mitch," she said quietly. "But you keeping this from me is bullshit and you know it."

Brent and Cole both had the decency to appear regretful. Berkley sat there, staring blankly at Lexie, as though trying to find a way to diffuse this situation before it became a full-blown scene in the middle of this restaurant.

Which would not be good considering they were dining with two of Detroit's premier athletes.

That thought was a bucket of cold water over Lexie's head, and all the fight left her instantly. The last thing she ever wanted was to cause problems for Brent and Cole.

"I deserved to know," she said, meeting Berkley's gaze.

"We know you did," Brent said. "We should've told you last week when Cole and I went to see him—"

"You what?" Lexie hissed, looking quickly between him and Cole.

"We had some Warriors' business to take care of that involved him," Cole said with a shrug.

"I can't..."

Lexie didn't even know how to finish that statement. There were a number of things about these last few minutes that were unbelievable.

Mitch was back in Michigan. No one had told her. They thought she wouldn't care to know. Brent and Cole had *seen* him.

The anger that had dissipated so quickly moments before was back with a vengeance.

She pinned Brent with a glare. "I don't understand how you're so cool with this. He left you, too, Brent. He left all of you," she said, also connecting gazes with Berkley and Cole.

"Look," Brent started. "I know things with you guys didn't end well..."

"Did he tell you what happened?" Lexie asked quickly, terror zipping down her spine at the thought.

That last night hadn't been her finest moment.

The night he walked out. The night she *let* him leave.

The last time she had seen him not on television or through a thick sheet of glass.

When he had still been *hers*.

"No, he didn't," Cole told her. "He said he had enough shit going on in his life right now to get into it."

Well, thank God for that, she thought.

"It's not important anyway," Lexie said dismissively, though it was extremely important. To her, anyway. That night was the downfall of the best—and only—relationship she'd ever had. And she would spend the rest of her days kicking herself for letting him go so easily.

But he hadn't even tried to fight for her, had chosen instead to use his trade as an escape hatch, a way to completely wash his hands of her and the four other people seated at the table with her tonight.

Of the Warriors.

Of Detroit.

She wasn't willing to forgive that as easily as Brent and Cole, and even Berkley, were.

"You should know, Lexie..." Brent said, trailing off.

"What now?" She ground out, jaw aching from clenching her teeth together to keep from saying things she couldn't take back.

She learned her lesson last time.

"I'm going to ask him to be my best man."

"You've got to be fucking kidding me."

Berkley, who had been annoyingly silent this entire time, piped up. "Well, it was either him or Nate, and you've slept with both of them so..."

"You bitch," Lexie said with mock affront.

The whole table seemed to relax at its appearance.

"Look," Brent said. "I know you're hurt, and I get that the way things ended was messy, and he handled leaving badly but...I think you should go see him."

"Why would I do that?"

"Because he deserves a second chance," Brent said simply.

For nearly two weeks, Lexie waffled between whether or not to go see Mitch.

During that time, she took a trip to Boston, wanting to give Amelia's readers the winter-on-the-East-Coast vibes without dealing with the absolute madness that was New York City. Boston was an all-American city but more subdued than NYC.

Since Lexie had been clued in on the ruse, Amelia's column in the magazine she worked for had changed considerably.

Initially, Amelia was using Lexie's mid-twenties, single-girl work trip adventures as fodder for her blog, and it attracted a lot of people that were in the same season of their lives.

But when Lexie finally became aware of what Amelia was doing, and decided to continue helping her out, they thought it would be a good idea to expand their reach by including not only things for young, single women, but also events for families, and historical sites for people who wanted to experience some culture while they traveled.

So while she was in Boston—where everyone but Amelia assumed she was for such a long stay because she was trying to land a particularly difficult client—Lexie had a jam-packed itinerary.

As she was here on her own dime and not that of her company, she didn't put herself up in a swanky hotel like the one she'd stayed in Dallas, choosing instead to book a room at the local Comfort Inn.

That was the first tip Amelia—by way of Lexie—gave her readers: don't splurge on hotels. There are plenty of nice, clean hotels, motels, and inns out there that won't break the bank. On vacation, most people are only in their rooms long enough to change, shower, or sleep. It made no sense to Lexie to drop a ridiculous sum of money on lodging when there were a million other things travelers could save for.

Like experiences.

The first day she was there, she simply wandered the city.

Her hotel was near Clam Point, and practically right across the street from the Boston Winery and Boston Harbor Distillery, so she took a little stroll along the Neponset River and stopped into each place for a drink, noting the pricing, atmosphere, and offerings for the magazine piece she and Amelia would later cobble together.

After a few beverages, she took an Uber from South Boston up to Beacon Hill, where Boston Common was located.

Boston Common is a fifty-acre park smack dab in the middle of Beacon Hill. During the American Revolution, it played host to British troops. Now, it was a great green space in the middle of a concrete jungle.

Boston Common had a beautiful public garden, the Frog Pond on which people liked to skate in the winter, and several statues in monument to people like George Washington, Wendell Phillips, Charles Sumner, and Edgar Allan Poe, plus a Boston Massacre/Crispus Attucks Memorial.

Lexie wandered the fringes of the Common, slowly making her way down the sidewalk along Tremont Street, searching for somewhere to have dinner.

The options were limitless within these few square miles, but Lexie found herself craving pizza and steered herself into Sal's Pizza.

After she gorged herself on two slices of extra cheesy pepperoni and a couple glasses of beer, fighting off advances from men who wondered why she was here alone, Lexie caught an Uber back to her hotel and fell asleep the second her head hit the pillow.

The next day, she made her way back to the Common, this time walking the entire perimeter, interviewing local shop owners, taking notes on the picturesque streets and buildings, and making a list of her favorite things in this area of the city.

From there, she spent the next week traipsing across the city, checking out the museums and historic districts. She walked King Street—now State—where the Boston Massacre took place in 1770, and down to Congress Street to check out the Boston Tea Party Ships & Museum.

As it was December, she couldn't attend a game at Fenway, but she did walk by, taking pictures and imagining what this section of the city must be like on those hot summer days when the Sox were playing.

On the West End, she bought a ticket to the Golden Bears game that night in a moment of what could only be described as pure insanity. They played the Florida Thunderhawks and won by two goals. Lexie had to admit, without the added pressures of cheering for the Warriors—or more specifically, her friends that played for the Warriors—she enjoyed herself.

Maybe she was becoming a hockey fan after all.

After that first week, she spent some time visiting a few of the bigger colleges and universities within metro Boston. The number of private, public, specialized, and research facilities in the area totaled a staggering forty-four. Still, she chose to focus on the major ones, like Berklee College of Music—where she bought Berkley a souvenir t-shirt—Boston College, Boston University, Brandeis, Harvard, Northeastern, and the University of Massachusetts. Both she and Amelia agreed that it was in their best interest to highlight the social scene at the local level, but academics as well.

Everywhere she went, she took photos. Of beautiful architecture and snow-covered streets. Of children walking hand-in-hand with their parents, bundled up in thick coats and scarves and mittens.

Of couples enjoying the magic of the holiday season.

Every time she encountered a pair strolling along the powder-dusted sidewalks or pausing outside an eatery to steal a kiss before popping inside for a meal, a sharp pang echoed through her chest.

She could've had all of that and *did* have all of that. As hard as she fought it, her relationship with Mitch had been the best thing that ever happened to her, and she had planned to spend forever with him.

Unfortunately, she could never get out of her own way, and now here she was, in a romantic city like Boston, nostalgic for everything she'd lost, for everything she'd thrown away.

Despite the melancholic ache that had set up camp in her chest thinking about Mitch, she felt more at ease, more clear-headed than she had in months. She couldn't help thinking that *this* was what she was meant to be doing—not jetting across the country on the whims of someone else, trying to convince annoying brainiacs to take jobs, but exploring new places and sharing those experiences with others.

Those two weeks flew by, and Lexie was not looking forward to going home and facing all that awaited her there.

She had just touched down in Detroit and turned her phone on when Berkley called.

"I literally *just* landed, Berk," Lexie said, exasperated. The weather had kept them grounded from takeoff in Boston far longer than she would've liked, and now all she wanted to do was get home and take the world's longest, hottest bath.

"Since you freaked out on us last time for not telling you, I wanted to give you a Mitch update."

Lexie's heart sank as her pulse sped up. If Berkley was calling about Mitch, it wasn't good news.

"What's up?" She asked, struggling to keep her voice steady.

"He had a bit of a setback," Berkley said.

"What kind of setback?"

Berkley's frustrated sigh blew into Lexie's ear. "I don't know, Lexie. I'm not Nate. You know my eyes glaze over when anyone starts talking about medical shit. Something to do with the broken vertebra. He had to have surgery to repair it."

"When?"

Berkley didn't answer for long enough that Lexie knew this wasn't a recent development. Her anger spiked. "Damnit, Berkley. When?"

"Last Tuesday," Berkley said quietly. "And before you start shouting at me, I wanted to tell you right away. The boys made me promise not to say anything until we knew he was in the clear."

"Berkley..." Lexie said, heaving a deep breath. "Last Tuesday was six fucking days ago."

"I'm aware."

"And it took six days to make sure Mitch was going to be okay?"

"Well, no..." Berkley said. "But I knew you were on an important work trip and figured you had some big client to close if you were gone for so long, so I didn't want you rushing back here if something happened. Or if nothing did."

This girl, Lexie thought, *is trying to kill me.*

For all Berkley's talk of hating surprises and disliking people making decisions for her, she sure pulled the same shit on other people often enough that it made Lexie want to rip her hair out.

"So why are you telling me now?"

"Because I figured you needed a kick in the ass to go see him."

Berkley knew her too damn well. The majority of the time, it calmed Lexie, easing whatever pressure she was feeling, knowing she wouldn't have to explain herself and what she was feeling or thinking to Berkley.

And then there were times like this, when she'd like nothing more than to take a pair of scissors and snip right through that connection.

Or maybe a hatchet.

In truth, Lexie *still* hadn't made up her mind about going to see him. But now that he was laid up? And she would have the upper hand because she could turn and leave at any time, and he wouldn't be able to follow her?

The idea was appealing for a number of reasons.

"Fine," she finally said to Berkley.

"Fine what?" Berkley asked hopefully.

"Fine, I'll go see him. Have Brent text me all the info I'll need."

"Oh, Lex," Berkley said. "I'm so proud of you. I think this will be really good for you. You can see him, get some shit off your chest—within reason, of course; the man is laid up in a hospital bed. Then you can finally move on."

Lexie rolled her eyes. Women like her didn't simply *move on* from men like Mitch.

There had been so many years that Lexie spent believing she was undeserving of love. Her parents had refused to give it to her, so why would anyone who didn't share her DNA be bothered?

And then Berkley, Amelia, and Kimber came into her life, showing her she *was* deserving, if only that friendship kind of love that close girlfriends experienced.

But with Mitch...Mitch had pulled the wool from her eyes and helped her realize she didn't have to live her life without romantic love, too. That there had never been anything wrong with her simply because her parents refused to see what a gift she was.

Mitch helped her realize that she could have it all.

And when she'd finally taken the leap with him and opened herself up to the possibility of allowing someone into her heart in a way she'd never done before...

It was *magic.*

Until he left.

And when he was gone, the beautiful, fragile thing they had grown together withered and died.

CHAPTER ELEVEN
Lexie

Two days later, the night before Lexie planned to visit Mitch, she found herself at Brent and Berkley's house.

Brent was on the road, somewhere on the West Coast, and Berkley knew Lexie was stressed about the next day, so she invited her over for a girl's night.

The girls were spread out in the basement in front of the sixty-five-inch television that dominated one wall.

When Brent and Berkley bought the house, the basement had been unfinished. Since then, they've converted it into a dual-purpose space: half was a small in-home theater with cushy leather couches, a popcorn machine, and a bar stocked with all manner of snacks and sweets, plus soda, water, and an assortment of alcoholic beverages. The other half was an in-home gym for summer days when Brent didn't feel like driving into the city—a scant ten miles that could feel three times as long depending on traffic.

Berkley had always said, in the year since they bought the house, that it was way too much space for the two of them, and usually, Lexie was inclined to agree.

Except for nights like tonight, when she had a particularly full glass of wine on the table in front of her, and she was curled up in one of the aforementioned leather chairs with a thick blanket wrapped around her legs and a bowl of popcorn mixed with M&M's on her lap, the TV playing a cheesy romcom that neither she nor Berkley were actually paying any attention to.

"You nervous for tomorrow?" Berkley asked her.

"Of course I am," Lexie said honestly. "I've been thinking of ways to get out of it ever since I agreed to go."

"Lexie..." Berkley started, but Lexie held up her hand to silence her.

"I know I need to go," she said. "I need to see him with my own two eyes, if only to confirm he's okay. I don't expect anything from him. The way we left things...it wasn't great. And it fucked me up for a while. But I'm better now. Aren't I?"

Lexie met Berkley's gaze, and her friend shrugged. "I can't answer that for you," Berkley said.

"I feel better," Lexie said.

"I consider it a win that you're no longer drinking your meals, honestly," Berkley said with a giggle.

Lexie threw a piece of popcorn at her and sighed. "It was touch and go there for a while, wasn't it?"

Berkley nodded solemnly. "I was really worried about you those first few months. You were walking around like a zombie. The only time you showed any of your old spark was when you'd get drunk and hook up with those random guys."

Lexie wanted to argue, but Berkley was right. The number of men Lexie had left in her wake in the first few weeks and months after Mitch left wasn't an amount she was particularly proud of. But after their fight, and his trade, she went numb. And she was so desperate to feel something, anything, that she drank herself stupid five nights out of seven and slept with someone new nearly as frequently.

One night the previous June, after the Warriors had been knocked out of the playoffs, Brent and Berkley hosted their official housewarming party. It may have been six months after they moved in, but between hockey season and Berkley's work schedule, the couple had no free time before then to even think about throwing a party.

That night, Lexie once again attempted to drown her sorrows in tequila and a meaningless hookup. A couple of Brent's teammates had been looking particularly delicious, and she was about to make her move across the back patio toward one when an arm clamped down on her wrist and towed her inside.

Brent dragged her through the kitchen and living room before bringing her upstairs and depositing her on the bed in one of the guest rooms.

Her head was spinning from how quickly Brent had moved her from the backyard to this bedroom—the tequila hadn't helped matters—but the fog cleared enough for her to find herself face to face with Brent, Berkley, and Amelia.

"What the fuck is this?" She slurred, clumsily gesturing between the three of them. "Some sort of intervention?"

"That's exactly what this is," Berkley said, crossing her arms over her chest and glaring down her nose at Lexie.

"Why?"

"Because we can't keep watching you drink and whore yourself out like this," Amelia said.

Lexie scoffed. "Don't call me a whore. That's not nice."

"Lexie," Berkley said, kneeling in front of her to look her in the eyes. "This is serious. You're hurting, we get that. But you're also hurting the rest of us by acting like this. You need to get your shit together."

Lexie glanced up to find tears lining Berkley's lashes.

Her best friend was crying.

Because of her.

What the fuck was wrong with her? It was one thing to have a good time, drink casually, and screw around when she felt like it. But since Mitch had left, she'd made an Olympic sport out of getting drunk and fucking.

Up to that point, Lexie hadn't felt like she was doing anything wrong, or that anyone cared one way or the other.

Clearly, she'd been mistaken if even Brent was standing in this room with her, the man who loved her best friend deeply but also loved—and had been left by—his own best friend.

Only when Lexie pulled Berkley in for a hug and buried her face in her neck, whispering, "I'm sorry," over and over did she realize she'd been crying herself.

Now, Berkley reached out and grabbed her hand. Lexie gave her a watery smile and said, "I'm sorry I put you guys through that."

Berkley shrugged and squeezed her fingers. "It's okay. It's no different than you throwing me in a shower fully clothed."

Lexie boomed out a laugh at the memory of Berkley's wallowing in the wake of her breakup with Brent. It made her feel better, knowing she wasn't the only one who had reacted poorly to the loss of the best relationship they'd ever had.

The only difference—and it was a big one—was that Berkley got hers back.

"I truly thought you were going to kill me for that," Lexie said.

"I definitely thought about it," Berkley told her. "But surprisingly, I was uninterested in going to prison for murder. Do you know what would happen to me on the inside?"

Lexie giggled. Berkley in prison? She'd be eaten alive.

Lexie sighed and said, "Tomorrow is going to be really hard."

"I know it is," Berkley told her. "But you'll feel better once it's over."

"I hope you're right."

Berkley had always been an optimist, especially where Lexie's relationship with Mitch was concerned. She had always chosen to see the bright side of things, to focus on the fact that two people she loved so much had found each other, had *loved* each other.

In Berkley's mind, that was everything.

But Berkley still didn't know the full story behind that last night, and Lexie didn't know if her best friend would be so optimistic about tomorrow if she did.

Eventually, Lexie would have to tell her and deal with the consequences. Knowing Berkley, she would not react kindly to the truth of their breakup and Mitch leaving.

Lexie had fucked up.

And so had Mitch.

It kept Lexie up that night, the memories of those final days. Of ignored phone calls and broken bottles and so many tears.

How could she walk into the hospital tomorrow with her head held high, knowing the part she had in destroying what they'd built?

How was she supposed to walk in there and look into the face of the man who had so thoroughly broken her?

How could she give him the power to do it again?

With each exit she passed on I-96 heading in the direction of Ann Arbor the next morning, Lexie nearly took the off-ramp and turned tail back to Detroit.

But she didn't, and those forty-two miles passed in the blink of an eye. Before she knew it, she was pulling up in front of the University of Michigan's Physical Medicine and Rehabilitation center, where Mitch had been staying since he came back to Michigan and was now recuperating from his most recent surgery.

Before stepping out of her car, she sucked in several deep breaths, took a fortifying sip of her lukewarm black coffee, and wiped her sweaty palms on her dark jeans. It was mid-December, the temperature moderate but nowhere near what Lexie considered warm, and yet she was seconds away from sweating through her sweater.

Finally, she unbuckled and unfolded herself from her vehicle, her long legs gobbling the distance between the parking lot and the reception area.

The automatic doors opened to a large lobby where a reception desk sat off to one side, the space beyond it narrowing into a hallway where people bustled in and out of rooms.

The desk was decorated with twinkle lights and garland, and a soaring pine tree to her right reached toward the skylights in the vaulted ceiling, decorated in the University of Michigan school colors.

As a Michigan State University alumna, the sight of all that maize and blue made Lexie want to vomit on the gleaming marble floors.

Honestly, it wouldn't take much; her stomach was already twisted in knots and unsettled over why she was here.

She approached the desk and said, "Hi, my name is Lexie. I'm here to see Mitch Frambough? He's in rehab."

The woman quirked an eyebrow. "Honey, this entire place is rehab. You're going to have to be a little more specific."

Lexie's hackles rose, but getting in a shouting match with a receptionist when her nerves were already completely frayed was the opposite of a good idea. She pasted a saccharine smile on her face and said, "He just had surgery. Spinal injury. Hockey player. Ridiculously tall, shoulder length blond hair, green eyes. Ringing any bells?"

The woman stared Lexie down for several long seconds before turning and tapping away on her keyboard. A moment later, she said, "Third floor. Take the first elevator bank on the left. It'll open up to reception up there, and Denise will direct you to the correct room."

Lexie tilted her head to the side and grinned. "Thank you so much for your help," she said with fake cheerfulness, then turned on a booted heel and strode away.

The reception area on the third floor was similar to that downstairs but on a much smaller scale. Lexie reached the counter and repeated her spiel.

"Give me just a second, hun, and I'll ring his room for you. What did you say your name was again?"

"Lexie Monroe."

The woman—Denise—picked up the phone and dialed, smiling at Lexie while she waited for someone on the other end to pick up.

"Good morning, Mr. Frambough," she said when Mitch picked up. "You have a visitor."

Mitch said something, and Denise responded with, "Well, don't you want to know who it is first? She could be a bad person."

Again, Mitch spoke.

"Yes, *she*," Denise replied. "She said her name is Lexie Monroe."

Mitch's voice rose through the receiver as he started talking a mile a minute, though Lexie couldn't understand a word of it.

Even Denise looked shocked by the outburst, but a moment later said, "Okay. Yes, I understand."

Denise hung up the phone and shot Lexie a pitying look. "I'm sorry, dear," she said. "It appears he doesn't want to see you."

Lexie's cheeks flamed instantly, but she stood there staring dumbly at the woman, processing what she'd just said.

It appears he doesn't want to see you.

He. Doesn't. Want. To. See. You.

That fucking bastard.

"Oh," Lexie said quietly. "Okay, no problem. Thank you for your time."
And then she turned, and she ran, bypassing the elevator completely
and speeding down the three flights of stairs two at a time, dangerously
careening around the sharp corners, before bursting out on the main floor
and sprinting into the cool December air.

She slowed to a walk when she reached the parking lot but still arrived at
her car quickly and shoved herself behind the wheel moments before the
dam broke.

After all this time, she knew she shouldn't be crying over Mitch. Truthfully, she hadn't even known she still could. She thought she'd got all the
tears out in those early days, before she started drinking and sleeping her
way over him.

After everything he'd put her through, leaving the way he did, making
her love him only to take that away from her. Pushing her into a relationship that she told him from the very beginning she didn't want. She wanted
to strangle him for then, after all that, having the gall to say *he* didn't want
to see *her*.

It should've been the other way around.

Coming here had been a mistake, and as her tears of embarrassment
slowed and finally stopped, anger bubbled under the surface of her skin.

Anger at Mitch. Anger at the game of hockey and the city of Detroit.
Anger at Brent and Berkley and Cole and Amelia and everyone else who
thought it was a good idea to come here today.

But mostly?

Anger at herself.

For letting things get so bad when she had learned long ago never to trust
anyone with her heart.

When she knew damn well, all anyone ever did was break it.

CHAPTER TWELVE
Mitch

TWENTY MONTHS AGO...

M itch woke up just as the sky began its shift from black to grey, blinking slowly, trying to figure out what pulled him from his slumber. And then he hears it: soft humming floating through his condo. The only people with the code to the door were his mom, the cleaning lady, and Lexie, and he knows without a doubt that neither his mom nor the cleaning lady would be here this early.

Clad in only his boxers, he padded out into his kitchen to find Lexie standing at the counter, a full fast food breakfast spread out on the island in front of her.

Wearing nothing but one of his well-worn deep blue Warriors tees that hit her mid-thigh, the curve of her ass peeked out below the hem when she moved.

Walking up to her, he slid his arms around her waist and pressed a kiss into her hair. "Did you just get here?" he asked.

"No, I've been here for an hour or so," she said.

"Why didn't you wake me?"

"You looked so peaceful," she said with a shrug.

"How are things with Berk?"

"Not great. I ended up spending all night with her. First holding her while she cried and then holding her hair while she puked up the three bottles of wine she chugged."

"Christ," Mitch rubbed a hand across the stubble on his jaw before jerking a hand through his hair to comb out the tangles. "That bad?"

Lexie nodded gravely. "It wasn't pretty. She and Brent broke up, Mitch."

Mitch stared at her, dumbfounded.

"Are you serious?"

The night before, the Warriors had won at home against the Buffalo Regents, allowing them to advance in the playoffs. It should've been a perfect night, full of celebration.

And it had been a great night, up until the moment Brent found out that Parker had attacked Berkley back in October.

Then all hell broke loose.

If management ever found out that Brent had punched his teammate not once but twice, Brent would be in more trouble than Mitch cared to consider, and they couldn't afford to lose one of their top forwards in the middle of a playoff run.

After the display Brent and Parker had put on, Berkley fled the loft, and Brent chased after her. He and Lexie had assumed they'd talk and smooth everything over.

Unfortunately, that wasn't the case, and Berkley called Lexie sometime later, crying and begging her to come over.

Apparently, she had dumped him, telling him she couldn't be with him anymore because they were too different. Mitch was honestly surprised Brent hadn't called him to tell him already.

"I can't believe they're just...done," he said. "I really thought they were endgame."

Lexie nodded. "Me, too. She's such a mess. When I got there, she was crying so hard she could barely form sentences. She finally fell asleep in the middle of the night, but I didn't want to just leave her."

He reached for one of the coffees, taking a long pull from the cup–black, exactly how he liked it. "You're a good friend," he told her.

She shrugged. "I try. I just wish she wouldn't self-sabotage herself like this."

"She must get that from you," Mitch said and instantly regretted it.

There go your chances of getting her naked this morning, Frambough, he thought.

"What's that supposed to mean?" she asked.

"C'mon, Lex. You know..."

"I most certainly do not. How exactly do I self-sabotage myself?"

"This really wasn't how I wanted to have this conversation," he muttered. "But Lex...since we started sleeping together and hanging out, you've done nothing but remind me at every turn that it's just sex. That we can never be anything more to each other. Don't you think it's time to give up the act?"

She settled her arms across her chest, glaring daggers at him. "It's not an act," she said defensively. "I can't give you anything other than sex."

He stood then, hoping his size would intimidate her into finally telling the truth. "Damnit, Lexie. Don't you see that you already have been this entire time?"

"We're not talking about this right now," Lexie said, settling onto a barstool and taking a massive bite of her breakfast sandwich, effectively ending the conversation. Resigned, Mitch sat down beside her and dug in.

Their meal was a tense affair. Mitch desperately wanted to have this conversation: about what they were doing and where they were headed. Lexie was as taut as a rubber band pulled tight, and Mitch braced himself for the inevitable snap.

But it didn't come. When they finished eating, Lexie quietly got up and collected their trash, walking it over to the garbage before leaning over the sink to wash her hands.

Mitch watched her, desperate to bridge this sudden gap between them.

So he did the only thing he could think of, the one thing that would put them on an even playing field.

The one thing that would bring her back to him, if only for a moment.

Mitch stalked up behind her at the sink, pressing his chest against her back, and said, "Do you have any idea how sexy you are in that t-shirt?"

Lexie's shoulders hunched, a giggling escaping her when Mitch trailed his nose along that ticklish spot on her neck. "It was the first thing I found in the dresser," she said.

"It's giving me all kinds of ideas," he said.

She spun around, and he braced his hands on the counter beside her, bracketing her in. In the dim morning light, her eyes appeared darker, more brown than their usual golden. "Like what?" she asked.

"Like propping your pretty little ass up on this counter, throwing your legs over my shoulders, and making you come with my mouth," he said, leaning in to run his tongue from her collarbone up her neck to her jaw.

Lexie's breathing picked up, and she reached for him, stroking her fingers along the dips and ridges of his back in slow, maddening circles. He wanted that touch lower. "What else?" she asked, tilting her head to capture his earlobe with her teeth.

"After that," he said, snaking his hands under the hem of her shirt and skating them up her sides, pausing when his thumbs brushed the undersides of her breasts. He moved his mouth a breath away from hers. "I'm going to bend you over that island and fuck you until you're screaming loud enough to wake the neighbors."

Lexie pulled back enough to look into his eyes and said, "I love it when you talk dirty."

Then she rose on her tippy toes and sealed her mouth over his. Mitch opened for her, running his tongue over hers. Mouths still fused, he trailed his hands down over the slope of her ass before cupping them around her thighs and lifting her. Lexie let out a squeal when the backs of her naked thighs met the cold marble counter. Mitch sank to his knees before her.

Lexie leaned back on her hands and studied him from her perch. "You look so good like this," she said as he smoothed his hands over her calves, knees, and inner thighs. She rose off the counter so he could hook his thumbs in her underwear and pull them off. "When your hair is all mussed from sleep," she continued as he ran a finger through her wetness, catching her eyes as he sucked it clean. On an exhale, she added, "That little pillow crease on your cheek. All that smooth skin on display. I love it when you're on your knees, worshiping me."

Mitch was hard as a rock, his dick tenting the front of his boxers. But he refused to touch himself. Not until she was satisfied. "I will worship at your feet every day if you let me."

Shifting closer, he reached out and hooked one of her legs over his shoulder, pressing a kiss to her inner thigh before repeating the process on the other side.

The first stroke of his tongue had Lexie's head falling back and smacking into the cabinet behind her. Mitch carried on when she didn't cry out in pain, only loosing a moan of pleasure.

Over the course of the last few months, Mitch had paid attention to Lexie in bed, quickly learning exactly what she did and didn't like, what got her there quickly and what wouldn't get her there at all, when she wanted it quick and dirty and when she needed to be teased.

On this slow, lazy morning, Mitch could tell she wanted to be teased. Unfortunately for her, thanks to all their verbal foreplay and her breathy moans and pleas, he was desperate to be buried in her.

When he shoved two fingers inside her and pumped them in and out a few times before pushing them in and curling them, leaving them there while he continued to work her with his tongue and teeth and lips, her quiet pleas grew in volume, quickly becoming begging shouts of *please God Mitch please please please.*

"I'm not God," he said against her clit, "but since you asked so nicely."

He made short work of her after that, her orgasm surprising both of them. Mitch loved how she clenched around his fingers as he continued to stroke her through it and how her legs twitched by his ears and her heels dug into his back.

Mitch was greedy for his own release, and to feel her tightening around his dick, so he barely let her settle before pulling her off the counter and spinning them toward the island. Lexie pressed her mouth to his, kissing him fiercely, their teeth knocking together.

He set her on her feet and spun her away from him. "Shirt on or off?" he asked against her ear.

Lexie responded by whipping the material over her head and tossing it across the room. Her long, dark tresses cascaded down her back, nearly brushing the dimples bracketing her spine above her ass. She bent at the waist and laid across the marble, letting out a small "oh" of surprise when her nipples encountered the cold surface. Mitch dropped his boxers and stepped out of them, kicking her feet wide and settling his hands on her hips, pressing into her without warning.

She arched, and he reached one hand out, scooping her hair off her back and wrapping it around his wrist while he held her in place with the other.

Then he lost himself, the sounds of their frantic joining filling the apartment.

"Mitch," Lexie breathed. "Oh, God, right there."

He had shifted his hips to the side a bit, the new angle apparently very good for his partner.

"You almost there?" He asked through gritted teeth. His balls had tightened near to the point of bursting, and he'd be spilling himself into her in a few more thrusts.

Her head bobbed as she nodded and said, "Give me your hand."

Their position made it nearly impossible, but Mitch would do anything to satisfy this woman, so he wedged his hand between her thigh and the counter, deftly finding her clit and pressing hard against it, moving in tight circles.

"Mitch, I—" her sentence was cut off by a half cry, half moan as her second orgasm barreled through her, and that clenching around his dick and her tiny, jerky spasms had his own bursting free. He draped his body over hers, resting his hands on either side of her torso as he emptied himself.

Lexie laid her head on the counter, body rising and falling below him, her back meeting his chest with every inhale.

When he pulled free, she said, "We should do that more often."

Mitch turned and ripped off a length of paper towel from the roll, using it to clean her up. She lifted herself when he was done and turned to face him. "It was one of my better ideas," he responded with a smirk.

"I'm surprised that's the first time we've fucked in here." She bent to collect her underwear and shirt from the floor.

"Me too," he said, and followed her as she moved from the kitchen and down the hall toward his room.

"I could go for a nap," Lexie yawned, slipping the shirt back over her head but foregoing her panties before crawling under his puffy, deep blue comforter.

Sliding in beside her, he wrapped an arm around her, pulling her close and closed his eyes.

"Wanna go again?" she asked.

Mitch cracked an eyelid to look at her. "Didn't you just say you could go for a nap?"

In response, Lexie simply trailed her fingers in a path down his torso toward his cock, which was already half hard again.

He couldn't and wouldn't ever say no to this woman.

Reaching out, he pulled her on top, and she lowered herself onto him, that t-shirt of his bunched around her waist. The sun had just cracked the horizon, the fresh rays of a new day spilling light across Lexie's bare legs, setting them glowing. Mitch caught her gaze, the moment stretching between them. Mitch didn't move, and neither did Lexie. She simply stared at him, some emotion Mitch couldn't quite name passing over her features, softening them, her eyes shining brighter than normal in the dawning morning light.

And when she finally did begin to move, that emotion morphed into something Mitch *could* name: adoration.

The recognition of it on the face of this woman who rarely shared exactly how she felt with *anyone*, least of all him, unlocked something in Mitch's chest and the quiet moment passed. It transformed into something that set his heart galloping as he pumped his hips up to meet her, his release barreling down his spine far sooner than he anticipated, unexpectedly throwing him off a cliff.

What surprised Mitch even more was the fact that she followed him right off that ledge, wrapping her arms tight around his neck and burying her face against his skin as she panted and twitched through the shockwaves.

"What the hell just happened?" she whispered in a daze when their shuddering ceased. "I have never come from just penetration before."

"I..." Mitch broke off, throat clogged with something he wasn't ready to reveal to Lexie quite yet.

Because he was falling in love with her, and had realized it as soon as he pressed into her minutes ago. He was falling for this girl, who was so incredibly smart, funny, loyal, sassy, and a slew of other things that would take Mitch days to articulate, but also guarded her heart like it was as fragile as a newborn baby.

And to her, he supposed it was. He had to tread carefully here; the last thing he wanted to do was scare her away.

Everything between them had changed after Dallas, even if Lexie continued to bury her head in the sand. That night, which was basically their first date, Mitch's feelings for her morphed from a magnetic sexual attraction to something softer, something more enduring. Physical connections were fleeting, but the tiny ball of *something* that had lodged itself in his chest that night only grew by the day. Lexie was dangerously close to capturing his entire heart, and he'd gladly give it to her, but not at the risk of getting nothing in return.

Not after spending his childhood giving his love to a parent who couldn't have cared less about him.

She rolled off him, and he pulled her close, clamping an arm tight around her, lest she try to run away before they could talk.

"Lex," he began, and she groaned.

"Can't you just let me enjoy this bliss for a few minutes before you go and get all serious on me?" she asked.

"No, because if I don't bring it up while you're too tired from sex to fight me, we'll never get anything accomplished."

She tilted her head back to glare at him. "I can assure you I am not too tired to fight you."

Mitch rolled his eyes. "You are exhausting, and we're having this conversation whether you like it or not."

"Fine," she said, awkwardly crossing her arms over her body despite being on her side and smushed up against him. "You can talk. That doesn't mean I'll have anything to say."

"Look..." he said, unsure of how to begin. It had been a very long time since he'd had a conversation like this, and this might be the most important of them all. There had never been so much on the line. If he couldn't get Lexie to see his side of things and understand that even if they hadn't officially labeled anything, they were as-good-as in a relationship, he didn't know what he would do. Because if this conversation didn't go well, he would likely lose her completely.

And that was unacceptable.

"I'm just gonna say it. I'm crazy about you. And this," he gestured between their naked bodies, "isn't enough for me anymore, and I think you feel the same."

"I don't," she said, propping herself on her elbow to turn away from him, but Mitch held fast, wrapping his arm tighter around her. She wasn't going to get away that easy.

"And I don't believe you." He sat up and rolled so she was trapped under him. "Lexie, this hasn't been just sex for us in a long time. It's been seven months since we met. Why are you still lying to yourself? And me? You're only hurting us both right now, honey," he said, tracing his fingers along her cheekbone and jaw.

"Because I don't know how to do this!" She shoved him so abruptly that the sheer surprise of it had Mitch sitting back on his heels, giving her the opening she needed to put some distance between them.

"And you think I do?"

"I think you're a lot better at deeply emotional relationships than I am," she whispered, hanging her head.

Hopping off the bed, Mitch moved so he was standing in front of her, struck by how strange it was to have such a serious conversation when they were both completely naked.

But if that's what it took to make this woman his girlfriend, his *everything*, then so be it.

"Lexie, honey," he said, scooping her hair out of her face and lifting her chin to gaze into the golden depths of her eyes. "We've been doing this relationship thing for months without putting the actual label on it. You realize that, don't you?"

Lexie shook her head violently, sending her dark hair flying, disagreeing with him without ever opening her mouth.

Mitch blew out a long, exasperated sigh, then reached for her. He trailed the fingers of his left hand over the jut of her cheekbone and across the edge of her jaw, sliding down the smooth column of her neck. He ran them over the sharp line of her collarbone and slope of her shoulder, along the soft skin of her arm, and chuckled when she shivered under his touch.

Lightly, he grasped her wrist between his thumb and forefinger and pulled her flush against him, using his right hand to tip her chin up, forcing her to meet his gaze. "Lexie," he tried again. "I want to give this thing a real shot, and I think you do, too."

She stared at him for a long, tense breath, eyes belying her anxiety. She tried to turn her face away, but he held fast. "I don't know how," she said again, quieter this time, the words a plea.

Show me, her eyes begged him.

"But?" He prompted.

"But I want you," she whispered, "in any way I can have you."

A smile threatened to tug the corners of his lips up, but he resisted the urge. Leaning closer, he pressed his forehead against hers, he said, "You can have all of me. It's already yours."

She leaned back, and her gaze softened on his.

Hope bloomed in his chest, wild and unbidden.

"Okay," Lexie finally said.

"Okay?"

She nodded. "Just...don't ask for too much too soon, okay? It took me seven months to agree to be your..."

"My what?"

She released a frustrated sigh, her breath warming his chest, right above his heart. "Your girlfriend, Mitch. I'm your girlfriend. Is that what you wanted to hear?"

"Fuck yeah it is," he said, face splitting into a grin so large his eyes became mere slits. Picking her up, he tossed her onto the bed and crawled up next to her, planting kisses along her impossibly soft and warm skin until they were eye-to-eye. "And I'm your boyfriend."

She rolled her eyes, and Mitch studied her face as she fought a smile. Finally, she gave in, her grin growing steadily until it matched his own.

Then she flipped onto her stomach and screamed into the pillow.

Mitch settled a hand on her back, rubbing soothing circles over the bare skin and ends of her hair despite the fact that he was laughing.

His girlfriend. Lexie Monroe was his *girlfriend*.

Lexie lifted her head then and said, "We can't tell anyone. Not yet."

All his mirth left him instantly. "And why the fuck not?"

"Are you forgetting that Brent and Berk *just* broke up? Like a few hours ago? I'm not going to shove my happiness in her face right now, and you are not going to shove *yours* in Brent's."

"Okay, okay, fair." He turned onto his side and pulled her flush against him. "Happiness, huh?"

Lexie rolled her eyes. "That would be the part you latch onto. But yes, happiness. A foreign concept for me, I realize. But for you...I'm willing to try it on for size."

Mitch grinned and leaned forward to kiss her, unable to help his elation, despite knowing that across the city, two hearts were breaking, hearts of people he cared about very much.

But with Lexie in his arms, finally *officially* his, he was the happiest man alive.

CHAPTER THIRTEEN
Mitch

Now...

L exie had come to see him. And like the little bitch he was, he turned her away.

The boys were going to kill him.

Berkley was going to kill him.

In his defense, he wasn't ready. When Denise called to tell him he had a visitor, he assumed it was one of the boys. Due to the fact that he was currently on bed rest until the most recent surgery to his back healed, guests had to be admitted to his room; they couldn't walk in without permission.

So when Denise told him it was Lexie waiting for him at the desk, his heart nearly gave out. Knowing she was in the same building as him, a few hundred feet away, sent goosebumps across his skin. He had waited for this moment for so long—over a year, to be exact—and he couldn't wait to see her.

And then he glanced down at his body, currently prone on a motorized bed, clad in a pale green hospital gown and nothing else, and the excitement from a moment before was doused by cold reality.

He couldn't let her see him like this. He refused.

So he did the only thing he could think of to get her to leave.

"Tell her I don't want to see her. Do whatever you have to do, just please make sure she leaves."

The words were shards of glass lodged in his throat, cutting him from the inside as he spoke them.

"Okay. Yes, I understand," Denise said, then hung up.

Mitch pictured Lexie's face then, knowing exactly how she would react when Denise relayed his message. A flinch of embarrassment, cheeks heating against her will. Then she'd set her jaw, murmur a thank you to Denise, and hightail it out of the building.

It appeared he couldn't stop hurting this girl.

While he recuperated, Mitch had a lot of time to think. And figure out what was next for him.

After Brent and Cole approached him about consulting for the Warriors, and endless hours spent with only his mind for company, he had a solid plan.

One evening a few days after his latest surgery, his mom stopped by to visit and sneak him a piping hot bowl of her classic chicken and dumpling soup. His mother, the southern woman she was, believed good food was the way to cure all sorts of ailments. Mitch wasn't about to argue; he loved his mom's cooking.

"So," he started. "I think I figured out what I want to do with my life now that I can't play hockey anymore."

His mother reached out to squeeze his hand, and he gave her a grateful albeit wobbly smile. This woman had always been his rock, and he was more thankful than ever that he struck gold in the mother department.

"And what's that, honey? I thought you were going to consult for the Warriors?"

"Oh, I'm definitely still doing that. I can't pass up the chance to be around the game, even if I can't play. But I thought I might like to go into real estate."

"Real estate," his mother said slowly. "In what capacity?"

"All capacities," he said, and ticked them off on his fingers. "Commercial. Residential. Buying and selling. Development. Eventually a brokerage. I want to do it all."

"Don't you think that's a bit ambitious right out of the gate? What do you even know about real estate anyway?"

"Mom, I've been successfully renting out my loft for years now."

"You have been? By yourself? I thought the team realtor handled that for you?"

He shook his head. "Nope. I listed it on one of those rental sites. I made sure to block out home game nights since we usually ended up there afterward anyway, but otherwise it was fair game."

"What kinds of things do people rent it out for?" She asked.

"Wedding receptions, birthday parties, holiday parties for local businesses, baby and bridal showers...I could go on."

His mother held up her hand, smiling. "Not necessary. I get the idea. So what, you're going to start buying up more properties to do the same thing? Where? Here in the city? Across the state? Across the country?"

"All of the above," he said with a grin. "I'll start by buying a few more properties locally. I'm thinking of more multi-use spaces like the loft."

"How many?" She asked.

"I've been in touch with the Warriors realtor and she's been helping me out. Right now, I've got leads on ten more properties."

"Ten?" His mother exclaimed. "That's...a lot."

"Well I'm not going to buy all of them, Mom," he said with an eye roll. "I haven't even looked at them yet, seeing as how I'm not exactly ambulatory."

She reached out and patted his leg, and he was reminded how lucky he was that he could even feel her touch.

"Okay, fair enough. Then what?"

His eyebrows drew together in confusion. "What do you mean?"

"I mean, once you build your multi-use venue empire, then what? What's next?"

"Well since I've been talking to Sherry—that's the Warriors realtor—she suggested I get my real estate license. So I will start those online classes next week."

"Oh honey, that's great!" His mom said.

He gave her a smile. "I think so, too. It'll be nice to have something to do with idle time while I'm stuck here. Eventually, though..."

"Yes?"

"I'd like to start developing some low income housing. For college students who are surviving on financial aid and bartending tips. For those people who work their asses off and just to turn around and pour every penny they have into rent." He looked up and met her eyes then. "For single moms who just need someone to cut them a break."

Exactly like their landlord had done when she and Mitch first moved to Ann Arbor from Georgia in a beat-up Chevy truck with nothing but a few measly suitcases of clothes, Mitch's hockey gear, and less than a thousand dollars to their names.

Mitch wanted to be there for people on their worst days, even if all he could do was give them a place to live that wouldn't leave them destitute while they got back on their feet.

"Oh honey," his mom said, lashing brimming with tears. "I did okay with you, didn't I?"

"I'd say you did more than okay, Mama."

He and his mother sat in companionable silence for a moment, both remembering what it had been like when they first moved to Michigan.

Mitch had made fast friends with his United States National Team Development Program teammates, and spent several nights a week at one of their houses while his mom was working or in night school. He was old enough to take care of himself, but he hated being alone in an unfamiliar city, and his teammates and their families—some of them billet families—didn't mind having him over for dinner. Mitch was an only child, so his teammates, wherever he was, had always become family to him. They'd always become like his brothers.

Those teammates had become an extension of the small unit that contained him and his mom, and though they were now in their thirties and spread far and wide across not only the U.S. but also the world, they still kept in touch.

And despite his tumultuous childhood, Mitch had always been a good student. He learned quickly, paid attention in class, and never missed assignments. Because of that, his teachers took a liking to him, always providing a solid, stable place to go for advice when his mom was busy.

He had said it before, and he would most certainly say it again, but moving to Michigan had been the best thing that ever happened to him and his mom.

And he had hockey to thank for that. Even if his playing career was over, he could never resent the game, not after everything it had given him.

Not after it had saved him.

A few weeks later, Mitch was back on his feet and back in Detroit for the first time since April, his trip through the airport when he arrived from California notwithstanding.

It was nearing Christmas, and his usual sure and confident stride had turned slow and stilted in deference to his back.

But he finally made his way into the arena, the barn he had called home ice for nearly five years. It was surreal being back in the building and walking down the tunnel where the ceiling soared. The rafters were full to capacity with all of the banners from the championships and other titles the Warriors had won in their long and storied franchise history.

He took a deep breath and started back down the tunnel, heading toward the locker room.

Nerves tightened his chest. He hadn't seen these guys in almost eight months, and though not all of his former teammates would be behind that door, he had to mentally fortify himself for the blast of nostalgia he would experience when walking inside.

Finally, he couldn't put it off any longer.

"Frambough!" Someone yelled from across the room, and soon he was wrapped in a bear hug, clutching his cane for dear life.

"Bro, my back," he said to whoever was crushing him.

"Oh fuck, I'm so sorry," he said, backing away, and Mitch smiled at Hank "Rat" Ratelle. "I was just so excited to see you. I can't believe you're back."

"But don't think you're getting off easy, leaving us the way you did," Tommy Grey said, walking up to clasp Mitch on the shoulder. "We're still pissed as hell about that."

Mitch nodded. "Understandably so. It's a long story but basically..."

"You don't have to explain anything to us now," his former captain Jordan Dawson said as he walked up to join their little pow wow. "We all just assumed it had something to do with Lexie."

The room filled with awkward chuckles and snorts, and Mitch grimaced.

That woman followed him *everywhere*.

Eventually, he would have to come clean about what happened between them, and his part in the destruction of the best relationship he'd ever had.

The relationship he thought he'd have forever.

He shook off that thought and made his way over to his old stall, which was now filled with the gear of Joel Schmidt, a young goalie they brought in to backup Brandon Roberts, the Warriors' veteran starter.

He sat down heavily on the cushioned stool in front of it, lifting his head and finding his former teammates staring at him expectantly?

"What?" He asked.

"I think they're expecting some kind of speech," Coach said as he walked into the room. "The prodigal son returns and all that."

Mitch swept his gaze around the room. "Don't hold your breath."

Everyone laughed, and the tension that filled the air moments before dissipated instantly.

Coach walked up to him and shook his hand. "Good to have you back, Mitch."

"It's good to be back. What do you need from me?"

"Right now, we're about to head out to skate. So once we start running scrimmages, keep an eye on the d-line and see if there's anything we can do to shore it up. Then if you don't mind sticking around after, you can run through some video with the guys and break down what you're seeing and what you would do in situations?"

Mitch grinned. It wasn't the same as being able to get out on the ice with them, but if he could help this team win, this team full of guys who were his brothers for all intents and purposes, he'd do it.

It should worry him how quickly his thinking shifted away from LA and back to Detroit, but it didn't.

"Sounds good to me."

The next two hours passed in a blur. Being in the rink again was a feeling Mitch couldn't accurately explain. It had only been a little over two months since he last skated, since he last went through practice with a team, but it was too damn long.

It felt good to be back.

After practice was over, the locker room cleared out quickly, the guys heading back to their respective homes to pack and prepare for their upcoming road games. Mitch wouldn't be joining them, his back not yet stable enough to spend hours on a plane.

He found himself in the video room with Brent and Cole, watching film from the Warriors' game against Pittsburgh earlier in the season. They'd be heading east this weekend, working their way across Pennsylvania, up to Boston, and through New York over the next week before heading home to play in Detroit on New Year's Eve, as was tradition.

Brent broke the companionable silence when he turned to Mitch and blurted, "There's something I want to ask you."

Mitch's eyebrow rose, and Brent and Cole exchanged a look.

Since when were these two all buddy-buddy, able to convey thoughts with quick glances?

"It's about my wedding," Brent said.

Mitch's pulse kicked up, his heart pounding against his ribs.

"Okay..." Mitch said slowly. "What about it?"

"I want you to be my best man?"

Brent phrased it like a question, closing his eyes and turning slightly away from Mitch, as though he were bracing himself for Mitch's response.

A thousand different scenarios ran through Mitch's mind in the last several seconds, but that one wasn't even in the realm of possibility.

Brent's best man? Him? The man who had taken the coward's way out after getting his heart broken and left all of his friends—his *brothers*—behind without so much as a goodbye?

"Why?" Mitch blurted. "What about your brother? Or Cole? Why me?"

Brent snorted, and Cole said, "I asked him the same question." Cole met Mitch's gaze then. "Look, bro. I'm all for second chances, and I'm not gonna lie, I missed you while you were gone. While this dude—" he pointed at Brent "—is willing to forgive and forget, I'm not so easily swayed. You fucked up, and you hurt a lot of people."

Mitch nodded, understanding completely where Cole was coming from. He looked at Brent.

"Cole said it. I'm willing to forgive and forget. You're my best friend and, not to get all sappy here, but seven months apart hasn't changed that. No offense, Cole," he said, shooting a sheepish grin at the blond. "I had always planned on asking you to be my best man once Berkley and I set a date. Now that you're back in our lives...I still want you standing next to me."

"Then what about your brother?"

"I love my brother," Brent said. "But he's so busy with med school and has his head so far up his own ass that all I'm expecting from him is to show up at the wedding and drink his weight in booze."

Mitch laughed; it seemed as though nothing had changed with Nate Jean in the past seven months.

"So will you?" Brent asked.

"Of course," Mitch said, throat tight with emotion. "I'd be honored."

A thought struck Mitch then, and his heart plummeted.

His face must have betrayed him because Brent choked on a laugh, taking a sip of water as Cole pounded him on the back before saying, "You just realized who the maid of honor is, didn't you?"

"Berkley didn't happen to choose her sister for that role, did she?" Mitch asked.

"Not a chance, bro," Brent said. "Berkley's maid of honor is none other than our dear girl, Lexie."

Mitch's head dropped into his hands as he sucked in deep breaths, and Cole laughed.

"You are so fucked."

Mitch's head spun. There wasn't anything he could do but ride it out, knowing that in a few months, he and Lexie would be walking down the aisle together, doing all sorts of things jointly as best man and maid of honor.

"Speaking of Lexie," Brent said, "did she come to see you?"

Mitch's chest squeezed at the mention of her name. He knew it was for the best, turning her away, but the thought was little comfort. "She did."

"And?" Brent asked, completely ignoring the game playing on the massive screen in favor of turning his attention wholly on Mitch. Cole did the same.

"And I said I didn't want to see her."

The room grew so quiet that Mitch could've heard a pin drop.

"I'm sorry, what?" Cole asked, breaking the silence.

"When the nurse called to tell me I had a visitor, and told me it was Lexie...I panicked." Mitch hung his head, ashamed even now. "I told her to tell Lexie I didn't want to see her."

Mitch had figured Brent would call him an idiot, and that Cole might smack him upside the head for being an asshole, but he never could've imagined Brent's reaction.

"What the fuck is wrong with you?" Brent yelled, shooting from his chair so fast the cushy seat bottom sprang upright with a loud thunk, and Mitch flinched.

"Seriously, dude, you're such a dick," Cole said.

Brent was pacing, pushing his fingers aggressively through his hair, an outward manifestation of the rage surely boiling under his skin. "Do you have any idea how hard that was for her? The fuck, bro?"

Mitch hung his head, unable to meet his friend's eyes. "I'm embarrassed, okay?" He said, gesturing down his body. He was in much better shape now than he had been when she came to see him, but even now, he wouldn't want to see her. "I don't want her to see me like this."

"That's the dumbest shit I've ever heard," Brent growled.

"Ditto," Cole quipped, and Mitch shot him a glare.

How did he explain this to them? They could both move on their own two feet without the help of a wheelchair, cane, or someone to lean on.

They could *skate*.

Mitch was on the mend, yes. Thanks to his athletic lifestyle and the fact that, prior to his injury, he was in peak physical condition, he was rehabbing faster than the doctors expected. But he would never be able to play hockey again.

And *that* was the man Lexie had known and loved. The man who skated fast, hit hard, and scored a modest amount of goals for a defenseman.

Mitch Frambough, professional hockey player.

Top-tier defenseman.

What would she want with him now that he was damaged goods?

"I don't even understand why she came," Mitch said. "She made it perfectly clear she didn't want me anymore."

Brent blew out an exasperated breath, and Mitch caught his gaze then. His friend was practically vibrating with anger and frustration. "I don't get you, Mitch. You're the one who left her. And she went there because, despite all that, she cares about you. And you basically told her to fuck off."

Mitch started to speak, to explain the situation and how those final days—that final night—had shaken out, but he bit his tongue. It was too late now, and there were too many mountains standing between them, mountains he didn't have the strength to climb.

"It's not important," Mitch said. "What is important is that I didn't want to see her. That's all you need to know."

"You know what?" Brent said, glaring daggers down at Mitch.

"What?" Mitch asked, annoyance lacing the single syllable as it left his mouth.

"Fuck you," Brent said, then turned and stormed from the room.

Mitch sat there, mouth agape, staring after him.

"He's right, you know," Cole said. "You're the one who left. I get that we don't know the whole story. There was some big fight? Okay, fine. But you didn't even try. And just because things with Lexie looked bleak in the moment didn't mean you had to give the rest of us the finger after the trade. And you have no idea what we've all been through dealing with that. Lexie had it worst of all because of who you were to her. Who you are to her. Looks like your time in LA changed you more than we thought it did."

Then he followed Brent out.

Mitch sat there for a long time after they left, watching the game film until its conclusion, one thought circling his brain.

My how the mighty have fallen.

CHAPTER FOURTEEN
Mitch

Eighteen Months Ago...

Thankfully, after Lexie and Mitch knocked some sense into their respective best friends, Brent and Berkley got back together after Berkley's law school graduation.

All was once again right in the world, especially since Mitch and Lexie were finally about to tell the world they were together...officially.

In the few months between their time in Dallas and Lexie finally agreeing to be his girlfriend, she and Mitch hadn't exactly been quiet about the fact that they were sleeping together. Both of them enjoyed public displays of affection—to an extent—and could frequently be found holding hands, with arms wrapped around each other, or stealing kisses.

Tonight, they were at the loft. The night before, the Warriors had been knocked out of the playoffs and had taken the evening to mourn the end of their season as a team.

Now was time to celebrate the start of summer. The off-season sucked, especially when their playoff run had been cut short, but Mitch was excited about spending the next few months with Lexie and their friends.

They hadn't agreed to make some big proclamation about the change in their relationship status, but understood that Brent and Berkley deserved to know before anyone else. They were their best friends, and sort of the reason they were together.

So when the couple walked into the loft and headed for where Mitch and Lexie were posted up near the bar, Lexie wasted no time, blurting, "Mitch and I are dating."

Berkley stopped dead in her tracks, forehead scrunching in confusion. "I thought you were dating anyway?"

"Told you," Mitch whispered, and chuckled when Lexie smacked him.

But he *had* told her. They *had* been dating all these months regardless of whether they had labeled it or not. In his eyes, she'd been his since Dallas.

Actually, long before that.

She'd been his since the moment he first laid eyes on her.

"We were," Mitch said with a pointed look at his girlfriend. "But I finally got her to label it."

"Like boyfriend-girlfriend kind of labels?" Brent asked, grin growing.

"Those exact ones," Mitch said proudly.

Berkley beamed and walked up to grab Lexie's hands. "Look at my little baby, all grown up."

Lexie pulled her hands away and swatted at Berkley. "Don't be annoying. It's not a big deal."

"Lexie," Brent said. "I've known you less than a year and even *I* know it's a *huge* deal."

Lexie scoffed, but Mitch said to her, "He's right, babe. You're not exactly the relationship type. And you made it pretty clear from the beginning that this between us would never been more than sex. It's a very big deal that you're now my girlfriend."

"What changed your mind anyway?" Berkley asked.

"Have you seen this guy?" Lexie replied, taking a half step away to look Mitch up and down appreciatively.

Berkley snorted, and Brent pulled her into his side. "Well, we're happy for you," Brent said. "Does that mean you'll be sharing a room when you come up to New York in August?"

"New York?" Lexie asked.

"Brent turns thirty at the beginning of August, so we're planning a trip up to his family's cabin for a week or so. You know, so we can celebrate before training camp starts and life gets crazy again."

Lexie looked up at him. "Did you know about this?"

"Of course I did," he said. "Brent mentioned it months ago. How did you not know?"

Lexie shrugged. "I've been a little preoccupied."

That she had. Ever since she agreed to be his girlfriend, Mitch had barely let her out of bed.

And now that his season was over, he didn't plan on letting her leave his sight for the foreseeable future. They'd already discussed him traveling with her when she had to go out of town for work, and they never spent nights apart if they could help it.

She'd also surprised him by clueing him in on her deal with Amelia. From the very first moment they met, this woman had barricaded her heart with rebar-reinforced concrete blocks so thick Mitch never expected to break through them, though he'd been more than willing to try. The fact that she was willing to open up to him now...they were leaps and bounds from where they'd started, and he was incredibly proud of her. And proud of himself for being the kind of man she could trust and lean on.

Telling their friends about the change in their relationship status was incredibly painless. Not a single person that knew them was surprised, which made the announcement smooth sailing.

But now...it was time to tell their families.

Well, it was time for Mitch to tell *his* family.

Lexie avoided contact with her parents like the plague. She still hadn't fully opened up to him about what the Monroes were like and why her relationship with them was so strained, and he wasn't about to force her to. Eventually, she'd trust him enough to tell him.

It was a spectacularly sunny day in late May. There wasn't a single cloud in the sky and just enough of a breeze to keep the eighty-five-degree heat from being suffocating with humidity.

They were on the way to his mother's house.

So she and Lexie could meet.

And Mitch was absolutely giddy, despite Lexie being pale-faced and uncharacteristically quiet in the passenger seat next to him.

He reached across the center console and took her hand. "You okay, babe?"

She shook her head. "No, I'm not okay. I'm nervous as fuck."

Mitch chuckled, but asked, "How come?"

"I'm not the kind of girl you bring home to mom, Mitch."

The admission punched Mitch in the gut. How could she ever think that? This insanely talented, smart, funny, driven, loyal woman?

"You absolutely are the kind of girl I'd bring home to my mom, Lex. Otherwise we wouldn't be doing this."

"What if she hates me? She knows about all the bullshit I put you through."

"She's not going to hate you. Yes, she knows about all of that. But it was just growing pains. She has to understand that you don't open up to people easily. And that the way our relationship has unfolded so far is exactly how it was supposed to happen." He brought their clasped hands to his mouth and kissed the back of hers. "Plus you're stuck with me now, so she's going to have to get used to it."

"Stuck with you, huh? I think you're the one who's stuck with me. God only knows why you want to be," she said with an eye roll.

Mitch sighed. "One day, Alexandra Monroe. One day I'm going to make you see yourself through my eyes. Then it'll all make sense."

She gave him a dubious sidelong glance, but didn't argue.

When they arrived in front of his mother and stepfather's stately white brick house, Lexie turned a terrified gaze on him. "I can't do this."

He rolled his eyes. "Stop that right now and get out of this vehicle."

"Make me."

He stared her down. "Lexie, now is not the time for one of your games." He nodded his head in the direction of the house, where his mom was waiting on the columned front porch. "Besides, she already saw us."

"Fuck," Lexie whispered, then got out of the vehicle.

"Mrs. Scott," Lexie said, walking up to hand her the big bouquet of flowers they'd picked up at Trader Joe's on the way.

"Oh please, call me Georgie," his mom said. "And in this family, we hug." She wrapped her arms around Lexie's middle, and after a moment of stiff surprise, Lexie hugged back, her face softening.

As Mitch anticipated, Lexie and his mother got along perfectly. Lexie asked a million questions about what Mitch was like growing up, laughing her ass off at his terrible haircuts and gangly body when his mom brought out the photo albums.

Mitch's entire body went stiff when Lexie continued to shuffle through the pictures and came across one featuring a toddler-sized Mitch, his mother, and his father.

"Is that your dad?" Lexie asked.

"Sure is," he said tightly, hoping she could sense his discomfort and let go of any further questions she might have.

He should've known better.

"What happened to him?" She asked quietly.

His mother, unaware that Mitch had told Lexie his father was dead, said, "Oh he's back in Georgia. I have no idea what he's up to other than still trying to drink himself to death."

Lexie looked at Mitch questioningly, hurt and anger flaring in her hazel eyes, but wisely didn't press the issue. This was a conversation for later.

Instead, she said to him, "You never talk about him."

"Not surprising," his mother said. "That man was horrible to Mitch. Horrible to both of us. If I hadn't used every spare penny I had to make sure Mitch could play hockey, and if he hadn't been picked up by the U.S. development team..."

She trailed off, her eyes shining in the sun coming through the living room window. "If we hadn't moved here, I can't even imagine where we'd both be right now," she finished.

Lexie reached out and took his mother's hand. "I'm sorry you went through that," she said with a squeeze.

His mother pulled free from Lexie's touch and waved a hand in the air, brushing the conversation and pity off. "Well it's all over now." She looked at Mitch and smiled. "We got out, right honey? That's the important thing."

Mitch could only nod, his words strangled by admiration and love for his mother, and fear for how he was going to explain this to Lexie and still keep her.

It was such a stupid thing to lie about, and he wasn't entirely sure why he did it. That date in Dallas was when Lexie had finally started to share her past with him, and he knew how difficult that was for her. He just hadn't been ready to do the same, and telling her that his father was dead was the most sure-fire way he could think of to nip that conversation in the bud.

But there were a million other ways he could have gone about explaining his father's absence, ways that didn't have her glancing at him with that betrayed look all over her face.

He's not in the picture. They didn't speak. He's a raging alcoholic who wasted their money on getting wasted and beat on him and his mother.

Reliving any moment from the first fifteen years of his life always reminded him of how weak and powerless he'd been. How, until the U.S. development team had taken an interest in him, he and his mother had lived their lives treading on thin ice, never knowing when their next step would suck them under. How he hadn't been able to protect her for so long, and how the guilt ate him alive for years after the move.

It was why he wanted to be a defenseman when he first started playing hockey, to protect people. Grudgingly, he supposed he had his father to thank for that. He and his mother spent so many years under the thumb of a man who was mean and suffering from a horrible disease that seeped into everything around them. All Mitch ever wanted to do was save himself and his mother.

Hockey had allowed him to do that in more ways than one.

After that depressing topic of conversation, the remaining time he and Lexie spent at his mother's was strained. Thankfully his mother appeared completely oblivious, but every once in a while, Mitch caught Lexie shooting him sidelong death glares.

If looks could kill...

When it came time to leave, he wrapped his mother in a hug, cocooning her smaller frame inside his large one, and whispered, "I love you, Mama."

"I love you, too, baby. I don't know what happened here today, but fix things with that girl. She's a dream and if you screw this up, I'll never forgive you."

Mitch pulled away, stunned. All he could do was nod before his mother pulled Lexie into a hug, telling her they would have to get together again soon.

The drive back to Detroit was tense. All Mitch wanted to do was reach for Lexie, take her hand and assure himself that she was still here, still in this with him. But Lexie's entire body from head to toe warned him not to go there. She sat in his passenger seat, curled in on herself, facing out the window, watching the world fly by.

When they arrived back in the city, Mitch drove them to his condo, his body tensing when he pulled into his space in his building's underground garage and turned the car off, half expecting Lexie to bolt.

But she didn't move, which he took as a good sign.

"You coming up?" He asked.

She only nodded, then unfolded herself from the car and stalked across the garage toward the elevator that would take them upstairs. Mitch heaved a sigh and followed her.

The second they were safely inside his apartment, she whirled on him, her arms crossed over her chest, eyes narrowed.

"I know how this looks," he said, holding his hands up in what he hoped was a placating gesture.

Lexie still didn't talk, barely moved save for the tapping of her foot on the ground.

"Can we sit down? Please?"

She turned on her heel and strode into the living room, throwing her body on his plush dove grey sofa and tucking her legs under her.

He sat on the opposite end and took a deep breath. "I told you he was dead because to me he is."

"That's such bullshit," Lexie said, speaking for the first time since they left Ann Arbor nearly an hour before. "For someone who wanted this relationship from the beginning, you sure have a funny way of showing it."

"What do you want from me, Lexie? That night in Dallas...God, that night was the first time you looked at me like I could be anything more to you than a warm body. What was I supposed to do? Unload my years and years of childhood trauma on you over burgers and fries? Say, *hi, my name is Mitch and my dad is a raging alcoholic and a piece of shit father?*"

"That's not what I meant and you know it," she said, leaping to her feet. "You could've said literally *anything* else, Mitch. That he's not in the picture because he's a bad guy. That you don't have a relationship. That you haven't spoken to him in years. I would've understood! I have a shitty relationship with both of my parents. At least you got one good one."

He stood and moved toward her slowly, then faster when she didn't move away. Hooking one hand loosely around her arm above her elbow, he used the other to tilt her head up to meet his gaze. "What do you want to know? I'll tell you anything. I'll tell you *everything*. Just please don't pull away from me right now."

"What happened when you left Georgia? *Why* did you leave? How did you even get out?"

Mitch sighed, then tucked Lexie under his arm and led them back to the couch. He nestled himself against the armrest and pulled her into his lap, needing her as close as possible for this conversation. "You know I played in Ann Arbor with the NTDP for four years," he said, and she nodded. "That call came shortly after my fifteenth birthday."

"When is your birthday, anyway?"

"October 22nd," he said and watched her eyes close as she did the math in her head. "We met a week after my thirty-second."

She blinked, surprised. "I had no idea."

"Well, why would you? We hadn't met yet. I only know your birthday because we celebrated it together."

"Fair enough," she said. "Continue with your story."

"When that call came, there was no question we'd be moving to Ann Arbor. I was barely back on my feet after a car accident about six months before left me pretty banged up, so I still don't even understand why they wanted me, but I thank God every day they did."

Mitch couldn't, in fact, *refused*, to tell her about the particulars of that car accident. That was a conversation for a different day...like never.

"At that point, things with my dad were really bad. Bad enough that he was controlling every facet of our lives, including my mom's money. But my mom...well, you've met her. She's smart, and she got crafty and started leaving money with a trusted neighbor in a little safe she bought. Only she and I had a key, and the agreement was that if things got bad enough, we'd take the money and run. We had officially reached the breaking point when Ann Arbor gave us a legitimate reason to leave. The same neighbor who was keeping our money safe also had an old Chevy truck with the registration in his name. One day, when my dad was out on a bender, Mom and I packed up what we could and hightailed it out of there, stopping along the way only to buy a couple new cell phones—those prepaid ones—and get gas and eat. We drove for fourteen hours, straight through the night, to reach Ann Arbor."

Mitch would never forget the terror of those early hours as they passed through Georgia. He hadn't taken a full breath until they'd crossed over into Tennessee, and even then, the weight on his chest hadn't lifted until they were safely within Michigan state lines.

"I still don't know if he ever tried to find us or was too drunk and stupid to care, but I didn't hear from him for a long time after that."

"When was the last time you talked to him?"

"The day after I got drafted by Columbus," he said.

"I'm sure that wasn't a pleasant conversation."

Mitch shook his head and wrapped his arms tighter around her. She reached up and tunneled her fingers into the hair at the nape of his neck, rubbing soothing circles along the base of his skull, grounding him.

Though Mitch and his mother had changed their numbers and moved clear across the country to get away from him, his father still somehow tracked him down and called the morning after the Columbus Ice drafted him. He had prattled on and on about how proud he was that his boy was going to be a big NHL star. How he wanted to come visit, that he was clean and deserved a second chance.

"And I almost bought it," Mitch told Lexie, running his fingers through the long, silken strands of her hair, absently wrapping a chunk around his wrist and letting it slip free. "I really should've known better after all the years I watched him pull the same shit with my mom. He'd go on a bender and smack us both around, disappear for a few days and come home saying he changed and he was going to be better."

"And he wasn't?"

"All he wanted was money, Lex," he said, and his cheeks burned with embarrassment. "He started asking me about my signing bonus and my rookie contract. When I told him I had no idea on numbers yet and I was just happy to get a shot at making a professional career out of the game I love so much, he told me to let him know what his cut was once I figured it out."

Lexie gasped. "Mitch..."

"When I asked him what he meant, he told me he deserved a piece of the pie after all the years he spent taking care of my ass, paying for gear and travel expenses and just a whole slew of other things."

"What did you do?"

"I lost it. I told him the only thing he ever gave me was black eyes, and that my mother was the only parent who ever gave a fuck about me. That my mom, my sweet, kind, generous, loving mother is the only reason I'm the man I am today. And that I thank God for the one good parent I got."

"I take it he didn't react well."

Mitch snorted. "Of course not. He started spewing all kinds of bullshit and finally I had enough. I told him he was dead to me and hung up the phone. That was almost fifteen years ago."

Lexie skated her fingers down his throat and over his collarbone, settling her hand over his heart. "I'm sorry."

He covered her hand with his, his heartbeat pounding against them both. "Don't be. It's over. He can't hurt me or my mother ever again."

"I wish you would've told me all this before," she said quietly. "I don't appreciate being lied to but...I get it."

He buried his face in her neck and planted a kiss on the soft skin where her shoulder curved up. "I don't deserve you."

She pulled back to look at him, taking his face in her hands. "No, *I* don't deserve *you*. My childhood was shitty. My parents were literally never around, but I was well-taken care of in terms of the fact that I never wanted for anything except love and attention. You...God, you dealt with so much. And you're the best man I know. You came out on the other side, maybe not entirely whole, but still willing to give your heart away and allow people in. I've spent my whole life shoving people away."

"Until me," he said quietly, and as he so often did, wondered *why*?

She nodded, swallowing audibly. "Until you. I got so tired of fighting it. And you...you never gave up on me. So truthfully, Mitch. I don't deserve you. I don't know how you put up with me."

"Because I love you," he said.

He had never said those words to a woman who wasn't his mother before, and had never wanted to.

Once again, he was reminded of how *everything* was different with Lexie.

But he should've known better, because the affection and softness on her face a moment before was replaced instantly with absolute terror.

"What? No!" Lexie jumped up and stalked away from him. "What did I tell you about pushing too much on me too soon? This is the exact opposite of that, Mitch!"

"I just figured that since you—"

"Don't even finish that sentence. I have zero desire to know what synapses misfired in that beautiful mind of yours to make you think this was a good idea."

"Lexie..."

She sat down hard on the opposite end of the couch and tunneled her fingers through her hair, bowing her head over her lap. "I asked you not to push this," she said quietly, raising her head to meet his gaze, searching and pleading for an easy way out. But he couldn't give it to her, couldn't take back what he'd said. Couldn't, and didn't want to. "I'm trying, Mitch. I'm trying for *you*. You have to give me some time to adjust."

Mitch moved next to her, curling his arm around her shoulders. "Can I ask you something?"

"Technically, you just did."

"Alexandra..."

Lexie chuckled at the use of her full name, but nodded for him to proceed.

"Do you think you *could* love me?"

Her head whipped up, gaze locking on his. She clearly had not been expecting that question.

"Yes," she whispered after several tense moments. "I'm falling so hard, so fast, and it terrifies me."

Once again, he pulled her onto his lap and leaned them back into the couch cushions. "I know it does, honey. But as long as you're in this with me, and willing to try, it'll all be alright. Can you do that?"

She met his eyes again, a small smile tipping up the corners of that beautiful mouth of hers. "Yes, Mitch. I can try."

They both leaned forward at the same time, mouths crashing together. And soon, they lost themselves in each other right there on the couch, Mitch thinking over and over as he drowned himself in her warmth that he loved her, that she was falling for him, and that everything was going to be okay.

CHAPTER FIFTEEN
Lexie

Now...

The holiday season had come and gone, and they were in that exhausting phase of late-March Michigan weather where Mother Nature couldn't make up her mind on whether or not she wanted to keep them in winter's clutches a little longer or let go and allow spring to bloom.

The night before she was set to leave for Seattle, Lexie had dinner and drinks with Berkley and Amelia. It had been a bit since they caught up, with Lexie constantly out of the state and Berkley back in school, on top of preparing for a wedding. Lexie wrapped her cardigan tighter around her, giving into a shiver as she stared at her friends across the table.

"Speaking of the wedding," Berkley said when Lexie mentioned how soon it was, "you guys need to pick out your bridesmaids dresses. I'm not having one style for everyone because I don't want anyone to be uncomfortable. So Lexie, you're wearing burgundy and Ames, you and the rest of the bridesmaids will be wearing navy."

"Warriors colors?" Lexie asked. "Seriously?"

"Burgundy and navy are hardly Warriors colors," Berkley scoffed.

"Close enough," Amelia muttered, and Berkley threw a half-chewed piece of garlic bread at her.

"Who all is in this wedding, anyway?"

"You guys, Jess, and Mackenzie."

"What about Kimber?" Lexie asked, surprised the fourth member of their tight-knit college crew wouldn't be standing up for Berkley.

"She's just...not really in my life anymore, you know? We catch up on occasion, mostly communicating through Instagram story replies and reactions, but it's not like it was before. I love her dearly, but I want my family up there with me, and she doesn't really fit the bill anymore."

Lexie couldn't help but be proud of Berkley at that moment. She knew her little blonde friend well enough to know that Berkley had most likely agonized over this decision, and had not come to it lightly. Still, the fact that she was sticking up for herself and getting exactly what she wanted when it came to her wedding was impressive for the girl who typically liked to keep the peace at all costs.

"What about groomsmen?" Lexie asked.

"Mitch, Nate, Logan, and Cole."

"Wow, Lex," Amelia said after she chewed and swallowed a mouthful of salad. "You've slept with half of the groomsmen. That's impressive."

"Not nearly as impressive as the black eye I'm about to give you will be if you don't shut your mouth," Lexie said.

Amelia rolled her eyes but didn't argue.

Berkley, however, didn't let Lexie's attitude go unchecked. "What is wrong with you lately?"

"Nothing," Lexie said with a shrug, downing the rest of her wine and signaling their waitress for a refill.

"No, there's obviously something. You've been acting like a colossal bitch for the last three months. Ever since you found out Mitch was back."

"Mitch has nothing to do with this," Lexie growled. "Mind your own fucking business."

"You *are* my business, Lex. You're my best friend, my fucking maid of honor. I can't have you acting like this when I'm only a few months away from getting married. I need you on top of your game."

"And what exactly makes you think I'm not on top of my game?"

"The constant partying, the endless drinking, the sleeping with random guys. You're acting exactly like you did right after Mitch left."

"What exactly is wrong with me partying and hooking up?" Lexie asked, seething. How *dare* Berkley throw Mitch's leaving in her face right now. "If you're not doing it, I'm not allowed to either? I'm not a little girl, Berkley, and I don't need you mothering me."

"I'm not mothering you, Lexie. I'm standing here begging you to start taking care of yourself. You keep doing this. Blowing everything off, acting like nothing matters but what you want and how you feel. You should be trying to fix things with Mitch! Instead you're getting drunk off your ass and fucking randos every night."

"I'm sorry," Lexie said quietly.

"I know him leaving was hard, but you can't keep doing this to yourself. Or us."

Amelia studied Lexie, then asked, "Are you ever going to tell us what happened with you guys before the trade, anyway?"

If Lexie had her way, they would never know. But Berkley couldn't get much madder at Lexie than she already was, right?

So she opened her mouth, and the entire story spilled free. How her parents came to visit and acted like they always do—Berkley and Amelia had met Robert and Christina Monroe enough times to know how they were—and instead of keeping his head down and his mouth shut like she'd asked, Mitch defended her. And it blew up in their faces.

"I broke up with him," she said. "I told him I couldn't love him like he deserved and to leave. I didn't think he'd take it literally and leave the fucking state."

"What is wrong with you?" Berkley hissed. "Why are you so fucking selfish?"

Berkley's words were a slap to the face for Lexie, partially because she deserved it and partially because Berkley rarely, if ever, spoke to anyone like that.

"Selfish?" Lexie asked, incredulous.

"Berkley," Amelia warned.

Berkley cut her eyes to Amelia and said, "No, she needs to hear this." Then she leveled that steely blue gaze back on Lexie. "Yes, selfish. You pushed him away so when he got traded, he left all of us! We could've spent this entire time still being friends with him. Instead you did what you always do, and ruined the best fucking thing you've ever had."

"Berkley, you weren't there," Lexie said, voice pleading. "My parents...they were horrible. To me. To him. He was doing the right thing in standing up to them."

Because I was too weak to do it myself.

"Then why did you break up with him? Seems to me that if you loved him that much, and he did the right thing in standing up to your asshole parents, then you had no reason to push him away."

Lexie looked Berkley dead in the eyes and said, "I'm a master of self-sabotage. I seem to recall you know a little something about that."

Berkley's cheeks turned pink, and Lexie knew she had struck a chord. Berkley had broken up with Brent for the same reason: to protect her heart.

"That still doesn't explain everything afterward," Amelia said. "The days between that fight and the trade? The day of the trade. Why didn't you call him?"

"I did," Lexie said. "I called him upwards of forty times when I heard the news. I even went to his apartment to see him. He was just...gone."

"Okay, fine," Berkley said. "The way he left was shitty. We know this. But when he came back and was in the hospital, why didn't you go see him then? You clearly still love him."

"I don't—" No, she wouldn't admit her true feelings. Not yet. Possibly not ever, so she focused on Berkley's question. "I did go see him."

In the wake of Mitch's most recent rejection, Lexie had shut down and reverted to old behaviors. It was the only thing she could do in the face of her heart potentially cracking wide open again.

When Lexie had talked to Berkley after attempting to go see Mitch, as soon as she was back in Detroit and the tears had dried and she'd once again gone numb, she'd lied through her teeth.

In her mind, it was better to look like the bad guy, the one who couldn't take that step forward, than to be the one rejected. She couldn't suffer the embarrassment, or the pity Berkley would certainly dish out.

So she'd told Berkley she changed her mind and hadn't gone to see him. Berkley was, understandably, upset. But not nearly as upset as Lexie was.

She wasn't proud of her behavior in the three months since that day. Growing up, she had tried everything to get her parents' attention. Drugs, alcohol, sneaking out of the house, and staying at random house parties until all hours of the morning, indiscriminate sex. The final straw for them had been when she brought her first boyfriend home, a guy ten years her senior who was covered head to toe in tattoos, piercings peppering his ears and face.

They didn't stay in Baltimore long after that.

This was what she did: she drank and fucked her way through the pain and loneliness.

After Berkley, Brent, and Amelia had staged their intervention last summer, Lexie had thought she'd moved past this kind of behavior.

But apparently, old habits really did die hard.

Berkley's mouth opened and closed like a fish out of water, unable to form a sentence. "I—what?"

"I *did* go to see him."

"But when we asked about it, you said you chickened out. Why didn't you just tell me?"

"He didn't want to see me," Lexie said, hanging her head. With the admission, her cheeks flamed, exactly as they had that day. "It was dumb anyway, thinking after everything, after so much time had passed, that he'd be willing to see me."

"He didn't want to see you?" Berkley asked dumbly.

"That's fucked up," Amelia said.

"So that's why you went off the rails again," Berkley said softly, and Lexie looked up to meet her pitying gaze.

"Don't look at me like that," she said, pointing her finger at her friend. "Yes, he didn't want to see me. Yes, I went on a bender for the last three months because of it. No, I don't want to talk about it anymore."

"I wish you would've told me. I can't believe you just let me scream at you and call you selfish."

"Yeah that was a low blow, Berk," Amelia piped up, and their blonde friend hung her head, chastised. "Lex is one of the most selfless people I know. In fact..."

Lexie's head snapped up, guessing what was about to happen. "Ames, are you sure? You don't have to do this."

"It's time, Lex. I need to come clean."

Berkley's puzzled expression would've been funny had Lexie not been terrified of her reaction to the bomb they were about to drop on her.

Amelia took a deep breath and said, "Lexie's been helping me with my magazine column."

Berkley's eyebrows drew together in confusion. "You...what? Helping how?"

Amelia's shoulders relaxed, and she launched into the whole tale. From stealing Lexie's travel stories and passing them off as her own, to Lexie finding out and agreeing to help her.

"She's been traveling double to make sure I don't lose my job."

"But...why?" Berkley asked.

"It's not that I don't *want* to travel," Amelia said. "Actually, that's a lie. I don't want to travel. I want to open my own fitness center. Lexie is helping me earn money to do that."

"I don't even know what to say," Berkley said, picking up her full wine glass and draining it in one go. "Seems like a lot of work to go through for money."

Lexie shrugged. "Honestly, I love it. It gave me something to focus on after Mitch left. I spent a few incredible couple weeks in Boston in December, just wandering the city. If I didn't love Detroit so much, I'd move out there for sure."

Amelia smiled and reached out to grasp Lexie's hand, squeezing it and mouthing, "Thank you."

"I thought you were in Boston for work!" Berkley exclaimed.

"Well, I mean...I kind of was. And actually, Ames, I've been meaning to talk to you about this."

"About what? You're not bailing on me, are you?"

"No, of course not," Lexie said. "I want to make this a full-time gig. Start our own blog or magazine or website or whatever."

"But our arrangement is working so well," Amelia whined.

Lexie laughed. "Sure it is, for the magazine. But you're making pennies off your stories, can't work with any sponsors, and I'm not making anything at all. Why not keep doing what we're already doing, but do it for ourselves? You can keep writing the stories, and maintain the social profiles, the website, whatever else. It'll give you more free time to open your gym, and then we can expand the scope of whatever platform we decide to use to include fitness tips and workouts and such, too. Since I'm already doing all the traveling, and I have a business degree, I'll manage everything, broker our sponsorship deals and handle partnership requests. The day to day stuff. And I get to keep traveling full time, which is really where my heart is at these days."

Berkley looked impressed, and a stunned Amelia said, "You've given this quite a bit of thought."

Lexie shrugged, feigning nonchalance when truthfully, she'd been able to think of little else since the idea took root in her brain.

For years, she'd been watching women—and a lot of men—monetize their social media presence. Lexie herself had been approached with numerous offers since graduating college, but she'd never had the time or energy to make a commitment with an already crazy and exhausting work schedule.

But now? Now she was ready to dive in head first.

"What exactly would I be doing while you travel, then?"

"Opening your gym," Lexie said. "Writing programs and buying equipment and doing whatever other shit you need to do to get a gym up and running."

"Are you going to help me with that stuff?"

"Of course I am," Lexie said. "We're going to be partners in all of this. Hell, I'll even ditch Brent and Berkley and start using your gym instead."

"Rude," Berkley said, "but I'm in. Lexie and I are young and fit. We're the perfect people to help you market this thing."

"Hell yeah," Lexie said. Then she dropped her voice to a stage whisper. "And I don't know if you know this, but Berkley is about to marry this super famous professional athlete. I bet he could help us out, too. Maybe offer to carry FLEX products in the gym as a quid-pro-quo type thing."

"You've been spending too much time with me if you're saying shit like 'quid-pro-quo'," Berkley said.

"Okay wait," Amelia said, waving her hand at the two to silence whatever argument they were about to have. "Let me get this straight. You want to quit your *incredibly* lucrative career as a headhunter, something you're very good at, to start some travel blog with me that has the potential to crash and burn miserably?"

"Pretty much," Lexie said brightly. "With a few amendments to that statement. First of all, you've already been doing this for like three years. Longer, even. We all know you're good at it. Second, as previously stated, I have a business degree, and as much as I loathe my parents, they're good at what they do and have taught me a ton along the way. Especially what not to do. We have a lawyer best friend who can make sure we're getting the most bang for our buck with brand partnerships, and she has a hot, super famous fiancé who can help spread the word about your gym. I think we've got this in the bag, honestly."

"And Brent also has business and finance degrees," Berkley reminded them.

The waitress came to their table then, topping off their wine glasses and promising she'd be right back with their food.

Honestly, the last ten minutes had been so tense that Lexie had forgotten where they even were.

She looked at Amelia, who was staring into her wine glass as though expecting it to reveal the secrets of life. A glance in Berkley's direction revealed that she was tapping away on her phone, presumably a message to Brent.

It was several minutes after the waitress finally brought their food that Amelia said, "I'm in."

Lexie grinned. "Fuck yeah. This is going to be amazing, Ames, I promise. I'll even foot all the start-up costs. We can do a combined fitness and travel blog. Whatever you want."

"Okay none of that is necessary. We'll split start-up costs. I'll make the down payment on my gym myself."

"Fuck that. I'm investing."

"Me too," Berkley said. "Have you found a space yet?"

"I haven't. I've been looking, but since I thought I had more time, I haven't actively been going to showings or anything."

Berkley had that gleam in her eye, like she was concocting a plan and they were all simply about to be along for the ride. "I might know someone who can help. Hold please."

Lexie and Amelia exchanged looks as Berkley picked up her phone and tapped the screen a few times before lifting it to her ear.

"Hey Mitch," she said a moment later, and Lexie's heart sank.

"Berkley," Lexie warned. Berkley just waved her off.

Lexie was going to kill her.

"Okay so I'm at dinner with Lexie and Amelia and...Yes she's good. She's fine. Amelia is good, too, thanks for asking." Mitch said something that had Berkley snorting. "Anyway, the reason I called. Amelia is in the market for a space she can lease or buy for a fitness center. I figured that's something you can help her out with." Berkley listened, murmuring affirmatives as Mitch spoke. Then she said, "Okay, great. I'll give her your number. Thanks Mitchell, love you bye!" And hung up.

"Berkley, what the fuck!" Lexie whisper-yelled. "We didn't ask for Mitch's help. What exactly could he do anyway?"

"He just got his real estate license," Berkley said. Then she tapped her phone screen a few more times, and a moment later, Amelia's dinged. "That's his contact info. He said give him a call tomorrow and you guys can schedule some time to sit down and talk specifics."

"Berkley, thank you!" Amelia said, leaping up from her seat and rushing around to give Berkley a hug. "You didn't have to do that."

Berkley shrugged. "We've all got connections. Might as well use them. But you're not signing a lease or any sort of contract without me looking at it first."

"Aye aye, Captain," Amelia said, giving Berkley a mock salute.

As the two chatted excitedly about names for both the gym and the new travel blog, Lexie checked out of the conversation completely.

It seemed these days, she was the only holdout. The only one unwilling to let Mitch back into her life.

But she had tried, hadn't she? She'd gone to Ann Arbor and walked into that hospital with every intention of extending an olive branch, of attempting to bridge the gap between them that now only grew wider by the day.

And he hadn't wanted to see her. That wasn't her fault.

So why was everyone acting like she was the bad guy here?

CHAPTER SIXTEEN

Lexie

THIRTEEN MONTHS AGO...

"What is all of this?" Lexie asked once she'd shed her coat and walked into Mitch's kitchen that evening.

"I'm cooking us dinner," he said, curling an arm around her waist and pulling her in to drop a kiss on her head. She snuggled closer, letting his warmth chase away the frigid November air still clinging to her from outside.

Lexie raised an eyebrow as she surveyed the scene. The normally pristine white granite counters looked like a bomb had gone off. There were ingredients everywhere: raw chicken, half-chopped vegetables, bottles of spices and sauces. A pot on the stovetop was coughing steam into the air, and something smelled vaguely burnt.

"Since when do you cook?" She asked, walking over to the stove to find spaghetti noodles boiling in an over-large pot. A pan with some questionable-looking red sauce bubbled next to it.

"Since it's our one year anniversary," he said, walking over to give the sauce a stir. It hissed when he scraped the spoon through it, alerting them both that *it* was responsible for the acrid scent in the air.

"Mitch, I appreciate the effort and all but we didn't start dating until April."

"It's not our one year *dating* anniversary," he said. "It's our one year *fucking* anniversary." He turned and pointed the spoon in the direction of the front hall. "Don't you remember that wall? That's where I fucked you for the first time and then you pulled up your pants and left."

Lexie snorted. She had worked so hard in those early days to keep this man at arm's length, because she knew what would happen if she didn't.

And now look at her, celebrating the one year anniversary of the first time she had sex with her now boyfriend.

Life came at her fast.

Everything had been good since their fight about his father on the day she met his mom. Better than good, actually; they'd been amazing. It scared her a bit how easily she had fallen into a steady rhythm with Mitch, how quickly he had fit into her life, the life she had so carefully cultivated around herself on the assumption that she would never need or want anyone to share it with.

From the very first moment she laid eyes on him, she should've known that Mitch would be the one to change all of that.

For all her talk of not knowing *how* to be a girlfriend, she and Mitch had fallen into an easy pattern. Being reminded of where they'd stood a year ago, so close physically but a chasm gaping between them emotionally, was sobering. Lexie had almost let this man, who could not cook to save his life but had still donned a little beige canvas apron over his jeans and black and white flannel, and destroyed his kitchen in an attempt to make today special for her, walk away because she'd let her past insecurities get the best of her. His patience in all things in life was something she'd always admired about him, but never more so than when it came to waiting for her while she navigated this new terrain.

She stepped away to study him, loving these quiet moments when it was just them. With them both barefoot and casual, about to settle in for a night in front of the TV while the city rushed past below. They had so few of these days, when they were both in the city and not busy with work or practices or games, and Lexie savored them, tucked them away in her chest and brought them out to keep her company on the days they were apart.

"Why exactly are we celebrating that?" She asked as she climbed onto a stool at his kitchen island. "If it means we end tonight with sex against that wall again, I'm not going to complain. No offense, but I'm not eating anything you've got cooking in this kitchen right now."

Mitch sighed and removed his ball cap to scratch at his scalp. Then he stalked over to the stove and turned all the burners off before moving toward the refrigerator, where he pulled out two beers. Seconds later, the caps pinged against the counter as he removed them, then he slid one in front of her.

"I don't know why I thought I could cook," he said with a chuckle, leaning over to open the drawer to the left of the sink where he kept takeout menus. He fanned them out in front of her face. "What are you thinking tonight?"

She gestured to Mitch's ill-advised cooking experiment. "Italian sounds amazing."

"Italian it is," he said, shuffling through the stack until he found the one for Crispigna's, although Lexie didn't know why he bothered because they got takeout from there enough to know the menu by heart.

Once he called and placed their order for delivery, he settled them on the couch with their beer, and she curled up in her favorite spot—her back to his chest with his strong arms wrapped around her middle, one hand resting just above her belly button while the other clasped his beer.

"So you know celebrating the first time you hook up with someone isn't exactly normal, right?" she said.

"Of course I know that. But nothing about our relationship has ever been normal, so why start now?"

Lexie shrugged. The man had a point.

"Don't worry, honey. I'll do something really big for our dating anniversary."

Lexie growled at him. "You've been spending too much time with Brent if you think a grand gesture is the key to my heart."

"No, I know the key to your heart is good sex," he said with a wink.

Again, the man had a point.

But with Mitch, it was more than sex; she could admit to herself now that it always had been. The first time she locked eyes with him at Contour, all bets were off. Somehow, *this* man, this kind, selfless, generous, incredibly sexy man, was willing to stick around and fight for her when she couldn't even fight for herself. It meant the world to her, that she meant that much to someone. And it was why she was sitting here right now.

"Okay, question for you," she said sometime later, after their food had arrived and they were spread out on the floor around the coffee table.

"Shoot."

"What would you do if you weren't playing hockey?"

"I haven't given it much thought," Mitch said, a frown turning his lips down. "Why are you asking?"

"I mean...don't all professional athletes need to have a backup plan? Brent's got FLEX, and when he's done playing for good I know he'd ultimately like to manage a team or even own one. Don't you have dreams and goals like that?"

"Growing up, I honestly never thought too far ahead. Now that I'm older, and settled, though..." His eyebrows drew together, something like embarrassment passing over his features. She reached up and brushed her thumb over the lines there, and his face softened. Whatever he was thinking wasn't something he had shared with many people, if anyone at all; she knew him well enough to know that. So she waited him out.

"I'd always thought I'd get involved in real estate somehow," he finally said. "As an agent, or as a property manager. I mean, I already manage the loft."

"Wait, what?" Now Lexie's eyebrows reached for each other. "I thought you just bought that for personal use."

"I did originally," Mitch said. "But after a few months, I had people reaching out asking if I was interested in using the space as an event venue. And I thought...I didn't need the money, but the loft just sat empty for days, sometimes weeks, at a time when we were too busy or on the road for long stretches. So I said what the hell, and listed it on one of those property rental sites."

Lexie was stunned, but not because Mitch had been offering his space up to people for, God, almost three years now? No, she was stunned because she hadn't known.

"Why have you never told me this before?"

Mitch shrugged. "It never came up."

She smacked him. "You're a pain in my ass," she said, "but it doesn't surprise me in the slightest that you'd do something like this. Let me guess, your cost to rent is a rock bottom rate, too." She rolled her eyes when he didn't disagree. "I'm sure it's something so insanely cheap that people regularly offer you more money because they feel like they're taking advantage of you."

Mitch's cheeks turned pink, and Lexie giggled, knowing she'd struck a nerve.

This man of hers. *Sigh.* There was no one more selfless. Add it to the long list of things she loved about him.

"It was never something I had planned to do," he told her. "Like I said, I never thought too far ahead. Playing hockey for a living was always the dream, and when I was younger, there were days when I wasn't even sure I'd see the next sunrise."

Lexie's face slackened in shock. Mitch didn't talk about his childhood—or his dad—much, so she remained silent while he continued.

"He was always smacking me around," Mitch said quietly, and she didn't have to ask who *he* was. After meeting his mother and knowing the things she did about Mitch's dad, the admission from him didn't come as a shock. But being unsurprised didn't lessen the clench in her heart, thinking of all Mitch and his mother had endured. "One of my earliest memories is him literally kicking my ass because I fell off my bike and cried when I skinned my knees. When I got big enough to start hitting back, he'd slap my mom around, or threaten to, just to keep me in line. Then there was that car accident when I was fourteen, right before Ann Arbor called."

"What happened?"

"We went out to a local restaurant for a family dinner. It was one of those rare weeks when my dad seemed to have gotten his head on straight for a few days in a row and wanted to treat me. You know, an attempt to make up for lost time and the fact that he was a shitty human. Anyway, dinner started off fine. We ordered drinks—water—and our meals. When the waitress brought out our food, my dad decided he couldn't eat his prime rib without a beer.

"From there, our nice, quiet evening turned into a drunken public disturbance in a heartbeat. My dad, naturally, got hammered and made a scene when he got into a fight with another patron over the football game on TV. The restaurant owner was seconds away from calling the cops when I finally got him outside. I tried to take his keys from him, but he wouldn't listen to me. It was late, and it was either I walked the ten miles home, or I got in the car with him."

Lexie reached out and grabbed Mitch's hand, and he squeezed back.

"We were about a mile from the house when he just...lost control. I don't know if I can't remember what happened because I don't want to, or because it all happened so fast that my mind can't accurately recall it. But one second we were cruising along just fine, and the next we were slamming into a tree at sixty miles an hour."

Lexie's face blanched. "Oh my God, Mitch."

"I still don't know how any of us actually survived. The car was..." He shook his head, as though dispelling the memory. "It was a twisted hunk of metal."

"Were you injured?"

He nodded. "My dad ended up with a concussion. I ended up with a broken leg and a two inch piece of glass stuck in my back, barely missing my spine. It would've been a lot worse if I hadn't been wearing my seatbelt."

Lexie was familiar with the scar, the thick, puckered line along his lower back that she had brushed with her fingers many times over the course of the last year. But she'd never asked about it, figuring it was a souvenir from his childhood, a memory too painful to recall. She had a few of those herself.

She crawled into his lap and threw her arms around him, pressing her face into his neck. "I'm so sorry, honey."

"It's okay," he said, his voice thick. "We survived and, as you know, Ann Arbor called not long after."

Lexie couldn't stop the tears that flowed free, and though Mitch surely noticed as they dampened his shirt along the collar, he didn't say anything, didn't move save for rubbing his hands up and down her back.

Her upbringing wasn't something she looked back on fondly. In fact, she'd rather erase it from her memory completely. But where her suffered brand of torment and poor parenting was general neglect and emotional detachment, Mitch had suffered physical damage at the hands of his father, injuries that he bore the proof of on his skin every day.

"What're you thinking about?" He asked her, reaching over to lace his fingers through hers.

"You. How strong you are despite everything you've been through."

"I mean, I work out regularly in order to be this strong," he said, attempting to lighten the mood.

"I don't mean physical strength," she said, pulling back to look up at him. "I mean emotional. You easily could've ended up just like me. Terrified of commitment, of letting people close enough to hurt you after all you'd endured growing up. One good parent or not, Mitch...you could be a very different man right now. How? How are you so...perfect?"

He snorted, but cupped the back of her head to pull her in for a kiss. "I'm anything but perfect, Lexie," he said against her mouth, then leaned away. "But you're right, I had one good parent. My mother is a saint. You've met her, you know. Even the massive, unending storm cloud that was my father couldn't dampen her shine. Even when we were struggling, she put on a brave face, tried to see the good in everything. And eventually, things got better. But I had hockey, too. The game saved my life, and hers, and has given me more than I could ever give in return."

"I wish I'd had something like hockey growing up," she said wistfully.

As much as she tried to deny it, and tried to ignore the wounds her parents had left on her...it was a lot like having a bruise. She completely forgot about it until she pressed her finger to it, and the pain flared up again.

"What are your parents like?" Mitch asked quietly.

"Mediocre at parenting, but great at business. They're not bad people I don't think. Not at their cores. They just didn't—don't—give a fuck about me. All they care about is money and their pristine reputation. To them, I think having a child was more about acquiring a status symbol, some sort of physical proof that they were good, solid family people."

"You've never really talked about it, you know."

Lexie looked at him with an eyebrow raised. "And I suppose that's your way of asking me to talk about it now?"

He shrugged. "I *did* just bare my soul to you. I'm here if you want to talk about it, but I'm not going to force you."

And that was the million dollar question, wasn't it? Did she *want* to talk about it? The short answer was a hard *no*. But she couldn't deny that things with Mitch were getting more serious by the day, and holding such a big piece of her life back from him, the piece that quite literally made her who she is and shaped so much of the way she moved about the world, didn't make sense anymore.

"Things were good early on, I guess," she started. "We all look happy in pictures, but in those days I was too young to vividly remember anything. I get flashes. Playing in a sandbox on a warm summer day. My mom curled up beside me in a tiny bed, reading me a story. My dad holding my hand as we walked down the street. By the time I was old enough to start actively recalling things that happened, those days were long gone. They made their first big investment, the one that took off and opened a thousand doors for them, when I was five."

"What is it they do again?" Mitch asked.

"They're venture capitalists. Filthy rich. Heartless. You know the type."

"I doubt they're heartless," he said.

"Oh they definitely are. Or if they do have hearts, there's just a giant hole where the love for their daughter should be. We never stayed in one place for long. Sometimes it was a month, sometimes longer. I think the longest we ever stayed in one place was Chattanooga. We were there for about six months when I was ten. I had absolutely no stability. It's why I said yes to the first job opportunity that came my way when college was wrapping up."

"Where else have you lived?"

"Everywhere," she said, turning her body and throwing her legs over his lap. Now that she'd cracked the box open that held all of these moments from her childhood, she figured she should get comfortable. They'd be here for a while. "But that's not the point."

"What is then? That your parents wanted to be successful and provide for their daughter?"

"You don't get it, Mitch," she said, leaping from the couch. She stalked to the windows and stared out at the city, the Detroit River a wide, glittering ribbon below, the lights of the Ambassador Bridge blotting out the stars. "They left me alone on Christmas."

"What?"

"Christmas the year I was twelve. I was barely old enough to stay home alone, but do you think the parents of the year cared about that? No. They didn't. Up to that point, I had been moved around so much and left alone so often that I had to figure out ways to fend for myself. I never expected..." She took a fortifying breath. This was the one memory she always buried deep, the one that hurt the most to recall. Her parents had said and done a lot of damaging things over the years, but this one...

"It was a few days before Christmas when they told me they had to go out of town. Apparently, they needed to put out some fire with one of their investments. Naturally I whined, not wanting them to leave me so close to the holiday. But they promised me they'd be back in time for presents on Christmas morning, and that they had called one of the local nanny services to have someone stay with me. My mom said I'd only be alone for a few hours.

"I was alone in that big, stupid house in Connecticut for three days, Mitch."

Mitch sucked in a breath and stood, his footsteps sinking into the carpet closer and closer until he wrapped his arms around her from behind.

"I survived on cereal, soup that I microwaved, and popcorn. I spent Christmas by myself. The only saving grace was that I searched that house top to bottom and eventually found my presents."

"I bet your parents felt horrible."

Lexie snorted derisively. "Of course they didn't feel horrible. They blamed me."

Mitch's eyebrows drew together. "I don't understand."

"I was always a bit of a loner. I had to be to survive. But I was also incredibly smart. Precocious. Resourceful. My parents assumed that I just called the nannying service and cancelled my sitter so I could stay home alone and *destroy their house*."

Those had been her mother's exact words when she yelled at Lexie after they'd returned to find the kitchen a mess of empty tin cans and cereal boxes. The living room was overflowing with shredded wrapping paper—they must have felt extra guilty for being shitty parents that year, because she never received as many gifts before or after—and Lexie had been found in the center of it all, reading her new set of Harry Potter books while lounging in her dad's recliner.

Her parents had screamed and screamed and screamed. And then they called the nannying service to scream some more about leaving a twelve-year-old unattended.

Until the woman informed them they had never called to have anyone watch Lexie in the first place.

"It was like a flip had been switched," Lexie told Mitch as he settled them back on the couch. "They were the ones who fucked up, so they went out of their way to make it up to me. A few days after Christmas, my mom took me into New York City on a shopping trip. Anything I wanted, she didn't say no to. It was a fun kind of game for me. I would pick out the most outrageously priced little bauble in the store and tell her I had to have it. And she didn't argue. Didn't fight me on any of it. Just let me have whatever I wanted. I learned then that she and my dad were the kind of people who thought they had to buy affection, that it couldn't be given freely."

"God, Lex," Mitch said as he pulled her onto his lap. "I'm so sorry."

"It's fine," she said, desperately wanting to wrap up this conversation.

"It all makes sense now," he said.

"What does?"

"Why you fought this so hard."

"*This*?"

"Us. Why you fought giving us a chance, giving *me* a chance."

"And why exactly does it make sense now?"

"You're scared," he said gently. "You've always been scared."

"What makes you say that?"

"Because you think you're unlovable and easy to leave. Because the two people in the world who were supposed to love you the most and without conditions, who were supposed to make sure you felt safe and wanted every day, spent your entire life acting like you were some cross to bear instead of a gift." He snuggled closer and cupped her face in his hands. "I am not your parents, Lexie. You *are* a gift. The greatest one I've ever been given. And I'm going to spend forever proving it to you."

He was right, and he was so very wrong. She wasn't just scared; she was petrified. To her, there was nothing scarier in the world than this man and her feelings for him.

Lexie could do nothing to stop them as her tears flowed, even if she wanted to. A dam had broken inside her, spilling free all of the things Mitch inspired in her that she had tried so desperately to bury. With his arms wrapped around her, she felt safe. She felt loved and wanted and treasured, all of those things her parents had denied her all those years.

She finally felt like she was *home*.

So she said the only thing she could think of at that moment, the only thing she *wanted* to say. She looked him dead in the eye and, in no uncertain terms, said, "I love you."

Mitch's answering smile could've powered the entire state of Michigan.

CHAPTER SEVENTEEN
Lexie

The Warriors' regular season had wound down, with the team finishing in third place in the Eastern Conference. Mitch had a short break before gearing up for the playoffs, and he decided now was the time to meet Lexie's parents.

"I can't believe I was crazy enough to let you talk me into this," Lexie said as she blew through her condo like a tornado, tidying everything in her path, straightening throw pillows, making sure the rug was laying perfectly straight in relation to the crisp ivory-colored couch, and cleaning dust from every surface.

"I let you meet my mom," Mitch said. "Besides, we've officially been together for almost a year now. It's the right time."

Lexie shook her head vigorously. There would never be a right time for Mitch to meet her parents. Half the time, she pretended they didn't exist.

Quite frankly, she didn't even understand *why* he wanted to meet them. He was well aware of how they had treated her growing up and continued to only acknowledge her presence when it suited them.

Like now, for example, when they were in Detroit potentially investing in a new company and wanted Lexie to join them for dinner with their potential investee. Apparently, family was important to this guy, and her parents were nothing if not excellent actors. They had invited themselves to dinner at her place tonight under the guise of wanting to see their daughter, but Lexie knew there was an ulterior motive.

Lexie refused to cook for her parents, so she ordered takeout from one of the fanciest restaurants in town.

Well, *Mitch* had ordered it, throwing around his weight as a professional athlete.

But just because she refused to cook for them didn't mean she wanted to serve them out of cardboard boxes and plastic bowls—she'd never heard the end of it—so she hustled into the kitchen to plate the food.

Wanting to do one last spot check of her condo's social spaces, she tried to brush past Mitch quickly, but he grabbed her wrist and pulled her flush against his chest. Where her heart was pounding rapidly behind her rib cage, Mitch's was a steady drum in his chest. "Honey, you need to relax. I'm sure it won't be that bad. They'll probably be on their best behavior because I'm here."

Lexie snorted and reached up to *boop* him on the nose. "Aww, it's sweet how clueless you are."

"You think they'll make a scene in front of me?"

"I think they'll take any opportunity to point out what a fuck up I am, so yes."

Mitch's forehead bunched as his eyebrows drew together in confusion. "I'm not going to pretend to understand your relationship with them," he said. "But what exactly am I getting myself into here? All I know is that they left you alone one Christmas and were generally absent from your life."

"That pretty much explains it all," Lexie told him. "They saw me more as a representation of this perfect family life they trotted out for potential investees and not as an actual daughter. I was something to be used."

"That's the only reason they're coming by for dinner tonight. First, to convince me to attend some function with them and play the perfect daughter. And second, to make sure the man I've chosen to spend my life with is someone worth being seen in public with."

Lexie realized what she said the moment Mitch's eyebrows rose up his forehead. He captured her chin between his thumb and forefinger, gazing deep into her eyes. "The man you've chosen to spend your life with, huh?"

"Don't read too much into it," she said, cheeks heating as she pushed away from him. "If we survive this dinner, I'll consider having a conversation about it."

Mitch chuckled. "Good enough for me."

She heaved a sigh, and said, "Look, this isn't going to be easy for me. They will inevitably say things about me that will piss you off. I'm asking you not to react. The sooner we get this over with, the sooner they get the fuck out of here, and the sooner we don't have to see them again for a good long while. Just please trust me on this. I love you, but don't go all big bad overprotective hockey player on me, okay?"

He nodded and bent down to kiss her forehead. "I'll be on my best behavior."

Studying him then, she knew full well just how much she didn't deserve him. The fact that he knew her well enough and loved her enough not to fight her on anything right now, when her nerves were frayed live wires over the impending arrival of her parents, further illustrated that point.

Truthfully, she didn't know how she got so lucky, but now that Lexie had him, she was holding on for dear life.

Stepping closer to him, she tipped her face up in invitation. Mitch got the hint and lowered his mouth to hers, tongue sweeping inside almost instantly. Those brief moments when they lost themselves in the kiss, like being in a vacuum that sucked all light and sound from the world, were pure bliss.

And they were over too soon.

Lexie had just slipped her hands under the hem of Mitch's shirt—flannel, of course—when there was a knock on her door.

"Fuck," she whispered against his mouth. "Do you think if we pretend we're not here, they'll just go away?"

"Not a chance," he said, giving her one more light peck before pulling away and turning her toward the door, swatting her ass when she made no attempt to move toward it.

Finally, she sucked in a deep breath and went to let her parents in.

"Oh, honey," her mother said the moment she opened the door. "You kept us waiting long enough."

Lexie barely contained an eye roll and stepped forward to peck her mother, then father, on the cheek. "Sorry," she said.

"And where is this boyfriend of yours?" Her father asked.

"I'm right here, Mr. Monroe," Mitch said, stepping forward.

Lexie got her height from her father. Her mother was average, around five-five, but her dad was a tall man, coming in at just over six feet.

Mitch still towered over him. Not only because he was nearly six and a half feet tall, but because everything about him was big. Broad-shouldered, big hands, thick, muscular arms and legs. He was intimidating as hell, even under the flannel and dark wash jeans, and Lexie bit back a smile of satisfaction to see her father cower a bit in his presence.

"Pleasure to meet you, Mitch," her father said, shaking Mitch's proffered hand. "Call me Robert."

"Likewise," Mitch said, then turned to her mother. "And you as well, Mrs. Monroe."

Her mother actually *blushed*. "Oh please, call me Christina," she said.

Lexie clapped her hands together. "Shall we eat?"

Mitch cut her a glance, an eyebrow raised.

What could she say? She wanted to get this over with as fast as possible.

"So how's work going, sweetheart?" Her mother asked once they were seated, the food served and wine poured, voice dripping with disdain.

"Oh, it's great," Lexie told her. "I'm heading out east next week."

"Where, exactly?" Her father asked. "Hopefully not one of those Po-dunk towns that are woefully beneath you."

Lexie sat momentarily stunned. That was the nicest thing her father had ever said about her. "I'll be in Pennsylvania. Philly, actually."

"Philly," her mother snorted. "What a dump. There's nothing there."

Lexie's eyebrows drew together. *Nothing there?* It literally used to be the capital of the country, but okay.

"Then I'm heading up to Connecticut."

"New Haven?" Her father asked.

She nodded, swallowing hard, and Mitch's hand settled on top of hers under the table. New Haven was where they had been living when her parents left her alone for Christmas that one year, and she hadn't been back since.

"Now that was a great little town," her mother said. "You loved it there, Lexie."

"It was okay," she said quietly.

"Remember that Christmas we lived there? You spent hours in your father's chair reading those Harry Potter books we got you, and I loved being so close to New York City. You had the time of your life the day I took you shopping."

Was she fucking serious right now?

Her father nodded in agreement. "We had a lot of good times in that house. You know our lifestyle is where Lexie gets her love of travel from," he added to Mitch.

More like I love traveling so much because I never had a home and never knew anything else growing up.

"Our girl has been turning heads across the country since she was a little girl," her mother said proudly. "But Lexie, I really wish you would change your look. All that black washes you out, and your hair is so outdated. But I suppose as far as trophy wives go, Mitch, you could do worse."

Mitch's hand tightened around hers, grinding her bones uncomfortably together, but the pain felt good, grounded her, stopped her from leaping across this table and throttling her parents.

Trophy wife? God, this had been such an epically bad idea. She mentally reminded herself to make Mitch pay for forcing her into this later.

Maybe she'd withhold sex for a few days.

Then again, that would be torture for her just as much as it would be for him.

"I think she looks great," he said, leaning over to peck her cheek. She smiled up at him, grateful for his presence.

An uncomfortable silence descended as they dug into their food, interrupted by her parents attempting to make small talk with Mitch that consisted of subtle jabs at Lexie, as if they were trying to get him on their side, to see what they see in her.

"So Mitch," her father said, "how's your hockey season going? I'll admit I'm more of a football guy myself, but if you and Alexandra stay together, we'll have to change that."

Mitch smiled. "It's good. I think we've got a real shot at the Cup this year."

Only Lexie could see the strain in that smile, and understand what it meant—he was worried he might not even be here for the playoffs.

With the NHL trade deadline looming, there had been rumors circulating for the last month or so that the Warriors were shopping Mitch around. According to *inside sources*, they were interested in trading their star veteran defenseman for speed and scoring ability.

Two things they already had plenty of in Brent, Cole, Rat, and Gray, to name only a few of the Warriors' talented forwards.

Parker had left the team at the end of the previous season when his contract expired, moving on to some team out east that Lexie never cared to remember.

Good riddance to that guy.

Since then, Mitch had been paired up with the Warriors' captain, Jordan Dawson, on the blue line. And as luck would have it, the two played even better together than Mitch and Parker had.

Lexie didn't understand the rumors, and she hoped they were just that. She knew very little about the game of hockey other than broad terms and how the Warriors were playing, but she had spent enough time around Brent and Berkley and Mitch, to know that trading a franchise player like him when everything was going so well for the team made no sense.

It was constantly on Lexie's mind, the thought that Mitch could be traded and move away. What would happen to their relationship then? Would they survive long distance?

Would he even be *interested* in long distance?

She had meant what she said earlier—she was choosing to spend her life with him. All of it. Forever. The thought that it could all be taken away from her so soon was terrifying, to say the least.

"That's great to hear," her mother said. "I don't know anything about sports other than what Robert tries to explain to me, but we've been to a few hockey games over the years with potential investees. Never a Warriors game, but we've seen the Quakers, Regents, and Voyageurs when we lived on the East Coast, the Knights, Bullets, and Wolves."

"Wow, impressive," Mitch said.

Lexie held back another eye roll. Her parents were laying it on pretty thick, trying to get in Mitch's good graces because he was rich, famous, and incredibly good-looking.

The fact that they were reacting to him this way was a ringing endorsement.

The thought should make her happy, that her parents deemed him worthy, but instead, it made her skin crawl. To them, he was just another person to be used to get what they wanted. And what they wanted was more money.

It was always about the money, and Mitch was made of it.

"So how exactly are you managing your money, Mitch?" Her dad asked.

See? She wasn't making this shit up.

"What do you mean?" Mitch asked.

"I mean, I did some research on you before we came here and your last contract was for a pretty hefty sum. And you're young. What exactly are you doing to protect yourself in the long run?"

Lexie opened her mouth to object to this line of questioning, but Mitch squeezed her hand under the table, silencing her. "I've invested some of it," he said. "Real estate, mostly. I own a building in Greektown. The entire top floor is a converted industrial loft space that I rent out for special occasions, and it's also become sort of a notorious hangout spot for me and my teammates."

"What else?" Her mother asked, leaning her elbow on the table and resting her head in her open palm, the picture of curiosity.

"I recently invested in my friend's athletic wear company. He started it last year, and it's been doing really well, but I asked if I could provide some capital to help grow the company even further, and he agreed."

"A friend?" Her father said, dubious.

"He's a teammate, actually. Brent Jean. He and his sister own an activewear company called FLEX."

"Oh, we've heard of that!" Her father said. "We actually reached out to be initial investors, but that Brent kid is stubborn. He wanted to pour all of his own money into getting it off the ground, and he couldn't be persuaded otherwise. We would've liked to have that one under our supervision, especially with the way it's taken off."

Lexie's eyebrows drew together as she studied her father. They had wanted to invest in FLEX? And Brent blew them off?

She always knew Brent Jean had a good head on his shoulders.

"Brent's got a great head on his shoulders," Mitch said as if reading her mind. Freaky shit like that happened between them all the time, and she'd long since gotten over the shock of it. "He's got business and finance degrees from Michigan State, so he definitely knows what he's doing."

"Well that's great to hear," her mother said, her tone indicating it was anything but. Her parents hated nothing more than when a solid, lucrative investment opportunity slipped through their fingers. "And I take it you've seen an excellent return on your investment?"

"Yes ma'am," Mitch said, throwing a little of his country boy twang into the words, making Lexie smile.

"That's good," she said, spearing a piece of asparagus with her fork and pointing it in Lexie's direction. "This one always needed someone to take care of her. She's got expensive tastes, so it doesn't surprise either of us that she's dating a professional athlete."

What the fuck?

Lexie's cheeks burned in embarrassment, and she sputtered, desperately trying to come up with a way to defend herself without causing a huge scene in front of Mitch.

This is exactly what she had been afraid of. When her parents looked at someone, anyone, all they saw was what that person could do for them. It didn't matter who they were. They could be the pope or a serial killer on death row. Her parents would still only wonder what they could get out of the relationship.

A trait they've mistakenly assumed they passed onto their daughter.

Lexie, once again, opened her mouth to speak up for herself, but Mitch beat her to it.

"With all due respect, Mr. and Mrs. Monroe, Lexie works her ass off. She doesn't need me to take care of her. She can take care of herself just fine."

"Are you sure about that?" Her father asked. "We raised the girl. I think we know her a little better than you do."

"I'm going to have to disagree with you there. You didn't raise Lexie. She raised herself. And somehow, despite the fact that you are two of the most self-centered and money-hungry human beings I have ever met, she turned out perfect. Kind, hardworking, incredibly loyal, doesn't take shit from anyone. And none of that is thanks to you. In fact, she is who she is *in spite of* who *you* are and how she grew up." Mitch stood and swung his arm out, gesturing at her massive condo with its floor-to-ceiling windows that looked out over the Detroit River. "You think you had any part in this? No. She pays for this all on her own, with money she earned on her own merit. So forgive me, but I don't think you know your daughter at all."

"Actually, she has a trust fund she's had access to since she was twenty-one," her father said smugly.

True, Lexie thought. And Mitch knew it.

But while she may have access to it, she hadn't touched a single penny. Mitch knew that too, but he also knew her parents wouldn't believe it if they told them, so he wisely didn't press the point.

Once she entered her late teens and started college, Lexie did everything she could think of to wriggle out from under her parents' thumbs. Turns out, the trick was streaking naked across Michigan State's campus in the middle of the day at the end of her senior year.

After they bailed her out of jail and paid to make the whole thing go away, they asked why she did it, and what it would take for her to get her act together.

She told them plainly: "I want my trust fund."

By then, she didn't need it. She'd already signed the contract with the headhunting agency and made more than enough money to finish school and relocate to Detroit. It just happened to be the only thing they could still hold over her head, and they would've continued to do so until she was thirty.

Thankfully, they signed off, and Lexie walked away from them, a very rich young woman.

"Mitch..." Lexie said, reaching for his hand. At that moment, she didn't know who she was more embarrassed by: her parents, or him.

He pulled away. "No, Lex. They need to hear this. They need to know that the first time you ever went home with me, you told me you don't believe in love. And they," he said, pointing at her parents, "are to blame."

"Now you listen here, young man..." Her father started, rising from his seat as angry red splotches rose from the collar of his shirt, spreading across his neck and face. "I don't know who you think you are but you don't get to speak to me like that in my daughter's home. You're a guest, and this is family business."

"That's what you don't understand," Mitch said, shaking his head. "*I* am her family. Brent, Berkley, Amelia...*we* are her family. You two are just a sperm donor and an incubator."

Her parents reared back as though they'd been slapped.

And then they both turned their gazes on her.

"You're just going to let him speak to us like this?" Her mother asked.

"I..." Lexie didn't know what to say, couldn't find the words to placate her parents. And the longer she stood there, searching for a way out of this, the more horrified her parents became, taking her silence for agreement with Mitch's words.

And the thing was, she *did* agree with him. But now was neither the time nor the place for this conversation.

Never would be more acceptable.

"Well if that's how you feel," her father said, "then we'll just see ourselves out."

"Goodbye," Mitch said.

"Stop it," she admonished him quietly. "Mom, dad, please don't go. Mitch is a hockey player. Being protective is in his blood, and he loves me so he's especially protective of me."

Her parents ignored her, instead shrugging on their coats and heading toward the door. "I am appalled that you allowed someone like that into your life," her mother hissed as her father yanked the door open and attempted to usher her out. "Into your *bed*."

"Mom...I'm sorry."

"We'll discuss this at a later date," her father said diplomatically, trying to protect their perfect image, even now.

And then they were gone, the door slamming shut behind them echoing through her apartment.

Mitch came up behind her. "I'm sorry," he said. "I just couldn't—"

"Couldn't what?" She said, whirling around and cutting him off. "Couldn't let us enjoy a quiet, drama-free meal with two of the most hard-to-please people on the planet? The worst part is they *liked* you! Before you ripped into them, they actually liked you."

"They liked my money, Lexie," he said. "They liked what my money could do for you, for them. They couldn't care less about who I am as a man."

He had a point, but Lexie was fuming, too angry to care. "You had no right to speak to them that way. I specifically asked you not to do this, and you completely ignored my wishes! What the fuck were you thinking?"

"What did you expect me to do? Sit there and let them call the love of my life a gold digger? Let them degrade you and diminish everything you've worked so hard for and not take a swing at them? Like you said, honey, I'm a hockey player. Protecting what's mine is in my blood."

"I told you so many times how they are. You *knew* what we were walking into. And the second they made some snide comment about me, you couldn't let it go. You couldn't just let us survive this day. You had to go and make it a big thing."

"I won't apologize for having your back, for caring about you. If that's what you expect from me, I don't know what we're doing here."

"Neither do I," Lexie said quietly.

All the fight left her at that moment, because she knew the way out of this wasn't *through*. The way out of this mess was to end it. Here and now, before it got any harder to do so.

It was the absolute last thing she wanted to do, but...

She had told him from the beginning, and several times since then, that she didn't believe in love, that she didn't know how to love. Against all odds, she had fallen for him. But she lived in constant fear of him walking away and leaving her all alone like her parents had been doing her whole life. And now, after this evening turned into a disaster of epic proportions, she didn't know what she was doing anymore. Her parents would always be her parents, whether she liked it or not, and she couldn't do this to herself every time they were forced to spend time together. What if she and Mitch got married? What about children?

Deep down, even when she had resigned herself to being single forever, Lexie had always believed she wanted a man who fought her, who kept her on her toes, kept her honest, but one who also made her feel safe and loved and protected.

But when confronted with that man, with Mitch, and witnessing how he'd reacted to a few slights from her parents when she specifically asked him to let it roll off his back...maybe he wasn't the one for her after all.

Maybe *the one* didn't exist for her.

"What are you saying right now?" He asked, stepping closer and grasping her chin, forcing her to look him in the eyes. "You're not...you can't be serious."

She tried to look away from the hurt swimming in his eyes, but he held her in place. "We can't do this anymore," she said. "I thought I could. But it's painfully obvious to me after this disastrous dinner that I'm not cut out for this."

"That's bullshit and you know it," he said. "After everything, this is how it ends? With you pushing me away again?"

She jerked her head out of his grasp and stepped back out of his reach, needing the distance to breathe, to corral her thoughts and explain this in a way that would make the most sense to him, that would show him she was well and truly done.

She had always been a good liar, but she was about to put on the show of a lifetime.

"It might be bullshit to you, but it's who I am. You just met the people who raised me, who made me like this. I told you from that very first night I don't believe in love, that I don't do relationships. And you kept pushing and pushing until we ended up here. I never wanted to be here!" She cried, voice rising as she unloaded all her pent-up fears on him. "I begged you not to push this. Not to push me. And now here we are. Well...I'm out. I want out. This is over."

"Lexie..." He took half a step forward, but she backed away.

"I just can't love you the way you deserve, Mitch," she said quietly. "You deserve someone who can give you the beautiful, happy, fairytale life that your big, perfect, romantic heart deserves. And I'm just not that woman."

Mitch sighed. "You don't mean that," he said. "How is it that after all these months you still don't realize that you're *exactly* what I want and *everything* I need? You're the love of my life, Lex. Why doesn't that mean anything to you?"

"It means everything to me," she said. "I've never had anyone love me the way you do. And I can't keep pretending it's a love I deserve. I'm messy and emotionally stunted and screwed up and I can't give you what you want or need. I can't give you my whole heart. It's time you realize it. Trust me, I'm doing us both a favor by ending this now."

He stared at her, expression blank, blinking slowly like an owl, then his gaze darkened, the muscle in his jaw jumping as he clenched his teeth together. "You don't get to tell me you love me and, in the same breath, tell me to leave. That's not how this works."

Biting her trembling lower lip and looking away from him, she said, "Please don't fight me on this." Her voice was cracked and shaky. "Please just go."

She turned her back on him fully as he stalked into the foyer, fighting back tears as he put on his shoes and dug his jacket out of the closet. A second later, the door clicked open, but it didn't shut. Instead, he spoke.

"You can try to deny and fight what's between us all you want, Alexandra," he said. And God, she loved the sound of her name as it fell from his lips. She almost went to him then, instead digging her nails into her palms, the tiny crescents of pain grounding her, keeping her rooted in place. She *had* to see this through. "But one day, you will give in. Because we're endgame. We always have been."

A moment later, the door slammed shut behind him, the sound a bullet to her heart.

And as though she'd been shot, Lexie crumpled to the ground and cried.

CHAPTER EIGHTEEN
Mitch

"**G**ood morning, Jackson," Mitch said. He was standing at his kitchen counter, a protein shake in one hand, phone in the other. Moments before his agent's call came through, Mitch had sent another text to Lexie, begging her to reconsider. These last three days without her had been torture. He knew she was reading his texts, but she had yet to reply to a single one.

"So I've got some news," Jackson said.

"Shoot," Mitch replied. "Is it some new partnership deal?"

"Not exactly..." His usually-effervescent agent sounded formal and subdued, and Mitch's stomach dropped out.

"Don't say it," he said, already guessing what news was coming. "I don't want to hear it. Just...fix it."

"I'm afraid it's a done deal, Mitch. There's no fixing this one. The Warriors have dealt you."

"Where," he said flatly.

"The Knights. Pack a bag. I'll meet you out there this afternoon."

Mitch hung up on Jackson without saying anything further and sat down hard on his couch, staring at the blank television screen.

Then he swiped across his phone and dialed Lexie's number.

Given the circumstances, he would do anything she needed him to in order to fix this before he left. He *had* to make things right.

It rang and rang and rang until her voicemail picked up.

"Hey, it's Lexie. Don't leave a message because I won't listen to it."

"Fuck!"

Two excruciatingly long hours later, after a brutal phone call with his mother during which she sobbed endlessly about her baby moving across the country, there was still no answer from Lexie, and Mitch was running out of time before he had to leave for the airport.

Were things between them well and truly over? She hadn't exactly left any room for arguments when she kicked him out of her apartment three days before, but he thought they'd have more time than this. That he'd be able to show up at her door, wear her down, and beg her to reconsider.

To remind her that he loved her, and that everything would be okay as long as they had that.

He scrubbed a hand over his face. It was all so messy, so complicated, and unfortunately, he didn't have the time to sit her down and make her see the error of her ways.

Was that for the best? Some small, long-forgotten piece of his heart whispered, *yes, it is. Let it go.*

He had his phone clenched so tightly in his hand that the vibrations from incoming texts sent jolts all the way up his arm. He dared a glance at the screen and wished he hadn't.

Endless notifications of texts and calls poured in, completely overwhelming his already overloaded emotional circuit board.

Mitch threw his phone against the wall, shattering it, effectively silencing the endless beeps and buzzes from the onslaught of texts.

Former teammates.

Because he had been fucking *traded.*

To fucking *California.*

Mitch had been aware this was a possibility for the past few weeks leading up to the trade deadline. The rumor mill was a deadly beast, and he'd assumed that's all the talk was: rumors from someone out to cause him emotional distress.

He never thought it'd actually happen.

"This is such bullshit," he said to his empty condo.

He had been in Detroit for five years, and in a blink, it was all wiped away. Five years he spent becoming a family with the men he went to battle with every night—five years of sticky-floored dive bars, of late nights at the loft or the casino in Greektown.

Two years of Lexie. Not long enough. Not *nearly* long enough.

It was almost hard to believe it had been almost two years since that day he turned around at the bar to find Berkley and Lexie standing behind him, waiting to get a drink. Had he known his life was about to change so drastically, he might have acted a little differently.

But then again, it had always been Lexie for him. He had learned that early on, and there had never been any sense in fighting it. So he hadn't, even when she had.

But God, when she stopped, when she had finally given herself to him completely, it had been the best day of his life.

The last year spent with her by his side, his in every way, had been nothing short of bliss. The life and love he'd always dreamed he would one day call his own.

And now, here he was, living a nightmare. Losing Lexie and his brothers in the same week. Destroying his phone had been stupid. He wouldn't be able to say bye face-to-face—his heart couldn't handle it—so a phone call would've had to suffice.

But, thanks to the shattered phone, that was out of the question.

Mitch couldn't help thinking maybe it was for the best. He would miss his teammates, absolutely. And he loved Detroit. The city had become more like home to him over the last five seasons than Georgia had ever been in the fifteen years he lived there.

And, of course, there was Lexie. A bright spot, but also a giant thorn in his side, especially after their last fight, when she told him she couldn't love him the way he deserved and kicked him out of her life.

So maybe leaving wasn't all bad. He'd get the chance to start fresh, to move on from the woman he loved who didn't want him back.

Lexie was scared. He knew that. Her childhood had certainly not been easy, and it made it difficult for her to be vulnerable with anyone. After meeting her parents, he now understood how deeply those emotional scars ran.

Join the fucking club, he thought.

That didn't give her the right to make decisions for him. But she had, and there was apparently no coming back from that. Not for her. It devastated him, left his heart bleeding and broken on the floor, but he had no choice but to accept it. For the last three days since their fight, he'd tried. Tried calling, texting, showing up at her building, and doing whatever he could to make her talk to him. To fight for her.

Every single time, she blew him off, going so far as to have the security guard at the desk of her building not even let him upstairs when he went there yesterday.

He was done fighting.

Moving methodically around his apartment, he blindly tossed clothes and toiletries into his duffel bag, thankful something nudged him to bring his skates home after their game the other night. Normally he wouldn't have, but now he was glad for it. This way, he wouldn't have to go to the rink to pick them up before going to the airport.

Just in case, he remembered thinking. In case he never came back.

He couldn't believe this was happening.

His flight took off in about three hours, which meant if he wanted to make it to the Verizon store to get a new phone and number, and get through security to reach his gate on time, he had to go now.

No more flying private for him. At least, not until he was settled in LA.

God, when was the last time he flew with people he didn't know? People who weren't his teammates?

The thought of the guys he was leaving behind was a punch to the gut. With a broken phone, a broken relationship, and a ton of unavoidable changes coming down the pipeline, Mitch had to admit he was a little freaked out. And without Lexie there to walk by his side through it all, maintaining his ties to Detroit simply didn't feel as important as it would have a week ago.

He loved this city, and the Warriors, but they apparently didn't love him back. He was moving to LA whether he liked it or not; there wasn't a damn thing he could do about it.

This was his chance to make a clean break. From everyone and everything. And it had to be all or nothing. If he was going to leave Lexie behind, Berkley had to join that list. As Lexie's best friend, she would only serve as a constant reminder of what he'd lost. And as Berkley's other half, Brent had to be cut off too. Which meant *all* of his teammates had to go.

Former teammates, he reminded himself.

Keeping them in his life would only be rubbing salt in the wound.

He wasn't proud of himself for the decision, but the way he saw it, this was the only way to survive. Change his number. Delete his social media profiles. Throw himself one hundred percent into helping his new team win games. Do his best to keep his head down, move forward, and forget about Detroit. Forget about Brent Jean and Berkley Daniels. Forget about Cole Reid and Jordan Dawson and all of the other Warriors he had spent the last five years with.

Forget about Alexandra Monroe, the woman he had *planned* on spending a lifetime with.

When he landed in Los Angeles, he deplaned to find it was pouring outside, a weather pattern that, though a rarity in Southern California, suited his mood perfectly.

He powered his phone on and waited for the notifications to come through. When the only text he received was one from his agent telling him to let him know when he landed, he was reminded he had changed his number.

No one from his old life was coming after him. No one could; he'd made sure of that.

Crazy how it had only been about eight hours since he got the call and he was already referring to it as his *old* life.

There was something so freeing in that notion, that his new life in California really was an entirely clean slate, and yet, something so fucking depressing that Mitch almost started crying right along with the sky.

But Mitch Frambough did not cry. Ever. Hadn't cried since he was a child and his father beat his ass anytime he did.

He ordered an Uber as he walked through the crowded terminal toward baggage claim. Truthfully, he could've skipped checking a bag altogether, and he didn't know why he hadn't. He'd packed in a hurry, so all he had with him on this side of the Mississippi was a duffel bag full of clothes and his skates. Clothes that, he soon realized, would be woefully out of place in the California heat. Back in Detroit, the ground was just starting to thaw, and all of his summer clothes were still in storage.

This was certainly going to take some getting used to.

Mitch climbed in when his Uber arrived, an expensive black Escalade with chrome rims and a hulking African American man behind the wheel.

"Where you headed?" The man asked.

"Can you just take me to the arena?"

The driver raised an eyebrow at him in the rearview mirror. "Which one?"

"Ahh fuck," Mitch said. What the fuck was the name of it? He'd played there enough times over the course of his professional career, and was now completely blanking. "The one the Knights play in."

The man still looked dubious, but pulled away from the curb anyway.

The second they were flying down the freeway, Mitch called his agent.

Jackson picked up on the second ring. "Hey, Mitch. You make it to Cali okay?"

"Yes," he said. "I'm in an Uber on the way to the arena. Can you meet me there so we can get all this shit sorted out face to face?"

"Yeah, sure thing! And look. I know this isn't what you wanted, but there was really nothing we could do. I promise, this is going to be great for you. And think about it this way: you no longer have to deal with the temperamental Midwest weather!"

I like that temperamental Midwest weather, Mitch thought. *And my temperamental Midwest woman.* "Yeah, sure, dude. Whatever you say. See you in a few."

"First time in LA?" The driver asked when he hung up.

"Nah," Mitch said. "I've played here before."

"Let me guess, you're a football player?"

Mitch snorted. "I could say the same about you! But no, I actually play hockey. Which is why I'm having you drop me at the Knights' arena."

"Oh right," the driver said. "That was going to be my next guess. Who do you play for?"

"Up until about twelve hours ago, the Warriors, but I just got traded to the Knights."

The driver whistled low. "Shit, man. I'm sorry. How long were you in Detroit?"

"Five seasons," Mitch told him, his heart squeezing with the memories of his time there.

Faces flashed through his mind, those of his former teammates, his friends. Brent and Berkley.

Lexie.

He winced, and the driver must have caught it because he said, "Sorry, man. It must be hard. I won't bring it up again."

Mitch shook his head. "Nah, it's all good. Just sort of left a mess in my wake. Going to take some time to get over it all, you know?"

The man nodded solemnly. "I get it bro. Being traded sucks."

Mitch glanced at him questioningly. "You played football, didn't you?"

The driver laughed. "Donovan Barnes, at your service."

Mitch's eyes widened. Barnes had been a six-time Pro Bowl offensive lineman for the Atlanta Falcons for years before he was traded to the Chargers. Two seasons into his stint in LA, he'd taken a bad hit and broken his back. The injury had ended his career.

Mitch couldn't even imagine, having everything he'd worked so hard for taken away from him in the span of a breath.

"So now you're driving an Uber for a living?" Mitch asked, unable to keep the incredulity from his voice. "You played fifteen seasons. Surely you're not strapped for cash."

Donovan snorted. "Nah, I'm not," he said. "I have enough that I never have to work again. Plus I coach at my son's high school. I just like driving. It's relaxing."

Driving in LA was *relaxing*? Mitch didn't press the issue, though it made no sense to him; he simply nodded. "Well hey, more power to you. I don't know what I would do if I couldn't play anymore."

"Trust me, kid," Donovan said as he pulled up in front of the Knights' arena. "That day is coming sooner than you may think. You better figure out a backup plan."

Mitch wouldn't, but Donovan didn't need to know that. Like he'd told Lexie before, he considered real estate. But he wouldn't give any serious thought to it until the day his career was over, which would hopefully be several years into the future yet.

Jackson was waiting for him on the curb, so Mitch tapped a few buttons on his phone to leave Donovan a large tip, gave him a tight smile, and got out of the Escalade.

"Good to see you, Mitch," Jackson said in greeting, shaking his hand. "How's LA treating you so far?"

"My Uber driver was Donovan Barnes," Mitch said.

Jackson's eyebrows shot up. "Like...*the* Donovan Barnes?"

Mitch nodded, still somewhat in shock. As a professional athlete himself, he shouldn't be starstruck, but he couldn't help it. "LA is weird," he said out loud.

Jackson laughed. "There's a reason they call it LaLa Land," he said, and led Mitch inside.

"So we've got a few contracts for you to sign. You'll meet with the equipment manager to get your gear squared away. I'll have the general manager, Dan Boyd, give you a tour of the arena so you two can get acquainted. You'll also be meeting the Assistant GM, head coach, Vice President, and the head of public relations."

They walked along the concourse to an inconspicuous elevator door, and stepped inside.

Mitch groaned. "Do we really have to do all of this today?"

Jackson side-eyed him. "Do you have somewhere better to be?"

Mitch opened his mouth to respond, then snapped it shut. He didn't even have anywhere to live at the moment, so he supposed this was better than listlessly wandering the unfamiliar city.

As if sensing the direction of his thoughts, Jackson said, "I'll set up an appointment with a realtor for this afternoon. For now, you're going to have to stay in a hotel."

With all the traveling he'd done in his career, Mitch was no stranger to hotel rooms. "That'll be fine."

"Great!" They reached the ground level where the offices were located, and Jackson led the way to a door behind which Mitch could hear voices. Jackson paused. "Just...try to see the bright side here, Mitch. I know you loved Detroit, but this is happening. There's no going back. All I'm asking is you give this team and franchise one hundred percent, just like you did the Warriors and Detroit. It'll make both of our jobs a lot easier."

"I promise I'll make the best of it," he told Jackson truthfully.

It was his only option.

Jackson nodded. "Good. Now let's go meet your new bosses."

Later that evening, Mitch sat in his hotel room, Chinese takeout containers spread on the table in front of him, staring out the window as the sunset lit the city on fire.

He had spent several long hours in meetings with the Knights' brass, hearing endless monologues about what they expected of him and the franchise moving forward.

We wanted you because we know you'll be a major asset to this team for a playoff push.

We're honestly still in shock Detroit gave you up.

We could go all the way this season with you on the roster.

Blah blah blah.

To Mitch, it was all bullshit. The same tired lines rolled out by every General Manager across the U.S. and Canada, welcoming newcomers into the fold with open arms, hoping all those useless platitudes would ease the sting of their former team not wanting them.

Mitch refused to be bitter. After all, nothing could be done about it now. But he hoped they didn't expect him to acclimate fully right away. A new team. New facilities. New city. New everything.

It was a lot at once.

But that also meant a new Mitch. And a new Mitch would take some time to craft, a prospect he couldn't deny was kind of exciting. The only thing he didn't expect to change was his personal style of play, but even that was a stretch given the fact that the Knights were not the Warriors, and he would have an entirely new defensive partner.

Mitch hated change. As a hockey player, he liked his routines. When he'd signed with Detroit five years ago, by choice once his contract in Columbus was up, he had settled in easily. The move from Columbus to Detroit hadn't been the culture shock coming to LA had been. He had easily become great friends with his teammates, genuinely loved the city and all it had to offer, and had been proud to play for the Warrior franchise, where so many greats had paved the way before him. Not to mention, he'd lived in Michigan for four years when he played in Ann Arbor, so it had been a homecoming for him, and his mother had been ecstatic to have him only forty miles down the road again.

Eventually, there was the girl.

Sitting there staring out at his new city, he made a plan: here in LA, he would live a surface-level existence. Only get to know his teammates well enough to help them win games. Short-term leases on apartments that came fully furnished. Acquaintances only outside of the rink; no deeper friendships allowed.

And absolutely no serious, emotional relationships with women.

He'd take a page from the playbook of one of the best: sex only.

Now, in that quiet hotel room, it was the first time since he'd gotten the trade news that he'd been completely alone. And unfortunately, with no distractions, Mitch couldn't stop his brain from circling around one thing.

Lexie.

He wondered what she was doing right now. If she had been trying to reach him. If she missed him. If she regretted their last conversation.

He knew he did.

His phone buzzed on the table, pulling him from his thoughts, a number with a Detroit area code showing up on the readout. Anxious that Lexie or someone else had managed to get his new number, he let it go to voicemail, watching the screen like a hawk until the notification popped up, then eagerly picked it up and played the message.

"Hey, Mitch, this is Sherry, the Warriors' realtor. I got in touch with your agent about taking care of some housekeeping stuff now that you're no longer with Detroit. If you could give me a call back as soon as possible, that would be great. Thanks."

Mitch sighed. He supposed there was no better time than the present to take care of this shit.

He redialed the number and waited for Sherry to pick up.

"Hi, Mitch," she said. "Thanks for getting back to me so quickly."

"Not a problem," he said. "Sorry I missed your call."

"Not a problem at all," she said. "So like I said in my voicemail, we've just got some housekeeping things to do, and I've got some questions."

"Fire away," he said, putting the phone on speaker and leaning back in the incredibly uncomfortable hotel chair that had not been designed with guys like Mitch in mind.

"First, what do you plan to do with your condo?" She asked.

Cutting right to the chase then. Wonderful.

"I..." Mitch paused, marshaling his thoughts. "Look, Sherry. I literally just arrived in LA. I hadn't really thought much past getting myself and my skates out of Detroit."

"Fair enough," she said with a little chuckle that grated on him. As though he were being funny by not having his shit together.

As if it was hilarious that his whole entire life had been turned upside down in the span of sixteen hours.

"You have a couple options," she was saying.

"And those are?"

"Well, sell, of course. You should be able to receive a great price for it in the current market. Or you could keep it."

"What exactly would keeping it entail?"

As a professional athlete, Mitch didn't have a mortgage or rent or any of those tedious things. He had purchased his condo free and clear the first day he laid eyes on it, feeling completely at home under the vaulted ceilings and the view of this city stretching out beyond the soaring windows.

"I'm not sure I understand what you're asking," Sherry said.

"I mean, what do you need from me in order to keep it? My mom lives in Ann Arbor, and while I know it's not that far of a drive, if she ever has to come into the city for work in the winter, I'd like for her to have somewhere to stay."

"Oh, uhh..." Sherry sounded as though Mitch had caught her off guard. If he had to, he would hazard a guess that she had been banking on a huge commission check from the sale of his condo.

Sorry to dampen your mood, sweetheart, he thought. *Sometimes we don't always get what we want.*

The hell he was currently living was proof of that.

"What do you need from me to make this happen, Sherry?"

"Nothing, actually. The condo is yours to do with as you wish. All I would recommend is having a cleaning service come in semi-regularly. In case you ever do have guests there."

"I have one." He was man enough to know where his limits were. Homemaking certainly fell beyond that line.

"Okay, great," Sherry said, the clicking of a pen echoing into Mitch's hotel room. "That settles that. So now there's the matter of the loft."

"I'm keeping that, too."

"But why?" She asked, clearly exasperated, her voice on the edge of whiny.

"It's a great investment, and properties like that don't go on the market every day. I'd rather not let it go just because I don't play for the Warriors anymore."

"So what are you going to do with it from all the way across the country?"

"I'll keep it listed on all the property rental sites it's currently on," he said. But then another thought occurred to him. "How do we go about getting Brent Jean added to the title?"

Mitch could practically hear Sherry's scowl through the phone, and he held in a laugh. This woman had clearly expected this to be a very different phone call, one with her garnering a hefty payday for her efforts.

"I can fax you over some paperwork to sign. It's basically a deed. It'll go from just being you on the property to you and Mr. Jean. If that's what you want..."

Adding Brent to the title of the loft was a risky move, one that Brent might see as Mitch trying to cover his ass in the wake of the trade and hightailing it out of Detroit. But on those days when the Warriors were home and needed somewhere to unwind after a game away from the prying eyes of the city, he wanted them to make use of the space.

"It's what I want. How soon can you get me that paperwork?"

"End of day tomorrow?" She said, phrasing it like a question. "Would that be okay? It's nearly seven here, but I can get to it first thing in the morning."

Mitch checked his watch. Shit, it was after dinner time there. The time change was going to take some getting used to. Then again, with no one but his mother back in Michigan to keep in touch with, maybe it wouldn't be so bad.

"Great, Sherry. That's perfect. Just fax it to the conference center here at my hotel and I'll take care of the rest."

"Sounds good, Mitch. I can do that."

"Great. And could you make sure Brent knows the loft is now his as well? I'll continue to pay for maintenance and all that jazz, and handle the bookings for rentals. Just let him know he can use it whenever he wants."

"You don't want to tell him yourself?"

Mitch considered that. It wasn't too late to take back what he'd done. His radio silence wouldn't be surprising. In fact, Brent would understand. A broken phone in the heat of the moment was a solid excuse. But, he couldn't so easily explain away the deleted social media profiles or the changed phone number and not even trying to say goodbye.

No, he was better off this way.

They all were.

"No, I don't. Bye, Sherry."

CHAPTER NINETEEN
Lexie

A s she had done every morning for the last three days, Lexie rolled toward her nightstand the second she woke up and grabbed her phone, unsurprised to find several notifications of texts and phone calls from Mitch on the screen.

In the end, she deleted the notifications without reading them.

Desperately, she wanted to talk to him and even went so far as to type out a response on several occasions, begging him to come over. Telling him that she fucked up and hadn't meant any of it. That she loved him and needed him, and they would figure out the rest together.

But, she had made it pretty clear when he left her apartment three days before that she never wanted to see him again, that she *couldn't* see him again.

It seemed Mitch wasn't giving up without a fight, and she knew she couldn't give in.

Being with him...it was too hard.

But that was beside the point. She had a life to live and a job to do, so she crawled out from under the covers and padded into the bathroom to take care of her morning routine.

Ten minutes later, she walked into her kitchen and poured a cup of coffee, setting a bagel in the toaster.

While she waited, she stalked into the living room and turned on the TV, instantly reminded that the last time it had been on was when Mitch was here that night, watching highlights on NHL Network while she got the condo ready for dinner with her parents.

God, what a stupid fucking idea that had been.

When she returned from grabbing her coffee and bagel, she settled herself on the couch and pulled the coffee table toward her, draping a blanket over her lap. It was early April, and she had turned her heat off already, but there was still a twinge of chill in the air.

Lexie tuned out much of the broadcast, which featured four men in suits seated around a table discussing the latest trade news and how the playoffs would look now that rosters were being shaken up.

A jingle sounded from the TV, a BREAKING NEWS banner ticking across the bottom, and Lexie waited to see who the next big name changing teams would be.

"We've just received word that Mitch Frambough has been traded from Detroit to Los Angeles," the announcer said.

All the blood drained from Lexie's face, and she stood quickly on stiff legs, almost falling over in the process, sprinting to her room where she had left her phone.

"Please pick up, please pick up, please pick up," she chanted as it rang.

"Hello, you've reached Mitch. Leave a message."

Lexie swallowed hard around the lump in her throat, forcing herself to take a couple deep breaths.

"Okay," she said out loud to no one. "Okay. It's fine. He'll call me back."

When hours passed without a call or text back from Mitch, Lexie's panic had reached astronomical levels. The constant spike of anxiety-induced adrenaline had her fingers shaking and her head feeling as light as a balloon.

So she did the only thing she could think of: she got in her car and drove to his condo.

The security guard at the front desk greeted her with a strained smile, saying, "Good afternoon, Lexie."

She nodded in response, hurrying toward the elevator banks and up to Mitch's floor.

When she reached his door, she didn't bother knocking; she simply punched in the code and burst inside, her voice a strangled cry as she yelled his name.

Sprinting from room to room, she was sure she'd find him in his office or lying in bed, his phone off or broken or something.

And she did find a broken phone, along with an accompanying dent in the living room drywall.

But Mitch was nowhere to be found.

Her anxiety was now full-blown hysteria as she dialed his number for, according to her call log, the fortieth time.

"Hello, you've reached Mitch. Leave a message."

"Fuck!" Lexie yelled into his empty apartment. She tossed her phone down on his couch and dug her hands into her hair, pulling at the strands near her scalp.

Why the fuck isn't he answering?

A loud buzzing echoed through the room and she snatched her phone up, hoping it was him.

But it wasn't. It was Berkley, who had been calling off and on all day.

Lexie was terrified to answer, knowing what it would mean, but she needed to get this over with.

"Berk, what the fuck is going on?" She asked by way of greeting.

"I...Have you talked to Mitch?"

"No! I've been trying him for hours and hours, but his phone keeps going right to voicemail. I got so worried I came to his condo but...he's not here. What is this I keep seeing about him being traded? Please tell me those are just rumors."

"Lex..." Berkley said, her voice cracking on the word.

And Lexie knew. Had known since this morning when that well-groomed NHL Network announcer had said Mitch's name. She sat down hard on the couch, her legs collapsing under her. "No."

"Lex, I'm so sorry...But it's true. Brent confirmed with management."

"So Mitch is just...gone?" Lexie surprised herself by how calm she sounded. In the middle of this shitstorm her life had just become, she was a rock. Steady. Immovable.

At least until she got off the phone with Berkley.

"I'm going to try calling him again," Lexie said. "I want to hear this from him."

"Let me know if you get through to him," Berkley said. "He hasn't been picking up for me or Brent or any of the other guys either."

Fuck, Lexie thought. *This is bad.*

"Yeah, I'll let you know."

She disconnected and tried Mitch again.

This time, it rang only once, and hope leapt into her throat, her heart pounding harder with the shot of adrenaline.

They would talk, and she could tell him she loved him and that they would find a way to make this work, and it would all be fine. That the fight had been stupid, that she had been stupid to send him away. Right?

Wrong.

"We're sorry, the number you have dialed is no longer in service. Please hang up and try again."

This time, there was no soft couch to cushion the blow as she chucked her phone across the room as hard as she could and watched it shatter against the wall, creating a near-identical dent and joining the scraps of his on the floor.

Their two phones, side-by-side in pieces on the carpet in his living room, felt like a too-accurate representation of the state of her relationship with Mitch.

But she couldn't leave them there, so she dropped to her knees and attempted to pick up the pieces. Absently, she brushed her fingers across his phone screen, hoping it would come to life. Instead, her pointer and middle fingers snagged on a jagged piece of the screen, and blood welled.

"Fuck!" She yelled, then hopped up and stomped toward the hall bathroom, tears gathering along her lower eyelid.. Brushing at her eyes with the back of her hand, she used her uninjured one to rifle through the cabinets.

All of his stuff was still here. Q-Tips and bottles of pain meds and a myriad of skincare products. And her stuff was there, too. A small bottle of her favorite lotion that she wore in lieu of perfume. A stray hair tie. A half-dried tube of mascara.

Abandoned.

Exactly as he had abandoned her.

Mitch was gone, had completely cut himself off from everyone and everything in Detroit, *including Lexie,* and that was the end of it.

She would likely never see him again.

Her temper rose as she stalked into the kitchen in search of a bag. When she left Mitch's apartment, it would be for the last time, so she might as well collect her things while she was there.

The blood boiling in her veins held the tears at bay, anger driving out all other emotions. Single-minded focus propelled her forward, down the long hallway and into the master bedroom, where she carefully averted her gaze from the king-sized bed piled high with pillows–half of which Lexie had bought–and made a beeline for the dresser.

Yanking open the top drawer where her delicates lay, she hastily stuffed them into the recyclable grocery bag. Methodically, she made her way through the dresser.

The majority of Mitch's clothes were artfully organized in his walk-in closet; he had used his dresser mainly for athletic shorts and old, faded t-shirts. When he and Lexie got serious, and she started spending more time in his space, he had presented her with drawers of her own, his cheeks burning with embarrassment. The emotion was so out of place against his tan skin that Lexie thanked him the only way she knew how.

First, she towed him across the room and pushed him down so he was perched on the edge of his bed.

Then, she stepped back and slowly stripped out of her clothes, tossing them onto the Warriors' blue duvet cover next to him.

Then, she stepped forward as Mitch reached for her. His fingers grazed up her thigh and backside as she turned away from him and folded her clothes before she walked them to the dresser, throwing a cheeky grin over her shoulder, and gently laid them inside.

Moments later, she was on her back on the bed, Mitch looming over her with a wicked grin curving his full lips.

Lexie pulled open the bottom drawer, confronted with her clothes from that day stacked neatly next to a few of Mitch's threadbare Warriors' t-shirts, the sight a gut punch.

Her anger reached a crescendo, and she tore into the drawer, removing the clothing and tossing it around the room, then stomping into the walk-in closet and taking her rage out on his suits, so carefully hung in neat, color-coordinated rows.

"Fuck you, Mitch," she seethed as she ripped his replica jerseys from their hangers and tossed them onto the floor, jumping up and down on them for good measure.

Moments later, with her chest heaving, she spun in a circle, eyes widening as she took in the carnage of her fit of rage.

"Fuck," she said quietly, moisture welling in her eyes, as she fell to her knees to run her fingers over Mitch's name on the back of his dark blue jersey.

That's when the tears began to fall in earnest. She curled herself into a ball atop the mass of clothing blanketing the floor and let it all out, sobbing and screaming until her throat was raw.

None of it was fair.

Not him being traded.

Not him letting her push him away.

Not him making her fall in love with him.

None of it.

Some time later, she heaved herself into an upright position and crawled into the bathroom, ripped off a length of toilet paper, and loudly blew her nose. Coming here had been a horrible idea, only serving to show her exactly how big of a disaster her life had become.

What did she do now without him?

Once she gathered herself enough to venture out in public, she sped back to her condo. When she walked in the door, she dropped the bag of her stuff unceremoniously by the door, walked into the kitchen, and pulled a bottle of tequila from the freezer. She had already broken down into a sobbing mess, and now she was going to handle this how she handled everything else: with alcohol and bad decisions.

Two hours passed and the tequila she consumed made the world feel a lot less shitty. Lexie was laying upside down on her couch, the top of her head brushing the floor, when the pounding at her door began.

"I'm coming, I'm coming," she grumbled, stumbling her way to the entry, not from the tequila but from all the blood rushing from her head. She pulled the door open and found Berkley standing there.

"What the fuck is wrong with you?" Berkley yelled. "Mitch goes MIA, and then suddenly I can't get you on the phone either?"

"I broke it," Lexie said with a shrug, extending the bottle of tequila out to Berkley. "Want some?"

Berkley considered her for a moment, as if deciding whether to call Lexie on her shit, or facilitate whatever mess she would surely get herself into this time.

Berkley chose the latter, swiped the bottle of tequila from Lexie's hand, and took a long pull.

Lexie grinned, eyes squinting to focus on Berkley's face. "My girl."

Somehow, Lexie talked Berkley into going to The Backdoor. Admittedly, there wasn't that much convincing involved. Lexie said she wanted to get drunk—ignoring the fact that she was already halfway there—and dance. Berkley, who had spent days in a red wine-induced haze after she and Brent broke up last year, wisely didn't argue. She simply went along with whatever Lexie asked.

Brent was standing at the curb waiting for them when they reached the bar, a tall man who bore a striking resemblance to him at his side.

Well, well, well, Lexie thought, eyeing up Nate Jean. *Tonight just got far more interesting.*

Lexie couldn't ignore the thrill that crept up her spine at seeing that pretty face close enough to touch. When Lexie met Nate the year before, in Brent's suite during their first playoff game that season, she'd been intrigued by his soft features and full, pouty mouth. Had she not been with Mitch, she might've taken him for a test drive.

Mitch, she scoffed to herself. *Fuck that guy.*

"Hey, babe," Brent said to Berkley, stepping up to peck her on the cheek. He nodded at Lexie. "Lex, you remember my brother, Nate, right?"

"Sure do," Lexie said with a smirk, trailing her eyes up and down Nate's body. He wasn't as chiseled as Brent, but that wasn't to say he wasn't as attractive. While Brent was all hard muscle and sharp angles, Nate was softer and leaner, as though someone had blurred his edges, though he was just as tall as his brother. Lexie had a feeling those clear blue eyes saw everything, and that he knew exactly what to do with that pretty mouth of his.

"Good to see you again, Lexie," Nate said. "I wish it were under better circumstances."

Brent groaned, but Lexie ignored the passing mention of Mitch. "I think these circumstances are perfectly fine," she said, strutting past them and into the bar.

The room was hazy from the smoke machine set up near the dance floor, and bodies flailed almost violently under the flashing strobe lights. Lexie stopped at the bar only long enough to be served, telling the bartender that her friend Brent Jean would be along to pay shortly. The bartender shouted after her, but she ignored him, choosing instead to grab Nate's hand when he walked up behind her and towed him to the dance floor.

If she was going to make bad decisions tonight, she might as well make them with someone most likely to piss Mitch off if he ever found out.

No, she admonished herself. *You will not think about Mitch. Not now, not ever again.*

This was about her and having fun. And she wanted to have fun with Nate Jean.

She quickly lost herself in the feel of Nate's hands on her hips, his fingers digging into her exposed flesh along the edge of her tank-top as they rocked together. She ground her ass into his lap, swaying back and forth to the beat of some top-forty hit, loving how his hard length, already ready for her, pressed up against her backside.

She didn't stop him when he bent his head and pressed an open-mouthed kiss to her neck. Or when he trailed his fingers across her stomach, sending shivers up and down her spine.

She *definitely* didn't stop him when he spun her in his arms and whispered in her ear, "Let's get out of here."

Giving him a playful grin, she said, "But we just got here."

"I can guarantee we'll have a lot more fun alone."

Lexie had to admit she was weak for that kind of confidence in a man, and if what she had felt pressed up against her ass moments before was any indication, he could absolutely back that claim up. Knowing full well there would be hell to pay in the morning, Lexie said, "All right. Let's go back to my place."

Nate's answering grin was wicked, and Lexie had a feeling this was about to be a lot more trouble than it was worth.

Unfortunately, she couldn't find it in herself to care.

They made a mad dash for the door, sneaking past Brent and Berkley, who were standing at the bar waiting for drinks. But they'd discover soon enough that both Lexie and Nate were missing, and would eventually draw the conclusion that they had left together.

It wouldn't take a rocket scientist to figure out what they were doing.

Once ensconced in a cab on the way to her place, Lexie couldn't help remembering how much different this felt than that first night with Mitch. With him, it had been frantic groping, unable to keep her hands or lips to herself, acting every bit like a teenager trying to sneak in a quickie before her parents came home. The draw to him. How that big body, those kind green eyes, and killer smile pulled her in like a magnet.

Whatever this thing with Nate was, it would surely be nothing like that. For starters, she didn't feel compelled to make out with him in the backseat of a taxi.

When they arrived at her apartment, there was no urgency to get upstairs, no near-suffocating tension between them as they stood on opposite sides of the elevator. Nate certainly didn't lift her off her feet and press her into the wall outside her door, so hungry for her that he couldn't even wait until they were inside.

No, Nate stood next to her like a gentleman, patiently waiting as she punched in her code and turned the knob. As she shed her coat and hung it in the closet. As she kicked off her Converse and padded barefoot down the hall into the kitchen. As she pulled out yet another bottle of tequila from the freezer—what could she say, she stayed well-stocked—and poured them each a shot.

Through it all, Nate followed her, those bright blue eyes tracking every movement. It struck her then how strange it was to have a man that wasn't Mitch in her home. It felt...wrong.

Hell, she still had some of Mitch's clothes in a damn drawer, his razor on her bathroom counter, and body wash in the shower.

And yet, she hadn't been able to get out of her own way long enough to fight for them.

God, she was so stupid.

Another shot of tequila chased that thought away.

Now was not the time. He might not be blond, green-eyed, or built like a linebacker, but Nate was a man who was here with her. Who, if the bulge in his jeans was any indication, *wanted* her.

For right now, that was enough.

Sex, after all, was all she could give someone right now.

It had been all she thought she could give Mitch, too, and look how that turned out.

Stop it, Alexandra.

So when Nate moved around the counter to stand next to her, and dropped his mouth to hers, if she couldn't stop herself from imagining that big-bodied blond who had shattered her heart in a thousand pieces instead of the trim brunette in front of her, well...no one had to know but her.

Waking the next morning was like swimming to the surface after a deep plunge into the water. Slowly, everything became clearer and sharper, until suddenly, she was breaking the surface of consciousness.

Eyes still closed, she snuggled into the warm body next to her, trailing her fingers over the forearm, lightly dusted with soft hair, that was thrown casually over her waist, thankful Mitch had chosen to stay the night.

The last few days had to have been a highly vivid nightmare.

"Morning," he said, and Lexie stiffened.

Definitely *not* a nightmare. And definitely *not* Mitch.

The events of the day and night before came rushing back, and Lexie choked on a breath, the influx of emotions nearly ripping a sob from her throat. She took several deep breaths and said, "Morning, Nate."

She hopped out of bed, staggering a bit as she got her hangover legs under her, and scrounged around on the floor for something, anything, to cover her naked body with. She found an oversized Warriors tee—which had once belonged to Mitch—and slipped it over her head.

Then she turned to survey the damage.

Nate turned onto his side and propped his head up on one hand, a lazy, satisfied grin settling on his lips. Lexie blinked, shaking her head. He looked so much like Brent at that moment that Lexie suddenly understood why he and Berkley spent so much time in bed.

It was also incredibly disconcerting because...ew, she had zero desire to bed Brent Jean.

Just his brother, her bitch of a conscience reminded her.

Not helpful, she shot back.

But now was not the time to be arguing with herself. No, getting Nate out of her apartment as quickly as she could needed to happen *right now*.

"I had a great time last night," he said, the grin growing as he took in her miles of bare leg. Her sheets rested low on his hips, leaving his smooth chest and ridiculously abdominals on full display. Wasn't this guy, according to Brent, married to med school? How the fuck did he have the time to look that delicious?

Focus, Monroe.

"Me too," she said out loud, tugging on the hem of the shirt and squeezing her eyes shut, begging her mind to dredge up some sort of memory of their time together.

Unfortunately, her tequila-soaked brain was, at the moment, entirely useless, which was honestly probably for the best. The most she could conjure up was the shots of tequila they'd taken in the kitchen when they got back from the bar. After that, it was flashes of tongues and teeth and lips and hands and *finally* the release that put her blissfully to sleep.

She had never been one to regret her sexual encounters, but sleeping with someone as a way to ease the pain of Mitch leaving, and not just anyone but Brent Jean's brother, was a bad decision she could have lived without.

But she couldn't go back. The best she could do at this point was try to minimize the damage, which meant getting Nate back to Brent and Berkley's as soon as possible.

And making sure no one, especially not Mitch, ever found out about how she spent her time mere hours after he pulled his disappearing act. Only the four of them—Brent, Berkley, Nate, and herself—would know what happened last night.

"Do you need me to call you a car or something?" She asked, wincing at her bluntness. Turns out, hungover, heartbroken Lexie wasn't one for mincing words.

Then again, neither was stone-cold sober Lexie, so it was honestly par for the course.

"Oh," Nate said, eyes widening. He tossed back the covers and scooted to the edge of the bed. "Sure. Thanks."

Lexie spun away from the sight of all that naked, bronzed skin and stumbled around the room, looking for her phone. It was only when she padded out into the living room that she remembered: she had shattered it against the wall in Mitch's apartment yesterday, which precipitated Berkley coming to check on her, thus leading them to the bar and her current predicament.

Well fuck, she thought. *Who knew a little phone could cause so much trouble?*

She spun on her heel and backtracked to her room. "Sooooo...small problem. I sort of broke my phone yesterday."

Nate laughed, a low, husky thing that had the muscles of his abs clenching in a truly distracting way. Lexie had to admit that the boy was a smoke show. But she needed him out. She needed time and space to pick up the literal pieces of her phone and figurative pieces of her life.

And she couldn't do that with a naked man in her bed, a naked man who was decidedly *not* Mitch Frambough.

She sighed. *You dumb bitch.*

But again, now was not the time. She could shame-spiral *after* Nate left.

"Don't worry, Lexie," Nate said, standing to dress. Lexie quickly averted her eyes. "I'll be out of your hair as soon as I find my pants."

She spotted them on the floor in front of her and picked them up, tossing them to him behind her back.

"Look," she croaked, then cleared her throat and tried again. "We can agree no one can ever find out about this, right? I..." she trailed off, unsure how to explain.

She what? Was a fucking mess? Was in love with another man?

"Say no more, Lexie," Nate said, slipping his shirt over his head and finally concealing the skin Lexie now distinctly remembered running her tongue *all* over last night. "My brother knowing is bad enough. We had fun. That's all. We don't have to make a big deal out of it."

Despite the regret and shame roiling in her gut, Lexie's shoulders relaxed. "I agree. Thank you."

Once fully dressed, Nate stopped next to her to give her a brief peck on the cheek and then disappeared. Seconds later, her front door opened and clicked shut behind him.

Only then, for the second time that week, when the quiet pressed in around her, did she fall on the floor, curl herself into a ball, and cry.

CHAPTER TWENTY
Mitch

Two days after leaving Detroit, Mitch stepped into the arena for his first practice as a member of the Los Angeles Knights.

And he'd be damned if it wasn't the strangest sensation.

Walking into a new locker room was reminiscent of being the new kid on the first day of school. Mitch didn't know anyone, didn't know his way around, or yet understand the social hierarchy among his new teammates.

Having done this once before, the whole getting used to a new team and city thing, Mitch knew it wasn't always an easy transition. He'd lost so much in this trade, but these players, his new teammates, had lost something, too. They had lost a teammate, a brother, and surely felt exactly how his former Warriors teammates felt.

But, fitting in when he arrived in Detroit had been easy, the guys welcoming him with open arms. He could only hope the same would be said for the Knights.

"Everyone, this is your new teammate, Mitch Frambough," Coach said when he led Mitch into the locker room. "I'm going to pair him up with Huntley today, and we'll see how that goes. I might end up doing some shifting later on, but right now, based on style of play, that seems the best fit." Coach turned to Mitch. "Your stall is that empty one over there. All of your gear should be exactly what you asked for."

Mitch nodded to Coach and started across the room. Gabe Huntley clomped over to him on his skates. The Knights' captain was several inches shorter than Mitch, probably only six-foot-one, but barrel-chested and ridiculously fast. He was one of the top defensemen in the league.

Next to Mitch, of course.

"Gabe Huntley," he said, sticking his hand out, which Mitch grasped and shook. "Nice to have you here, bro."

Mitch gave him a small smile. "Thanks, man. Appreciate that."

"I know being traded isn't ideal. You were in Detroit for, what, four seasons?"

"Five," Mitch corrected him.

"I'm sorry, truly. I can't imagine how hard this all must be. But all I ask of you is that you do everything you can to help us win."

"Trust me, I plan on it."

"Good. Then we'll get along just fine."

Mitch snorted. "You're kinda stuck with me, anyway."

"That may be true," Gabe said. "But I could easily make your life hell. And the last thing we need is animosity among teammates, especially when it looks like we'll be partners."

"I get it, man. I can assure you I will do my job to the best of my abilities."

"Perfect." He spun, stalking across the room and through the door that led to the ice.

Mitch appreciated Gabe's no-nonsense attitude. Having been on the de-livering end of such a conversation a few times before, he could understand the sentiment Gabe was trying to impart.

Mitch shook his head and turned to his locker, quickly scanning all of the gear to make sure he'd have everything he needed. Each piece of his equipment was new and shiny, with the exception of his skates. Those he had brought with him from Detroit, because any self-respecting hockey player knew that breaking in a new pair of skates was a bitch, and he didn't have time to go through that whole ordeal right now.

He stripped out of his street clothes and donned his new practice gear: black pants, white socks, and a silver jersey with his name and new number—91–on the back. In Detroit, he had been 87.

Next, he dropped onto his stool to lace up his skates, shaking off the memory of Detroit. LA was his team now. There was no changing that or going back. He had decided to forget about Detroit, forget his teammates and his friends. Forget Lexie. It wouldn't do him any good to drag all of that into a new locker room. Not when he had to go out onto the ice in a few minutes and show off his skills to a new group of guys.

Rising to his feet, he made his way across the room and stepped out into the hallway, moving down the tunnel until the arena opened up around him.

It was no Detroit, but he had to admit the Knights had spared no expense in the construction of their arena. Only five years old, it was filled to the rafters, which were lined with an impressive number of banners, with cushy faux-leather seats for fans to enjoy the game in comfort. The Jumbotron was the size of a house, an impressive sight to behold even now when it was dark.

The ice called his name, and he answered, placing one skate down and pushing off, gliding to the far boards, then picking up his pace as he turned to take a lap around. Several of his new teammates stopped to watch him skate. He had played against them just a few weeks ago, so his speed shouldn't come as a surprise.

He took a few loops around, warming up, before heading down to where Gabe was participating in a passing drill with a few other guys.

"Everyone knows Mitch, right?" Gabe asked.

The three others nodded or mumbled their affirmation, and Mitch struggled not to roll his eyes.

Here goes nothing, he thought.

Practice went surprisingly well; the guys were welcoming and helpful. As a veteran player, Mitch didn't have to get used to the pace of an NHL game, or learn any of the minutiae of the game that changes from college to the pros, but he did have the unenviable job of getting used to a new offensive system.

His team in Detroit was full of scorers; any one of the four lines was capable of producing a goal at any given moment.

The same could not be said for the Knights. They were a defensive-heavy team, relying on their blue line to keep them in games.

Why they traded a forward to Detroit in exchange for Mitch made sense in the way that it further strengthened their already solid defensive core, but Mitch thought that they really could've used a high-scoring forward. Unfortunately, no one asked for his opinion.

After practice was over, and Mitch had showered and redressed in a bro tank and cargo shorts, two of the only summer-like articles of clothing he'd had the foresight to bring from Detroit, he slung his bag over his shoulder and made for the door.

All things considered, the day had gone better than he'd expected. Maybe this trade wouldn't be the worst thing that ever happened to him.

"Hey, Mitch!" He whirled to find Gabe hurrying toward him with his own bag slung across his chest, Hawaiian-print shirt buttoned haphazardly over his chest, as though he'd dressed quickly.

"What's up, Gabe?" Mitch asked.

"Let's go get dinner. I'll show you the city and we can get to know each other a little better."

Mitch pondered for a moment. Quite frankly, he was starving, and didn't have anything better to do. "Fix your shirt and you got a deal."

Gabe looked down at his shirt and grimaced, quickly unbuttoning and straightening it.

They exited the arena together, and Mitch was suddenly grateful for the offer so he could bum a ride back to his hotel after. He didn't yet have a vehicle in LA, and he was getting sick of dealing with Uber drivers.

Gabe led him to his car in the player's lot, a bright white Range Rover. They stashed their bags in the back, settled onto the black leather seats, and set off.

"I'm going to take you to WeHo," Gabe told him, using the abbreviation for West Hollywood. "It's got some great restaurants, for sure, but I figure if you're in LA, you should be exposed to the Bravo TV hot spots as soon as humanly possible so you never want to go back."

"That bad?" Mitch asked with a laugh.

"Not bad, exactly. Just...overwhelming. I prefer downtown."

Mitch gazed out the window as the streets rolled by, the buildings an amalgamation of chrome and glass, wood, and Spanish-inspired architecture. The sun was a bright, near-white ball in the sky, heating this corner of the earth to what would be mid-summer temps back in Michigan. Palm trees cropped up at regular intervals, towering over the sidewalks packed with a melting pot of people from all walks of life.

He definitely wasn't in Detroit anymore.

But he had promised himself he would give this city and his new team his all, so he turned to Gabe and asked, "How long have you been with the Knights?"

"Six seasons," he said. "Since I graduated college."

"Really?" Mitch asked, studying his new defensive partner. Gabe didn't look old enough to have already been in the league for six seasons, especially not if he went to college first. "Did you leave school early?"

Gabe shook his head. "Nope. Got my degree and everything."

"How old are you?" Mitch asked.

"Thirty."

"Wow," Mitch said, genuinely surprised. "I thought you were way younger than me."

"You're like, what, thirty-three?" Mitch nodded. "I don't know why, but I always thought you were younger, too."

"Seriously? Have you seen me?" Mitch asked, gesturing to his massive body.

"You move like you're a lot younger," Gabe said with a shrug.

"I'll take that as a compliment," Mitch said. "And so do you."

Gabe laughed, and pulled to a stop in front of a white stucco building, a sign out front announcing Mexican food. "I'm really glad we're getting out now, because things just got a little weird in here."

Mitch laughed with him, feeling lighter than he had since arriving in LA.

They made their way inside and were seated almost instantly, seemingly catching the restaurant in a weird lull between rushes.

Gabe ordered a margarita, so Mitch felt comfortable doing the same. After all, he wasn't driving, and he was sitting across from his lone maybe-friend in the city. That alone was worth celebrating.

Their drinks arrived, and both chose their meals. While they waited, he studied the room, and couldn't help but think that this would be the kind of place Lexie would like to go on one of their dates, or the kind of place Brent would like to visit when in town for a game.

He missed Brent and the rest of the Warriors, and goddamnit, he missed Lexie. So many times over the last few days, he had nearly picked up his phone and called her. But what would he even say?

Sorry I left you without saying goodbye?

Sorry I didn't fight harder for us? For you?

There wasn't anything that could take back what he'd done. It was pointless to even consider the what-ifs.

His face must have shown his anguish because Gabe said, "Tell me about her."

"What makes you think there's a her?" Mitch asked, nonchalantly taking a sip of his drink. Tequila mingled with lime juice and a burst of salt exploded across his tongue, and he greedily sucked down more.

"Look, man," Gabe said, and Mitch felt he was about to get an earful. "I typically don't pay attention to the gossip that follows other guys into our locker room. I know you were a huge piece of the puzzle in Detroit. We're damn lucky to have you."

"But?" Mitch prompted.

"But..." Gabe looked him dead in the eye. "But a former teammate of yours spoke to a national media outlet about how you disappeared. That you didn't bother to reach out to any of them to say goodbye. Changed your number. Deleted all of your social media profiles. Basically wiped yourself off the face of the planet. I've been around this game long enough to know that's not a typical reaction to being traded. There's nothing in the rule books that says you can't remain friends with your old teammates, Mitch. So it would stand to reason that you were running from someone, and the trade was the perfect opportunity to make a clean break. And since you did that, I can bet you haven't had anyone to talk to, making me your only friend in this crazy city. And the only way we're actually going to be friends, and start clicking on the ice as defensive partners, is if you tell me what's going on."

Mitch sat, still as a statue, blinking at him. Did Gabe live inside his head or something? Since he moved here, he'd spent three hours total with the man, and Gabe already had him figured out.

"That's a neat trick," Mitch said, again reaching for his margarita glass and draining it.

Gabe shrugged. "I'm good at reading people."

Mitch would later learn that Gabe had studied psychology in college, intent on becoming a therapist if hockey didn't work out.

Reaching up to flip his hat around so he could hang his head in his hands over the table, Mitch sighed and said, "Her name is Lexie."

"What happened?"

While the absolute last thing Mitch wanted to do was dive into his woe-is-me tale in the middle of a quiet Mexican restaurant with a guy who was practically a perfect stranger, he knew he'd feel better if he got it off his chest.

So he started speaking, the words flowing from his mouth like water gushing over the edge of a cliff. He couldn't stop them, not when he started talking about Lexie. The night they met. The first time they had sex. All of the little, perfect, endlessly frustrating moments that had let up to that fight right before he got traded.

"We weren't exactly speaking when I got traded," Mitch said. "I thought we were done. It was just...easier."

"Easier for who? Because I gotta be honest with you, man, you seem pretty fucking miserable."

"Moving on is going to be easier here, far away from her. This is just the...early stages."

"Of?"

"Grief."

Gabe stared at him, as if weighing his next words carefully. "I think you should call her. Or at the very least reach out to your old teammates. You can have them in your life and still give your all to the Knights. The two aren't mutually exclusive, you know."

Before Mitch could respond, their food arrived, and they both dug in, leaving him to marinate in his thoughts.

What Gabe said made perfect sense, but Mitch hadn't exactly been in his right mind when he left Detroit. He left in a hurry, and not by choice. At the time, Mitch thought he'd been making the right decision to burn those bridges. As far as he was concerned, Lexie had made it perfectly clear where they stood, and it was at odds with Mitch's own stance on their relationship.

After nearly two years of the constant back and forth with her, the will-we-or-won't-we, the emotional whiplash, he couldn't do it anymore.

She had said what she needed to say, and Mitch hadn't agreed with her. When she asked him to leave, her voice breaking, unable to even look at him, it felt final. Like they were finally, well and truly done. It wasn't going to be one of those instances where one of them broke down a few days later and called the other, asking if they could talk. That talk wouldn't lead to sex, Mitch giving in when Lexie used her body to distract him from all of the things she wasn't saying to him. There would be no blissful few days or weeks when everything seemed as though it was back on track, that they would live happily ever after. There would be no fixing it this time.

And he *had* tried those last few days before the trade. Texting and calling and showing up at her place.

It still felt so *final*.

Happily ever after wasn't in the cards for them anymore; he knew that. He had most likely known it all along, in some deep, dark corner of his mind that he actively chose to ignore.

And so, the clean break had been the only logical choice, the only thing that was going to get him through this.

The only thing that would ever allow him to fully move on from Alexandra Monroe.

CHAPTER TWENTY-ONE
Lexie

Now...

One year to the day after Mitch got traded, Lexie woke up and poured Bailey's in her coffee.

She followed that up with a Bloody Mary.

By noon, she had switched to beer, and by dinner time, she was taking pulls of tequila straight from the bottle.

She had turned her phone off, wanting to mourn the anniversary of the death of her relationship in peace.

She really should've known it wouldn't be that easy.

The pounding began shortly after seven that evening, and Lexie experienced an acute sense of déjà vu. Had she lived this before? She must have, but she was too drunk to remember when.

Lexie didn't bother getting up to answer the door, already able to guess who would be standing there and knowing full well that person had the code to get in.

Seconds later, a series of beeps followed by the loud *snick* of a lock opening sounded through the apartment.

"Lexie, so help me God if you're dead in there, I'm going to kill you!"

"That makes exactly zero sense," Lexie said as Berkley stalked into the living room, where Lexie was seated on the floor, takeout containers from four different restaurants spread out in a semicircle around her.

"Thank God," Berkley breathed when she laid eyes on Lexie. "I was having flashbacks to this time last year."

"This time last year?" Lexie asked, though she knew exactly what Berkley was referring to.

"Don't play dumb with me, missy," Berkley said, stalking across the room and collecting an armful of beer bottles. "You may be drunk, but you're not stupid."

"What are you doing here?" Lexie asked.

"We couldn't get a hold of you!" Berkley yelled from the kitchen over the sound of clinking glass as she settled the bottles in the recycling. "So I wanted to come check on you."

"Why?"

"Lexie..." Berkley said as she re-entered the room, gaze softening. "I miss him too."

Lexie held up her hand, barely holding the tears at bay in her inebriated state. "Don't. Don't talk about him. I can't do it. Plus he's back in your life anyway."

"It's not like I spend time with him. The Warriors are about to go on a Cup run. Brent is never home. He and the boys, including Mitch, are always at the rink," Berkley said. "But like...you can't keep doing this."

"Don't lecture me right now, please," she said. "When you and Brent broke up, you survived on red wine and chocolate for like a week. I don't want to fucking hear it."

Berkley held her hands up in surrender. "I said what I needed to. I really came over to see if you want some company."

"If you can keep your mouth shut and the judgmental, pitiful glances to a minimum, I'd love some."

Berkley mimed zipping her lips closed and throwing away the key. Lexie shook her head.

"What are we watching?" Berkley asked.

"*Love is Blind*," Lexie told her. "I'm just drunk enough to find it interesting instead of depressing as fuck."

Berkley laughed, then turned on her heel and left the room. The fridge door opened and closed, the tinny sound of a bottle cap bouncing on the counter following swiftly behind. Berkley came back in with a beer pressed against her lips and sat on the couch behind Lexie.

"Help yourself," Lexie told her.

"I need to be your level of drunk if I'm going to watch this show," Berkley said with a shrug.

"You're going to need to start shotgunning them if you want to get on my level before midnight," Lexie told her, and Berkley chuckled.

They sat in companionable silence until one episode switched to the next. Lexie tried to tamp down her need to talk, desperately wanting to ignore that urge in her chest to purge her feelings to Berkley. Unfortunately, her mouth had other plans.

"I miss him," she said quietly.

Berkley, still seated behind her, leaned forward and began combing her fingers through Lexie's thick, dark hair in the way she had been doing for Lexie for years. It reminded Lexie of being a little girl and having her mother brush her hair every night before bed.

Before she and her father got too busy to be parents.

Emotional intimacy had been in short supply in the Monroe household while Lexie was growing up. She didn't have any siblings, and once her parents' venture capital firm took off when they landed their first six-figure payoff, they just sort of...disappeared. With the constant school changes, Lexie struggled to connect with anyone, and rarely made friends. Her formative years were not meant to be spent friendless at school and parentless at home, but that's exactly what happened.

Lexie had been a plaything for her parents, a trophy daughter. They trotted her out to parties and meetings, putting on a show for potential business partners. It was their way of saying, "Hey, look. We're family people. We have a beautiful daughter whom we love dearly, so you should definitely trust us with your money."

Truth be told, her parents didn't even particularly like each other outside of the fact that they worked well together and had an image to maintain.

On the surface, Lexie had been what they needed her to be; she didn't see the point in fighting it when they refused to realize how fucked up the way they treated her was. On the inside, she was a tangled mess, her self-worth tied wholly to what she could do for other people. By the time Lexie had reached her teen years, and puberty came and went overnight, a growth spurt along with it—not only her height but her chest as well—she stopped striving to make lasting, emotional connections with people and instead chose to use sex to fill that void inside of her.

Berkley, Amelia, and Kimber and the friendships she'd formed with them had helped repair a lot of that emotional damage, and Lexie was terrified to think of where she might be now had she not met them all that first week of classes at Michigan State nearly a decade ago.

And, of course, she had never been in a serious relationship before Mitch, had never *wanted* to be. She'd had flings, of course, but never something that she saw lasting past a few weeks and certainly never something she wanted to keep for life. But being with him...she had thought that maybe someone finally *saw* her, saw all the rough edges, the sharp words she wielded as weapons, the hole in her heart she thought she couldn't ever fill, and loved her anyway. But they say hindsight is twenty-twenty, and Lexie was living with the consequences of her actions. She never gave herself fully to another—mind, body, heart—and this was exactly why: it had been a year since Mitch had left, and she was still nursing the wounds.

But she was the one that had pushed him away. Maybe if she'd bothered to fight for him, to tell him she messed up and beg for him to take her back, to respond to one of his damn text messages before he changed his number and moved clear across the country, things would be different now.

The worst part about it was that Mitch *knew*. He knew about all the times when Lexie was barely old enough to be trusted not to wet the bed that her parents would travel for business, leaving her to fend for herself in whatever fancy apartment they would rent in the city of the month.

And he still left anyway, without a goodbye, without giving her something to hold onto.

He had promised to spend every day reminding her that she was a gift, and the second she tried to push him away, he gave up.

She couldn't decide which of them she was angrier with.

"I miss his eyes and his hair and that Greek statue body of his," Lexie continued when she came back to the present. "But I also miss his laugh, and how kind and gentle he can be with other people.

"And I hate that I miss him, you know? He gave zero fucks about leaving me behind, came back to Michigan and turned me away when I tried to see him, and I can't seem to get over him." She stood abruptly, completely ignoring the beer bottle she knocked over as liquid began to pool on the floor. Berkley hopped up to grab a stack of napkins leftover from Lexie's earlier feast, but Lexie kept talking. Now that she had opened the floodgates, there was no stopping her. "I had to move into a new fucking apartment just to get away from him! Everywhere I looked in that place, there sat his ghost. Eating at the kitchen island. Shaving in the morning, a towel wrapped around his waist, water from the shower still glistening on those ridiculous muscles of his. Asleep next to me in bed." She gripped her hair at her temples and pulled, the sting returning some of her sanity. "I don't know how I'm just supposed to forget everything we had. How was it so easy for him?"

Berkley wrapped her arms around Lexie's waist, resting her head on Lexie's boobs. Lexie couldn't help but laugh, their height difference as comical as ever. But before she knew it, she was choking back a sob, and then all at once, she was crying, her tears dampening the top of Berkley's head.

"I wish I could give you some quick fix potion to make this easier on you, Lex," Berkley said, her voice muffled against Lexie's chest. "But I can't. The only way out is through."

"This is fucking bullshit," she said, reaching up to wipe her tears away with the back of her hand.

"A good place to start would be not bottling everything up for an entire year until you're drunk and sobbing into your best friend's hair with a stupid ass reality show on as ambient noise," Berkley said, pulling away to smile up at Lexie.

"This show really is awful, isn't it?"

Berkley giggled, and soon Lexie joined in, the crying stopping almost as quickly as it had started. "You need to talk to me more," Berkley said.

"I know."

"I know it's not exactly your cup of tea, but it's going to help. That I can promise. Plus, you're going to have to spend a lot of time with him at the wedding."

"God, don't remind me," Lexie groaned, throwing herself dramatically onto the couch. Berkley plopped down next to her.

"It's the biggest day of my life, Lex," Berkley said. "Surely you can hold it together long enough to let Brent and I have a happy wedding day. I know it's not going to be easy, and I honestly wish things could be different, but...I can't tell Brent who he can or can't have as his best man."

"I just wish..."

"What?" Berkley asked when she didn't go on.

"I just wish I could talk to him before then. Clear the air at least. I'm not happy with him. In fact, I might be liable to punch him the first time I see him. But he and I need to talk at some point, right? I really don't want the first time we see each other to be at your fucking rehearsal dinner when we have to walk down the aisle together."

"I've tried to talk to him about it," Berkley admitted. "We all have. But he's just not interested."

That didn't make any sense to Lexie. Why should he be the one holding all the cards here? He's the one that left. If anything, he should be crawling on his hands and knees back to Lexie, and Berkley and Brent and everyone else, begging for a second chance.

Although, it seemed he'd already done that with Brent and Berkley.

So why not her? What the *fuck* was his problem?

"I don't get it," Lexie said. "And I think that's the hardest part. Why is he perfectly okay with you and Brent and the rest of the boys coming back into his life, but when it comes to me, the girl he loved, the girl he was planning a future with, he just has zero interest in any sort of relationship? What did I do wrong?"

She had asked herself that question a lot growing up, too. What had she done wrong to deserve parents like hers? What had she done wrong to be treated like a trophy to show off instead of a daughter to love and be proud of?

Lexie had never felt good enough, but during the year she spent with Mitch, she had started to believe in herself again. She had started to feel loved and safe and happy.

And then he left and took it all with him.

Lexie was so damn tired of all of it.

She wished she'd never met Mitch Frambough.

CHAPTER TWENTY-TWO
Mitch

"**G**oddamnit, Grey!" Coach yelled from his perch next to Mitch on the bench. "You were so far offsides you might as well have been walking down Woodward!"

Grey skated back to center ice with his head down, mumbling "I'm sorry" under his breath.

"Kid's been in the pros for three seasons and is still regularly going offsides."

"He's like a puppy," Mitch said with a laugh. "Just too excited to get to the puck."

"Well he needs to knock that shit off," Coach said. "We're going on a playoff run. The time for childish mistakes is over."

Mitch nodded in agreement. Grey was young yet, barely twenty-three, but if he was good enough to find a permanent home on the Warriors' second line, he shouldn't be screwing up the small things.

"Alright," Coach yelled. "I've seen enough."

Several of the Warriors sagged in relief, shoulders drooping dramatically as they skated toward the bench. They'd been out on the ice for two hours, running drills and listening to Coach scream.

Mitch sat by and watched it all unfold, almost thankful he wasn't out there letting Coach chew his ass out for missing a pass or reading an odd-man rush wrong.

Almost. Because truthfully, he'd give just about anything to be able to play again. Acting as an assistant coach for his old team wasn't quite the same, but being near the game and helping the Warriors win games was a huge blessing, and more than he could've ever hoped for after his injury.

Once the skating portion of practice was over, Mitch and the guys headed into their media room to breakdown some game footage of the Toronto Tritons, who the Warriors would play in the opening round of the playoffs. They settled in to dissect not only game tape from the last time the Warriors had played Toronto, but also the Tritons' last few games of the season.

"That goalie's stick side is so weak," Brandon Roberts, the Warriors' veteran net-minder, said.

"Yours is, too," Coach said.

Roberts scoffed but didn't argue. Most goaltenders were weaker on their stick sides, so it wasn't necessarily a bad thing. They chose to focus on stopping shots with their bodies, gloves, and lower pads instead of waving a stick through the air, hoping to magically fend off a puck.

So while the Tritons' goalie may have been weak on his stick side, he didn't appear to have any other holes in his game. The game they were watching was between Toronto and the Philadelphia Mustangs, a team that had also made the playoffs. In their final game of the regular season, when the Tritons and the Mustangs faced off, the Toronto net-minder only allowed one goal, a five-hole shot that got lost in traffic and snuck past him.

The Warriors would certainly have their work cut out for them, but they had speed, experience, and a strong defensive core on their side, not to mention three of the league's top ten goal-scorers in Brent, Rat, and Grey.

"That guy is a brick wall," Cole said. "Gonna be a tough four wins."

"Let's not get ahead of ourselves here," Brent said. "One period at a time, remember?"

The room chorused their assent, and they spent the next two hours in much the same manner, with Coach breaking down plays and the guys offering up minor commentary here and there.

For a moment, Mitch felt like one of them again. If he didn't think too far ahead, didn't look past this moment in time, he could pretend that in a few days, he too would be lacing up and skating out onto the ice down the hall, the arena erupting in cheers around him as he went to battle with his brothers.

But unfortunately, the daydream was short-lived.

He would never leave the bench, would never suit up again.

All he could do now was move forward, and with Brent and Berkley's wedding coming up in a few short months, there was a lot to look forward to.

Being back in Detroit was strange, though. His tenure with the Warriors had been recent enough that even now, he still got recognized on the streets, and fans regularly asked for autographs and pictures despite the fact that it had been over a year since he last played for the Warriors. They told him how upset they were when he went to LA, that it was bullshit he was traded, and that they're glad to see him back in the Motor City.

It was jarring how much had changed in the span of a year. Last April, one phone call upended his entire world. Earlier that same week, the love of his life told him she couldn't be with him anymore.

And then, in November, when he'd injured his back and his career had ended, he thought he'd never catch a break. The hits kept coming, and for months he braced himself, waiting for the other shoe to drop.

After his last surgery in early December, he couldn't help waking up every morning for weeks and asking himself, *what will go wrong today?*

Thankfully, it had been relatively smooth sailing since then, even if he experienced a pang in his chest every time he entered the arena and reminded himself he couldn't suit up with the guys. One day, he might be able to skate for fun, but it would never be his career, his *life*, ever again.

His mom talking him into moving back to Michigan for rehab had been a game-changer for him, though. While he was a born and bred Georgia boy, he had really grown up in Michigan, becoming the man he was always meant to be—once he was finally out from under his father's thumb and had legitimate, solid male role models to look up to. At this point, he had called Ann Arbor and Detroit home for nearly half his life, nearly as long as he'd been in Georgia.

Luckily, his old friends and former teammates had welcomed him back into the fold with open arms, and being a short car ride away from his mother instead of a several-hour long flight was honestly the best thing to come from breaking his back. He still kept in touch with Gabe and Cally, plus a few other guys from Los Angeles, but after deciding to cut ties with the Knights in order to join the Warriors' coaching staff, many of them avoided him. And he was okay with that. At the end of the day, he had to do what was best for him, and ultimately that was coming home.

When he wasn't working with the Warriors, which was only when they went on the road since flying still made his back pain flare up, he was building his real estate portfolio. He'd received his license the month before and had been working closely with Sherry, the Warriors' in-house realtor, to develop his client list.

Mitch was surprised when Berkley called him at the end of March asking for help finding Amelia a space to lease or buy for her gym.

Mitch had an idea for the perfect space, but he didn't want to present the option until he was one hundred percent certain it was possible. He didn't want to let anyone else down.

Unsurprisingly, Berkley had been hesitant to let him back into her life when he'd returned to the Mitten. Where her fiancé accepted him without question, shocking them all by asking him to be his best man, Berkley had taken her sweet time warming back up to him. He couldn't be entirely sure if it was because he had hurt her, or because he had hurt Lexie. Honestly, it was probably a bit of both.

And speaking of Lexie...

He'd been kicking himself every day for not letting her see him at the hospital after his last surgery. Who knows where they'd be now if he had. Would they be back together? Friends? Tentative acquaintances?

Anything would've been better than Mitch walking around this city with a hole in his life the exact size and shape of her. When he'd come back to Michigan, the first thing he should've done was shown up at her door, got down on his hands and knees, and begged her to take him back.

Looking back, Mitch wished he had fought harder for her. He wished he hadn't given up so easily when she told him it was over and kicked him out. When he got traded, the second after his agent called him, he should've gone to her, told her he loved her, that he knew she was scared and things were changing so fast, but she was *everything* to him, and that he would do whatever it took to make long-distance work.

Things might be different if he had simply *stayed* after that dinner with her parents. If he had only held his ground as he had every time before when she'd tried to push him away.

But it was too late now to go back and change anything.

All he could do now was beg for forgiveness and hope some piece of her still loved him.

"I'm pulling a page from the Brent Jean playbook," he said to the man himself. After Warriors practice was over that afternoon, Mitch, Brent, and Cole settled in a booth at a diner near the arena. Cole was next to him, Brent across the table, and both looked at him as though he'd spontaneously sprouted a second head.

"I'll bite," Cole said, turning his back to the wall to give Mitch his full attention. "What page would that be exactly? Hooking up with random waitresses in Nashville? Crashing a graduation ceremony? Or my personal favorite, throwing a surprise birthday party for a girl you don't even know?"

Mitch snorted and Brent tossed his straw wrapper at Cole's face. It bounced off the tip of his nose, and Cole yelled, "Hey!" indignantly.

"I'm talking about making a grand gesture," Mitch said. "But there will be no surprise parties involved."

"Who's the lucky lady?" Brent asked, unfazed by the content of this conversation.

"Are you finally going to pull your head out of your ass and fight for Lexie?" Cole asked excitedly.

"My head isn't in my ass," Mitch said defensively. "But yes. I'm finally ready."

"I should tell you that we know what happened between you two before your trade," Brent said.

Mitch stared at Brent, stunned. After a year, Lexie *finally* told Berkley? Why now?

"I didn't fight for her hard enough," he said quietly.

"Look," Brent said, "I've been there. When Berkley told me we were done, I should've stayed there and begged her to reconsider. Instead, I left, and we lost two weeks of time together."

"Brent, I appreciate the sentiment and all, but Lexie and I lost an entire year. It's not the same."

"It *is* the same," Brent insisted. "Unfortunately for us, we've chosen two of the most stubborn and independent women on the planet." Cole snorted, and Brent glared at him. "When they dig their feet in about something, there's nothing you can say or do at the moment that's going to change their minds. All I'm saying is you two need to sit down and have a conversation."

"That's not the worst idea, Jean," Mitch told him.

"But what makes you think she wants anything to do with you anyway?" Cole asked.

Mitch looked at Brent, who was no longer looking at them, but down at the table, wringing his hands in front of him. Mitch's hackles rose. Brent knew something, and Mitch was going to find out what.

"You tell me, Jean," he said, and Brent's gaze snapped up to him. "Something happened, didn't it?"

Brent heaved a world-weary sigh. "I've been sworn to secrecy, but because I love you both and genuinely think you're made for each other, I'm going to tell you. Berkley spent the last couple days at her apartment. Apparently, she spiraled on the anniversary of your trade."

Mitch experienced a bubble of joy in his chest that quickly popped. She was clearly not over him, which was a good sign, but he had hurt her badly, which was the last thing he ever wanted.

"Okay, so she's definitely still into you," Cole said. "What are you going to do? You should plan a romantic dinner at the loft or something."

"I considered that," Mitch said, "but ultimately decided that she wouldn't show up. I think I'm just going to show up at her condo and beg her to forgive me. Bring her flowers. Keep it low key, but show her I miss her and I fucked up."

"It's a bit on the small side in terms of grand gestures," Brent said, "but I like it. I'm proud of you for finally fighting for her. It's about fucking time."

"There's only one problem."

"What's that?" Cole asked.

"I don't know where she lives. I showed up at her building last week and there was some middle-aged couple living in her condo. I don't suppose either of you two know where she moved to?" He asked, gaze zeroing in on Brent.

"Goddamnit," Brent said. "Berk is going to kill me. I'll give you her new address if you promise me you'll lie and say you used your real estate connections to get it."

"Deal," Mitch said.

Mitch didn't want to make any rash decisions in the heat of the moment, so he waited a few days before going to Lexie's.

Actually, he waited nearly a week, choosing to make his move when the Warriors were up in Toronto for games three and four of the opening round of the playoffs. They'd split at home, winning game one handedly but dropping game two in overtime. Mitch wanted to travel with them, but unfortunately, his back had other ideas.

Thus, with the team out of town—and all of his friends with it—he decided tonight was the night.

But first, he had a phone call to make.

"Berk," he said when she answered.

"Mitchell," she replied, and he smiled.

"I need a favor."

"Okay..." she said, suspicious. That attorney's mind of hers was probably working overtime, wondering what he could possibly need in the middle of the day on a Tuesday.

"I need you to make sure Lexie is at home this evening. Around...six, let's say."

"I...what?" Berkley asked dumbly. "Why?"

"Because I'm going to surprise her."

"Jesus Christ," she said. "You idiots and your surprises. And tell me, Mitch. How the fuck do you know where she lives? I'm assuming by now you've learned she moved."

"I...used my real estate connections?" Mitch said, knowing as the words left his mouth that Berkley would never buy it.

And he was right.

"He told you, didn't he?" She said, resigned.

"Don't be mad at Brent," he said. "He just wanted to help me get my girl back."

Berkley was silent for long enough to make Mitch antsy.

"I'm not mad at him," she finally said. "But Lexie is going to kill me. And I have to ask...are you sure about this?"

"More sure than I've ever been of anything," he said without hesitation.

"I love you, Mitch, you know that. But I'd be remiss if I didn't go to bat for Lexie right now. She's my best friend, and you really hurt her. With that said...she misses you. She rarely talks about it, but I know she does. She hasn't dated anyone seriously since last summer, and even that was more a fling than anything. I think you two are the real deal, but be prepared for a fight because she's not going to make it easy on you."

"You do know *she* broke up with *me*, right?"

"And you're the one who left without saying goodbye."

"Fair enough," he said diplomatically, unwilling to argue the point further.

"Look, I know how things went down with you two. That she pushed you away. But with how her parents treated her, you *have* to know that leaving the way you did was going to fuck with her."

Mitch winced. He would never forgive himself for that, for treating her like someone disposable, exactly as her parents had for her entire life.

"I know. And I'll spend forever apologizing for it."

"That's all I'm asking."

"So are you going to help me or not?"

"Of course I am," she said, and they hatched a plan.

Three hours later, Mitch found himself at a local florist, hoping to pick out the most obscene bouquet of flowers he could manage.

"What says I'm sorry, I love you, and I miss you all rolled into one?" He asked.

The two women standing at the counter, who had been staring open-mouthed at him since he walked in and nearly knocked over an expensive-looking vase filled to the brim with an assortment of flowers, exchanged a look.

"Oh dear," the elder of the two said. "If you don't mind waiting, we'll whip up just the thing for you."

Mitch smiled, turning on the charm. "Perfect. Money is no object, either."

The women shared another glance and Mitch's smile turned brittle. He should've kept his mouth shut and asked Berkley for help, because these women were surely about to take him for everything he's worth.

Twenty minutes later, after a sizable chunk had been deducted from his checking account, Mitch walked out of the shop carrying a bouquet big enough to partially block his line of sight as he strode down the street toward his Suburban.

As he drove toward Lexie's new apartment, his mind flicked through all possible outcomes of this encounter.

Would she fall into his arms and confess that she had never stopped loving him?

Would she punch him in the face or kick him in the balls?

Would she even let him in the door?

It was the last one that scared him the most, and honestly, he wouldn't blame her. She had come all the way to Ann Arbor, made an attempt to start patching things up between them, and he had turned her away.

He was a fool, and he hoped like hell she was willing to overlook it.

By the time he pulled into the parking lot that wrapped around her building—some new construction clear across the city from where her old place was—his palms were clammy and nervous sweat beaded his hairline along his forehead and the nape of his neck.

"Alright, Frambough," he said out loud to himself. "Game time. Go in there and get your girl back."

And so, he stepped out of his Suburban and made his way into the lobby.

Brent had told him she lived on the eighth floor, so he pressed the UP button at the elevators and impatiently waited for the car to reach the main floor. When it did, he stepped inside and shifted the weight of the massive bouquet to his left side, pressing the eighth-floor button with the shaky fingers of his right hand.

When the elevator reached Lexie's floor, and the doors slid open, Mitch stood frozen in place.

He loved Lexie, and every moment of the last year spent away from her had been akin to living with half of his heart missing. Now was time to fight for her.

Except he was scared—terrified. If she told him to fuck off and slammed the door in his face, he might never recover.

But if he didn't try now, didn't show her he was willing to fight for her, then nothing would ever change. He would never know how she felt, if that spark between them was still there, simply waiting for one of them to reignite it.

With a deep breath, he strode into the hallway and toward Lexie's door.

CHAPTER TWENTY-THREE
Lexie

T uesday afternoon, Berkley called and invited herself over, saying she was lonely with Brent out of town and wanted to watch his game with Lexie at her place.

Lexie obliged, if only because she was about to head out of town for a week. This time, she was heading to sunny Florida, specifically 30A. It was an area that had been garnering a lot of buzz from the major Instagram influencers, and she and Amelia both agreed it was time to check it out for themselves.

Lexie had to admit, she was excited to see what all the fuss was about.

Ever since the month before, when she and Amelia had agreed to give this blogging thing the old college try, Lexie's life had changed drastically in some ways and stayed exactly the same in others.

She was still traveling all the time, now to places she *wanted* to go instead of spending a week in Cleveland trying to sign some nerdy college dropout who was apparently the next Steve Jobs, or four days in some backwoods town in West Virginia recruiting an agricultural whiz kid for a new sustainable farming outfit in Indiana.

Although that trip to West Virginia hadn't been all bad. She'd met the most wonderful older couple—Jack and Alice—who spent half their time on the farm they owned and the other half in Charleston, South Carolina, where Alice owned a renowned restaurant.

The two were so clearly in love it nearly made Lexie's heart clench with jealousy, and when she discovered that they had been separated for thirty years before finding their way back to each other, well...Lexie couldn't help thinking that maybe all was not completely lost for her and Mitch.

Some of the drastic changes had come in the form of the excessive amount of brand partnerships she'd been offered.

However, the first person to reach out, and the one person she didn't even have to think before saying yes to, was Brent.

Berkley's fiancé rarely called her, so the month before, once he'd heard about her and Amelia's decision to quit their jobs and make blogging a full-time gig, Lexie answered his call with shaky hands, and said, "What happened to Berk?"

Brent laughed. "Nothing happened. She's fine. Currently in her office studying for some final she's got next week. I offered to help, but she told me I'm too distracting."

Lexie heaved a sigh of relief and sat down on a barstool at her kitchen island. "So why are you calling me, then?"

"I'm formally offering you a job as a brand ambassador for FLEX."

"Yes."

"You haven't even let me lay out the terms!"

"Doesn't matter," Lexie said, pulling her phone away from her ear and tapping the speaker button so she could text Amelia. "We're in."

"We?" Brent asked.

"You don't think I'm doing this without Amelia, do you? She's the one opening a gym, after all."

"Oh, of course. She was going to be my next call, actually."

"Don't sweat it," Lexie said when her phone vibrated with Amelia's incoming reply. "I texted her and she's in. She also wants to know if she can buy some stock at wholesale to sell in her gym."

"Hell yeah," Brent said, and Lexie smiled at his excitement. "I can't believe how easy this was."

Lexie let out a laugh. "You really thought we'd turn you down?"

"I figured you'd at least make me work for it a bit," he said.

"I mean, in that case, we can hang up and try this again."

"Not necessary," Brent said. "I'll email you over the contracts."

"Send them to your fiancé, first. She is my attorney, after all."

Brent chuckled and said, "I'll bring them to her right now."

"What made you decide to switch from a single hired model to brand ambassadors, anyway?" She asked him.

"It was Berkley's idea, actually," he said, and Lexie wasn't surprised. His fiancé's mind for business was nearly as sharp as her legal mind. "When she started talking about you and Amelia and what you're doing with your blog and whatnot, she kept going on and on about how social media influencers are making brands all kinds of money these days, because they're the people that the general public look to for recommendations for everything. Print catalogs and billboard advertisements just don't get the same level of attention as they used to. The more I dug into it, the more I realized Berkley was right."

"She usually is," Lexie said.

Brent laughed. "True. But I started doing some of my own research, especially on Instagram. And when I realized I had spent my entire professional career as an influencer for hockey-related brands, and had been earning those companies money all this time, I figured it was time I took a piece of that pie."

"Whatever you need from us," Lexie told him. "We're in."

"It's all outlined in the contract," he said. "I'll have your attorney look it over once she emerges from her cave. I'm sure she'll call you later."

After that conversation, the offers came pouring in. Not that Lexie hadn't received several brand partnership offers before. Still, someone, somewhere must've found out she was now open to the possibility of accepting them, because they came in like a deluge.

She had decided to work with only good people, to represent brands that were socially and environmentally conscious, as well as ones based in the United States.

Right out of the gate, she and Amelia signed contracts with a mineral-based skincare and makeup company that planted a tree with every refill purchased, Grove Collaborative for household cleaners and supplies, and a clothing company that produced all of their products in America.

Her previous employers had been sad to see her go, even going so far as to offer a raise and less time on the road, but she couldn't be persuaded to stay. Deep in her bones, she knew this new path was the right one for her. Already, it was paying off in spades, and she and Amelia were just getting started.

But she was spending the evening with Berkley, watching hockey, and hoping she didn't see Mitch's face on the screen or his name mentioned at all during the broadcast.

She was putting the finishing touches on their evening snacks—a full charcuterie spread complete with cheeses, nuts, slices of fancy meats, jams, crackers, and an assortment of fruits and vegetables—when a knock came at her door.

As she made her way across the apartment, she grumbled, "Berkley, you know the code. I don't understand why you insist on knocking every single time you come—"

Her words died in her throat as she flung open the door.

And came face to face with Mitch *fucking* Frambough, an oversized bouquet of flowers weighing down his hands.

If his appearance hadn't rendered her momentarily mute and frozen in place, she would've slammed the door in his face, because to see him showing up here unannounced felt like a slap in the face would be the understatement of the century.

"Hey, Lex," he said, a sheepish grin turning up the corners of his lips.

"What the fuck are you doing here?"

He winced, and she'd be lying if she said it didn't feel good to hurt him. *Welcome to my hell, you bastard.*

"I wanted to see you."

"Oh *now* you wanted to see me? Have you lost your goddamn mind?"

"It's good to see you haven't changed any, Lex," he said. "Can I come in? We have a lot to talk about."

Lexie was so stunned she could do nothing but step aside as he crossed the threshold into her condo, uninvited and unwanted.

And still, she couldn't deny the way her body felt drawn to him, like it had before. He looked as at home in this new place as he did in the old one, taking up more space than anyone had the right to.

Wasn't she just thinking about that road trip to West Virginia, and Jack and Alice and the thirty years they'd spent apart, and how it made the year she and Mitch spent apart seem measly in comparison?

When confronted with him like this, dressed in his usual flannel and those jeans that hugged his thighs and perfect ass, Lexie nearly lost her mind and threw herself at him.

But as he stalked further into the condo, turned in a circle, and said, "Nice place," she violently shook her head, reminding herself that they were not the same people they were a year ago.

As desperate as she was to put space between them, while the only thing that would truly suffice would be miles, she settled for the ten by eight-foot granite slab that served as her kitchen island.

The quiet between them stretched thin and unending as Mitch twisted his hands in front of him, a nervous gesture Lexie had never seen on him before.

"I'm sorry about hockey," she blurted, unable to handle the silence.

Mitch shrugged. "Thanks. Hockey was everything to me. You know...until it wasn't."

"What changed?" She asked despite already knowing the answer.

"You. You changed everything for me, Lex."

You changed everything for me, too, she thought.

But God, how did they come back from the last year? From everything weighing the air between them? She was still so *mad* at him, her heart still badly bruised in her chest. With him standing in front of her, once again in her space, trying to work his way back into her life, she desperately wanted to say fuck it and run into his arms.

He would let her, too; his showing up here today proved that.

But if she didn't stand up for herself now? After how he left? After how he refused to see her when she tried to visit him in Ann Arbor?

She'd never forgive herself–or him–if she gave in so easily.

"What do you want, Mitch?" She asked, infusing her voice with as much venom as she could muster, even though her insides were tangled in knots that would take days to unravel.

"I told you, I wanted to see you. And we have to talk."

"The time for talking was, oh, I don't know..." she said, tipping her wrist up to check her imaginary watch, "a year ago. Or maybe five months ago when I came to see you and you sent me away like a fucking coward."

"Lex," he said, exasperated.

"Stop calling me that! You don't get to call me that anymore. You lost that privilege the day you left."

"Lexie, please, just listen to me."

"No, you are going to listen to me." She took a deep breath and finally cracked the lid on that little box she'd kept buried deep in her heart since he left. All of the hurt, the anger, and the *embarrassment*, spilled out with her words. "Do you have any idea what I've been through since you left? What I've had to deal with? You cut off contact with everyone, Mitch. Your teammates, that's one thing. It's a job and you have to adapt. I get it. Trying to fit into a new room has to be hard. What you did was shitty, but I can understand. But I'm not your fucking teammate, and I was *never* part of the job. The way you just walked away without a backward glance and left me to pick up the pieces was so cowardly it makes me sick. You broke my heart. I spent months after you left crying. You made me feel so stupid for loving you that I suffered in silence so I wouldn't have to admit it to anyone and feel ashamed. I've just barely managed to put myself back together, and now you walk in here acting like everything is fine? It doesn't work that way."

"How could I break your heart when you never even gave it to me?" He asked, eyes on the floor.

The fact that he had the gall to ask her that, after *everything* she had given him...

"You're so fucking dense if you honestly believe you didn't have it the whole time," she said. "Remember how I told you that you were either going to be the best or worst thing that ever happened to me?"

Mitch, who still couldn't be bothered to meet her eyes, mumbled, "Yes."

"I figured out which one it was the moment you left without saying goodbye to me. Now get the fuck out."

His gaze snapped up to hers then, the first time their eyes met since she opened her door ten minutes before, and she'd be damned if it didn't make her a little weak in the knees. That single-minded focus, those bright green eyes that always cut right to her soul, she nearly hurtled the counter and threw herself into his arms.

But she wouldn't, *couldn't*, make this easy for him.

She felt a lot like a feral cat at that moment: malnourished, entirely forgotten, and ready to lash out at the next person who tried reaching for her.

And here Mitch was, extending that olive branch she'd been so desperate for during the deepest, darkest parts of the last year.

Only now, she didn't want it.

"Lexie..." his voice cracked, but she refused to cave.

"Seriously, Mitch. Get. The. Fuck. Out."

Mitch half-turned, but stalled and spun to face her again, jaw set in what she recognized as grim determination.

"Not until you listen to me. I know I fucked up, and I'm going to spend every moment from here on out making it up to you. Whatever you want, I'll do it. Do you want me to get on my hands and knees right here and beg you? Just say the word. But the one thing I'm not going to do is let you run away again. You ran away a year ago, and yeah, I didn't fight for you like I should have. I let you push me away instead of holding on for dear life. But that's not going to happen again. I'm here for good, and I'm not letting you get away again. I refuse."

This time he fully turned away from her and walked toward the door. Lexie trailed after him like a puppy, telling herself it was because she wanted to make sure he actually left and not because some quiet, hopeful part of her heart wanted to believe what he was saying. When he set his hand on the doorknob, he looked back at her over his shoulder and said, "Or have you already forgotten? We're endgame, baby."

And then he was gone as quickly as he came, and Lexie rushed to where her phone was resting on the kitchen island, dialing Berkley's number with shaking fingers.

"Hey, Lex," Berkley said.

"I'm going to kill you," Lexie responded, then hung up.

It came as no shock that Berkley let herself into her apartment twenty minutes later.

Lexie greeted her with a glass of wine and said, "You made good time."

"I didn't tell him where you live," Berkley said, accepting the glass and taking a large mouthful. "Brent did."

"But you did help him make sure I'd be home tonight, didn't you? Were you even planning on coming over?"

"Of course I was. As soon as he left. And look...I made it!"

Lexie lifted a chunk of cheese from the charcuterie board and chucked it at Berkley, who ducked out of the way.

"I hate you," Lexie said.

Berkley didn't say anything, simply gathered the cutting board loaded with snacks and carried it into Lexie's living room. She came back a moment later for her wine, dragging Lexie along behind her.

No words were exchanged as they nestled into the couch and turned on the Warriors' game.

It was late in the second period, a full bottle and a half of wine gone, the charcuterie board picked nearly clean, when Berkley finally spoke.

"It didn't go well, did it?" Berkley asked, walking around the counter and setting her wine glass down so she could wrap Lexie in a hug.

"We talked, I yelled, I told him to get the fuck out, he reminded me we're endgame. Same shit, different day."

Because she and Mitch had been through this song and dance before, hadn't they? Every single time things between them had gotten too serious, she'd done everything in her power to push him away. And he kept coming back, kept holding on, holding out hope that maybe one day she'd get her shit together and love him back the way a man like him deserved to be loved. With her whole heart, her whole mind, body, and soul.

It should have been painfully obvious to him after their disastrous dinner with her parents that she couldn't, and never would be, that girl for him. That she was entirely incapable of giving that kind of love to someone. How could she, when she had spent her entire life without receiving it?

"Things are better this way," she told Berkley quietly. "He just doesn't know it yet."

"Lexie..." Berkley said, and held up a hand when Lexie tried to cut her off. "What was it you told me when Brent and I broke up? You have to decide here and now to either find a way to trust him and love him how he deserves, and let him love you back, or you move on. This limbo you've got yourself caught in isn't hurting just you anymore. It's hurting all of us."

"I can't love him like he deserves," Lexie said.

"I know you think that, but I'm calling bullshit. You've been loving him, Lexie. For the better part of two years. Hell, since you met him. I understand if you want to keep running scared. You know how hard I fought falling for Brent. But at the end of the day...he's the love of my life. I can't picture living without him, and I'm willing to bet you feel the same about Mitch. That's why you've been miserable since he left.

"So you decide here and now, Lex. You keep running, or you stop and let him catch you."

"I don't know how."

"Having a legitimate, meaningful conversation with him without either one of you ambushing the other would be a good place to start, in my opinion."

"I'm just not ready to forgive him yet, Berk," she said, burying her face in her hands. When she spoke again, her voice was muffled. "It's been so long, and yeah I played a part in the breakup. Hell, I instigated the breakup. But he didn't even try to fight for me, didn't try to say goodbye." She whipped her head up as the tears started flowing. "He wouldn't even see me when I went to Ann Arbor," she choked out.

Berkley scooted closer and wrapped her arms around Lexie, much in the same way Lexie had done for her the night she and Brent broke up. "I know it's not easy, giving your heart to someone. But other than the shitty way he left Detroit, there's nothing about Mitch that tells me he wouldn't take care of it. That he wouldn't protect you with everything he has. And I think you know that."

Lexie could only nod, slanting sideways so she could rest her head on Berkley's lap.

The thing was, she *did* know that. From the moment she met him, that first night when he stuck around after their hookup was interrupted to take care of Berkley, Lexie had known Mitch was one of the good ones. The best one. And somehow, someway, that man had fallen in love with her, and still loved her despite the time and distance, plus the baggage she carried.

"He hurt me so badly, Berk. I haven't always been open about my childhood, but being abandoned like that? It's a trigger for me. And he knows that. I've told him all about my parents, and about that Christmas they left me alone, and all the other times they'd deposit me in some rented McMansion while they went off making money and ignoring me. I just...being left like that? By someone who promised to love me and never hurt me? It sucked."

"You pushed him away first," Berkley said quietly.

Lexie choked on a laugh. Leave it to Berkley to call her out when she was baring her soul.

It's what made her the best friend Lexie had ever had.

"I know that," Lexie replied, resigned.

"Look, I know nothing is going to change overnight," Berkley said. "But...give him a chance. I can tell he's serious about this, and he deeply regrets the way he left. Do you think Brent would've let him back into his life so easily if he thought Mitch would do it again? No, he wouldn't. It's not going to be easy. But just...try."

Lexie had never believed in soulmates, and made her feelings on the subject of love abundantly clear to anyone who would listen. But Mitch made her want those things. And more than that, he made her believe in those things, and believe that she could have them.

With him.

Even after a year apart, and all the casual hookups and nights she spent trying to drink his memory away, she still missed him in that bone-deep way, like half of her had up and walked away.

Finally, she sat up and wiped her tears with the sleeves of her sweater.

"I can try."

CHAPTER TWENTY-FOUR
Mitch

The Warriors were about to play their biggest game of the twenty-first century, and Mitch was watching from the bench.

Over the course of the last few months during the Warriors playoff run, he'd gotten used to being on the sidelines. It still stung, but generally speaking, he was happy to be around the game that had been his entire life for so long.

Nights like tonight, when it was game six of the Final, and the Warriors were one win away from bringing the Stanley Cup back to Detroit, Mitch would give anything to be suiting up with the guys.

The Warriors had a three games to two series lead over the Colorado Chargers, and each of the first five games had been a low-scoring affair. Thankfully, Brandon Roberts had been standing on his head, stopping shots that lesser goalies would've missed, but unfortunately, the Chargers' goalie had also been a brick wall.

"Score early, score often," Coach said once the team was dressed, each player seated at their stall.

Mitch and the Warriors waited for him to continue, to make some grand, Herb Brooks-worthy pregame speech.

Instead, Coach turned on his heel and walked down the tunnel.

"Uhh...alright boys," Jordan Dawson, the Warriors captain, said awkwardly, standing and strapping his helmet on. "Let's go to work."

There was no fanfare as the group of men made their way from the locker room and down that long red carpet in the direction of the ice. The closer they got, the louder the crowd noise became. And when Jordan skated onto the ice, the rest of the team following swiftly behind him, it rose to a crescendo.

There was nothing like the atmosphere of a hockey game, especially at the professional level, and it was difficult to explain without having experienced it firsthand. The earthquaking roar of the fans when a goal was scored, the collective gasps, boos, and yells of outrage for big hits, missed opportunities, penalties, and fights.

And during the playoffs? *All* of those emotions were drastically heightened.

Mitch missed being on the ice, being the one the crowds cheered for, but he was happy to be here nonetheless.

The second the puck dropped, Mitch knew it was going to be a hard-fought battle, a win earned by pure grit and physicality. The Chargers didn't allow the Warriors to demonstrate any of their usual finesse with the puck, instead using their brute force and big bodies to create choppy gameplay full of starts and stops.

Within the first period, each team had fifteen penalty minutes, five of those from major penalties, when one of the Warriors' fourth liners got into a little fisticuffs with a Chargers' defenseman.

The game progressed the same way through the first half of the second period until around the twelve-minute mark when Rat scored on a breakaway, teeing up a shot on a beautiful pass from Grey. Had anyone but those two attempted to make that play, the game would still be scoreless.

After the excitement and brutality of the first period, things settled down in the second, and the Warriors took a 1-0 lead into the locker room at the second intermission.

Coach stood in front of his team and scrubbed a hand down his face. "Is there anything more stressful than only being up a goal going into the third period?"

"Yeah," Brent said. "Being down a goal going into the third period."

His teammates laughed, some of the tension in the room easing.

"There's nothing I can say right now that you don't already know, that you haven't already heard," Coach said. "We have twenty minutes. The next goal, whichever way it goes, is going to be the most important one in this game. Let's win this one at home, okay?"

The Warriors nodded and mumbled their agreement, the game clock on the wall showing less than two minutes until the puck dropped on the third period.

When they trotted back down the tunnel, the fans in the stands were quieter, more subdued than they had been at the start of the game. They were all on the edges of their seats, hoping and praying that the game ended in favor of the home team.

And Mitch had a good feeling it would, when a scant two minutes into the period, Brent beat the Chargers goalie high on his glove side, the lamp behind the net burning red, the goal horn lost in the deafening roar of the Warriors fans as they lost their collective minds over the goal.

Mitch couldn't help but grin when, moments later, the arena broke into a "BRENT JEAN" chant.

The Warriors were flying high for the next ten minutes, zipping around the ice, blocking shots, stealing pucks, and laying big hits on opponents.

Until the clock ticked under five minutes remaining, and a few seconds later, traffic in front caught Roberts blind and the Chargers snuck a goal past him.

Two-goal leads really were the worst in hockey, and the Warriors' had been cut in half.

Mitch had played hockey long enough, and been involved in enough close games like this one to rarely—if ever—let the stress and sense of urgency get to him.

But tonight, he wasn't playing, and he'd be damned if he didn't have to ball his hands into fists at his sides to keep from chewing on his nails as those final seconds ticked off the clock.

A late whistle stopped play in the Warriors' defensive zone, setting up a face-off in the circle to Roberts' right with under a minute to play.

Arguably, this was the biggest face-off of the game, and Mitch hoped to God that Cole had one last win in him.

Everything seemed to move in slow motion as the Warriors and Chargers moved into their positions around the face-off circle, Cole's back to Roberts as he hinged forward, angling his stick in preparation of the puck dropping and sweeping it behind him to Brent.

Fifty-five seconds stood between them and a championship.

Mitch blinked as the ref dropped the puck onto the face-off dot, staring in horror as the Chargers' player won the duel and tipped it behind him to a teammate, their goalie rushing toward the bench in the same instant to give them an extra skater.

The extra skater crossed into the Warriors' zone and zipped into the corner, where the player on the blue line who had the puck attempted a long, cross-ice pass to him.

But Cole was there to cut it off.

In the span of another blink, Cole skated into the neutral zone, narrowly avoiding an open-ice check from a Chargers' player. He reached center ice and slid a soft shot on net.

The crowd noise faded to a dull buzz as Mitch's eyes darted from the puck to the game clock, hands curled around the edges of the half-wall in front of him, knuckles blanched white.

The puck sailed across the goal line and into the empty net.

Mitch was on the ice before the goal horn even sounded, his dress shoes sliding all over as he rushed toward Cole.

"Mitch!" Coach was yelling behind him. "Get your ass back here!"

Mitch would do no such thing, and a moment later, with thirty-five seconds still on the clock, the entire Warriors bench, save the coaches who weren't Mitch, was gathered at center ice, a mob of cheers and tears.

"Hey!" Jordan yelled above them all. "We're not done yet! Get your asses back to the bench if you weren't on the ice for that goal."

Grins stretching each of the Warriors' faces comically wide, they all skated back to the bench, Mitch following slowly behind, his grin more sheepish than outright ecstatic as Coach shot him a glare.

When the final buzzer sounded, sealing the Warriors' victory, and all the players hopped over the wall, mitts and helmets and sticks flying through the air in celebration, Mitch remained on the bench, taking it all in.

Back when he and Lexie had been together, there was a weekend stretch when Detroit got hit with a monster winter storm. Mitch had a few days off, and though Lexie was supposed to fly to California for work, the snow had all flights grounded.

"What should we watch?" She asked one morning as Mitch brought their mugs of coffee into the living room in his condo and sat on the couch, holding his arm out to let her curl into his side.

"Whatever you want," he said, dropping a kiss to the top of her head.

Lexie started scrolling through Hulu, talking quietly to herself as she paused on and quickly discarded numerous shows and movies.

"Oh my God," she said. "I haven't seen *One Tree Hill* in forever."

"I've never seen it," he told her. "What's it about?"

"It's one of those older CW dramas. It's a high school basketball drama. Well, it starts that way anyway. It's one of the best shows ever, and we're watching it."

Mitch shrugged and settled in, fully preparing himself for some cheesy chick flick that he would endure for Lexie's sake.

In the end, he was pleasantly surprised to find that *One Tree Hill* was actually an incredible show, if a bit unrealistic. But it made him think about a lot of things, take a deep long look at who he was as a person and what he brought to the world.

There was one line in particular that had stuck with him since then, and at this moment, when the Warriors were on the ice celebrating, their families having joined them, the crowded arena going nuts in their seats, that Mitch was reminded of:

When all of your dreams come true, who's the one you want standing next to you?

Not that all of Mitch's dreams were coming true.

Not in the way he had always hoped, anyway.

To be even a small part of winning a championship was an amazing accomplishment for him when, seven months ago, he hadn't even been sure he'd be able to walk again, much less be involved in the game of hockey in any way.

Knowing his name would finally be stamped on one of those silver rings alongside guys like Brent and Jordan Dawson was an incredible feeling, but also bittersweet at the same time.

He would've preferred to have played, naturally.

But coaching was just as rewarding, and to be living this moment was nothing short of a miracle.

The only thing that was missing was Lexie.

She was the one he wanted next to him when all of his dreams came true.

Since their showdown in her apartment nearly two months ago, he'd left her alone in the sense that he hadn't tried to ambush her again.

But that didn't mean he was letting her forget his presence.

Flowers, chocolates and other candies, plus a selection of travel-inspired gifts had been sent to her condo regularly. Anytime Brent and Berkley went out, Mitch turned it into a group hang, knowing Berkley would drag Lexie along.

They kept their distance for the most part, but he didn't miss how every single time he looked at her, she was already looking back.

He would make her forgive him and win her back if it killed him.

Once the Cup and Conn Smythe trophy had been presented, and the on-ice celebration died down, the Warriors players and the team's various staff proceeded to the locker room, where they pulled out bottles of champagne, passed around cigars, and took turns holding and posing for pictures with the Cup.

And exactly like old times, Mitch yelled, "Loft party tonight! Attendance is mandatory!"

A cheer rose from the guys, and after that, everyone hurriedly showered and changed, preparing to head out into the night and continue this celebration away from prying eyes.

Because Mitch didn't have to go through the whole post-game shower routine anymore, he changed out of his suit and dipped out ahead of everyone else, calling Berkley as he headed toward the parking lot.

"Hi, Mitch!" She squealed in his ear. "I didn't catch you on the ice, but congratulations! I know it's not the same as if you were playing, but I'm proud of you."

Mitch's heart swelled. He adored this girl, and was thankful she and Brent had found each other, and thankful she was still in *his* life after everything. "Thanks, Berk. Look...where are you? I'm having a loft party and I was going to see if you wanted to help me get set up?"

"Sure!" Berkley said. "Can I bring Lexie and Amelia? Oh, and Reece and Harper are around here somewhere."

He stopped listening after she said Lexie's name, knowing what the answer would be. "Hell yes. The more the merrier. I'll meet you in Greektown in ten."

"Deal," she said and hung up, already in a conversation with someone in the background on her end.

Mitch hadn't been to the loft since he'd returned to Michigan, so he wasn't sure what he was in for upon stepping inside. He knew for a fact Brent and the guys had never used the space, so Mitch mentally prepared himself for dust and cobwebs, possibly some vermin, and an empty bar.

So when he pulled open the door and flipped the lights on fifteen minutes later, Berkley and her crew in tow, he actually gasped.

Not only was the loft free from dust, dirt, and pesky rats, the bar was stocked and gleaming, the couches and chairs clean and arranged in their normal conversational groupings. The game tables in the back had been wiped down and laden with empty solo cups in preparations for the night's festivities.

Everything was perfect, as though Mitch had never left.

He looked at Berkley, mouth agape. "You did this?"

She nodded. "Brent and I thought—hoped—we'd end up back here one of these days. I wasn't even a little bit surprised when you called me as we were leaving the arena."

Mitch walked up to her and scooped her off her feet in a crushing bear hug. "Thank you," he whispered, then set her down.

"I guess the only thing left to do now is party!" he said.

Within an hour, the loft was packed wall to wall with Warriors players, staff, coaches, brass, friends, and families.

Mitch set up camp near the bar, as he always did during loft parties, and watched the night unfold in front of him. On more than one occasion, a female approached him and made him an offer a weaker man wouldn't be able to refuse.

It had been an embarrassingly long time since Mitch last had sex. Like, before his injury. It wasn't lost on him how easy it would be to take one of those women into the bathrooms and fuck their brains out, then send them on their merry way.

But he couldn't, because the only woman he wanted was the one woman who had been going out of her way to avoid him all night.

After he turned down a fifth proposition in less than an hour, Mitch decided it was time to change that.

Lexie was at the beer pong tables playing flip cup with Amelia and Reece, one of Berkley's old law school classmates, when Mitch stalked up to her and pressed the front of his body along her back. He had to breathe deeply to keep his dick from reacting to her nearness. All that did was fill his nose with that cinnamon and vanilla scent of hers, and he knew he was a lost cause.

He took it as a good sign when she leaned into him, so he bent his head close to her ear and whispered, "Can we talk?"

She glanced at him over her shoulder, pupils blown from alcohol consumption, nearly gobbling up that gold-flecked hazel he loved so much, and nodded.

The second his hand closed around her wrist, he nearly let go, the contact sending a jolt up his arm, a sensation Mitch couldn't deny he had missed desperately since the last time he'd touched her. Tugging her across the space, he led her to a dimly lit corner in the back, far enough away from the noise and the crowds that they wouldn't be bothered or overheard.

Lexie sat down in an overstuffed chair and crossed her arms and legs. *So it was going to be like that, huh?* Mitch thought.

"Have you been getting my gifts?" he blurted.

She nodded. "I've been out of town a lot, but yes, I have them."

"What, no 'thank you'?"

"I'm not going to thank you for attempting to buy my affection, Mitch."

Embarrassment heated his cheeks as he mentally smacked himself.

There were women out there who would give anything to be courted by a professional athlete. They were the kind of women who looked at men like Mitch and only saw the dollar signs he represented, not what kind of man he was.

And he knew Lexie, knew her well enough to know that she certainly didn't fall into that category. So why had he been treating her as such?

Her parents had spent her entire life using her and attempting to buy her love and affection, and here he was, pulling the same shit.

He was such a dumbass.

So finally, he said, "Tell me what I need to do then. Tell me what it's going to take to get you to stop looking at me like that."

Her thick, perfect eyebrows drew together, and she said, "Like what?"

"Like you want to rip my balls from my body."

Lexie snorted, and Mitch relaxed a bit. If she was laughing at him, that was a step in the right direction.

"I just need some time," she said quietly. "You leaving was...hard. And I know I told you it was over and made you leave that night we had dinner with my parents but..."

She swallowed hard, and Mitch could tell she was at war with herself on whether or not to voice her thoughts.

"But what?" He prompted.

"You were the one person, other than Berkley, who knew how bad it was for me growing up. How the only way I could get my parents attention was by acting out, and even then all it ever accomplished was getting us moved to a new city. They didn't love or care about me or even really want me." She lifted her hand and swiped at her eyes, but Mitch didn't dare move a muscle, no matter how badly he wanted to cradle her in his arms and promise her he'd never leave her again. "You were the one person who promised never to go, who promised to spend every day proving to me what a gift I am. Those were your exact words, Mitch." She lifted her head to meet his eyes then, and for the first time, he truly understood how hard this last year had been for her. How broken she was.

And it was all his fault.

The strength of this woman, after everything her parents put her through, to be sitting across from him now...it was awe-inspiring.

"I am so sorry, Lexie," he said. "There's no excuse. Nothing I could ever say will erase the last year."

"Why did you do it?"

It was then he realized that not a single person had asked him that in the months since he'd come back to Michigan. It had been so easy to slip back into his old life and to be around his old friends.

"I was angry," he said. "At you, about the trade, at everything. I didn't know how to fight for you from across the country. At the time, everything felt so broken that it just made sense to cut ties, burn every bridge, and move to LA with a clean slate.

"Leaving your apartment that night after dinner with your parents was the hardest thing I've ever done. I wanted nothing more than to fall to the ground at your feet and beg you not to push me away. But you're so damn stubborn, and that night had already been so emotionally draining on both of us. We never talked about it, and I know how mad you were at me for talking to your parents the way I did but...I'm not going to apologize for it. I will *never* apologize for having your back. I would've done and said a lot worse to them if I felt the need to. The way they spoke to you, *about* you, even with you sitting mere feet away from them...it still makes me angry. And the worst part was that you just sat there and took it. I was almost disappointed in you. That you, this stubborn, independent, beautiful woman who found the strength to love me back when you'd grown up with those people as parents, didn't even bother to fight for yourself. You let them walk all over you, and chew you up and spit you out just like they'd been doing for your entire life. I was disappointed, and I was heartbroken for you.

"And when you finally sparked to life, and your anger wasn't even directed at them but at *me*?" He said, stabbing a finger into his chest. "That was the moment I realized how deep their brainwashing of you had gone. I just needed some time to figure my shit out. And let you figure out yours. And I tried to talk to you after that all went down, but you ignored every attempt. What more could I have done?"

Lexie studied him for several long moments, and he had to work hard not to squirm under her gaze. He felt stripped bare when she looked at him like that, as though she could see beneath his skin and bones right to the heart of him. It was an uncomfortable sensation, but for this woman, hell, he'd run around this loft naked if she asked.

"I guess I understand why you did what you did," she finally said. "But it doesn't mean I just magically forgive you. Everyone else seems to be happy you're home and comfortable with moving on as though nothing happened, but...I can't do that. I'm just not there yet."

"So where do we go from here?" He asked.

"I don't know, Mitch," she said. "I still just need time."
And then she got up and walked away from him.
Time? He could give her that.
But she never said she needed space.

CHAPTER TWENTY-FIVE
Lexie

Three days after the Warriors won their Stanley Cup clinching game, Berkley had transitioned fully from WAG mode to wedding mode. And Lexie was along for the ride.

With the wedding taking place at the Jean family cabin in New York, Berkley had been forced to delegate a lot of the planning to her future mother-in-law, a task that rankled her nerves to no end.

At that moment, they were sitting in the bridal shop, Lexie, Amelia, Berkley's sister Jessica, and Brent's sister Mackenzie all seated on a plush white couch, each with a flute of bubbly balanced in one hand while they picked at trays of hors d'oeuvres with the other. Berkley was in the changing room, her voice carrying over to them as she yelled at someone on the other end of the phone about table linens.

"Someone should go save her," Jessica said.

"As her sister, that's *your* job," Lexie told her.

"Actually, as her maid of honor, I think it's yours."

The kid had a point, and a moment later, Lexie made a beeline for Berkley. Without preamble, she pushed open the fitting room door to find

Berkley clad in only her underwear and a nude bra, face beet red as she argued with whoever was on the other end of the line.

Lexie snatched the phone from Berkley's hand, said to the woman on the other end, "Berkley is going to have to call you back," and promptly hung up.

"What the fuck?" Berkley said, her fury almost comical given how tiny she was.

"We're here for dress fittings," Lexie said calmly. "Now get your cute little ass in that dress and come out here with the rest of us. We don't have all day."

Truthfully, they had nothing but time. It was nearing the end of June, and Berkley was on summer vacation from classes. Since she was now working part-time, her schedule at the law firm was light enough that she'd managed to take all of July and August off in preparation for the wedding and honeymoon.

The blogging had taken off in a major way, and Amelia had finally opened her gym the week before. MissFitness was already wildly successful, having signed up forty clients in the first three days alone. Mitch had found Amelia the perfect spot, which, much to Lexie's dismay, ended up being the ground floor of his loft building.

Apparently, Mitch had been planning to convert the entire building into usable space for years. His hectic work schedule was the only reason why it had remained abandoned, out-dated apartments and storage space for so long. After consulting with the city commissioner and zoning board, he was approved for a commercial leasing license.

When he first approached Amelia about it—naturally cutting her a ridiculously cheap deal on the rent—she flat out refused. But once she and Lexie sat down and talked about it, and Berkley explained the contract she'd drawn up, they both agreed they couldn't have asked for a better space. It took some time to turn the former building lobby into a gym, but Lexie couldn't deny...it was perfect. Exactly what Amelia had envisioned, and they had Mitch to thank for it.

With the Jean-Daniels wedding happening in New York, Lexie was using that as an opportunity to head out east before the wedding and bum around NYC, and then spend some time exploring upstate afterward. She and Amelia had planned a fun series for their socials and the blog about the five boroughs in NYC, and Lexie couldn't wait to get started.

Working for herself had a lot of perks; the biggest of which was that she could make her own schedule.

As for Mackenzie and Jessica...

Well, Jess was on summer vacation as well, about to enter her final year of college before earning her teaching degree, and staying with Mackenzie in the city for the summer while she worked with one of the youth groups in the area.

And Mackenzie was still keeping FLEX from going off the rails while her big brother did his job winning the city championships. There had been talk of her enrolling in some college courses to expand her knowledge on business, financing, and marketing.

Her brother was a fount of information on those subjects, but Mackenzie didn't want to always rely on him for help.

"It's *our* company," she had told Lexie and Berkley over drinks one night. "I need to start acting like it."

All that was to say there was nothing in the world any of them *needed* to be doing that was more important than this.

"That dumb bitch wanted to send ivory table linens to the cabin for the wedding," Berkley said with an eye roll. "I specifically asked for *cream*."

Lexie huffed out a sigh through her nose. "I thought Sandra was handling all that bullshit?"

"She is, but somehow that company misplaced her number and called me instead. As if I don't have enough to worry about."

Lexie settled her hands on Berkley's bare shoulders, forcing her friend to tip her head back and meet her gaze. "It's going to be fine, Berk. I'm giving you two minutes to call Sandra and explain to her what's going on so she can fix it. Then you're putting that dress on and coming out of this cubicle. Deal?"

Berkley heaved a deep breath. "Deal."

Lexie rejoined the group outside a moment later. "Everything okay?" Mackenzie asked.

"Yeah. It was just something dumb about table linens. She's calling your mom to sort it and then she'll be out."

And when Berkley finally emerged from the changing room...

Lexie wasn't a crier, but tears sprung to her eyes as Berkley walked out and stepped up onto the dais set in front of a curving half-wall of lighted mirrors.

"Holy shit," Mackenzie whispered. "My brother is going to lose his mind."

Berkley looked at her future sister-in-law over her shoulder and winked. "That's the plan."

The sweetheart neckline and corset bodice left Berkley's arms, shoulders, neck, and chest bare. It was covered in lace and beads, with a row of tiny buttons up the back. There was a sash of silk cinching at Berkley's waist before a full skirt of silk overlaid with tulle fell to her feet.

It was stunning, one hundred percent Berkley, and perfect for an outdoor summer wedding.

"You're beautiful, Berk," Amelia said, hopping up from her seat to give Berkley a hug.

"My brother is a lucky man," Mackenzie said. "I don't know why you put up with him, honestly."

"I love him," Berkley said simply, turning back the mirror and lifting the skirt of her dress so she could twirl and watch it balloon out around her. "I feel like a princess."

Lexie stood and poured another glass of bubbly, walking over to Berkley and Amelia and handing one to Berkley. Jessica and Mackenzie soon joined them.

"No, Berk," Lexie said, raising her glass into the air. "You're a *queen*. And I hope Brent treats you as such every day for the rest of your life."

"To Brent and Berk," Jessica said, lifting her own glass.

"To Brent and Berk," they echoed, clinking glasses and giggling.

Berkley drained hers and handed it off to Mackenzie, clapping her hands together as she surveyed the group. "Okay, your turn!"

The girls groaned collectively, but skittered off to their changing rooms to don their dresses one last time before the wedding.

Berkley allowed the girls to each pick their style of dress, as long as they were all in the same color. Amelia, Mackenzie, and Jessica would be wearing navy. And Lexie, as the maid of honor, had the honor of wearing burgundy.

As she shimmied into her dress, which was floor length with a modest slit up the side, held up by two skinny straps with swoops of fabric that fell down her shoulders, she found herself wondering what a Lexie Monroe wedding would even look like.

Somewhere tropical, probably. A destination wedding, where she could keep the invite list small and bury her toes in the sand along some crystal clear body of water while she looked up at the face of the man she loved, was certainly her idea of a good time.

A knock at the door jarred her from her daydream. "Lexie, c'mon. Did you fall asleep in there?"

"No, I'm fine. I'll be right out."

She hurriedly zipped up her dress and adjusted the straps, exiting the changing room, the images of her dream wedding still clinging to the edges of her subconscious.

Because standing across from her in front of all their family and friends, exchanging vows and rings and a kiss to seal it all?

Lexie pictured Mitch.

Later that evening, after the dress fittings were done and the girls had driven to Novi and spent several hours wandering Twelve Oaks, Lexie found herself at Brent and Berkley's, enjoying a glass of wine with Berkley while Brent finished up some administrative work related to FLEX.

"We're going to head into the city for dinner and drinks with some of the guys," Berkley told her. "Do you want to join us?"

"Who exactly is 'some of the guys'?"

"Cole, Jordan and his wife, Naomi, Rat and Grey. You know, the usual."

"No Mitch?"

"I don't know if he's coming," Berkley said, and Lexie studied her face for any hint of deception, finding none. "He was invited of course, but he hasn't responded. He might be in Ann Arbor."

The chances of her running into Mitch tonight seemed small, but truthfully she could use a low key night out with Berkley and the Warriors, and she wasn't about to let the possibility of seeing him ruin her fun.

"Okay, I'm down," she said.

"Down for what?" Brent asked as he entered the kitchen and dropped a kiss on the top of Berkley's head.

"Coming out with you guys tonight."

"Oh shit yeah," Brent said, lifting his wrist to check the time. "We should probably get going if we want to meet everyone in time for dinner."

Lexie tapped her phone screen alive and noted it was nearing eight o'clock. She and Berkley simultaneously drained their wine glasses while Brent laced up his shoes and grabbed his keys.

They reached the city and arrived in front of the Hockeytown Cafe. The second Brent stepped out of the vehicle, he was swarmed. The man *had* scored the Stanley Cup-winning goal, after all. The attention was well-deserved. Berkley, who usually got annoyed when fans accosted them in public, gave him a small smile and a kiss on the cheek before she and Lexie made their way inside.

And when Lexie spotted that tell-tale backward ball cap with thick, dark blond hair curling along the nape of a strong, tanned neck, she wasn't even surprised.

For all her bullshit about not wanting to see him, she couldn't ignore the bubble of excitement that formed in her chest. This was a low-stakes social situation, where she could spend the evening avoiding him exactly as she had done at the loft after the Warriors won the Cup.

And if they did find a quiet moment together?

Lexie would be okay with that, too.

They walked up to the table, and Berkley immediately made her rounds, hugging everyone before plopping down next to Mitch. Lexie, having zero desire to be anywhere near him given the way her body still reacted to his presence, chose a spot across the table next to Cole, where she immediately engaged him in some benign conversation about the crowd outside and why they had chosen the Hockeytown Cafe of all places.

"This is a beer and pizza kind of night, Lex," he said. "Where else would we go but here?"

"I can think of about thirty other places in the city that serve those two things and aren't filled to the rafters with crazed hockey fans."

"Yeah but where's the fun in that? We want to celebrate with our city."

"Fair enough," she said.

Brent finally made it inside, completing the group, and they set about ordering drinks and food, the table dissolving into smaller conversations as the beer flowed.

Lexie was surprised to find that, for the most part, the other patrons in the bar left them alone. Sure, there was the occasional camera flash, and every once in a while, some brave soul would approach, asking for autographs from everyone, including Mitch, which always made Lexie smile when his face lit up like he was surprised these people cared about him.

His playing career may be over, but Mitch was an important part of this championship run and, before the trade, had been a big part of this city and the Warriors franchise. It made Lexie happy that he was still getting the recognition he deserved.

Eventually, after gorging themselves on thick slices of supreme pizza and several pitchers of beer, the group decided to move on.

"Shall we go to Contour?" Lexie asked when they reached the sidewalk. It was a Tuesday night in the summer, so the club wouldn't be teeming with college-aged girls screaming their heads off. Lexie only hoped the crowd of fans now begging for more autographs didn't follow them.

At her suggestion, Mitch caught her eye and cocked an eyebrow, an expression that was not lost on Lexie.

Or Berkley, who looked between them with a small smirk tipping up the corners of her lips.

Contour was, after all, where Lexie and Mitch had met.

Ground zero for the hell Lexie had been through the last two years.

And joy. There really had been so much joy before it all went to shit.

"I could get on board with some dancing," Berkley said, grabbing Brent's hand and towing him down Woodward.

Jordan and Naomi begged off, saying they needed to get home and relieve their sitter, but it seemed like everyone else was in. Rat and Grey were both excited about the prospect of meeting girls their age, Brent typically did whatever Berkley wanted, and Cole, like always, was along for the ride.

That left Mitch.

"What do you say, Farmer?" Cole asked, resurrecting Mitch's old nickname that everyone knew he hated.

Lexie dared to glance at him then, and found his eyes already on her. Without looking away, he said, "I'm in."

It was amazing to Lexie how much had changed in the nearly two years since that night she and Mitch met. For one, tonight, the bar was busy but not overcrowded. The group walked inside and up to the bar easily, and Mitch, as he had done that fateful late-October night, ordered them a round.

Moments later, they were settled in a rounded booth, and Lexie found herself sandwiched in between Cole and Mitch.

Mitch's tree trunk thigh pressed against the side of Lexie's own, and she shivered at the contact.

"You cold?" Cole asked her.

"Not really," she said. "Just one of those freak things."

"Why are we even sitting right now anyway?" Berkley asked. "I thought we came to dance?"

"You make a good point, Daniels," Lexie said, then turned to Mitch. "Can you let me out please?"

He licked his lips and settled his gaze on her mouth. This close to him, she was enveloped by his scent: classic Old Spice deodorant and one hundred percent American male. Mitch was a no-frills kind of guy and didn't care about buying the latest, trendiest, most expensive cologne on the market. In fact, he didn't even wear cologne. His scent was unique to him, bringing Lexie back to lazy days in bed, and curling up against his chest when one of them finally came home after a road trip.

Everything went a little hazy around the edges as they stared at each other in their own little bubble.

And then Berkley said, "You gonna move, Mitch?" And the whole thing popped, bringing them back to reality.

Mitch shook his head and instantly turned away from Lexie, unfolding his body from the booth before extending a hand to help her out of the booth. Reluctantly, she accepted it, goosebumps raising on her arm as it settled around her slender one.

The second she was on her feet, she pulled her hand free from his and practically sprinted toward the dance floor, Berkley hot on her heels.

"Is it just me, or is it hot in here?" Berkley said, fanning herself and raising an eyebrow at Lexie.

"I have no idea what you're talking about," Lexie said, spinning away from her friend and losing herself in the beat pulsing from the speakers.

It was apparently 90s night, and as one song blurred into the next, Lexie gave herself wholly to the music. It had been too damn long since she had let loose like this, and she was reminded how much she loved it. She didn't give a fuck if she looked ridiculous, jumping around and bopping her head, swinging her hips back and forth, or grabbing Berkley and towing her around the dance floor when a slow song came on.

Eventually, the boys decided they wanted in on the fun. Brent and Cole made their way into their little group, Brent settling his hands on Berkley's hips and pressing a kiss to her neck as Cole grabbed Lexie's hands and twirled her around to a one hit wonder while everyone shouted the words until they were breathless.

Cole had become a great friend of Lexie's over the course of the last year. First, as they bonded over Mitch leaving, and then became closer and closer the more time they spent together. Lexie considered him a brother, and he considered her a sister. But Mitch didn't know that, and when Cole spun her around and pulled her back to his chest, she laughed and tried to pull away.

"What are you doing?" She shouted at him over her shoulder.

"Trying to make Mitch jealous," he yelled back, that perfect smile settling into a wicked grin. "Let's see how long it takes for him to come out here."

"That's not what this is about," Lexie told him.

He leaned down and pressed his mouth right against her ear. "Look, you're hot. You know it, I know it. If you were anyone else, we'd already be in a cab back to my place. But you're not. Whether you're ready to admit it to yourself or not, there's never going to be anyone else for you but him. I'm not trying to get in between true love and all that. That's just bad karma."

She turned her head, and their faces were close enough that moving a scant inch forward would have her lips pressed against his. "You're ridiculous."

"But I'm also right." His head snapped up, and the heat at her back left.

"My turn," someone growled, and Lexie instinctively knew it was Mitch. She spun on him. "What if I don't want to dance with you?"

"Too damn bad," he told her, gripping her hips and pulling her toward him so that her front was flush with his.

The song changed to some Boyz II Men baby-making slow jam, and Lexie knew this entire night was a lost cause.

Given all the times she had found herself in this exact position with him before, it shouldn't surprise Lexie how well she and Mitch fit together. But it had been so long since he held her like this, and she couldn't help but marvel at how easy it would be to tip her head back and allow him to lower his mouth to hers.

But like she'd told him at the loft, she needed time. So much had happened between them. So much drama and bullshit and misunderstandings that honestly could've been solved with a phone call and a few words. Now it all just felt insurmountable, and she didn't even know where to begin to wade through it and come out safely on the other side.

So she rested her cheek against his chest as they swayed to the song. Familiarity and muscle memory took over, and Lexie couldn't help burying her fingers in the hair at the nape of his neck. She felt his breath hitch, and he bent his head, his lips coming to rest against the sensitive spot right below her ear. When she didn't move away, he pursed his lips and pressed a kiss there.

"I miss you so much," he whispered, his voice nearly swept away by the pulsing of the music. She shivered as his breath fanned over her skin.

Pulling away, she looked up at him, his eyes pleading, cutting right through her, nearly shattering her resolve. "I..." she started. "I'm sorry." She pulled away and sprinted for the bathroom.

"What the hell happened back there?" Berkley asked a few moments later when she pushed into the bathroom behind Lexie.

"I wanted to kiss him," Lexie blurted.

"Cole or Mitch?" Berkley asked, standing next to her at the counter with her arms folded over her chest.

"Mitch you dumbass," Lexie hissed, leaning forward to run the cold water and splash her face.

"Just had to be sure. So why didn't you?"

"I don't know! Everything is happening too fast. There's still so much baggage there that I don't know how to unpack. I don't know what I'm doing."

"I think you know perfectly well what you're doing, and you're just afraid."

"Yeah, well, no one asked you," Lexie told her, voice lacking any real venom.

"Lex, I love you and I only want you to be happy. I think it's time you want that for yourself, too."

Happiness.

She had once told Mitch that happiness was a foreign concept for her, but for him, she was willing to try it on for size.

Could she do it again? Throw herself into the fire and risk the burns?

"I don't know how," she said quietly.

"Well, my dear," Berkley said, reaching out to grab Lexie's hand and giving it a squeeze, "it's time to figure it out. Because that man isn't going to wait around forever, and you'll be kicking yourself for the rest of your days if you let him get away again."

As a rule, Lexie didn't believe in regret. It didn't make sense to her to wish so badly to change something that was exactly what she thought she wanted and needed at the moment. She preferred to look at those situations as learning experiences, so she would know what *not* to do next time.

But in this case?

Lexie couldn't help feeling like Berkley was right.

CHAPTER TWENTY-SIX
Lexie

I t was officially bachelorette weekend, and Lexie was more than a little excited to get out of Detroit—and away from Mitch—for a few days.

It was the final weekend of June, and when they touched down in Nashville, it was painfully obvious the city was gearing up for the Fourth of July. Red, white, and blue covered *everything*.

Not that Lexie was complaining. Independence Day was her favorite holiday because it was the only one she had never felt obligated to spend with her parents growing up.

As an adult, it was the perfect excuse to get drunk and let loose.

Basically, she was planning on a very long detox after this bachelorette weekend, the Fourth, and Berkley and Brent's wedding happening in such a short period of time.

Thanks to her newly minted influencer connections, Lexie cut them a major deal on the condo for the weekend. The owners were looking for some publicity, which Lexie offered to provide during their stay, as well as a feature on the blog afterward, in exchange for the nightly rate cut in half.

So here they were, with a condo in a building with an insane rooftop pool and lounge space only a block off Broadway.

The condo itself was all clean white walls, countertops, light wood floors, and plush cream-colored furniture. They even had a small balcony that looked out over the Cumberland River.

"I'm rooming with Berk," Lexie said as the group entered the condo. "I figured Ames and Kimber can share, and then Jess and Kenz together? Does that work for everyone?"

They all nodded their ascent, except Kimber, whose flight hadn't landed from LA yet.

"Perfect," Lexie said. "So how about everyone gets settled, and then we'll start drinking!"

In addition to featuring this condo this weekend, Lexie and Amelia had also teamed up with an app touted as "bachelorette party planning made easy." With so many personalities involved, and a bride who hated surprises, Lexie was willing to take all the help she could get.

Once Lexie and Berkley had set their bags in their room, changed, and freshened up, they settled at the kitchen island and clicked into the app.

"Okay so this app is awesome because not only can you look up excursions and other such things to do in the area, but you can also book directly in the app. It's honestly a no-brainer for anyone planning a bachelorette party. Amelia and I actually reached out to them about partnership, explaining what we needed it for and how we already have a huge social media following."

For a fledgling operation, she and Amelia had each amassed over fifty thousand Instagram followers in a few short months, and the blog traffic was steady.

Rarely did she and Amelia have to reach out to brands; typically the brands approached them. In this instance, however, both agreed making the first move was worth it to give Berkley the best possible weekend.

"It looks awesome," Berkley said as she scrolled through the app's landing page, which was highlights of the sights and sounds of Nashville. "I don't want to do anything that requires physical labor, though," she says, her finger hovering over an ad for one of those pub-on-wheels things. "I'm here to relax, not work out."

"Fair enough," Lexie said. "What exactly do you want to do then?"

"Drink," Berkley said simply. "And it's a bachelorette weekend, so shouldn't we find one of those Magic Mike-type shows, too?"

Lexie scrolled until she found what she was looking for. "Here, this is perfect. Music City Gents Male Revue. It's a choreographed burlesque show featuring hunky southern men," Lexie said, wiggling her eyebrows. "And we can book you your very own lap dance, too!"

"Did someone say lap dance?" Amelia asked as she padded out into the kitchen, Mackenzie and Jessica not far behind her.

"We're going to a show tonight, ladies," Berkley said. "And your girl is getting a lap dance from a cowboy."

Lexie laughed along with the rest of them, thinking how nice it was to see Berkley letting go and enjoying herself. Her best friend had a tendency to be uptight about a lot of things, and ever since the day Lexie met her, she had been working her ass off toward something. First, it was getting her undergraduate degree and getting into a good law school, then it was getting her law degree, passing the bar, and finding a job at a really good firm. Now it was getting her business degree—or whatever she was doing; Lexie truthfully didn't know exactly—and preparing to start her own agency.

But Berkley was about to marry the love of her life. And that wasn't something she had to work her ass off for. She already had Brent and would forever, wedding or no wedding. All Lexie wanted was for her to sit back, relax, and let loose, and she told her so.

"I fully plan on it," Berkley said seriously. "I'll even shut my phone off if it'll make you feel better."

"That's not the worst idea you've ever had, actually, but not necessary. I want you to be able to document your memories of this weekend. And send those cheesy little love notes to Brent when none of us are looking."

"My texts are *not* cheesy," Berkley said indignantly. "Besides, haven't you ever sent suggestive texts to a boyfriend?"

Lexie had, but only to Mitch, and it was never anything she wouldn't say to his face. Berkley must've realized her mistake, because she said, "Sorry, I didn't mean to bring him up."

"It's okay," Lexie said, waving her off. And she found herself actually meaning it. Mitch wasn't going anywhere. Not anytime soon, and if she was completely honest with herself, hopefully not ever.

The time for Mitch to prove himself to her had passed. In fact, she hadn't needed those reassurances from him in the first place. That tether between them was still there, still pulling her into his orbit, and if all of the months and miles that had separated them hadn't lessened that pull, Lexie had to admit nothing would. But before she jumped back in with him, if that was even still on the table, she wanted to make sure her head was on straight and that she was *ready* to give him everything.

She had tried to give him everything before and thought she'd succeeded. But that dinner with her parents...God, it was like being a teenager again and inviting her first real boyfriend over for dinner. The subtle digs at her character, at how the guy better be prepared to take care of her because she couldn't do it herself.

It was exhausting, a war she had been waging with them for her entire life. And having Mitch by her side? It should've fortified her, given her the strength to fight back. Instead, she had curled in on herself and then lashed out at him when he stood up for her.

She was embarrassed.

That's what it all boiled down to.

Mitch deserved someone to love him openly, without reservations or conditions. Not only was she terrified to give that much of herself—all of herself—to him again, but she didn't even know if she still could.

So yeah...she needed time.

At that moment, the door to the condo clicked open, revealing Kimber and driving thoughts of Mitch and her future straight from her head.

Berkley was on her feet in an instant, not having seen Kimber in nearly two years. Lexie, who had just seen her in the fall, hung back while the rest of the group greeted her.

"So that's the infamous Kimber," Mackenzie said, standing next to Lexie as the other three women exchanged hugs and compliments with Kimber.

"Sure is," Lexie said, turning to smirk at Brent's sister. "The party has officially arrived."

The sun was still a fiery ball in the sky, though slowly beginning its descent toward the horizon, when the girls left the condo and ventured out onto Broadway.

Surprisingly, Nashville was one city Lexie had never lived in growing up or visited while traveling for work, and stepping foot onto the infamous epicenter of country music was a bit of a shock to the senses.

Everything was lit up in neon, and twangy, guitar-heavy music blasted onto the sidewalk from every open door they walked past.

Commotion on the sidewalk in front of them had the group slowing, and the small crowd parted to reveal two men huddled together, a complicated-looking camera tripod set up between them.

Lexie halted in her tracks as the taller of the two turned, his dark blond hair and big body reminding her of someone.

"Mitch?" She whispered.

"Ladies!" He hollered in their direction, and Lexie shook herself. In the waning daylight, the man had looked so much like Mitch that Lexie thought he followed them here. With his green eyes and blond hair, he was a ringer for Mitch; it was kind of freaky.

And from a distance, his shorter, brown-haired friend looked exactly like Brent.

"Are you seeing what I'm seeing?" Berkley asked her. "I thought that was my fiancé right there."

Lexie exhaled. "Okay, I'm glad it wasn't just me."

The blond one stepped in front of them, blocking their path, and said, "You're here for a bachelorette weekend so we need to interview you."

Lexie raised an eyebrow. "And what if we don't want to be interviewed?"

He stuck his hand out. "I'm Weston King."

This was Weston King? Lexie had heard of him, of course. She and Amelia were influencers now; it was in their best interest to be aware of other big names in the industry. But she'd never actually looked him up and was surprised by how...good looking he was. Then again, with his YouTube presence and social media following, it made sense that the guy was attractive.

"And I'm Camden," his dark-haired friend said. "Wes is doing a series for his channel where he interviews drunk tourists on Broadway. Do you mind if we ask you some questions?."

"I don't know if you noticed," Berkley said, "but we're not drunk. In fact, we haven't even started drinking."

"Not to mention I have my own brand to think about," Lexie said. "And she—" a point at Berkley "—is about to marry a professional athlete. So thanks but no thanks."

"Wait, are you Lexie Monroe?" Camden asked, squinting at her. "And...oh my God. You're Brent Jean's girlfriend."

Lexie smirked and nodded. "Sure am."

"And technically, I'm Brent Jean's *fiancé*," Berkley said with a smirk, flashing her ring at him.

"My girlfriend is kind of obsessed with you," he said to Lexie. "And my family is full of Warriors' fans," he added to Berkley. "Mind if we take a picture? No one will believe me otherwise."

"Sure, why not! Ladies, huddle up!"

The group of girls formed a circle around Weston and Camden, who used their recording setup to take the picture for them.

"Thank you guys so much," Weston said. "Enjoy your weekend, and congrats on the wedding!"

The girls strode away, giggling as they made their way further down Broadway.

"Weston King is going to post a photo with us on his social media," Amelia said excitedly as she slipped her arm through Lexie's.

"I know." Lexie couldn't help the smile that overtook her face. "We're going to get a ton of engagement and followers from that."

"When we get back to Detroit, we should make a plan for how to capitalize on that. We can promote FLEX and the gym."

"Whatever you want, Ames," Lexie said, practically floating down the street. "But right now, we focus on Berk. Work can wait."

Amelia nodded and turned her head toward Berkley, who was on Lexie's other side. "What do you want to do, Berk?" she asked.

"Food," Berkley said, pressing a hand to her stomach dramatically. "I want food."

Lexie stepped ahead of them and stopped in the middle of the sidewalk, arms spread wide as she turned in a circle. "Take your pick!"

They continued down the street, pressing through the crush of foot traffic until Berkley was lured in by a bright red sign advertising Jack's Bar-B-Que.

Making their way inside, they were seated quickly at a table near the back next to a group of guys decked out in cowboy hats and boots.

Berkley was wearing a crown and sash that read "Bride to Be", so it surprised no one when one of the guys leaned over and said, "Bachelorette party?"

Lexie pointedly looked between him and Berkley's outfit, then said, "What gave it away?"

He smirked, and Lexie had to admit he was smoking hot. Deeply tanned skin, sparkling blue eyes, shaggy blond hair, his blue pocket tee clinging to his biceps and the muscles of his chest. The rest of his group was equally as attractive.

"What are you ladies getting into tonight?"

"Bumming around, getting some drinks, and then later we're going to a show," Lexie said.

"What kind of show?"

"The male stripper kind."

"Ahh, the Music City Male Revue," he said knowingly.

"You're familiar with it?"

"A bit. I've seen the show a few times."

"Let me guess," Lexie said. "You were dragged there by a girlfriend."

That smirk again. "Something like that."

Their waiter approached their table then, and the guy nodded at him. "I'll let you get to it. I hope you enjoy the show tonight."

"Do all the guys down here look like them?" Mackenzie asked, fanning herself with a laminated menu as she eyed the men.

"Don't even think about it," Berkley said, pointing her unopened straw in Mackenzie's direction. "Your brother would kill me if I let you get all tangled up with a cowboy."

Mackenzie rolled her eyes. "He's not the boss of me."

"Keep telling yourself that, kid."

The table erupted in laughter, each of them knowing full well how overbearing Brent Jean could be when he went into big brother mode.

The waiter reappeared a moment later with their beers, and Lexie raised hers to the center of the table. "To Berkley...and Brent," she said, winking at Mackenzie. They all clinked glasses and tipped them back.

By the time they made it to the Music City Male Revue a few blocks off Broadway later that evening, each of the girls was happily tipsy.

They made their way inside the club, the room illuminated by a sporadic placement of small lamps and fairy lights strung up, a big spotlight trained on a large black stage lined by thick black velvet curtains. They found seats near the front and settled in for the show.

Some time later, the opening bars of "Save a Horse, Ride a Cowboy" blasted through the speakers, and a single man stepped through the curtain from backstage, clad in a pair of soft leather chaps, tight black underwear, and a cowboy hat.

"Oh my God," Mackenzie said next to Lexie, and Lexie turned her head in that direction.

"What?" She asked upon seeing Mackenzie's jaw practically on the floor.

"You don't recognize him?"

Lexie's gaze whipped back to the stage, just in time to catch the wink of the guy from Jack's earlier.

"Holy shit," Berkley said. "You mean to tell me..."

"I guess that explains why every last one of them could've been a model," Jessica said with a giggle. As the group's youngest—and least experienced—Lexie worried about how she'd handle tonight, but she proved to be a trooper, the alcohol taking the edge off any anxiety she may have had.

The volume of the music lowered, and the guy on stage said, "How we doin' tonight, ladies?"

A loud cheer peppered with wolf whistles and catcalls went up, and the guy grinned. "That's what I like to hear. So how many of y'all are here for a bachelorette weekend?" He asked.

Berkley's hand rose to the air immediately, as did the hands of several other women scattered around the club.

"How about you gorgeous ladies come up on stage and we'll give you a little something extra to celebrate your last days of freedom?"

Berkley was all for it, rising from her chair before the guy had even finished speaking. Lexie couldn't help but laugh, reclining in her seat and watching as her friend hopped on stage, the height difference between her and the guy comical.

The girl was tiny.

"My, my, you are a pretty little thing. And I think I recognize you. Were you and your friends at Jack's earlier?" He asked.

Berkley nodded and pointed at Lexie and their table. "We were! Why didn't you tell us who you were?"

"Wanted it to be a surprise," he said with a wink. A moment later, the other bachelorettes joined them on stage, and two other heavily muscled and oiled men emerged from the back with chairs for them all.

"I'm Bobby, by the way," he said to the crowd. "I'll be your host for tonight. I hope you enjoy the show."

Lexie can confirm they did, in fact, enjoy the show.

Very much.

Afterward, they hung around the club for a few drinks, and were just packing up to leave when the dancers emerged from backstage.

"Y'all are still here?" Bobby drawled as he walked up to them, clad in jeans that hung low on his hips and the same tee he had on earlier. His palm settled low on Lexie's back, and she found herself annoyed by the familiarity in the touch.

"It's a bachelorette weekend," Lexie said with a shrug, stepping away from Bobby and resting her arm across Berkley's shoulders. "We're just about to head out, though. Long day and all that."

"No, don't go yet!" One of the other guys said, walking up behind Bobby. "Come get a drink with us."

"We could get a drink here," Lexie reminded him, gesturing to the full bar behind her and the cocktail in her hand.

"We hate drinking where we work," he said with an eye roll. "Let's go somewhere more fun. How about Jason's bar? Or maybe Blake's?"

Lexie's face must have betrayed her confusion because, with a chuckle, Bobby said, "Jason Aldean and Blake Shelton."

Oh, duh. Country singers, Lexie thought, mentally smacking herself.

She turned to her friends. "What do you guys think? More drinks, or back to the condo?"

She desperately wanted a shower and a soft bed, and she wasn't a fan of the way Bobby was looking at her, but when Berkley said, "Drinks!" Lexie had no choice but to oblige. This was Berkley's weekend, after all. What Lexie wanted didn't matter.

And so the group of them, ten in all, wandered out in the late night Nashville air and made their way back to Broadway which, despite the hour, was still teeming with life.

"So which is it?" Bobby asked Berkley. "Jason or Blake?"

"Jason!" She shouted, and Bobby smiled indulgently.

"Jason it is," he said, gripping her hand and towing her forward. Berkley reached behind her and snagged Lexie's wrist a second before she was lost in the crowd, pulling her along with them.

Jason Aldean's Kitchen and Rooftop Bar was a multilevel space packed to the gills with people. Each level had a small stage and was standing room only, with people sucking down bottles of beer or cocktails sweating in their hands—or sloshing all over them.

Bobby guided the group through the crowd on the main floor until they bellied up to the bar, signaling the bartender closest to them.

"Bobby!" She yelled, walking up to give him a complicated handshake over the bar top. "What brings you in? Didn't y'all have a show tonight?"

She noticed Lexie and Berkley standing there, Bobby's arm slung casually over Lexie's shoulders, the other guys and the rest of their friends standing behind them, and quirked an eyebrow. "I see. Picking up strays again."

Strays? *Again?*

"We're just here to have a good time," Bobby said smoothly. "Can you get me a round of My Kinda Party for me and my friends here?"

"What's that?" Berkley asked, tipping her head back to look at Bobby. "Other than the name of a song, of course."

"Some fruity drink that, despite being the manly men we are, we can't get enough of."

Lexie laughed, a full-bellied sound, and Bobby glanced sideways at her. "I like your laugh," he told her quietly.

She looked into his eyes, and her cheeks heated instantly.

Get yourself together, Monroe, she silently admonished herself. *You can't possibly be blushing over this cheesy cowboy.*

This was why Lexie wanted to go back to the condo and go to bed instead of joining these guys for more alcohol.

Because Lexie plus beautiful boys plus booze equaled bad decisions, and despite her misgivings about getting serious with Mitch again, she really was trying to get her head on straight.

The last thing she needed was a distraction the likes of some Nashville hottie to come in and fuck the whole thing up.

After the bartender delivered their drinks and Bobby paid, he led them up several flights of stairs to the rooftop, where they pushed a few tables together and settled in, comfortable in the balmy Tennessee summer air.

"So where are you ladies from?" One of Bobby's friends asked. Lexie later learned his name was Nash.

A bit too on the nose for her liking, but southerners were strange.

"Michigan," Lexie said, pointing at herself, Berkley, Amelia, and Jessica. "She"—a point at Mackenzie—"is from New York but now lives in Detroit, and she"—a finger in Kimber's direction—"is from California."

"And how do y'all know each other?" Bobby asked.

The girls explained their relationships, which truthfully weren't all that complicated: college friends and siblings.

After that, they spent some time getting to know each other, ordering more drinks and enjoying the Nashville evening above the hustle and bustle of Broadway.

Bobby found any excuse to touch Lexie, whether it was sliding a hand along her thigh before reaching out to snatch his drink from the table, or twisting a lock of her hair between his fingers as he listened to one of the girls tell a story. By the time bar close rolled around, and a bartender ushered them down the stairs and back into the night, Lexie's nerves were completely frayed.

Tonight, she had done everything in her power to avoid leading him on, leading them to this moment when he snagged her wrist and pulled her flush against his body right as she turned to go, but she knew Bobby's type. He was the kind of guy used to getting what he wanted, and tonight he'd set his sights on Lexie.

"You didn't think you were getting away without a good night kiss, did you?" Bobby asked her, licking his lips.

She pushed away from him, cheeks heating in embarrassment. She had tried so hard to be someone different tonight, someone other than her usual party-girl, boy-crazy self. It made her skin crawl that despite all that, this man still saw her as an object to be used, as someone who would kiss him, maybe go home with him for an orgasm or two, then leave and never see or hear from again.

It would be so easy for her to give Bobby what he so clearly wanted, but Lexie desperately didn't want to be that girl anymore.

Mitch's voice sounded in her head: *You are a gift.*

It was time she started treating herself as such.

"Lexie!" Someone yelled behind her, and she spun to find her friends waiting for her. Her shoulders sagged in relief.

"Sorry," she told Bobby. "Gotta go."

She ran to catch up with Berkley, who hung back as the rest of the gang forged ahead in the direction of the condo. "He tried to kiss you, didn't he?" She asked.

Lexie nodded. "I didn't want to."

"How come?" Berkley asked. "I mean, nothing was stopping you."

"Because I'm still in love with Mitch," she blurted. "I always have been. And I might be screwed up and drowning, treading water while I figure out what the fuck I'm going to do about it, but I love him. And I think he loves me. I can't do that to him...to us."

Berkley wrapped her arm around Lexie's waist and leaned into her shoulder as they walked. "About fucking time," she said.

CHAPTER TWENTY-SEVEN
Mitch

B rent's bachelor weekend was upon them, and Mitch was genuinely excited to get out of Detroit for a few days.

The only thing Brent had asked for was somewhere warm where they could go golfing, so as a group they settled on Hilton Head, South Carolina. Of the five of them—Brent, Mitch, Cole, Brent's brother Nate, and Berkley's brother Logan—three of them, Mitch's career-ending injury notwithstanding, traveled for a living, and the other two had seen enough places that it was difficult to find somewhere none of them had been. Berkley had actually been the one to recommend Hilton Head, claiming Lexie had been there before for work, and told her it was a great place to relax and spend the weekend on the links.

Cole had suggested they go to Vegas for the weekend to enjoy his final days as a single man, an idea Brent immediately shot down.

"After all," Brent had said when they started planning this trip, "I don't consider these my last days of freedom. They're just my last days before I get to marry the love of my life."

Mitch was envious of that, the confidence in his relationship, and the fact that he and Berkley were making their love for each other official in front of all their friends and family.

Mitch wanted that one day. And he couldn't help picturing Lexie up there next to him on that altar.

After their little heart-to-heart at the loft after the Warriors' Cup win, and the way she reacted to him the night they went to Contour, Mitch had to admit he was floating. He'd half expected her to call him the next day and finally give in.

But she hadn't.

And like a dumbass, he'd constantly been checking his phone since, waiting for a call that never came.

She said she needed time, but Mitch was growing impatient.

"Waiting for a call from your giiiiiirlfriend?" Cole sang when he caught Mitch tapping his screen for the millionth time on their ride from the airport to their resort. "Let me guess, you got ghosted. A little taste of your own medicine?"

"Shut up, Cole," Brent said from the front seat.

"If we can't joke about him dropping us all like hot cakes the second he got traded, what can we joke about?" Cole said with a shrug.

"That's enough, Cole," Brent growled.

Mitch caught his gaze and gave him a grateful nod, mouthing, "Thank you."

Brent nodded back.

This weekend wasn't about Mitch.

It was about celebrating the end of Brent's bachelor status.

It was about his best friend settling down with his soulmate.

Saturday morning, they were out in the hot sunshine on the ninth green at the Shipyard Golf Club. All five of the guys were extremely competitive, and there was a lot of money on the line thanks to various bets they had made over the course of the first eight holes.

"If I make this putt," Cole said, taking his stance and eyeing the distance from his ball to the hole, "you each owe me fifty bucks."

Logan groaned. Berkley's brother was a serious guy at first glance. But the more time he spent around the group, the more he relaxed, and the more he reminded Mitch of Berkley. He could easily see why the two were so close.

"You guys realize I don't make hockey player money, right?" Logan said.

"And I'm a poor as fuck med school student," Nate quipped.

"He's not going to make the putt anyway," Brent said with a shit-eating grin on his face. "Cole always chokes on easy shots."

Cole straightened and glared daggers at Brent. "I do not!" He said indignantly.

"I'm going to have to agree with Jean here," Mitch said. "Remember that game against Buffalo a few years ago where y'all caught the goalie on an odd-man and faked him out. Brent laid the most perfect pass of all time on your tape, and you still shot wide."

The group devolved into laughter as Cole's cheeks burned bright red. "Okay, that was one time," he said, resuming his stance and quickly tapping the ball toward the hole. It rolled slowly across the green, appearing as though it was going to drop in, before veering to the left and missing the hole entirely.

"I think that means you owe us fifty bucks," Logan said with a laugh.

"Nobody took my bet," Cole said, his cheeks still tinged pink. "I don't have to pay up if we don't shake on it."

Brent rolled his eyes but walked up to where his ball lay, bent into his stance, and executed a perfect putt that put the ball in the hole.

"I always was a better shot than you," Brent said to Cole with a smirk.

The back eighteen holes were much the same, with the guys good-naturedly ribbing each other, cracking jokes, and discussing what they were going to do later.

They decided on spending the afternoon in the pool. They'd finished golfing by noon and decided to use the rest of the day to relax before a late dinner.

The sun was a scorching disc in the sky, and as the guys stripped their shirts off and climbed into the pool, more than a few ogling glances from nearby women turned their way.

Cole and Nate had swam over to the bar to get them all drinks while Logan, Brent, and Mitch reclined near the edge.

"I wonder what the girls are up to," Logan said. As Berkley's big brother, he had always been overprotective, even though she had more than proven she could take care of herself. That, combined with her hockey-playing future husband, meant Berkley was always being fretted over.

Brent slid his phone out from under his towel, where he had stashed it so it wouldn't overheat, and thumbed through it.

"Looks like they're having a good time to me," he said, turning his phone to show Mitch and Logan the screen, which featured a picture of the girls on the sidewalk along Broadway, two tall, good-looking men—one blond, the other brunette—sandwiched between the members of their group.

"Who the fuck are they?" Mitch asked, his tone biting.

"Apparently some big YouTube star and his videographer," Brent said with a shrug. "I'm glad they're having fun. Broadway is wild."

Brent's nonchalance grated against Mitch's nerves, which were bubbling over with anger seeing some random guy with his arm wrapped tight around Lexie's waist.

"Don't you see the way those guys are draped all over them?" he asked Brent.

"Yeah, and?"

"And you're not mad?"

Brent gave Mitch a you have lost your damn mind look and said, "No, why would I be? I trust Berkley. Not to mention both of these guys are happily in committed relationships from the looks of their social media." Brent lifted his head and narrowed his gaze on Mitch. "And for the record, you have absolutely no right to be mad at Lexie."

Mitch glared at him, crossing his arms over his chest. "Oh, I don't?"

"No, Mitch, you don't," Brent said, standing to his full height in the water. With only an inch separating them, they were nearly eye-to-eye. "You gave up that right when you left her. And I know you want her back, and that you've been trying, but you have to give her time. She's only had a few months to wrap her brain around the fact that you're back for good, and that you want to resume a relationship with her. It's not that easy."

Mitch stepped back, water sloshing against his back and arms as he moved, surprised by the outburst and animosity in Brent's tone. "Since when are you Lexie's biggest champion?"

"Since the one man who was supposed to protect her heart left and threw it in the trash. Someone had to step in, and she's Berkley's best friend. I love that girl like she's my own sister," Brent said. "I imagine that's how you once felt about Berkley."

"I still do..." Mitch said quietly.

Brent shook his head sadly. "But you still left. And me and the guys and Berkley may have been able to easily forgive you and move on from it when you came back, but we weren't the ones in love with you."

"It doesn't feel like you've forgiven me," Mitch said.

"I have," Brent told him, and Mitch knew he was telling the truth. "But that doesn't mean I just magically forgot all those months you were gone, and all the times I had to stop Lexie from drinking herself to death in your absence."

Mitch winced. "It was that bad?"

"It was worse," Brent said. "But it's not my story to tell. All I'm saying is that you're over here spun out about her not giving you the time of day when..."

Brent stopped and lowered his voice. Nate and Cole were swimming back their way, and Logan was staring, eyes wide, as though they were a train wreck he couldn't look away from. "Look, I know I told you to fight for her, and I stand by that. But there's a fine line between fighting for her and pushing her too hard and scaring her off. If you thought she was skittish before, she's even worse now. Just give her some time."

Everybody kept saying that to him.

She needs time.

Give her some time.

Let her come to you.

Mitch liked to think he was a patient man, but at this point, he was starting to wonder if Lexie was toying with him. Was she drawing out this limbo they were in longer than necessary as some sort of retribution for the way he had left her last year? No. Lexie couldn't possibly be that vindictive, could she? Mitch didn't like to think so, but so much had changed in the last year that he honestly didn't know anymore.

Maybe it really was time to step back and let her come to him.

"What happened when you left anyway?" Nate asked as he reached their group and caught the tail end of his and Brent's conversation. "I was in Detroit when you got traded, and spent the evening with my brother and some of your other...friends. Everyone was distraught, almost like you had died."

Mitch took his hat off and ran a hand anxiously through his hair, dampening the strands. He didn't want to get into this. Not here, not now, not ever, and especially not with Nate Jean.

"It's an incredibly long story not worth repeating," Brent said, coming to his rescue. "We've forgiven him. That's all you need to know."

Nate raised his hands in surrender and swam away to where some girls were organizing a water volleyball game.

"I'm sorry about my brother," Brent said to Mitch in a low voice when the three others had abandoned them. "He's always been a shit-stirrer."

"It's okay," Mitch said. "I was a coward. Being reminded of that every now and then is good for me. Keeps me humble."

He gave Brent a wobbly smile, and his friend let the matter drop.

When they arrived back in Detroit on Monday, Mitch had every intention of playing it cool with Lexie until the wedding.

Once that weekend rolled around, and Brent and Berkley were married, all bets were off.

So it surprised him when his phone rang that evening, the screen flashing Lexie's name.

"Hey you," he said when he answered.

"Hey," she said, and they sat in silence for several long, tense moments.

"It's weird that you're calling me," he finally said.

"I agree, it is," she said with a laugh. "But well...I have a question for you."

"Shoot."

"Do you want to maybe grab dinner with me tomorrow? I'm going out of town on Wednesday but...I wanted to see you before I left," she added in a rush.

"Yes."

"You didn't even think about it."

Mitch's heart fluttered. "I don't need to think about it, Lexie. For you, the answer is always yes."

He could practically hear the smile in her voice when she said, "Tomorrow, then. Does six work?"

"Six is perfect," he said. "Where do you want me to meet you?"

"I'll pick you up," she said. "You're back in your old place, right?"

"Sure am." It turned out that hanging onto his condo when he moved to LA had been a good idea, not only so his mother could use it in case she ever found herself stranded in the city during bad weather, but also because he didn't have to hunt for a place to live when he moved back.

"Perfect. See you tomorrow, Mitch," Lexie said and hung up.

Mitch wished he could snap his fingers and make the intervening hours disappear, but he couldn't, so he had to find ways to keep himself busy. That included staying up late binge-watching Outer Banks on Netflix because he was too wired to sleep, running errands he had been putting off for days and even weeks, and cleaning his condo top to bottom—something he had never done before but found incredibly cathartic nonetheless.

Tuesday afternoon, an hour before Lexie was supposed to pick him up, Gabe called him, and Mitch answered in a hurry, genuinely glad for the distraction.

"Mitchell," Gabe said when Mitch answered. "I haven't heard from you in weeks so I'm doing a wellness check."

"I just texted you the other day."

"Yeah a screenshot of Cally's Instagram story, which I had already seen. What was even the point of that, anyway?"

Mitch snorted. Upon completion of his rookie season, Connor Callahan had decided to stay in California instead of returning to Pittsburgh, where he was originally from. After finishing the season third in points on the Knights and second among rookies league-wide, he was a bit of a hot commodity with the ladies, his already large ego inflating to a dangerous size.

The Instagram story in question featured Cally at a club in WeHo, eyes heavily-lidded, arms draped around two girls who looked to be straining under his weight.

"Mostly I just wanted to make sure we had receipts so we could give him shit for his drunken escapades later."

"Oh don't worry, I've already yelled at him for it."

Mitch laughed. "A captain's job is never done, hey?"

"Especially not with that kid on the team."

"So what's going on with you? How are things with Allison?"

"Allison and I broke up," Gabe said.

Mitch's jaw dropped. Gabe had met Allison at a Knights' charity function not long after Mitch joined the team, and they'd been head-over-heels for each other ever since. "What the fuck happened?"

"She got a job out east with her dream charity organization. She didn't see the point in long distance, so she dumped me."

"How long ago was this?"

"Like two weeks," Gabe said.

Two weeks. Mitch had been so wrapped up in his own shit that he hadn't known his friend was hurting. Mitch was familiar with a cross-country move costing him his relationship, and he should've been there for Gabe.

Instead, every waking moment—and a lot of the sleeping ones—had been consumed by thoughts of Lexie.

"God, man, I'm so sorry," Mitch said.

He could practically hear the shrug as Gabe said, "It's all good, man. I know you've got a lot going on."

"That's not an excuse," Mitch said, and he scrubbed a hand over his face, suddenly embarrassed.

He was constantly doing this to people—focusing on his needs and wants instead of what the people around him were going through. It had happened with Lexie that night they had dinner with her parents. Instead of respecting her wishes and surviving the evening without incident, the second her parents said something about her he didn't like, he went off like a bomb, leaving a Lexie-sized crater in the middle of his life.

She may have doused their relationship in gasoline when she pushed him away, but he was the one who lit the match and burned it to the ground.

"Look dude, it's fine," Gabe said to him. "I just wanted to call and check in. See how you're doing. See how things are coming on the Lexie front."

"Actually, she asked me out to dinner tonight," Mitch said.

"Damn son, look at you go. You sound excited."

"I am." He looked at his watch. "And she's actually going to be here soon, and I still need to shower. I hate to cut this short, but let's catch up for real soon."

"Maybe I'll come to Michigan for a few weeks next month."

"Deal. We'll make plans soon."

"Good luck tonight, bro."

Mitch smiled. "Thanks, man. Talk soon."

When the time came for Lexie to pick him up, he was freshly showered, dressed in khaki shorts and a short-sleeve button-down covered in pineapples, one of the few pieces from Bonobos that survived his move from LA. The second her knock came at his door, he was swinging it open, stuffing a bouquet of flowers under her nose.

Mitch had come to learn that Lexie's love language was a combination of physical touch and quality time, two things she had been robbed of as a child. She'd never much cared for gifts or words of affirmation or acts of service. Words to her were often hollow, and gifts or acts of service reminded her of the way her parents would bribe her into being the dutiful daughter they needed for the moment.

But when he'd been at Trader Joe's earlier that day, he couldn't resist picking up the cellophane-wrapped peonies for her.

She accepted the blooms, cheeks tinged pink to match the petals. "Thank you," she said. "They're beautiful."

"You're welcome," he said, stuffing his hands deep into his pockets, feeling for all the world like a teenager about to embark on his first date.

"You ready?" She asked.

"Sure am," he said, gesturing for her to exit.

As they made their way downstairs and settled in the car, they made stilted small talk. It was nearly comical to Mitch that after all these years, all the orgasms they had exchanged and sweet words whispered in the darkest hours of the night, that things between them were so uncomfortable.

He snorted, and Lexie cut him a glance before returning her gaze to the road. "What's so funny?"

"I mean...we've seen each other naked," he said. "Why is this so damn awkward?"

Lexie laughed, her shoulders lowering in relief. "I don't know. It feels like we're starting over, doesn't it? Maybe that's why."

"Is that what we're doing here?" He asked, turning his body in the seat so he was angled toward her. "Starting over?"

"I don't know," Lexie said honestly. "I think we're figuring it out as we go. If that's okay with you."

I'll take whatever you'll give me, he thought. But he didn't dare say it out loud, instead only nodding.

A few minutes later, Lexie pulled into a parking lot in Greektown, and Mitch's eyebrows scrunched together. "You're taking me to the loft? *My* loft?"

They were out of the car and down the block before Lexie responded.

"I didn't want to share you."

Oh boy. Mitch slowed his pace and let Lexie walk ahead of him so he could discreetly adjust his cock, which had thickened with those six words.

Nothing about the loft was different when they walked inside, save for a small round table and two chairs set up near the bar, which was loaded with takeout containers.

"I didn't know what you'd be in the mood for," Lexie said, "so I got a bit of everything."

I'm in the mood for you, he thought. *Just you.*

He studied her as she made her way behind the bar to grab them beers, her long legs toned and tanned and stretching from the hem of her pale pink sundress, setting off her deep tan perfectly, feet stuffed into a pair of white Chucks. The skirt of her dress swished around her thighs, offering only glimpses of the full shape of an ass that he'd always wanted to sink his teeth in—and had a few times. Her arms, shoulders, and chest were bared, dark hair swishing down her back.

She handed him a beer and he sat quickly at the table before he could embarrass himself. Lexie was quiet as they set about serving themselves the food, which consisted of dishes from all of his favorite restaurants in the city.

They dug in, but the tension between them was a living thing that Mitch itched to address.

He swallowed a mouthful of roasted green beans and said, "Why are we here, Lex?"

Her eyes snapped up to his at the use of her nickname. "I wanted to see you."

"But *why*?"

Lexie heaved a sigh and slowly laid down her fork, apparently resigned to the fact that this conversation was happening right now, whether she wanted it to or not. "I've had some time to think," she said.

Mitch's pulse kicked up, his heart pounding against his rib cage in an accelerated rhythm. This conversation could go one of two ways, and he would either walk out of here elated or devastated. There would be no in-between.

"Think about what?" He said, feigning nonchalance and failing miserably if the look Lexie gave him was any indication.

"You. Me. Us."

"What about us?"

Lexie took a deep breath and said, "When you left, I was a mess. I drowned myself in booze and sex, and only managed to pull myself out of it because Brent and Berk staged an intervention. Those first few months...they weren't pretty. It felt a lot like being a kid again, when my parents would disappear for days on end and I didn't know when, or even if, they'd come back for me. I did some things I'm not proud of, but I'm not going to apologize for them. For any of it." She looked up at him then, her eyes swimming with tears as though remembering it all put her right back in that place, when the pain was the most fresh. "You broke my heart, Mitch. And I wasn't sure it would ever heal."

"I understand," he said quietly. "And I'm sorry."

She waved him off. "I don't need your apologies anymore. You've made it perfectly clear the last few months that you regret what you did, and you've been trying to fix it. I'm not saying I agree with how you handled things, but I'm willing to forgive you. And I'm willing to admit to my part in things. If I hadn't pushed you away..."

"It's not your fault. I should've tried harder."

She glanced up at him, her smile wobbly. "We both should have. I think we can agree we both fucked up."

He gave her a small smile and nodded, tamping down on the full force of the one he wanted to unleash. If she was willing to admit she had also fucked up, and to forgive him, they were halfway there.

"So now what?" He asked, popping a piece of garlic bread in his mouth.

"I'm not ready to just jump back into things the way they were before, if that's what you're thinking. But I'm willing to go slow."

"How slow?" He asked. Now that she had taken a step back toward him and was making her way back into his arms, he was greedy.

He wanted everything.

"I was thinking we start by you being my date to Brent and Berkley's wedding."

Mitch was surprised by that. The wedding was still three weeks away, and his mood fell with the knowledge that she really meant it when she said *go slow*.

But again, this was Lexie. The love of his life, the only woman he'd ever wanted like this. The only woman he wanted forever. So he said, "I would love to be your date."

CHAPTER TWENTY-EIGHT
Mitch

Since their little date after Brent and Berkley's respective bachelor and bachelorette weekends, he'd hardly seen or heard from Lexie. He knew she had been out of town for work, and she'd made it clear she wanted to take things slow, but his chest still felt heavy with everything riding on making this weekend so perfect, not just for Brent and Berkley, but for him and Lexie as well.

As if sensing the direction of his thoughts, Brent asked, "So what's your plan for this weekend, Mitch?"

Mitch's eyebrows drew together in fake confusion. "You mean other than standing by your side as you marry the love of your life and getting absolutely shitfaced in celebration?"

Brent glared at him, as if begging Mitch to stop fucking around and give him the answer he really wanted. When none was forthcoming, Brent said, "For Lexie, bro. What's your plan for Lexie?"

"Oh."

"Yeah, oh. Don't play dumb with me. You've been trying to get her back since you moved back to Detroit."

"I hadn't really thought about it," Mitch said with a shrug. He was lying, and Brent knew it.

"Right," Brent said. "That's why you spun out when you saw that picture of her with a fucking YouTube star. And why you went on a date with her after the bach weekends."

"I didn't spin out," Mitch grumbled half-heartedly. "But how do you know about the date?" Then it hit Mitch. "Berkley. They've been talking about me?"

Brent nodded, a smirk gracing his mouth. "Sure have. I'll admit, your methods aren't as impressive as mine, but surely you've got something planned for this weekend? If not, I can help!"

Mitch had never considered asking for his friend's help before, and was quite frankly surprised Brent hadn't offered it. When he and Berkley were dating, Mitch had frequently tossed around ideas with Brent, nudging him in the right direction when it came to courting their favorite little blonde, even when those ideas backfired epically.

Truly, it was a gift from God that Brent had come to his senses before giving that speech at her law school graduation.

"I don't have a plan," Mitch told him honestly. "I'm just hoping she'll come to me naturally. We had dinner when we got back from the bach weekends and talked. She asked me to be her date to your wedding. She said she's willing to forgive me, but she wants to take things slow. I'm just trying to honor her wishes and let her come to me."

Now it was Brent's turn to snort. "Bro, have you met Lexie? Where in the manual on that girl does it say she's going to come to you?"

Mitch considered that, quickly realizing his friend had a point. Lexie wasn't going to come to him. At least not without some subtle nudging and hand-holding. The fact that she had invited him to dinner three weeks ago, and asked him to be her date for this wedding, was a big step for her, and completely out of character.

It made sense to him that she had all but disappeared after that, citing work and preparing for this wedding as excuses for why she couldn't spend any time with him.

If he knew Lexie, if she was still the same woman he'd fallen in love with underneath the emotional trauma he'd put her through, she had taken that step forward, gotten spooked, and was now trying to backtrack.

He wouldn't let her go that easily. Not again.

"I've got an idea," Brent said.

Mitch sighed, resigned to his fate. He supposed he should be grateful he was standing here with Brent, considering Lexie wasn't the only one he had left without a goodbye. "Let's hear it."

"First of all, as my best man, you'll have to walk with her."

"I'm aware," Mitch said drily. "Remind me to thank your fiancé for that one."

Brent clapped him on the back. "You leave Berkley out of this. Look, the fact of the matter is you're going to be stuck together doing lots of cheesy, couple-like things for the next few days. Sitting next to each other at the rehearsal dinner. Walking with each other during the ceremony. Dancing. Speeches. Photos. I'm just saying that there's lots of opportunity to start planting some seeds that you two could be here one day."

"Brent, I appreciate the thought, but that's not going to work on Lexie. The first time I told her I loved her, she practically ran screaming."

"That's because your dumbass said it barely two weeks after she agreed to be your girlfriend."

"It wasn't two weeks," Mitch said defensively. Then, "Goddamnit, that little lady of yours talks a lot."

Brent chuckled. "We tell each other everything."

"Everything?" Mitch asked, a jolt of fear shooting down his spine.

"Everything," Brent confirmed. "But look," he continued, shuffling over and placing a comforting hand on Mitch's shoulder. "Berkley and I can both tell she's thawing. She hasn't been with anybody since you came back. I think she's confused and conflicted, but I also think that this is your chance to shoot your shot."

The bare bones of a plan began to form in Mitch's mind. It wasn't anything as grandiose as what Brent would do. No, it was subtle, more a mind game than an outright physical display of his affection.

Weddings were romantic as hell, where people couldn't help but be blinded by the love the couple was pledging to each other.

As Brent said, if ever there was a time to shoot his shot, it was this weekend.

This was the love of his life on the line; everything had to be perfect.

And it didn't get more perfect than a wedding.

Two days later, Mitch found himself lined up at the back of the wedding party procession, staring down a trek up the dock to where Brent waited with the officiant, Lexie's arm wrapped loosely around his.

Next to him, she was stiff as a board, and she had barely glanced his way since they'd gathered here for the ceremony. It was amazing to him how she'd gone from wanting to take things slowly but give them a chance to acting like she didn't even know him in the span of a few weeks.

He bent close, the baby hairs escaping her braided crown tickling his cheek, and whispered, "Come on, Lex. It's a wedding, and your best friend's at that. At least try to look like you're having a good time."

She turned her head toward him, so close their lips nearly brushed, and Mitch pulled away as though he'd been shocked. "Don't talk to me," she said.

"I don't know if you realize this, Lex, but you're kind of stuck with me tonight. Can we tone down the animosity until our friends are married? Then you can go back to hating me."

It killed him to speak those words, imagining she actually did hate him, but he would do anything at this moment to get some sort of reaction from her.

She held his gaze for several long beats, until the processional music started up and the couples in front of them started moving forward.

And so quiet, soft enough that Mitch wasn't entirely sure he hadn't imagined it, she whispered, "I don't hate you. I never have. And that's the problem."

Well, okay then. They would be talking about *that* little admission later.

When it was their turn to walk down the dock, Mitch quickly glanced down at her, watching in awe as she squared her shoulders, lengthened that slender neck, and pasted an incredibly convincing smile on her face. But being pressed against her like this, Mitch could see her pulse ticking in her throat, fluttering much faster than normal.

Was he causing this reaction in her? Truth be told, touching her again, and having her nestled into his side exactly as she'd been so many times before, was wreaking absolute havoc on his nerves. He wouldn't be surprised if she could feel his heart pounding against his ribs where her arm was pinned between them.

They slowly made their way down the dock, the weathered boards creaking beneath them, a stiff breeze keeping them all from sweating profusely under the late-July sun. When he and Lexie reached Brent and the rest of the group, he reluctantly released her arm and took his place at Brent's side.

The crowd gasped a moment later as the song changed to an instrumental version of *I'll Be* by Edwin McCain, and Berkley and her father stepped out onto the patio behind the cabin.

Berkley was a fucking vision. Her dress flattered her small frame, her blonde hair unbound and curled and cascading down her back, topped with a crown of flowers to match those in her bouquet.

Brent Jean was a lucky man.

But truthfully, Mitch only had eyes for Lexie. It wasn't fair that she was so close, practically breathing the same air, yet he couldn't reach out and touch her. Couldn't brush his fingers over that impossibly smooth skin, followed by his lips. Couldn't bunch her dress around her waist and run his hands all over her long legs. Couldn't push her up against a wall and take her like he had that first time. Those brief moments when they'd walked down the aisle together were too much and not enough all at once.

Giving his head a shake, he cleared that image away and returned his attention to the ceremony unfolding in front of him.

Mitch couldn't deny he had a good feeling about tonight. Lexie's best friend was marrying the love of her life; the twinkling lights lining the ceiling of the giant white tent set up outside Brent's family cabin, tables laden with flowers, drinks flowing the moment the marriage license was signed, set the perfect scene. Romance was in the air, and Mitch was going to use that to his advantage.

Berkley had done a wonderful job planning the wedding, every single tiny detail exquisite. Mitch was unsurprised that the color palette matched that of the Warriors' jerseys. The arch her father had built was set up at the end of the dock and draped with navy and burgundy fabrics, adorned with large blooms in the same colors livened with greenery. Brent and his groomsmen, and Berkley and her bridesmaids would fan out on either side. The guests stood on the banks of the water some twenty feet away, watching as Brent and Berkley committed themselves to each other forever.

Coming back into their lives had been surprisingly easy, given how he left. Brent had been forced to spend time with Mitch at the rink anyway, considering he was now one of his coaches, and as he thawed toward his old friend, he made sure Berkley did too.

He had been honest with them, too: he was embarrassed about the trade and heartbroken over Lexie. When he left, he had been under the impression that his relationship was over. Lexie hadn't left much room for interpretation in her final words to him.

So he told them how he felt the only way to survive had been to cut everyone off completely, and it hadn't been easy to admit that, especially not after Berkley told him how cowardly it was.

We would've helped you through it, she'd said.

Lexie realized she fucked up pretty quickly, she'd said.

She would've given long distance a chance, but you didn't bother to fight for her.

Mitch winced. So much wasted time.

He shook his head, dislodging the memories and the guilt over things he couldn't change. Now was not the time to break open his old wounds.

Berkley reached Brent then, and her dad, Jay, extended his hand to shake Brent's and give him a hug. Berkley stood on her tip-toes to kiss her dad's cheek, then turned to grasp Brent's hands while her father retreated to his seat.

From his vantage point, Mitch couldn't see Jean's face, but he was confident that the love and adoration shining from Berkley's was mirrored there.

Mitch didn't cry as a rule, but he'd be damned if seeing these two get married didn't make him a little misty-eyed.

"Dearly beloved," the officiant began. As Brent's best man, Mitch's one job was to keep the rings safe and hand them off at the right time, and he tried to pay attention. But wedding ceremonies weren't exactly his idea of a good time; he preferred the party that came after. But soon, his gaze was drawn back to Lexie. She stood there in a wine-colored, floor-length dress with skinny spaghetti straps and swoops of fabric curving across her upper arms. The neckline hugged her breasts, dipping between them in a modest vee, like someone had cut the top of a heart off and sewed it onto the dress. It fit her tight through the waist before flaring out.

It was absolutely not the time, but Mitch couldn't help picturing her, again, with the silky fabric bunched around her middle, those legs hooked around his back as he pumped in and out of her.

Would sex between them be the same as before? Would it be like coming home?

He had to find out. That was his only mission tonight.

That and getting her to admit that she still loved him.

But one thing at a time.

Someone cleared their throat, and Mitch tore his eyes away from Lexie to find Brent, hand outstretched, staring at him expectantly.

"Oh, right, the rings," Mitch said, and the guests chuckled. He dug in his pocket and retrieved the velvet box, passing it to his friend, who opened it and removed the ring he would give to Berkley.

"With this ring..." Brent said, sliding the rose gold ring onto Berkley's finger.

A sniffle undercut Brent's words to Berkley, and Lexie once again captured Mitch's attention. Honestly, he couldn't be held responsible. He had always been drawn to her this way, like a magnet. It had been difficult to get her alone since he'd moved back to Michigan, and now they were stuck here, in this secluded, romantic-as-all-hell setting watching two of their very best friends promise themselves to each other.

And Lexie was crying. The Lexie that Mitch remembered didn't cry. She was like him in that regard: generally stoic unless she was turned on, angry, or messing with him.

It seemed a lot had changed over the last year, and Mitch was dying to discover every new thing about her.

Would she still taste the same? Make the same noises when she came? Love the same movies, take her coffee the same, get takeout from the same Chinese restaurant up the street from her building every Friday night if she wasn't on the road?

Well, the answer to that last one was probably no, considering she had moved.

And why had she moved?

When it came to Lexie, he was greedy and wanted everything. Neither time nor distance had lessened the hold she had on him. If anything, that year and those two thousand miles only made him realize that he should've spent that time fighting for her, begging for her to stay in his life no matter how hard it would get with half a country and three time zones separating them.

Mitch truly had taken the coward's way out when he left the way he did, and he would spend every minute of the rest of his life making it up to her if she'd let him.

Upon conclusion of the ceremony and the seemingly endless few hours spent taking pictures, having Lexie's body pressed against his for half of them, it was finally time for speeches and dinner.

And Mitch was a live wire. He was almost grateful not to have Lexie's heat pressed into his side any longer; he needed a moment to collect himself, cool himself off, and urge his dick down before he made a fool of himself.

Brent and Berkley let Lexie and Mitch choose between them who would speak first, and Lexie gave Mitch one look before shaking her head.

Guess that meant it was his turn.

He stood in front of the group that had gathered under the tent, which included several of Brent's teammates of past and present, Berkley's former law school classmates and current colleagues, some Warriors' brass, and Brent and Berkley's extended families.

Raising his champagne flute, he tapped a fork against the side, and all sets of eyes turned his way.

"Good evening," he said. "Most of you here know me, but for those of you who don't, I'm Mitch Frambough. Former Warrior and Brent's best man.

"Six years ago, after a few seasons in Columbus, my contract expired and I received an offer from the Warriors. Turns out, signing with Detroit was the best thing that would ever happen to me. I jumped at the chance to play for such a storied franchise, and after two seasons with the Ice where offense was hard to come by, I was excited by the prospect of coming to Detroit and playing with this stud named Brent Jean."

Mitch looked over at Brent, who was blushing, Berkley laughing softly next to him. She whispered something in his ear, but Mitch pressed on.

"If you know Brent, you know there is no better guy to have on your side in any situation. Whether it's down two goals with less than five minutes to play in an elimination game, or when you're dealing with life struggles off the ice. He's the most loyal friend I've ever had. And it should come as no surprise to anyone that he and Berkley found each other. To know them is to understand that they're two halves of a whole. They complement each other, picking up where the other falters, and have always loved each other through even the most difficult of life's trials. They've given me hope, and allowed me to believe that true love is a possibility, and soulmates do exist."

He caught Lexie's eye then, and she quickly turned away, taking an exaggerated swallow of her champagne.

Turning back to Brent and Berkley, he said, "I know it wasn't always easy, and you two went through a lot to get here. But none of us ever doubted you would reach this day. I am so happy for you both. I love you guys. Congratulations."

He raised his glass in the air. "To Brent and Berkley!"

The crowd echoed the sentiment, and Mitch returned to his spot at the head table, Lexie brushing past him to take her turn.

Lexie cleared her throat, then said, "When I first met Berkley, I hated her."

Berkley barked out a laugh, as did Amelia and Kimber, the four of them in on some joke from that first week of college when they'd all met.

"How could I not? This beautiful, tiny little thing who had her entire life figured out at eighteen. It was exhausting to be around, truthfully."

She glanced pointedly at Logan and Jessica. "You two grew up with her. You know."

Berkley's siblings nodded in agreement, and the crowd laughed.

"But...to know Berkley is to love her. It's funny that Mitch cited Brent's loyalty as one of his best qualities, because the same can be said of Berkley. Our freshman year of college, Berkley and I took an English class together, and one of the units that semester was dedicated to Shakespeare. When I look at Berkley, I'm reminded of a quote from A Midsummer Night's Dream, which is fitting because this wedding is a midsummer night's dream. The quote is, 'though she be but little, she is fierce.' I think of Berkley whenever I hear that quote. She is the best, most loyal friend I have ever had. The one who will go to bat for anyone she cares about in any situation, consequences be damned.

"And trust me, we've damned those consequences a time or two," she added with a wink in Berkley's direction, who laughed through her tears.

"I'll admit, when Brent first expressed an interest in Berkley, I was hesitant to let him anywhere near her."

"You scared the shit out of me," Brent said from next to Mitch, and the crowd laughed.

"These two...that first year, they went through the ringer. But to come through it on the other side in one piece, more in love than ever? They've proved to me, and everyone here, time and time again that they're the real deal."

Lexie paused and took a deep breath. "Berk. Brent. I love you both dearly. There aren't words to express how happy I am that you've found each other, and I'm so excited to stand by your sides as your future unfolds. For starters...I'm expecting a niece within a year."

"I second that!" Jessica and Mackenzie yelled in unison, and the crowd once again devolved into a fit of laughter.

She raised her glass in the air and said, "To a lifetime of love and happiness. To Brent and Berk."

The crowd echoed her, and Mitch sat back in his chair, gaze trained on Brent and Berkley as they exchanged a kiss and whispered to each other.

Lexie was still out in the middle of the dance floor, where Berkley's parents had approached her and wrapped her in a group hug.

"Damn, Lexie looks hot tonight," Nate said conversationally from next to Mitch, lifting his beer to his lips and taking a swallow while watching Lexie conversing with the Daniels. Her deep red dress hugged all of the soft curves of her body and molded to her chest, falling to the ground in a swath of fabric that swished side to side when she moved.

"Yeah, she does," Mitch said, the words clipped. Nate was right; Lexie was easily the hottest woman here tonight. But who the fuck did Nate think he was, commenting on his girl like that?

Then again, Lexie wasn't exactly his girl.

Not yet anyway.

Nate turned his body so he was facing Mitch fully. "Look man, I just wanted to say I'm sorry for sleeping with her."

Mitch's eyebrows drew together. "Uhh...thanks?"

"I knew she was an emotional wreck when you left and I took advantage of that. I knew it was a bad idea but...I mean, you've seen her. You know how she is."

Mitch did know how she was. "Yeah..." he said, voice unsteady with all of the emotions coursing through him.

"My brother already chewed my ass out for it, so I hope we're cool. I happen to like my face the way it is and I'd really prefer it if you didn't break my nose."

Nate continued to ramble about how sorry he was and how truthfully, if he was going to be mad about it, he should be mad at both of them because Lexie used Nate, too, but Mitch stopped hearing any of it.

Lexie had slept with *Nate*? What the actual fuck?

His memory snagged on something Nate had said during Brent's bachelor weekend.

I was in Detroit when you got traded, and spent the evening with my brother and some of your other...friends. Everyone was distraught, almost like you had died.

And something Lexie had said the week after.

When you left, I was a mess. I drowned myself in booze and sex. I did some things I'm not proud of.

The night he left.

She had slept with Nate *the night he left.*

He was out of his seat before he could think twice about it, stalking around the table and in Lexie's direction. When he reached her, her face lit in a tentative smile, as though she was happy to see him but didn't want to be. That smile quickly dimmed when he hooked a hand around her upper arm and towed her away from the crowd, ignoring her protests and the shocked expressions on Jay and Michelle Daniels' faces.

CHAPTER TWENTY-NINE
Lexie

Lexie knew she was in trouble when Mitch had approached her on the dance floor moments ago, rudely interrupting her conversation with Berkley's parents, that look in his eyes indicating the rage roiling under his skin.

The only problem was, she couldn't figure out what had pissed him off.

It had been a long time since she'd seen him this riled up, and she was anxious and excited to find out what caused it.

His grip on her arm was loose enough not to hurt her but firm enough to warn her off from attempting to get away. He towed her out of the tent and around the side of the cabin, pulling the side door open so hard it nearly came off its hinges.

Seconds later, he pushed her through the first open door they came to—which happened to be a bathroom—slamming it shut and locking it behind them.

"What the fuck are you doing?" She asked, putting as much space between them as possible in the small powder room.

"Nate Jean ring any bells?"

Lexie felt the blood drain from her face, fingers instantly chilled by the shot of adrenaline that spiked her blood. "Mitch..."

"Not a word, Lexie. Not until I say a few things."

She only nodded, and he continued.

"I know I hurt you. With the way I left, I don't blame you for going out and trying to move on the only way you knew how. Reverting back to those types of relationships after I had broken your trust so badly...I get it. But Nate *fucking* Jean, Lexie? That cocky fuckboy? And the day I left, no less?"

"I told you I did some things I'm not proud of," she said quietly.

"Yeah well I didn't think you meant mere hours after I'd been traded."

"What did you expect me to do?" She yelled. "You were gone! Do you know how many times I called you that day, from the second I heard the news? God, it had to have been upwards of fifty. And you blew me off every single time. I would've done anything to hear your voice. I even went to your apartment to see you, but you'd already left. No one could get a hold of you, and then you changed your number! What the fuck was I supposed to do?"

Her voice had risen to hysterical, and she hoped like hell no one would come inside the cabin right now, or they'd be getting an earful.

"I know, Lex," he said. "I know. But God, you could've at least waited a few weeks or months."

"And how long did you wait?" She retorted. "Before you fucked someone in LA?"

He didn't have an answer readily available, which led her to believe it hadn't been long after he moved. Probably not the same night, but soon enough after that she could be hurt by it if she wanted to.

If she hadn't already been drowning under the pain of losing him the way she had.

"That's what I thought," she said. "I regretted it the moment it happened. But I can't take it back. I missed you so fucking much I would've done anything to chase that feeling away. You hurt me so badly."

"And you think pushing me away didn't hurt me? Why are you acting like you're the only one who got their heart broken here?"

"Because you *left* me! You made it clear you didn't want me anymore. With the way I grew up, you had to know how that would affect me."

He stepped closer to her, pressing her back against the wall. "I have always wanted you," he said, voice low and full of gravel. "Every second of every day that I was gone, and all of the ones since I've been back. That has never changed. Leaving you the way I did and not fighting for our relationship is something I'll regret for the rest of my life. We can never get that time back, Lex, and that's on me. But you've always been safe with me, and I'm sorry I made you feel otherwise. I'll spend forever proving it to you."

"Then why are you so mad at me right now?"

"I don't like the idea of that little tool having put his hands on what's mine."

"Yours?" She asked, voice shaky. Unable to stop herself, she smoothed her hands over his chest and around his neck, burying them in his hair. It was a gesture she'd performed a thousand times, and he still reacted the same: eyelids growing heavy, hands snaking around her waist to cup her ass.

"Yes, Lexie. *Mine.* You have always been mine. Don't you know that by now?"

She answered by leaning forward and pressing her mouth to his.

They both whimpered. It was so familiar, his mouth as soft and warm as she remembered. And when he licked his way inside hers, he tasted strongly of champagne and vaguely of the cigars he, Brent, and the rest of the groomsmen shared after the ceremony.

She'd never been into smokers, but on him, it was intoxicating.

He pulled away, her bottom lip trapped briefly between his teeth. When he looked down at her, his pupils were blown wide with desire, no doubt mirroring her own. They stood like that, gazes locked, for several long seconds.

"I gotta ask, Lex," he said, grasping her chin in his hand. "Are you..."

"Clean? On something? Yes to both. I get checked regularly, and I have an IUD." She stared at him expectantly.

"I'm clean, too," he said. "I got checked not long after I came back to Michigan, and I haven't been with anyone since."

"Good." Lexie took a deep breath, the tips of her breasts brushing Mitch's chest, and his control snapped.

When he dove his hand under the layers of her skirt, deftly making contact with her sex, he groaned. "Why aren't you wearing underwear?"

The easy answer would be to say it was too hot, and this dress didn't require them.

But truthfully? "I was hoping this would happen," she admitted, leaning forward to nip at his ear while she worked his belt open and zipper down. She brought her mouth to his just as she wrapped her hand around his cock. "I wanted to be ready for you."

"Fuck, Lex," he said, sliding a finger through her wetness. "I'd say you're more than ready."

"So are you," she retorted, sliding her hand up and down his hard length. "So what are you waiting for?"

Mitch needed no further encouragement, and a moment later, Lexie's legs were wrapped tight around his hips as he pushed slowly into her.

"Oh my God," she said, head falling back and hitting the wall with a thunk.

In all of her fantasies of this moment, the moment they finally reunited, where Mitch was finally back where he belonged, not a single one of them could have prepared her for this.

His kiss had been familiar, like seeing an old friend after a long time apart.

But this? With him buried to the hilt inside her, stretching her in that delicious way only he could do?

It was exactly like coming home after being gone for too long.

"Mitch," she ground out. "Fuck, it's so good."

He pulled out and slammed into her again, her moans growing in volume as he picked up speed.

Mitch slapped his hand over her mouth to quiet her, burying his face in the crook of her neck to muffle his own noises.

But that didn't stop his relentless pounding into her. Something in him seemed to have snapped when he first slid into her, and he was picking up speed with each thrust, the mirror above the sink next to them rattling so hard Lexie was afraid it was going to crash to the floor at any second, giving them away.

Then Mitch slowed, and stopped completely, buried so deep inside her it *almost* hurt, hitting that one spot that only he had ever been able to reach, and said, "I forgot how good you feel."

And with those six words, she was once again lost, all other thoughts in her brain written over by the sheer presence of this man. Even after all this time, she was still utterly gone for him, swept up in the way he supported her entire body with his hips, one arm wrapped tightly around her waist as he pumped in and out of her. She was lost in the way her toes curled in pleasure when he moved his hand away from her mouth to shove it between them, toying with her clit even though there was barely an inch of space between them.

And she was completely lost in how fucking good it felt to have him wrapped in her arms again.

"No one feels as good as you," she breathed when he resumed moving in and out of her, so slowly that she dug her fingers into his ass, urging him on. "No one has ever felt as good as you."

"I know, baby," he said, teeth gritted as he continued pumping in and out of her, his shoulders bunching under her hands as she slid them up his back. She clung to him like a life raft in the middle of the ocean.

That's how it had always been between them: one step away from drowning, each other being the only thing keeping their heads above water.

"Mitch," she moaned, her voice half-strangled. "Don't stop. Whatever you do, don't stop."

"Never," he whispered, trapping her earlobe between his teeth.

Seconds later, as that pressure between Lexie's legs nearly reached its peak, someone pounded on the door, and Mitch froze, eyes wide as they looked into her own.

"If you're a really good girl and be quiet," he whispered, "they'll probably go away."

Lexie responded by burying her face in his shoulder, his dress shirt damp and sticking to his sweat-slicked skin, his linen jacket long since abandoned somewhere outside.

"Lexie?" Someone called. "It's Berk. Are you in there?"

Lexie lifted her head, opening her mouth to answer.

"What did I just tell you?" Mitch hissed.

She rolled her eyes at him. Even with his dick inside her, this man was infuriating. "And I told you not to stop, so I guess neither of us are very good at taking orders."

"Lexie?" Berkley asked again.

It was impossible to straighten her thoughts to form coherent sentences that weren't her moaning Mitch's name and begging for more. Her entire mind was focused on the spot where they were joined. Nothing else in the world mattered but that.

Well, except for Mitch getting her off, which had been about to happen until Berkley cockblocked her, and her body was not happy with being denied.

"I'm here, Berk. Just freshening up."

"Oh thank God," Berkley said, followed by a muffled thunk that set the door rattling on its hinges. Lexie flicked her eyes down and found the hem of Berkley's dress pooling against the bottom of the door, as though she had collapsed against it. "We couldn't find you, and Mitch has gone AWOL..."

"Shit," Mitch whispered. Lexie pressed a finger to his mouth, silencing him.

"Wait a minute," Berkley said, that big brain of hers drawing conclusions Lexie had neither the time nor mental capacity to deal with right now. "Is Mitch in there with you?"

Lexie huffed out a laugh, then winced, the tightening of her muscles reminding her that she had a very large, very hard dick still inside her. "Of course he's not!"

"Okay good," Berkley said. "I know weddings are all romantic and make people super horny, but you really do have to make him work for it."

"Oh trust me, I am," Mitch said quietly with a roll of his eyes, and Lexie pinched him.

"Shut up!" She hissed.

Berkley had gone on babbling about how exactly Lexie should handle the Mitch situation, which was honestly comical coming from the woman who had forced them to spend this entire weekend tied together as maid of honor and best man.

"Berkley, can we talk about this later? Maybe when I'm not in the bathroom with my dress up around my tits?"

Mitch buried his face in her neck, his body shaking in silent laughter.

What could she say? It wasn't a lie.

"Okay," Berkley said. "The dance floor is lonely without you, so hurry up!"

"I will!" Lexie said. "I'll meet you out there."

The hem of Berkley's dress disappeared from beneath the door, and the rustling of fabric faded into the distance.

"You have to make me work for it, huh?" Mitch asked, face smug as he cocked an eyebrow at her.

"I thought that's what you were already doing?" She said, gesturing between them.

Experimentally, Mitch pulled his hips back slightly and pushed back in. Lexie couldn't help it; she winced. Her hips were sore, quads burning from her legs being wrapped around Mitch's waist.

"Am I hurting you?"

"What? Of course not. The only thing hurting me was Berkley showing up right as I was about to come."

Mitch placed both palms flat on her ass, lifting her so his dick slid free a few inches, and Lexie winced again.

"I am hurting you!" Mitch said, pulling himself completely free and setting her on her feet, keeping his arms tight around her waist to steady her.

She studied him, his eyes hooded with desire, unreleased tension written on every line of his body. "Mitch, it's fine."

"It's not fine," he said. "As badly as I want to fuck you against that wall, I'm not going to hurt you to do it."

Lexie released an aggravated sigh through her nose. "Fine," she said, turning from him and stalking on stiff legs to the counter where she had left her small clutch, rifling through it for the tube of lipstick, a refresh needed now that what she had on was smeared all over Mitch's face and neck.

"Lexie," Mitch said quietly, coming to stand behind her. "Just because I don't want to hurt you doesn't mean I'm leaving this bathroom until I get you off."

She met his eyes in the mirror, and he gave her a wicked grin. "What did you have in mind?"

He spun her around and lifted her so that she was seated on the edge of the counter. He spread her legs wide as he lowered himself to his knees and stuck his head under the skirt of her dress.

As she rested her bare feet on his shoulders and steadied herself by digging a hand into his hair, slapping the other down on the counter next to her, Lexie had to admit, having Mitch on his knees, submissive, worshipping her with his lips and tongue and fingers, was preferable to the wall sex for a number of reasons.

By the time her second orgasm washed over her, and Mitch had pumped himself hard and fast to his own release with his tongue still circling her clit, Lexie was reminded exactly how good the boy was with his mouth.

And exactly how he had ruined her for anyone else so long ago.

When she stood, legs shaky, he once again snaked his arms around her waist and held her close, planting a series of sweet, soft kisses on her mouth. The taste of herself on his lips went right to her head, and she knew it would be impossible to keep what had just happened between them a secret the second they stepped out of the bathroom.

"This stays between us," she told him.

He looked like he wanted to argue, but nodded instead. "Whatever you want."

"I want you," she said honestly. "I've always wanted you."

He grinned at her and pressed a rough kiss to her lips. "We'll figure it out."

Now it was her turn to nod, throat too clogged with emotion to form words anyway.

They straightened themselves and exited, Lexie sneaking out first and checking the hallway outside for anyone lingering who could witness their little sexual reunion.

Confirming the coast was clear, she and Mitch snuck out and went opposite directions, Mitch choosing to walk through the cabin and around the front while Lexie slipped out the back door off the kitchen.

She had barely stepped foot on the patio when Berkley was on her.

"I know what you were doing in that bathroom, Alexandra."

Lexie whirled on her friend, hand flying up to her chest. "Jesus, Berk. You scared the shit out of me."

"Have a nice fuck?" Berkley asked, arms folded over her chest, a smug smile tugging at her lips.

Lexie sighed dramatically. "I have no idea what you're talking about," she said, turning on her heel to rejoin the reception under the large white tent erected on the lake shore.

"Don't play dumb with me, Lexie Monroe," Berkley said, walking quickly to keep up with her. "I know you were in there with Mitch. You think I don't know what blissed out, post-orgasm looks like? Please. Have you seen my husband?"

Lexie stopped and smiled at Berkley. It was the first time she had heard her friend call Brent her husband, and Berkley's face split into a grin.

Lexie wrapped an arm around her friend's shoulders, tucking her into her side. "I'm so happy for you, you know. It took a lot for you guys to get here."

"I know," Berkley said. "Thank you for being here with me."

"There isn't anywhere else I'd rather be."

"But stop trying to change the subject," Berkley said, pulling away. "Were you just fucking Mitch in that bathroom or what?"

Lexie's cheeks heated, and her grin turned sheepish. "Maybe."

Berkley slapped her arm playfully and squealed. "I knew it! I knew this weekend was going to be good for you two."

"Ugh, Berk," Lexie said. "It was just sex. No need to start planning the wedding."

Berkley looked at her as if to say *get real*. "It has never been just sex for you two, and you know it. Maybe one day you'll stop fighting it."

Berkley turned and surveyed the crowd spread out across the lawn of the cabin, groups of people dancing, drinking, playing yard games, and enjoying the gorgeous summer night in Upstate New York, celebrating her and Brent. "And trust me, when you finally do? It's the best thing that'll ever happen to you."

She patted Lexie on the arm and padded off to where Brent was standing with his brother and Cole. Lexie watched as Berkley slid a hand into Brent's and he dipped his head to plant a kiss on her mouth. The smile they shared had Lexie turning away, as though she were witnessing something sacred, something that she wasn't deserving of.

But truth be told, she *was* deserving. If her relationship with Mitch had taught her anything, it was that she was capable of loving and being loved. And if a man as good as Mitch was willing to take her as she was, and love her so fiercely that neither time nor distance had lessened his pull on her, then she must be doing something right.

CHAPTER THIRTY
Mitch

Lexie still wanted him.

That much was painfully obvious after their bathroom tryst, and Mitch couldn't wipe the smile from his face as he adjusted his clothes and ran a hand through his hair before rejoining the party.

Lexie was already back outside, standing with Berkley, whose gaze zeroed in on him the second he set foot on the grass, and Mitch gave her a sheepish smile, which only invited her to corner him.

"Have a nice time in the bathroom?" She asked when she reached him.

He shot her a smug grin. "Sure did."

Berkley shook her head. "You two are idiots," she said, "but I'm glad to see you're finally figuring your shit out."

"Glad" didn't even begin to cover the swirl of emotions Mitch was experiencing. Ecstasy, joy, hope, love...annoyance at Nate.

Mitch's eyes scanned the crowd and zeroed in on the little shit where he was sitting by himself at the head table, phone in one hand, a beer dangling loosely by the neck of the bottle from the other.

"Did you know about Lexie and Nate?" He asked Berkley.

Berkley's face drained of all color. "You were never supposed to find out," she said quietly. "She was hurting. She just wanted to make it stop, and she wasn't thinking clearly."

"But the night I left, Berkley? Really?"

"What do you want me to say? You broke her heart," she said, her voice cracking. "You broke mine, and Brent's, too. But it was different for Lexie. It was so hard for her to love you, to give herself to you like that. I've known her for nearly a decade and I've never seen her so gone over anyone. Not even close." She heaved a deep breath and released it slowly through her nose. "She made a bad call in the moment, and she's spent every day since regretting it. Cut her some slack. It's the least you can do."

Mitch only nodded. It's not as if he had been a saint while they were apart, even if he hadn't fucked someone new right away. They hadn't been together; Mitch put the exclamation point on that statement when he disappeared from her life.

He wasn't mad at her, but he'd be lying if he said the jealousy twisting in his gut wasn't a living, breathing thing. And the only thing that could lay it to rest was knowing Lexie was his forever.

Lexie joined them a moment later, gaze wary. "What are you two talking about?" She asked.

"You," Berkley said. "And the sex you had in the bathroom."

Lexie's eyes held Mitch's as she slipped her hand into his. "It was pretty incredible." Then she cut her eyes to Berkley. "Except you interrupted us."

"You look like you're doing just fine," Berkley said, eyes surveying Lexie up and down.

"That's because the boy is amazing with his tongue," she said smugly, and Mitch couldn't help but puff his chest out proudly. "Poor Mitchell had to finish himself off."

Berkley choked on a laugh as Mitch's cheeks heated. "I always knew you were selfish, Lex," Berkley said.

Lexie smacked her lightly on the arm, and Berkley darted away, back under the tent and into the waiting arms of her husband.

"You told her already?" Mitch said, snaking his arms around Lexie's waist.

"Have you met her? She's like a dog with a bone. And anyway, she figured it out herself."

Mitch nodded in agreement. Berkley was nothing if not persistent and far too perceptive for her own good.

"So before she cornered me," Mitch said, "I was thinking about having a little conversation with Nate. Care to join me?"

"Hell yes," Lexie said, immediately stalking away from him, Mitch could do nothing but follow her as she approached Nate.

"Put your phone away," Lexie said to him.

Nate raised his head and gave her a look that said make me.

"What can I do for you, Lexie? Looking for round two?"

Mitch caught Lexie's arm just as she pulled back, surely about to smack Nate.

"This is not the time or place for that, Lex," he said quietly.

Lexie dropped her arm to her side but continued to glare daggers at Nate. "We want to talk to you."

"Then by all means, talk," Nate said, settling back in his chair and propping his ankle up on his knee.

"Not here," Mitch said. "Let's go inside."

"I think this is fine," Nate said.

"Get up and come inside, pretty boy," Mitch said, turning away. "I'm not asking."

Mitch started across the yard and back into the house.

"What do you want, Mitch?" Nate asked once they were all inside the open concept kitchen-dining-living room, folding his arms across his chest.

"What the fuck is wrong with you?" Lexie asked Nate, and Mitch sat back, smug. Her ire was hot as fuck when it wasn't turned on him.

"You're going to have to be more specific. Emotionally unavailable, workaholic, so good in the sack I ruin women for everyone else...oh, is it that last one this little interrogation is about?"

"Why the fuck would you tell Mitch about us?" She asked. "When you left that morning, we agreed it would stay between us."

"But it didn't, did it?" Nate said. "Because you told your best friend, who told my brother, who gave me the ass chewing of a lifetime."

Lexie was unmoved. "First of all, Brent and Berkley were there that night. It doesn't take a rocket scientist to figure out where we disappeared to after leaving the Backdoor. And second, I don't feel bad for you," she said. "Why would you bring it up now, tonight of all nights?"

"Because I was bored," he said. "Watching you two moon over each other from afar was exhausting. I was only trying to help. And from the looks of it—" he gestured between them, no doubt noticing their unkempt appearances and satisfied faces—"it worked. You two had your little reunion. Now we can all live happily ever after."

"You expect me to believe that you told me about you laying your filthy fuckboy hands all over my girl because you wanted to *help* us?" Mitch asked, stepping into Nate's personal space and glaring down his nose at him. At the moment, Mitch's temper was a barely leashed thing, and the discomfort crawling under his skin needed an outlet. "Forgive me if I don't believe you."

Nate backed up a step, hands raised in surrender, before turning to stalk over to the fridge. He pulled out a trio of beers and passed them out before removing the cap and taking a pull from his own. "Anyone who looks at you two can tell you're still in love with each other."

Mitch glanced at Lexie, who appeared calm, and his heart swelled when she didn't deny it.

"That doesn't give you the right to fuck with other people's lives, Nate," she said. "For fuck's sake, you're 29 years old. Stop acting like a fucking child and get your shit together."

For the first time since they'd entered the kitchen, Nate looked thoroughly chastised.

"I'm sorry," he said quietly. "I'm sorry for meddling. But I'm not sorry that you two are...whatever you two are."

He continued to stare at them and, upon realizing no response from either of them was forthcoming, he spun and disappeared through the double doors onto the patio.

Several tense moments passed before Lexie said, "What are we, anyway?"

"I don't know," he said honestly. "I was hoping you could tell me."

She turned to him, tucking her hand into his. He marveled at how perfectly they fit—two halves of the same whole.

"How about we don't decide tonight?" She said, looking up at him, the twinkle lights outside making her eyes practically glow in the dark. "Let's go out there and celebrate our friends, and we can figure it all out in the morning."

"Deal," he said, bending forward to press a soft, sweet kiss to her waiting mouth. "For what it's worth, though...I—"

Lexie pressed a finger to his lips. "Don't say it. Not yet. Tomorrow. It's not that I'm not...that I don't feel it too. I just want to make sure we do it right this time."

He nodded, swallowing hard. He understood her hesitance, and he refused to push her.

And truthfully, he was standing on shaky ground himself. The way he'd left was shitty, yes, but she had pushed him away. He wasn't afraid of his feelings for her, but he was afraid that hers for him could possibly be weak enough that she could run from him again. If that happened...he wouldn't survive it this time. To live in a world without Lexie by his side would be like living in a world without the sun.

They rejoined the party, hand-in-hand, abandoning all pretenses that they weren't here together, letting the gathered crowd guess at what had happened between them over the last few hours that they were glued to each other now.

On the dance floor later, Brent shot Mitch a knowing look over Berkley's head when he wrapped his arms around Lexie's waist and planted a kiss on the side of her neck.

"You better be careful," she said, pulling back to look at him. "People might get the wrong idea."

"And what exactly would that be?"

"That we're back together."

"Honey, if people think that, they've got the right idea."

Lexie's face split into a grin, and she rose up on her tiptoes to plant a kiss on his lips.

They spent the next few hours that way, alternately kissing, holding hands, always touching in some way, and circling around their friends, belting the words to every single song the DJ blasted into the balmy New York summer night.

When the party disbanded, and the couples not staying at the cabin drove off—including both the Jean and Daniels parents—Lexie looked at Mitch. "You're sleeping with me tonight, right?"

"Define 'sleeping'," he said with a wide yawn.

"I mean, I'm not going to try and have my way with you, if that's what you're asking. We've just..." She trailed off, chewing on her lower lip.

"What?" He asked, sliding a finger under her chin and tipping her head back to meet her gaze.

"We've wasted so much time," she whispered. "I don't want to waste anymore."

His heart swelled, and he gathered her in his arms, planting a kiss on the top of her head. "I'm not going anywhere," he said.

She backed away with a smile and grabbed his hand, leading him inside.

When they'd first arrived here two days ago, Brent had explained to Mitch that the cabin had been about half its current size when two of his Jean ancestors bought it decades ago, the title being passed down through the generations until eventually, Brent's dad came to own it, free and clear. Brent had used his first big contract extension to purchase more of the shoreline and the neighboring property, which had been a vacant lot. This gave them a long swath of uninterrupted beach, the opportunity to add major square footage to the cabin, and to upgrade the interior with all the modern amenities.

On one end, the first floor contained a large open-concept kitchen, dining, and family room, with a sliding door that opened onto a flagstone patio. The opposite end housed two bedrooms, each with an attached bath, that Brent and Nate had long ago claimed as their own.

The second level was full of bedrooms—four to be exact, including another master suite for the Jean parents—and two bathrooms, with a loft that had a full wall of windows that overlooked the lake.

Mitch and Lexie entered the house through the patio door, Mitch snorting when he found Cole passed out on the couch. Apparently, he'd been too drunk to make the drive back to his hotel.

"Should we wake him?" Lexie asked. "There is an empty room."

"Nah, he's fine down here."

"If you say so," Lexie whispered, then strode away from Mitch to reach into the refrigerator and grab a couple bottles of water.

They snuck past him and up the stairs, Lexie wincing when one of them creaked.

Mitch felt surprisingly steady for the amount of alcohol he'd consumed, more drunk on the feel of Lexie's hand as she slid it back into his than any beer or wine could ever make him.

Brent and Berkley had long since disappeared into their room downstairs, and Nate was nowhere to be found, presumably in his own as well. Jessica and Mackenzie had opted to share a room for the weekend, leaving the remaining three rooms on the second level for Amelia, Lexie, and Mitch. Logan had opted to stay at the nearby bed and breakfast with his parents.

Upstairs was quiet, the doors to both Mackenzie and Jessica's, and Amelia's rooms closed, the sounds of soft, even breaths drifting out to them as they crept by.

The moment they entered the room and the door clicked shut behind them, Mitch had Lexie pressed against it. Now that he'd had a small taste of her earlier, and finally had her back in his arms after so much time apart, he wanted the whole damn meal.

"Now who's trying to have their way with who," she said breathlessly as he trailed kisses down the column of her neck.

God, he'd forgotten how soft her skin was, and how wild her favored cinnamon and vanilla lotion drove him.

Lexie put her hands on his chest and applied pressure, enough for him to yield a step, raising his head to look at her.

"As badly as I want to strip you down and ride you until the sun comes up," she said, "I want to go slow."

"How slow?"

"I want to make sure we've both got our heads on straight about this. That we're going into it with open eyes...and hearts. That we're clear with each other on exactly what we're expecting and what we can give in return. We did everything all wrong last time."

Kicking his shoes off, he scooped her up and crawled on to the bed, reclining on the mountain of pillows with her curled up against his chest.

"We're not the same people we were when we met, Lex," he said. "Hell, we're not even the same people we were when I moved back to Detroit. This time apart has been...difficult."

"You don't even know the half of it," she whispered.

He smoothed his hand over her hair, which she'd released from the braided coil on the top of her head sometime during the evening. It now hung down around her shoulders, a little tangled and half-wild.

"I'm afraid, too," he whispered to her. "But I also know I can't act like I'm okay living my life without you anymore. You're everything to me, Lexie. You always have been."

Saying those words out loud, after holding them in for so long...the weight that had been crushing his chest for so many months lifted. It was almost easier to say these things in the dark, when he couldn't gauge her reactions, when he didn't have to look her in the eye as he poured out his heart.

"What do you have to be afraid of?" Lexie asked. "You've always been the strong one. For both of us."

"I'm afraid of you pushing me away again. I only survived last time because I had to move halfway across the country, and even then I missed you like I'd miss a limb. You followed me everywhere. I can't do that again."

"I moved for that exact reason," she said.

Mitch had always wondered why she'd given up a perfectly nice apartment along the river to move further inland.

"I saw you in every inch of my old place. Your ghost...it haunted me. Some days it really did feel as though you had died."

Mitch's heart squeezed painfully. "I'm sorry."

She shifted herself so she could look up at him. "I'm not just afraid, Mitch. I'm terrified. But I need you more than I'm afraid of losing you."

He planted a soft kiss on her mouth once, twice, before pulling away and wrapping his arms tighter around her.

"So we take it one day at a time," he said. "No rush, no pressure. I want to make sure it sticks this time, and I think you do, too."

"I do, more than anything," she said, eyes glinting as they caught the twinkle lights from outside. "I'm ready to jump back into this with you."

He planted a kiss on her nose and nestled them deeper into the bed. "All you have to do is fall, baby," he said quietly. "I promise I'll catch you."

CHAPTER THIRTY-ONE

Lexie

R ising to consciousness the next morning was a disorienting experience for Lexie, who blinked open her eyes to sunlight streaming through the blinds on the window across the room, feeling for all the world as though she'd been here before.

The arm slung across her middle didn't help matters.

She squeezed her eyes tightly shut and forced herself to remember.

She *had* been here before.

A year ago, in this same room, waking up in this same place with a man in bed next to her.

For a brief moment, she wondered if she'd dreamed everything since then. The trips to LA, Boston, Dallas, Seattle, and several other cities across the country. Leaving her full-time, well-paying job as a headhunter to become a full-time influencer. Helping Amelia open her gym, Berkley's bachelorette party and wedding.

Mitch.

Mitch's injury, him moving back to Michigan, and her agreeing to give things between them another shot.

The arm around her stomach squeezed tighter and hauled her back into the hard body behind her, and the man said, "Good morning."

Lexie rolled over so fast to face Mitch that her elbow glanced off his forehead, and he let out a surprised, "Ouch!"

None of it had been a dream. Every single minute of sadness and heartbreak, of love and loss, of compromise and selfishness, had led her right here, to this single perfect morning, waking up next to the love of her life.

"Sorry," she said when she burrowed into his arms, stretching to kiss the red mark on his forehead. "I woke up this morning and had this moment where I thought everything that happened this last year was a really weird, vivid dream. I was right here a year ago," she added. "In this bed. With a different guy. And I thought..."

She buried her head in his chest, his voice rumbling through her as he said, "And you thought what?"

"Everything these last few days has been magical," she said, voice muffled into his skin. "I was afraid I'd lost it again."

Mitch tunneled his fingers in her hair and tugged so that she was forced to meet his gaze. "I'm not going anywhere," he told her, pressing a kiss to her forehead. "Ever."

She relaxed against him. "Good," she said. "I couldn't survive it again."

He rolled them so he was on top of her, hands still cradling her head as she instinctively widened her legs so he could settle between them.

Sometime in the darkest hours of the morning, Lexie had woken up to Mitch. They had fallen asleep with her curled up against his chest, and she carefully disentangled her limbs from his before quietly getting out of bed to strip off her dress and toss one of Mitch's t-shirts over her head. When she crawled back in next to him and even in his sleep, he reached for her. Surrounded by his strength and scent, Lexie had felt home for the first time in a long time, and slept soundly for the first time in months.

While Lexie had been asleep, Mitch must've woken up and shed his button-up and pants, clad only in his boxers, and the morning sun now lit his chest and abs, turning all that smooth skin golden brown. She couldn't help marveling at him. Even after months of no longer playing professional hockey, he still resembled a statue of a Greek god, all broad shoulders and muscles that rippled when he shifted. She wanted to lick every inch of him from head to toe.

Where their joining the night before was frantic, all wet mouths and nails dragging across skin, sex this morning was an entirely different affair.

It wasn't just sex; it was making love.

Slowly, Mitch trailed kisses across her throat and shifted down her body, nuzzling her breasts through the worn cotton of his shirt. When he sucked a nipple into his mouth through the fabric, Lexie's eyes rolled back in her head, and he chuckled when she dug her fingers into his shoulders and pushed him lower.

"You're awfully greedy," he said to her, lifting the hem of the shirt to pepper her stomach with hot, open-mouthed kisses. Then he ran a finger over her slit, which was already aching for him, and said, "And awfully wet."

Lexie squirmed under him. "This is what you do to me," she said, straining her neck to look down at him. "Now quit playing with me."

"I love playing with you," he said, hooking his fingers around the edges of her panties and pulling them down her legs, discarding them across the room. "It's been over a year since I've had you like this, Lex. I plan on taking my time."

And he did, starting with long, slow licks designed to drive her wild. After several torturous minutes, he inserted one finger, and then another, lazily pumping them in and out of her while still lapping at her clit.

By the time he closed his mouth around her nub, she was panting, and when he curled his fingers inside her and sucked her clit hard into his mouth, she went off like a bomb, back arching off the bed, screaming his name into the pillow she had covered her face with.

After all this time, he still knew exactly what to do to have her completely coming apart under his skillful mouth and hands.

He worked her through it, the shockwaves lasting for several long moments, and when she calmed, she mustered just enough strength to dig her fingers into his hair and pull him back up her body.

"I hate you," she said when he pressed his mouth to hers.

He grinned against her lips and said, "No you don't."

He was right; she opposite of hated him.

She stretched her arms over her head, arching her breasts so that they pressed against his chest, and then relaxed and snaked her hands between them, palming his cock through his boxers. "As much as I'd like to pay you back for that little performance," she said with a squeeze that had him biting off a groan, "I need you inside me right now."

Mitch needed no further encouragement, and she, once again, found herself amazed by how quickly he moved that massive body of his, even with a bad back. Quickly, he backed off the bed, stripped his boxers off, and jumped back on, settling himself between her thighs. He gripped his dick by its base and ran it along her sex, once again toying with her.

"Mitchell..." Lexie warned, lifting her legs and crossing her heels behind his back, trying to pull him forward.

"You want this?" He asked, giving her a smarmy grin like some male lead in a terrible old-school porno film.

"You know I do," she said.

"Come get it."

Mitch was on his back a second later, Lexie lowering herself onto him the next.

"Jesus Christ," he said, gripping her hips tightly as she started to move.

Lexie had forgotten how deep he got when they were like this, and her first couple of movements were shallow, barely coming off and barely lowering back on, until she had stretched enough to accommodate him.

And when everything had finally relaxed, she picked up speed, the bed rocking enough underneath them that the headboard repeatedly smacked into the wall.

Everyone in the house would be awake soon if they weren't already, and Lexie didn't give a single fuck.

Mitch reached up and tweaked one of Lexie's nipples between his thumb and forefinger, sending a jolt right to her clit, which in this position was rubbing against Mitch as she moved but without nearly enough friction. But her partner knew her well, and a second later, he rose onto his knees and pressed his thumb to her aching nub, still buried deep inside Lexie as she straddled his lap.

"Fuck," she breathed, dropping her head onto his shoulder as she continued to bounce up and down on top of him.

"I'm close," he said through gritted teeth.

She lifted her head and kissed him, rough and sloppy as she let him take over, trading his hand for hers, and he gripped her thighs as she ground down onto him, meeting every single one of his upward thrusts.

As she broke apart for a second time, she threw herself backward and pulled Mitch down on top of her, letting him frantically fuck her into the bed while he worked toward his own release moments later.

Sticky with sweat, limbs shaky, and thoroughly satisfied, they laid there in comfortable silence for several long minutes, curled in each other's arms and in no rush to get out of bed.

Then Lexie's stomach let out a loud growl, and Mitch rested his palm there. "I suppose I should feed you now," he said.

"I don't want to go downstairs," she whined, turning to bury her face in his chest. "But I suppose we're going to have to."

Mitch smiled. "No time like the present."

"Let me just swing into my room and grab some shorts," she said with a resigned sigh.

"And you expect me to walk down there like this?" He asked, gesturing to his bare torso and those long, sculpted legs of his. Not to mention his bare dick and ass. "You're wearing my shirt."

"I hope you brought more than one," she said. "Because you're not getting this back. And your boxers are over there," she added, pointing to the corner of the room.

He gave her a smug smile and stalked toward her, wrapping his arms around her and cupping her ass in his hands. "You look better in it anyway."

In short order, Mitch stepped away and pulled on his boxers, and scrounged up a different shirt and a pair of blue mesh shorts with the Warriors logo on them. Even clothed, the man made her mouth water, and she didn't let her gaze linger on him too long for fear that they might not make it out of the room for a long, long time yet.

As if reading her mind, he slid his fingers in hers and pulled her into the hall. She darted into her room and quickly threw on a clean pair of underwear and cotton pajama shorts.

When she came out, Mitch said, "Ready to face the firing squad?"

She gripped his hand and gave it a squeeze. "I am if you are."

When they entered the kitchen, Lexie wasn't surprised to find the rest of the house already gathered there. Amelia, Jessica, Mackenzie, Brent, and Berkley all sat at the long informal dining table while Cole and Nate moved around the kitchen. The scent of bacon hung in the air, and Lexie's stomach growled again.

"Good morning, everyone," she said cheerfully, dropping Mitch's hand and hurrying over to the coffee pot. "Coffee, Mitch?"

"Yes, please," he said, sitting on one of the island bar stools.

Lexie moved around the kitchen, pulling two mugs from the cupboard by the sink and filling them both to the brim with black coffee before walking over and taking a seat next to Mitch.

She took a fortifying sip and raised her gaze to find all her friends staring at them.

"What?" she asked, annoyed, and Mitch snorted.

"Are we not going to talk about the fact that you two came down here together this morning?" Berkley asked. "Or that you had sex in that bathroom last night?" She added, pointing down the hallway in the direction of the scene of the crime.

"Or that the entire house could hear you going at it this morning?" Amelia added.

Lexie really hated her friends sometimes.

"Berkley, Amelia," Brent warned. "Maybe don't put them on blast in front of everyone."

"They seem to be doing a pretty good job of that themselves," Berkley said, gesturing to where they were seated. Mitch had pulled Lexie's chair close enough that they were thigh to thigh, his arm draped casually—but possessively—across the back.

At that moment, Cole slid two heaping plates of bacon, eggs, potatoes, and fresh fruit in front of them. Lexie rose and grabbed hers. "We're taking things slow," she said, and stalked out onto the patio.

A second later, Mitch settled next to her. "That went surprisingly well."

"Berkley's got a big mouth," Lexie said around a mouthful of eggs. "This is hard enough as it is."

"But why? I thought we agreed to take it one day at a time?"

She nodded. They had agreed to that. But when Lexie woke up this morning, thinking that it had all been a fever dream, some idyllic version of her life her subconscious had shown her, but one she could never attain, she'd been terrified.

And when she thought she'd lost it...she knew what she had to do.

She hadn't asked for this, had never thought that a love like this was in the cards for her. But she should've known that very first night when their gazes locked over the top of Berkley's head at Contour.

It had been game over for her.

That he would be the one to make her believe in something again. That he would be the one to make her believe she was someone who could be loved, and love in return.

He was always referring to them as endgame, and now she understood *why*.

She finally believed it, too.

For her, it had always been him.

He had been so strong for her, so brave for them both, picking her up and carrying her when her past continued to drag her down into the deepest, darkest recesses of her mind. Into those quiet spaces where she was reminded of her formative years, of being that child whose parents were never around. That girl who moved around so much she could never fit in. The sullen teenager whose acts of rebellion were really just cries for attention from the people who would never give it to her.

She had found her home in Detroit. With Berkley and Brent, Amelia, and, surprisingly, guys like Cole, Rat and Grey. They were her family, the only people that had ever taken the time to break through her tough girl exterior and see the softest sides of her, the sides she hid behind sheer bravado.

And then came Mitch and her vision for her life changed, her focus no longer only on her career or her friends, but expanding to include him as well. She hadn't even known she'd been missing him, that she needed him, until he was right in front of her.

When he left, the world tilted on its axis, turning everything upside and sideways for over a year. Everything was dark, like the sun had gone. She had tried, desperately, to drown his memory in cheap sex and even cheaper booze. Anything she could get her hands on to make her feel something, to shake off the persistent numbness, the fog that had settled over her brain when he was gone.

And when he came back, a veil had lifted. Not entirely, but enough to remind Lexie that somewhere out there was a giant ball of light in the sky. That things could be, and had been, bright and warm and wonderful.

She had fought it for so long, too long, but she was finally ready. Finally, she was brave enough. Her world had been shrouded in grey, leached of color.

But no longer.

And so, with her next words, she banished all the clouds from the sky.

"I love you," she whispered. "I know I told you yesterday not to say it to me, that I wanted to go slow. But...I can't ignore it and pretend I don't feel it with every fiber of my being."

His eyes widened, and his mouth gaped like a fish out of water. "What did you just say?"

Louder, she repeated herself, her voice calm and steady. "I love you."

And the grin that overtook his face...Something so pure was surely far too good for her. Thankfully, he wasn't of the same opinion. In the next moment, she was out of her seat and crushed against him, his hands in her hair, anchoring her head in place as he gazed deeply into her eyes.

She saw it then, everything she had been missing all these years. His absolute devotion to her. His adoration. His respect. His pride.

His love.

She hadn't realized she was crying until he brushed his thumbs under her eyes, wiping away the moisture that had collected there. Distantly, she heard clapping, and a glance in the direction of the cabin showed Berkley standing at the screen door.

Lexie gave her the finger over Mitch's shoulder.

"I have waited forever to hear you say that again. And you know what?"

"What?" She asked, suddenly afraid he wouldn't say it back, but proud of herself for having taken the leap anyway.

One side of his mouth tipped up. "I love you, too."

She would have sagged to the ground at his feet in relief if he hadn't been holding her up.

"Thank God," she said. "I thought I just embarrassed myself for nothing."

"It's always been you, Lexie," he said. "You know that. I'm just glad you finally came to your senses."

She laughed, half choking on a sob as joy bubbled up her throat. "I'm sorry I kept you waiting."

"Don't you know that I would wait for you forever?"

EPILOGUE
Mitch

"Come on!" Mitch yelled down the hall, anxiously jangling his keys in one hand and Lexie's shoes in the other. "We're going to be late!"

"Hold your horses, old man," she said, finally emerging from their bedroom down the hall, her hair hanging in loose waves around her shoulders and down her back.

"Don't call me old man," he said. He was thirty-five. That did *not* make him old, no matter how often Lexie teased him about it.

"I'll call you whatever I want," she said, stalking up to him and sticking her tongue out before quickly snatching her shoes and darting away from him.

Almost like she knew that gesture would earn her a little smack on the ass.

"Seriously, Lex," he said, twisting his wrist so he could look at his watch. "We should've been there twenty minutes ago. We agreed to help setup."

Lexie sat on the end of the chaise and stretched her long legs out in front of her so she could lace her black combat boots up over her black pants.

"They can survive without us," she said, not looking at him. "There's probably a hundred people there already, and the damn thing doesn't start for another hour."

His girl had a point.

Baby showers happened all the time, but when the wife of a professional athlete had a baby, it became a thing.

Expensive catering. Swanky venue downtown, in this case, one of the many meeting rooms located at the Atheneum Hotel in Greektown. Something called a balloon arch and a flower wall?

Mitch honestly stopped listening whenever Lexie talked about it, but he supposed he was about to see for himself what all the fuss was about.

Lexie finally stood, her pale blue top contrasting her black lower half.

"What kind of person wears black to a baby shower anyway?" He asked her.

"The kind who wears black every other day of the year. Just because my best friend is having a kid doesn't mean I'm going to start wearing floral prints," Lexie said. "I conceded with this top. What more do you want from me?"

Mitch chuckled and hooked an arm around her neck, hauling her in for a kiss. "Fair enough," he said against her mouth. "But can we go now?"

"Yes," she said, snagging her coat off the hook by the door and slinging her purse over her shoulder. "Grab the gifts, will you?"

Mitch rolled his eyes but gathered up the stack of wrapped boxes and gift bags stuffed with tissue paper.

Admittedly, these gifts were from him as well.

It wasn't every day his best friend had his first kid, after all, and a boy no less.

"Poor Berkley," Mitch said out loud as he settled behind the wheel of his Suburban.

"How come?"

"Raising boys is tough work," he said as he pulled out of the garage. "Or so I'm told."

"Well yeah, if he turns out anything like Brent, especially in the looks department, those two are in for some hell. And if he's as talented of an athlete as Brent? Or as smart as Berkley? Or both? They're fucked."

Mitch nodded in agreement and reached over to grab Lexie's hand.

It was crazy to him how much could change in a year. Last January, he was barely moved back to Michigan, still on the mend from his career-ending back injury and heartbroken over Lexie.

And now...he glanced over at her quickly before returning his eyes to the road, grinning when he caught her already looking at him.

The last six months together hadn't always been easy. They fought about stupid shit, as most couples did, and he could've sworn she had steam coming out of her ears when he asked her to move in with him.

Much to his surprise, she acquiesced, but not without presenting him with a laundry list of reasons why it was a bad idea, and then, when he shot down every one of those, an even longer list of demands, the biggest of which being they would find a new place together.

That was only two months ago, but they had easily settled into sharing a space. Lexie didn't complain—much—when Mitch inevitably left wet towels on the bathroom floor, and Mitch didn't complain when she refused to put her clean laundry away, preferring to leave it spilling out of laundry baskets in the walk-in closet. They loved the same foods, and both were perfectly content to eat takeout every night instead of cooking, which was something neither of them was very good at.

The beautiful thing was they traveled together, which was the true test of whether or not their relationship would go the distance. Mitch's real estate portfolio continued to grow, now encompassing rental properties all over the country that he was converting into Airbnbs or low-income housing, and Lexie's infamy as an influencer rose daily.

The addition of her hot, former professional hockey-playing boyfriend to her Instagram didn't hurt matters, that's for sure.

When her parents learned that not only were they back together, but that Mitch was investing in properties all across the country, they showed up on Lexie's doorstep, unannounced, demanding to be allowed to help Mitch out.

Lexie, bless her, told them in no uncertain terms to get the fuck out and don't come back.

He was so proud of her for that, for finally standing up for herself. They were her parents, the two people who should've loved her unconditionally, and he knew some part of her still held onto the hope that one day they would. But in that moment, when they came back into her life only because of what she could do for them, she'd finally had enough.

And he fucked her senseless afterward in celebration.

"I can't believe they're having a baby," Lexie said when they pulled up to the Atheneum. A valet approached the driver's side and greeted Mitch before taking his keys. Mitch walked around and let Lexie out, giving her hand a quick squeeze before he shuffled to the back to retrieve the gifts.

"I can't either," Mitch said.

But truthfully, he could. Brent and Berkley were going to be the most amazing parents, and he was excited about the prospect of being Uncle Mitch for real. The little guy had no idea how blessed he was.

"Do you want kids?" Lexie asked conversationally as they strode through the front doors of the hotel and into the lobby.

Well, for anyone else it would've been conversational, but his girl didn't ask questions or make small talk for the sake of filling the silence. Her question had him stopping dead in his tracks, nearly dropping all the gifts on the floor. "Is this your way of telling me something?" He asked, heart beating almost painfully against his ribs.

"What?" Lexie said. "No! I'm just curious."

He did set the gifts down then and pulled Lexie into him. She came to him willingly, and he was surprised by how well they fit together, even after all this time.

Almost like they were made for each other.

"I never considered it," he said, "until I met you."

She gave him one of her smiles that conveyed she felt the same.

"One day at a time?" She asked.

"One day at a time," he replied, dropping a kiss on her lips. "I love you."

Lexie just nodded and mumbled, "Me too," before attempting to pull away. But Mitch held fast.

The words had never been easy for her to say, even if she'd gotten better about it since they got back together. Every now and then, he liked pushing her on it.

"'Me too'?" He asked, arching an eyebrow at her. "C'mon, Lex."

"What?" She asked, looking up at him and glaring daggers.

"You too what? I need to hear you say it."

For several long moments, during which she folded her arms over her chest despite the fact that he was still wrapped around her, she didn't speak, only continued to look at him as though he was the bane of her existence.

Finally, her shoulders slumped, and she placed her palm over his heart. The heart that beat only for her.

"I love you, too, you big dumb asshole."

Mitch grinned and pressed a kiss to the tip of her nose. "Thank you."

Then, together, they gathered the mountain of gifts and went inside to celebrate Baby Jean.

ACKNOWLEDGMENTS

To my parents and my sister, for being my biggest cheerleaders. I couldn't do any of this without you.

To my grandparents, the ones in heaven guiding my hands and the earth-bound ones cheering me on.

The Jennifer and Meredith, for being the best alpha readers a girl could ever ask for. This story wouldn't be half of what it is today without the two of you. Jen, your early notes, your constant and never ending patience while I rambled about plot lines and "what if I did this here" or "what if Lexie does this or Mitch does that" made this book palatable. Mer, thank you for being my favorite person to bitch to, and for reading four hundred and thirty-seven iterations of Chapter Twelve before I finally settled on one that didn't make me want to set this entire book on fire. I love you forever. You two know this story and these characters almost as well as I do, and I am forever grateful that you love these broken babies as much as me.

To my Burnt Pancakes, for so many things. Madison, Kelsey, and Juliana: thank you being my favorite people to laugh and cry with over our author woes, to beta reading and providing invaluable feedback, to being the people I can lean on in any situation. I love you dearly.

To the rest of my beta team: Abigail, Erin, Katie, MJ, and Tricia. Your enthusiasm for this project and endless notes and commentary about how much you love these characters means more to me than I could ever say.

To Samantha, for giving me the most beautiful cover in the world. I am so incredibly grateful for your friendship, your talent, and your endless patience.

To everyone who has read and loved and raved about *For the Boys*. Even on the hard days, you all and your enthusiasm are the reason I felt confident enough to write a second novel. I hope you loved Lexie and Mitch just as much as you loved Brent and Berk.

To Brit, for taking such good care of my baby. The polish you added to these pages made this story so much more perfect than I ever could've dreamed.

And lastly, to my family and friends, near and far, who have been nothing but supportive and excited for me as I embarked on this journey. The outpouring of love and pride I experience daily from you all, especially the residents of my hometown, make all of the long days and nights worth it. You're the reason I do this.

CPSIA information can be obtained
at www.ICGtesting.com
Printed in the USA
BVHW031218140223
658408BV00006B/336